M000079789

MY WEIGHT IN WANDS

WILLIAM LEE

Hi, Fernanda!
Thanks for your
interest in my book!
Look my forward to
your thoughts...
Bill Lee

Mixco Books

Copyright © 2020 by William Lee

All rights reserved.

No part of this book may be reproduced in any form or by any electronic or mechanical means, including information storage and retrieval systems, without written permission from the author, except for the use of brief quotations in a book review.

For more information write Mixco Books at mixcobooks@gmail.com.

First Edition

ISBN 978-1-7352224-0-0 (print)

This is a work of fiction. Names, characters, places, and incidents either are the products of the author's imagination or are used fictitiously. Any resemblance to actual persons, living or dead, businesses, companies, events, or locales is entirely coincidental.

Cover design by Tara Alexander

❀ Created with Vellum

For my Family
And all my barista-muses across the world that have nourished and
sustained me

PART I

The Warning Label

The type was too small, Aunt Ezra pushed the tube closer to the light. The warning label was something new, the hard orange color could have cut through skin: "Use not recommended for those 125 years or older." She indignantly tossed the tube of de-aging or de-icing or whatever the nasty-smelling creme was supposed to magically accomplish, back in the bag.

Aunt Ezra picked up her wine tonic instead and continued her spontaneous self-pity party: *That's a fine how-do-you do...* Such bullshit. I—*we*—finally get things to a fairly manageable place and then something like this silly irritant pops up and throws me off my game, pokes at my raised witchy consciousness.

Nothing to fret, it's simply adding a layer of complication that can, like so many others before it, be plucked away. The irony is that the whole of these conversations, these Coven "feel-good" sessions (with their pathetic goodie bags), is about *bringing the Blessed closer together*—and certainly not the other way around. (There's already enough animosity between *lineages* to last at least two red wolf moons...)

People, W's, *everyone* is simply bored. Society's in a slump and it's somehow decided the supernatural to be, well, "silly" and shopworn... Not all of it, just us W's—witches, warlocks (nasty, temperamental word anymore), wizards—and a few other untouchables that I won't bother about right now. To be completely blunt: *it burns my one-hundred-twenty-seven-year-old butt that suddenly I don't matter anymore!*

My physical body can only accomplish so much when there's this sad and pathetic sameness, a cosmological ennui—it can make one practically suicidal. Nothing's more ridiculous than a whiny, needy middle-aged (okay, slightly more than that) over-witch, surrounded by wildly talented, mostly oblivious and mostly beautiful underwitches... (Just put a Duraflame stake in it now and call me dinner.)

I may be an old hag, but I'd much rather be out there stretching and flaunting whatever magic muscles I have left as opposed to just sitting here with my wand, excuse me, *wands* up my ass... And *I'm sorry—why am I whining at you?* (Speaking of inappropriate *how-do-you-do's!*) I'll moan at Antonia in the morning; she'll swallow her medicine—one more bitter pill—like she always does... Like the good little witch she's always been.

SASHA WAS ORGANIZING HER BACKPACK. (She was always organizing something.) She was obsessively (and thereby happily) oblivious as she arrived at the kitchen table. She had no reason to consider that the average Tuesday breakfast would be anything other than *her* usual average. She slumped down with fork in hand, but the morning wasn't happening as per *her "usual."*

"Wait. Where's my waffle?" Sasha looked up at Soba; Soba looked at Tip—The Sisters beelined their scowls to their mother. Their parents were seemingly, suddenly immune to their daughters' glare.

Antonia taunted, "Right where it *shouldn't* be." (It was hovering above and just behind her, sneakily out of view; Antonia preferred deflection and befuddlement to get her parental concerns communicated and enforced—*that element of surprise works wonders!*)

"*This* is the morning you decide you're going to make a point about me going *craft-free?*" Sasha snapped.

Antonia smiled slightly, "Maybe... Can't be a real surprise—it's not the first time it's come up."

"*Maybe?!* Why this morning of all mornings?"

"Why not?" Antonia's responses were equally curt. Sasha's scowl deepened, *Especially on a Tuesday morning at 7:04, eighty-four minutes before my geometry final? What is the deal lately?* Tom Dad almost stabbed her with his fork (a love stab), but it wasn't an unfair question: why would she—*right now*—choose that particular Eggo to make her already moot issue even mooter?

The breakfast's milk and Eggo now floated over the cereal bowl and toaster, respectively, as if it was (or Antonia was) reconsidering if it would play the role of breakfast this morning or not. Sasha fixed her eyes (she could be *very* intimidating, whether she was actually aware of that or not), "If all magic within these four walls is now *verboten*—then what's *that?*" She glanced up at the pre-baked U.F.O. hovering over the counter.

Antonia and Tom Dad followed her eyes; Antonia sucked in her cheeks, her brow furrowed, trying to think as quickly as she could. Tom Dad, however, appeared unchanged. Sasha's very valid query seemed to burst the teachable moment, but Tom Dad continued pressing his position, looking at the anxious waffle then Sasha, "*That* is a perfect example of what *is* legitimate—magic that *is responsible.* Has a valid and useful reason for being, helping us illustrate our point." Tom Dad clearly felt validated; he consistently believed he was at his best when locating that happy middle ground—not black or white, exactly right or wrong, but the sweet grey middle. Antonia sat expressionless (it was time to remove herself from this conversation).

"So will I have to submit a formal written request before I throw any spells?"

Tom Dad sighed, "That's not my point at all, Sasha."

Sasha sat up, "Then I'm not sure why it's still even a discussion *at all*... Spell-making, W's, under- or overwitch—it's all so *not about* **anything** anymore. I mean, it's just so *boring* no one barely gives a shit."

Big roll of the eyes from Tip. She had been waiting for this moment; she knew it was coming—Sasha had gotten on her soapbox one too many times. She had placed bets with Soba when Tom Dad would finally relent and attack (as much *attacking* as Tom Dad could muster, anyway), *Surprise strike from the kitchen table's starboard side, Colonel Father successfully maneuvers the Antonia Grace into position and fires...* Tip had refused to choose a side, even though The Sisters had already tacitly acknowledged that their dad was going a hex too far with his spell-making rule. It was just another stupid thing they had to remember not to think about. And it only underscored yet another (in a series) of their father's rampant insecurities. *I mean, I love him like crazy, but this is some real corn-fed hoo-ha...*

Baby Girl Soba had, during the whole discussion and clumsy silence, assumed her default position, which was a fixed stare at their dog, Sput. It (and the dog) provided her a necessary safe space—her emotional rescue.

Antonia blinked, looked at Tom, "She has to eat something." The breakfast had landed, Mom zapped it back to temperature, Tom Dad couldn't believe she did that right while he was sitting right next to her... Life at the Tetersberg home proceeded as per the usual painfully hyperactive weekday morning.

DITAN IS DISTRACTED AGAIN, he looks carefully at Abyssinia a second time, leaning her into the light: So were you a "warm" witch or a "cool" witch?

Abyssinia stares right through him, at a complete loss for words: Um, I've really no idea what—

Ditan thinks a second more: I'm guessing "seasonless." You're too pretty, one of the lucky ones... *Abyssinia was still clueless,* Your skin tone, dimwit. Where'd you grow up? *Mars?* Every witch that's transitioned through here recently had had her colors done, seemed to be a trend... Thought I'd ask given the topic at hand.

Abyssinia shakes her head; she's getting impatient: Which is? The *topic,* I mean...

Ditan frowns, bewildered again: Which is, which was... *Oh yes!* The Energy Spectrum! It's demanding so much attention of late—another 'trend,' I suppose. But I was wanting to add something specifically about the Earth's plane... *What* was it?

Ditan suddenly jumps up, scaring whatever color Abyssinia had remaining out of her—he professes: The Earth should be for learning and leisure—to harness and grow whatever parts of your life you can! Grab for the energy, electricity—*look at those goddam colors! That proves my point: it's **as blue as blue can be**...*

And Frenchtown now seems the bluest-est of all! That *has* to be why we're starting here—even though this is just one of millions of moments and stories that are happening right now.

*Abyssinia isn't sure what to say next; she cautiously glances up. Ditan seems to be done pontificating—she **has** to change the conversation. Abyssinia thrusts her thoughts in front of him.*

Abyssinia: So, is this okay? Just keep going like *this?* It's my first time on this level; it's a little disorienting.

Ditan: A little? That's generous.

Ditan scans her parchment notes impatiently...

'Sasha is brilliant and driven, a linear thinker with sharp edges and even sharper magickal instincts. Tip is equally brilliant but maintains a more happy-go-lucky perspective; she's a passionate tree-hugger whose occasional craft-throwing recklessness could hex a random hundred other living things under said hugged tree. Sasha's bright, pointed beauty has always complemented Tip's delicate, pliable loveliness—two halves of a very enchanted whole. Soba is three years their junior and is painfully *competitive with her sisters, even her cute and rounded features adapt daily to the twins' aggressive charm. Soba has a spontaneous intelligence (sometimes spell-flavored) that's too quick and too eager—almost too everything...'*

Abyssinia: So, change something—or what?

Ditan: No, you're fine, just keep going. That's one soul's opinion, anyway.

Abyssinia: Not too fussy? And the girls'? Getting their gist?

Ditan: It is, it's good—just keep going...

They peer around the sphere; they're unexpectedly alone—where was everyone else? They become anxious; Ditan's wary stare makes Abyssinia nervous.

Abyssinia: What's wrong, what's happening?

Ditan: Well, they're gone now, so can't know for sure, but most times it's a good thing—they're trusting us a bit more than the others... Probably. Maybe.

Ditan reconsiders their conversation, the words still hanging close by, slowly dissipating... Abyssinia shakes her head: Well, I don't know how believable your last bunch of twaddle was—especially from where I'm floating, sitting, *whatever we're doing...* But who am I to judge?

They sit there silently for a few more minutes, now more frustrated than nervous. Then Abyssinia intervenes: Let's stop with our—your?—blathering... One of The Sisters should get to say *something*, no?

Now Ditan's miffed: Fine. But they just started eating.

Major eye roll from Abyssinia, she sighs: No, they just finished.

THE RACHEL MADDOW birds were up and at it again this morning, moping and yapping about every damn thing in the world, or so it seemed. Could they give my young, precocious and impressionable, slightly warped brain just a *little* more space first thing in the a.m.?

Sorry, I know I don't always make the best first impression—

I've been told that quite a few times. You should blame that on Antonia—the gods and everyone else do. *She's* the one that produced such an insanely talented and beautiful set of twins— *Tip's the insane one,* by the way. (I'm kidding... Kind of.) Antonia calls my humor "abrasive," which is *such* an Antonia-ish thing to say.

One thing I do know for sure is that my political persuasion is definitely *both* my parents' fault: I love my lesbian-ish liberal newscasters no matter how cranky they are... *Tip thinks so too.* (Our passion, however, is nothing compared to Tom Dad's obsessive-compulsive bleeding heart.)

There *is* a big homunculus-like elephant in the room, and it's something all of us with even a tiny bit of witchery or metaphysical mishegoss feel desperate to say: mortals used to take this magic thing *so* seriously—some still do—and I'm not sure why... Maybe it was a jealousy thing, maybe a cultural thing, but guess what—*the reality is not all that interesting.* Most of us can't even straddle a broom let alone fly one. True magickal talent or spell-crafting ability only happens once in a blue wolf's moon. So most of this myth-making crap about W's just isn't real—and what *is* real, *isn't "all that"...* (To be fair, maybe a couple centenary ago, Mom and Aunt Ezra like to brag *it was different.* And maybe it was —but *this* is *now...*)

Truth-be-told, I do like some of the ideas that Aunt Ezra goes all-Ephelba about—maybe I *am* ready for some of that *nasty old magic to be new again?*

Julie's text interrupts Sasha: she'll meet her at her locker first thing... *But what if I don't want to meet her first thing—or* **anything?**

THE INTENSITY of colors shifted again—now with more heat, shards of blood-red. Then some more teetering, shaking; the air remained clean and clear, though. It was Constance moving closer to the conversation, but it had to be more than just that—something temporal, tricking time somehow (or trying to).

Pilar: Love her! What tits-for-balls she has! Didn't get that from her mother.

Constance, bites her tongue, hard: Oh, I wouldn't say that. You're just getting a quick sense—keep peeling that onion... Their magic and craft is still so very young, but it will grow like every other part of them with every feeling they have.

Pilar, frowns, shrugs: Well that's obvious and boring. What are you reading from? Some old transcript you found floating around? Kind of makes Sasha's point.

Constance scowls: Not very confident in that, but let's keep going. Did you or any one mention The Spectrum yet—especially The Impeccable Blue?

Pilar: You were sitting right there—oh wait, no you weren't—so yeah, done.

Constance: And The Green?

Pilar: Too soon.

Constance, impatiently: The *Spectacular* Green?

Pilar: Too soon...

Constance: I'm not sure—they'll need to know what we mean, how to actually look at the world, all parallel realities, the different planes.

Pilar: I *know,* I get it. But it's too much *already—too **soon**!*

Constance let it drop, though not happily. (She knew too well that whatever needed to be done, she and Pilar would need to do willingly, and together.)

———————— ◆ ◆ ————————

SHE'S LATE AGAIN?! Sasha stomped the curb—a chip of sidewalk launched, dinged the street sign. Tip could have heard Sasha's toilet-mouth brain fart a mile away, *Sloppy, but now is hardly the time to mention it.* Three other dudes were at the corner of Earbuds & Happiness, oblivious, shifting and tapping and finger-dancing. Tip had always envied that ability—such an incontrovertible gift—to become immune to whatever was indisputably in front of you, demanding you take heed, *Must be a secret power all its own...* She could get close to some level of apathy, but it was all through spell-making (a wonky part of her craft)—it wasn't the same thing as *true* adolescent indifference. She was too self-aware, *too sensitive.* Always had been.

The bus turned onto Main, stopped at Ridge (the first of three on Main), but after a minute or five was still resting at Ridge. This of course only made Sasha more agitated (more illicit language and hand gestures ensued). Tip's defense: turned her music up, pretended to be looking for a song she already knew she didn't have. (To be fair, no one—not even a *good witch*—is at her best first thing in the morning.)

Tip already knew Sasha was primed for some sort of battle, so she got behind her to do whatever damage control she could. Sasha stepped-dragged herself, exaggerating one step (counting to five or so...) then the next. Bubby was at-the-ready since this was hardly the first time Sasha tried to hijack everyone's high school commute.

Sasha sneered, "It's not like any of us has a math test first thing this morning, Bubby. Don't worry about us!"

"I get it, I'm sorry, Miss Witchy-poo—now get your tuchus on this bus."

"Oh, oh, wait. Let's just sit here and watch the trees flower, what do you—*shit!*"

Tip had just given her sister a swift whatever-it-was straight up her boney white butt, then threw the thought, *What the hell? Just sit your ass down!* But Sasha, for some reason, was not deterred this morning...

Sasha stalled, "No, we deserve to *know;* I'm tired of all this *subterfuge.*"

Now her captive audience was turning against her, "Sit your ass down and shut the hell up!" yelled an irritated voice.

"Now, now, none of that." Bubby held up her hand and turned to Sasha, "Which would you have preferred, Miss Sasha, my taking a dump in that pretty pink bag of yours or at the Monroe's house on the corner?"

Sasha fizzled, surrendered—she sat hard, angling herself firmly into the rigid bus seat back. She straightened her shoulders into place; it was her small ritual, one that stamped the beginning of the school day in her mind.

T.G.I.F.F. ('*THANK GOD IT'S FREAKIN' Friday*'): For over one hundred Gregorian years, 1,200 Wiccan lunar months, and the attendant 4,800 Fridays, the Tetersberg clan (Tom and Antonia, its current iteration) religiously abandoned their Earth-bound responsibilities wherever they were working, conjuring, metamorphosing (when that was popular) and *got their high on*—The Lord of the Buzz would rule, and Cannabis was his queen (that primarily describes the present reign, to be clear). Tom and Antonia's dedication was commendable as was their ability to adapt to and/or deter various obstacles: limpid friends, an impatient Aunt Ezra, and children (mostly their own).

But as much Antonia would revel in her Fridays, she was equally wary about the first part of the week; the discomfort, mostly between she and Tom, had become strangely persistent, a nagging itch. It wasn't *necessarily* obvious and maybe all of that witchery—her preternatural gifts—helped keep the anxiety well hidden, much like it presumably had the last eighty of her one hundred twenty-four years. (She could pass for a mortal fifty, albeit a very well-worn fifty.)

And Antonia noted, for the fourth time that week, she was also more times outside of her body than in it. Taking stock of her current physiological state—she was not impressed. *This is all* *gross—and I'm **especially gross**—getting grosser by the moment.* Antonia could be too quick to admonish herself; she'd consider all her terrific creative output and recent accomplishments (her paintings were finally lucid, their intent fully realized) and then sprinkle it with what remarkable young women—*exceptional* soon-to-be underwitches—her daughters were becoming, but she'd ultimately felt the emotional equivalent of *nothing-but-crickets.*

When pressed, however, Antonia professed to hate *all* her work. Actually, *hate* is a mite too heavy-handed; she needed to qualify that: *love-hate,* no, *hate-love* would be more apt. She respected her thinking, the quality of the work, but—the right words always abandoned her. To quickly sum up Antonia's philosophical whining: *boredom.* She slashed her canvas with long, bold strokes of ennui every day, for as long as she could stand it.

Suddenly in her next breath she felt she was once again a small invisible Antonia, fluttering just above herself, patiently and painfully tracking her own movements, her will completely disabled. *This is like that podcast: 'When Bad Things Happen to Good Witches'...* An empty wine glass had materialized in her hand, actually there was one in *each hand*—her id was always the first to surrender to her spell-crafting instincts. (If nothing else, you need to stay good friends with your *yin,* always keep that top-of-mind...) She was compelled, moving toward the counter to get something to fill it with. The wine was in her sight lines, but this moment was demanding something much more substantial—the wine would just become water.

What time is it? It has to be five o'clock somewhere... That jokey reflex barely registered anymore, more embarrassing than anything else. *I guess I should give myself some measure of credit for trying to look like I give a shit what anyone thinks...* (Actually, she cared too much.)

And it is only 11:36 a.m. Friday... Antonia gradually exhaled and picked up the paint brush again.

The Sisters had ascertained and developed unique defense

mechanisms: they had concocted "tricks" (slightly lesser spells, not as long-lasting) to keep their perspectives intact. There were two types of tricks that the twins could do particularly well (even tag team if required) in the iffiest of circumstances. Sasha had been the first to discern, by trial and then more trial (very little error—we don't like error) what her mom's tipping point (a fun play on words if I do say so, simply trying to keep the mood upbeat) was when it came to her various highs of choice. They were very simple, functional spells: locking the car ignition upon the third unsuccessful attempt, conjured baby clouds of aural bliss that would float in one ear and out the other—dissolving desires for tequila shots, another "half a joint," etcetera, etcetera. Rather simplistic, I know, but they did the trick—all bad and unhealthy intent (at least, temporarily) aborted.

Sadly, painfully (fortunately and unfortunately), Tom Dad and Antonia performed as expected. If the fuss seems to be more about Antonia, it's because she was more predictable than not; Tom Dad liked to keep himself (and everyone else) guessing as to when and how he'd fail. It had been exactly that way all of his fifty-three (mostly) mortal years. There were several other semi-successful spells that were concocted from that original cloud-ear-worm spell, so in the spirit of full transparency, it's very true that last grouping *were* a drug of a sort, so not really helping truly solve anything for their addicted parents.

Sasha hypothesized that their family existence was like algebra: there was a formula first required to be understood and then, and only then, could it be used to figure out that problem's unique answer. This particular perspective, on a very basic level, gave Sasha at least some solace, a semi-logical solution.

TIP SLID INTO THE CAR... Antonia had already determined this token conversation would be her daily good deed for a daughter—any accessible daughter, one per day—regardless of its outcome.

Antonia had compelled (yes, there was a tad bit of mind control involved) Tip into the car with her; she'd forgotten gas and rolling papers. (*But does the mall offer pre-pot-party sundries?* Antonia would finally learn today.)

"How long have you been writing it?" Antonia actually looked *at* Tip with her question, which caught Tip completely off guard.

"It's not an 'it'—it's probably a lot of *its*. I mean there have been a lot of ideas, a lot of *good* ideas, I think. Too soon to know. But it *feels* good. Most of them do, anyway..." Antonia was nodding, looking left *again*; Tip almost wondered aloud how her mother was able to drive as efficiently and accident-free by only (or mostly) looking out of the left front door window. (Maybe her overwitch alter ego took the wheel during these random moments when cognizant Antonia needed to go somewhere else.)

They drove about three minutes farther—it seemed longer (driving always does).

Antonia abruptly continued, "So, it's a script?" (She must have gotten bored with looking at that one side of the road.)

Tip was getting impatient again (and too quickly, she took note), "If it's a script, it's more than *one*. Just said that. The process is very organic right now—could be written, a graphic novel that's craft-based, we just don't know exactly if it's—"

"So, it's a book? Who's 'we'?"

"Sorry, there's no 'we'—not sure why I said that, and there's no book. But..."

"But what?"

Tip bit down hard on her first thought, "No. Don't want to say."

Antonia was getting twitchy, distracted anyway—she went back to her window. (Two minutes more of driving.)

Antonia thought she'd be funny, "Um, is it pink?... Bigger than a breadbox?"

No answer. More minutes of driving—she decided to back into their parking space for a change.

Antonia was miffed, "You never take me seriously."

Tip shrugged, "Why would we? You're always stoned... A warm, funny, motherly—mostly—kind of stoned, but still stoned."

They got out of the car and walked into the mall without another word.

So THE WEEKEND began to take shape at just slightly ahead of the rate that it was already losing it; don't stress or fuss, this is very standard for not only the Tetersbergs but many of the well-placed homes and family mixtures in Frenchtown.

With the autumn chill, the competition at the Frenchtown Mall was fierce among the young female witches prowling the worn prefabbed concrete runways. No one offered any new or surprising strategies—the same was true for the male witches right off the bench. Teen mortal and halfling boys made a strong showing, but again that's par for this stage of the game—they *always* overcompensate. (Who can blame them? The female witches outnumber the males regardless of persuasion or geno-type almost two to one, so it can easily descend into something very post-Darwinian.) But nothing to worry, everyone and every-thing ended up in their rightful place: the younger players ending the first half either on their phones or notepads or already half asleep, floating homeward. (The one exception was Julie who had found a younger halfling teen [new to the mall] and was still exploring different applications of her Wicca tongue exercises in the back of his ancient Camaro.)

The more mature players—ages fifty to one hundred twenty-five or thereabouts—were appropriately inebriated and crawling their way to sleep, hopefully across their metaphorical goal line and in the comfort of their beds. Tom Dad and Antonia were still in overtime, slinging shots in their kitchen.

"Do the teachers know anything about it?"

"This isn't *Hogwarts*, nimrod, I doubt it. And why would they really care?"

The second period bell was two minutes late again; Sasha tried desperately to ignore it, since nobody else seemed to notice. But it was a strange thing to happen on a Monday morning.

Tom Boy's comments caught up with her, "Wait—each classroom is a *portal?!*" Sasha was as much dumbfounded as she was brimming, exhilarated. "I'm with bated, well, not just breath —everything!"

Tom Boy pressed reset, turned to Sasha and grumbled, "Cool your jets, Samantha. You're blowing this way out of proportion— and like I first said, I think some asshole was just bored and tweaked some thread." Tom laughed and looked at Sasha—she was transfixed; he almost thought aloud, *Could someone so smart actually be that stupid?* Tom Boy interrupted her strange reverie, "Sash, you look like I just told you Santa Claus existed. Just relax, like I said, I don't see how any of it could be actually happening, and anymore, it's boring, stupid shit. You've always had that geek aura going on, but you were always cool—let's not *not* be cool..."

Sasha was immediately defensive, "Screw you, Bright Boy. When did you become the Wizard Arbiter of Coolness?"

Now Tom Boy became unusually impatient, "*Wizards* aren't cool either, *by the way.*"

"Cool your jets is *right*, dickbreath."

"Nice." Deep groan from Tom, "Just leave Harry where he belongs, in Florida, will you please?"

(*Pilar is confused:* What's wrong with her? She's acting like some silly Sasha doppelgänger, boondoggled by some boy...

Constance shrugs: Well, she *was*... *Constance rolled her eyes:* and apparently, in spite of what she claims—still is.)

. . .

SASHA HAD ABRUPTLY CONVINCED herself (once again) that she felt *pseudo-committed* to the *"concept"* (again, her words) of her and Tom Boy's coupledom (at least for the duration of this convo—it had started out pretty well...). She pressed him, "So, what do *we* do?" Sasha really meant it; she needed Tom Boy to talk and logically make the words then ideas mean something. He could make people (especially Sasha) believe something and know what to do about it—that's what he did. Without a snippet of craft or a wink of a wand, he could sell anyone *anything*—it was his secret sauce, his own special potion. Tom Boy had devoutly believed it was his magical, witchy sixth sense but recently had deducted it was an unabashedly human talent, and he was no less proud of it. Tom Boy's overall intent, his unspoken goal, was to always help, not hurt.

The first bell rang, they started their Pavlovian stroll to Mr. Clarke's Wonderful World of Even More Wonderful World History. Tom Boy finally finished the conversation, "What do we do? Nothing, because there's nothing to do. It was just some stupid tweet."

Sasha needed a distraction, and she had predetermined that this distraction would come with Tom Boy attached to it. Their two-month, two-week relationship-that-wasn't-exactly-a-relationship was in dire need of some care and feeding—especially from Tom Boy. (At least that was Sasha's fixed perspective.)

She was staring hard at the back of his head, "But you said there were three or four of them—isn't that what you said?" Sasha felt suddenly irritated and impatient (her stated Tom Boy goal was apparently as capricious as she is).

"There's *always* at least three or four *thousand* them, Sasha," he looked back at her, incredulously. "*You* don't know that? And you want to be part of *BWB*?" (That was Tom Boy's pet acronym for their school club—currently sporting an entirely male membership—*The Boyz With Byte: Digital Machinations Society*... Always sounded kind of gay to Sasha, but she'd kept that to herself, *I can be gay if I have to...*)

Sasha mouthed the words, "*Eat my—* " when Mr. Clarke started class. She started to point at a part of her anatomy but couldn't determine exactly in that moment what would be the *least* apropos. And Tom Boy had already stopped paying attention.

SASHA SAW THE DIFFERENT (I.E., wrong) year on her favorite WWII poster in a crafty millisecond. It was her most favorite of several she loved; Sasha was passionate about certain periods of history (the more layered and socially complicated, the better). She could give two hoo-ha's about simple nation grabs or war heroes... Tip was the opposite: she tried hard to be her all-powerful sister's complement (or foil if need be). Tip loved it *all*— the nuances of the world she lived in, all the tints and shades of meaning she'd occasionally sense from her parallel (or wherever) realities.

(*Pilar starts looking more nervous than anxious:* Where the hell is Tip anyway? She was supposed weigh in by this point.

Abyssinia shrugs: That would make sense... *She glances through the next few pages and suddenly recalls,* I forgot. We shifted things around a bit, we sensed she wasn't quite "ready." She seemed pleased by that.

Pilar doesn't appear to remember, waves the concern away.)

MR. STEPHEN CLARKE loved his wall, and he love-loved that his students loved his wall, his very unique and "enhanced" poster collection. A veritable who's-what filled almost every available inch—his war posters dominated and they truly were fascinating. Clarke's spell-crafting strengths were middling at best, and liked to happen in fits; it was during one of those fits—a *"magical stroke of genius"* (his words, by the way; Stephen Clarke didn't struggle a smidge with self-adulation)—that he enchanted every poster hanging with its respective living history. The magical, animated result appeared more of a Cartoon Network promotional spot than anything ostensibly educational (ironically, much like Clarke himself). Mr. Clarke bragged (as the posters danced, fought, or sang—all silently—over his class) that anyone could "enter" any of the posters with the appropriate learning spell or "key"—but he couldn't guarantee they could find their way back out. (No one had ever attempted to prove him wrong, or right.)

After rambling on for a number of minutes, Mr. Clarke dramatically announced their next topic (with readings for tomorrow): "Post Invasion Policies: Spanish Influence in the New World" had jarringly become "The Rude (Though Eloquent) Pirates of Fernandina: the Politics of Please and Thank-you." Did this deserve yet another *what da freak?* Sasha scowled, *Was that Clarke's cover version of Rocky H.'s 'Doin' the Time Warp'?!* How did she miss the transition from the French coast to the United States? (Not to mention a rather significant gap of fifty-whatever years?) *And what the double-freak does one have to do with the other?*

Suddenly she caught Toby in her sideview, playing around with something under his desk that could be a wand, could be a—she stopped pursuing the thought... Toby had tested the limits of Mr. Clarke's sufferance by crafting a couple innocuous poster whammies: completely harmless (from *his* perspective) and just to see if he could get away with it—that had been Toby's *modus operandi* since Sasha could remember. But maybe this one time he swung that wand a little higher than his skill set? The affected posters had time-bounced *years* not minutes... *The 'real' damage is still, potentially, waiting to happen.*

Sasha reveled in these *potentially* superhero-super witch moments; she knew Toby would be bouncing to Math in a few minutes, so she mentally and then (when the bell rang) materially positioned herself directly in the middle of the hall. Toby saw Sasha, tripped over nothing but his nerve (or lack of it).

Chest out, he was on the defensive, ready, "What do you want?" *Avoid her eyes at all costs.*

Sasha knew the drill well; Toby was expert at the verbal duck and roll—before you knew it, he was off and spinning. Not this time.

"Since the start of our conversation, I think you've been lying to me, T."

Toby furrowed one brow, "But that's impossible."

Sasha was arch, "*Why* is that impossible?"

"Um, because we just *started* this conversation...?"

"Don't be a dick. I meant that *other posters convo,* when they were all green."

Toby started walking, sneering, "That *was* pretty funny. And nobody even said a word—poor Mr. Dickhead Clarke... Nobody but *you*, that is."

His nervous finger-fidgeting shifted to some strange form of knee-knocking. Girls were tricky in general, but Sasha triggered her own unique form of anxiety: it wasn't a crush (he liked black girls), it wasn't her magic (hot, but she never really pulled any even-a-little-bit-interesting spells), it wasn't a physical thing (on that he was sure something was wrong with him—Sash was frigging hot)... So, *what was it?* All his unanswered Sasha neuroses aside, he was pretty sure what she was quizzing him about, and for the first time in two years of lopsided passion *he* knew something *she* thought she needed.

Toby stopped still, "I never lie. It's outside of my code of ethics." She laughed; he kinda laughed. He meant it to be funny, but he also *meant it.* They had maybe a minute more so Sasha dug in: "Spill it, T. I know you know what I think you know." That didn't exactly come out how she would have liked, but there it was. Toby suddenly wasn't sure now where she was going with this. *I thought for sure this was about her "ship status" with Steve, but, alas, no...* Uh-oh.

"I'm talking about the *Lips* poster in Clarke's room, and everything you were screwing around with—or it." Sasha became a tad distressed, unsure, "All of the *time* behind it..."

Toby was coy, "Huh? You lost me. What about them—what would 'time' have to do with anything?"

Sasha abruptly sliced his response in two, "Did you change those dates?"

Toby's in play, "Change them to what?"

"To what you changed them to!"

Toby grinned wide... *I've finally impressed the queen.* (*Blam—that was the trick!* "*Caught in the act*"—*what a friggin' turn-on—even if I never did touch those stupid-ass dates!*) And Sasha, apparently, was especially clever at catching boys with their spell-casting pants around their ankles.

Sasha pressed, "You can't screw around with Time, dude... Even a little bit."

His ego flattened, Toby shot back, sans the cheesy smile, "I didn't change *anything*. Screw you." Then he was gone in a shot. (The difficult truth—for Sasha, anyway—*was the truth:* if Toby had done basically zilch, maybe some more coloring outside the lines at best, then what or *who* was flirting with paranormal disaster?)

Sasha was stymied, and not happily; the third-period bell shook her, stung a bit, *I **hate** when that happens.*

CONSTANCE PONDERS: Frenchtown, the social climate and such... How *The Sisters* think they fit, how they actually do, and don't. I typically like to wait until the dust has settled, or cleared (*we* always used to say *settled*) to start to consider it. But all of this doesn't seem very "typical" to me...

So, first and foremost, the magick—*the craft*. I think you'll be more frustrated now than surprised to hear it's become, how shall I say it quickly, *trite*—rather *silly*. But to be absolutely clear (fair?), that depends more upon the individual—the witch that's 'using'... I know you've heard the same issue (complaint? concern?) a few different times already. (One could make the argument that maybe we're not as immune or bored as is being suggested.)

Then there's this: there are larger machinations underway; it sounds ominous and perhaps it should. Even hints of that perpetually ridiculous but insanely effective patriarchal curse and malediction from decades ago (you don't retain much in a transition, but *that* is something I'll never forget). The prose, the details are gone, but the horrific essence of it will be etched in my amorphous mind forever:

To make women less than they are, to make them hateful and intolerable. Those that can't find the will to hate or are too weak to antagonize shall be expunged...

———————

Tip started to scribble: A Tree Grows in Frenchtown... *It has one small finger of a root wrapped carefully around another—the longest in the world! They're slightly different but mostly the same. The trees themselves are big but will become bigger. Two huge, remarkable and remarkably* **perfect** *trees...*

There'll be more magic in one seed of this maple than in all the demigods over, let's say, California. Myriad spells will help explain this perfect magic: in how things will grow, what they'll share with other beginnings is specific and very, very precious...

I'll get this lovely fact out of the way—if it isn't obvious already—I'm a major "tree-hugger" (a fave Tom Dad term) from *way* back, all of my interminable sixteen years... (*I'm kidding. Kinda.*)

I'm not only a *hugger*, I've been and still am an unabashed *tree-sleeper, tree-whisperer* (I *kind of* have proof of that, real *facts*—pics, actually), and Mom has said I basically have a very "unnatural" relationship (can we please label that *supernatural?*) with that perfect oak in our backyard... I'm not exactly clear what makes something *unnatural* versus, I suppose, *natural*, especially when you come from a family of witches and a father that (at the least) puts out a good effort, mostly in regards to the tolerance and patience thing.

So I've started this particular "wish list" maybe ten times—it's what I called them when I first started writing them, but they've become much more than just a "list" of wishes, dreams, or hopes (I counted the pages behind this one to be sure). But that fact isn't really important, not when compared to the wide variety of wish lists that I've concocted; some are completely grounded in this reality (very intentionally), but then others are probably more accurately described as *dream wish lists*. (I'm not being redundant at all, promise.)

Which is so often the case about facts, no? *Wobbly things facts are...* Whether they're real or magical, attached to one reality plane or another, whether you want to acknowledge them or not, whether you want to *believe* in them or not. Can be a tough call many times, at least for me.

I'm half-kidding (probably a little less than half): facts *are* always facts. It's how we want to *understand* them, and then how I decide (maybe not even consciously) how to explain, interpret and share the *story*, because the minute you try to explicate something, you necessarily influence it, change it. (It can happen in remarkably subtle ways, but it's inescapable.)

(I'm not sure I'm doing this correctly—haven't heard anything one way or the other...)

What else can I tell you right now? I'm boring until I'm not. I'm insanely crazy-passionate about *goodness*—I'm just as blah-blah as the next girl regarding magic and spell-crafting. I mean, *how many disappeared elephants that are found in someone's Mini car trunk* can a person find entertaining, or even a little bit funny? (Apparently *three*, and it was the same bunch of assholes each time.) Big friggin' deal, just because you discover you have that transmogrifying gene or trait, does that give you the right to inflict pain on the only elephant in a fifty-mile radius? Hasn't she or he been through enough trying to live its elephant life a zillion miles from where it *should be?* (Sometimes it just fucking burns my hot little wand...)

So, I don't know if this was helpful, completely boring and mindless (I personally didn't think so... *These notions just come into your brain, and you do your best to make some sense of them*).

Tip thought it was later than it was—still two minutes till the bell. She moved over a few inches out of the library building's shadow and swallowed as much sun as she could.

THE BUS LURCHED in any which direction, but each student's phone and its attached face seemed impervious, as if there existed an innate gyroscope function—nothing could or would disrupt the flow of their impregnable dialog and connection. (The Sisters were hardly immune.)

"O.M.G., why did you just write that?" Sasha challenged Tip; you could almost hear Soba's eyes roll as she scooted down into her seat, avoiding the impending line of fire.

Tip scowled, her eyes stayed fixed, "Because she *fucking* deserved it."

"Great, so you now you have 'fuck' all over your scroll."

Tip smirked, "It's not all over anywhere—it's right there. Once, *right there.*" Actually, it was quite a few other places and, actually, it might have been accompanied by some other select *bon mots*, oh, and some choice customized emojis, for added kicks. Tip found the convo funny, *What a freaky thing for somebody to get so weirded out about...* Especially your twin sister.

"Wait, you tweeted *the same message too?*" Sasha fretted aloud.

"Yeah, *so?*"

"*So?* So it's now imprinted on your social network thought stream, and you can never, ever do anything about it. To help yourself."

Tip dead-panned, "Uh-huh, that's weird—mostly because *you're* weird. No further comment."

The two glared at each other to a draw; this was and will continue to be the bane of their shared existence: Sasha worried about things she couldn't control, and Tip didn't seem to have the worry gene in any shape or form.

Tip relented, "So that's what's got your wands so wadded up this afternoon? I doubt just my 'doomed future'? Not even a single chirp about the Great Wall Possession?"

"You heard?"

Tip teased, "Not just heard—I *saw!*"

Sasha muttered, now strangely anxious, "Well, that's definitely bigger that one tweet... Actually, that's another something that's untweetable."

Tip was disconcerted—Sasha was avoiding something. She knew this nervous and erratic something-or-other was what her sister did when she didn't know what else to do, when she didn't feel *in control.* Tip didn't fret about Sasha's craving control, it was part of their innate yin and yang, but what she didn't like was when she sensed Sasha was lying, attempting to keep something from her.

She pushed her way into Sasha's very antic thought stream, *What the freak are you trying not to say? You know something, what is it?*

Sasha was nonplussed, pushing the conversation away with the palm of her hand. She blurted her made-up response, "No, I've moved on. You said last week you'd tweeted your last tweet."

"Oh yeah, I did say that. Hmm, guess I was joking. Or not. We'll see, '*time* will tell,'" said Mocking Tip, Patronizing Tip.

And that was the end of that. (Still nine rather fussy yet tense minutes till the corner of Line and Locust.)

The twins stomped down the steps. Sasha turned, "Wait, where's Soba?" Tip looked slightly surprised, then not, "She probably got off at Line and Oak. She's no dummy—I wouldn't want to be around us either." Sasha turned, huffed and puffed her way up the sidewalk. Tip lingered, pretending to check her messages, giving herself a safe distance from any further potential arguments.

There would be much out-of-body floating and not-especially-polite discussion between bedrooms tonight... (Or perhaps none at all.)

AUNT EZRA SLAPPED her coffee mug down on the table in praise! For once—a first—she concurred "one thousand percent," ten times more than her *very* occasional "enthusiastic agreement." The article was straightforward and specific (that was a happy surprise) and seemed to balance its point exactly on the tip of *her* wand: fight *"diminishment" with doing 'better.'* But: *"...it's the 'doing' and not necessarily the 'improving.'"* Yowza, what a Mr. (Miss?) Smarty-pants! (She'd forgotten the sex of the writer, which was a very good sign.) Aunt Ezra liked to pick on The Times, primarily because she believed they liked to pick on her—a love-*deteste* relationship. This was standard operating procedure for the majority of Ezra's relationships be they human, an over- or underwitch, digital or non-binary, or somewhat in the middle, etcetera and more etcetera. Aunt Ezra tended to behave as if she was much older and cultured and sage than she in fact was—not to suggest living for well over a century was a toss in the figurative cauldron. It wasn't at all, and she had all the emotional baggage, wand burn scars, anti-depressants, paranormal residue to prove it.

AS PER DITAN'S REQUEST, *Constance speaks louder (enunciate!) this time:* late April, 23 April to be precise. 1878...

> *The wedge between worlds, wasn't always like this,*
> *The balance made sense; nothing was missed, in the*
> *Shift from one plane to another below.*

If lost—a nose, an ear, a finger or two,
Would simply grow back, perhaps slightly askew.
And who's worse for that knowledge,
Of a nose tipped or tweaked,
Or an ear somewhat hampered,
By a drum that might tweet...
But the souls *that were lost—now* that, *to be fair,*
Could cause worse to worsen, and
Then more—and yet again! So be ready, be nimble,
Trip lightly and dare no one
To dawdle and stare.
These changes are real, and for all to contest,
For the wedge between worlds,
Gives lives much to protest...

Constance flips through the next few pages. (It was "cheating" but also habit at this point.) The rest was still unreadable, inscrutable. The text had done this every time she'd read this passage and nothing seemed to change; even more frustrating: the questions (by default) stayed the same as well.

She knows loosely about the future potential swirling around Ezra (at least the wildly varying conversations pointing to it). She tried not to have an opinion (she was required to remain neutral), but at times it was hard not to; all of those sects, especially the two covens, seemed to be inflating their hopes—all of Ezra's makeshift aspirations—a bit *unrealistically.* (At least that is Constance and especially Pilar's feelings; the covens were setting their own ambitions too high and didn't appear to care.) In Ezra (she was one of three potentates) they had at least found an over-witch whose overextended ego and vanity seemed to match their own.

Pilar's main frustration is the effect that all of this was begin-ning to have on Ezra's "niece," Sasha Tetersberg. *So hard to just float here and watch it all happen and not "react"—but that's the job...*

. . .

TOM DAD JUMPED for his phone, knocking the same charm (Antonia preferred the word "talisman") to the floor of his tiny, shared office space. This particular rune held a specific and unique "charm" unto itself: it was the Monopoly game piece that started their "archetypical" (*his* description) relationship, and he most certainly wasn't going to let that stray too far from where it needed to live.

To give this moment some quick context: it was sometime around '62, at a coffee shop where there was a Monday game night (before coffee shops and board games had an even glancing connection with being cool; actually, the word "cool" was just beginning to mean something beyond temperature). Magic-making was commonplace; the basic stuff—simple transformations, basic levitation, flying (as long as it wasn't any distance more than about a street block—too much effort otherwise)—was as complicated as walking and talking (*without* gum) at the same time. It was more a thing of convenience (even a sign of complacency or laziness). It wasn't anything to aspire to, but it wasn't anything to necessarily avoid or disparage as déclassé or low brow. (If you had the genes and the bones, and the will and the means—goody-good for you.)

It took a little extra energy to make it interesting—show a little creativity or personality; Antonia had been exceptionally blessed (one of the lucky ones), and Tom, well, kind of the other way around. He could barely transmigrate through a wall, but flying or any real-deal spell-crafting, not so much. He also wasn't that concerned about it; he was much more interested in the more practical magic that *words*—all by themselves—could offer. Antonia liked that: the fact that *he was different,* a uniquely *Tom* kind-of-different.

. . .

NOTE TO SELF: get a faster watch. Antonia sat back down. She looked at the last thing she wrote, the last time she was writing... *This has got to stop. There's no way I can keep up, or am I once again talking myself out of or into something?*

It *had* changed, but not to the degree she had once again begun chastising herself: the painting, the writing, the etcetera had all kept happening in spite of how she tended to dwell on how they weren't. Antonia excelled at whatever she set her mind to, and with all things equal, she actually was better than most, at least within her middling community of Frenchtown.

But suddenly, yet again, there was the burning issue of Ezra and their ostensibly indestructible friendship.

Maybe it's time for a break—a breather? It wouldn't be the first time: a friendship doesn't maintain its mostly healthy status without some occasional bumps in the formica. (Let's face it: one hundred five years is no, as they suggest, flash in the pan...) But the struggles seemed more frequent and overwhelming in a way Antonia couldn't quite get her head (or wands) around. Ezra had had her fatalistic phases, but she'd never before sounded threatening during them. She seemed to be demanding some sort of demonstrable change from Antonia, and she seemed to need to be able to "quantify" it on some level somehow.

Antonia glanced at her watch again; she had to leave now for her weekly *Ezra Tequila Therapy* unless she was going to "broom it," or fly. (One would think the fresh air would help enliven things, her mood, but it had more of a debilitating effect of late—*Or could it be more to do with the 'subject matter'?*) Antonia suddenly, strangely, surprisingly recalled a favorite talisman: one that had helped wrangle problematic personalities into a smaller, more manageable—and if necessary, squash-able—form. She had never posited it as a potential Ezra vaccination before because, frankly, it had never become an issue.

Then strangely, said talisman (a charm-size dusty silver fork being strangled by a spoon) was floating front and center, ready for action. Also burning bright—disturbingly so—in the box to the left were several shards of perfectly decorated wood, pieces of something that at some point was (it couldn't have been anything else) a wand.

I gotta get my fat ass out of here—but what's up with this smart-ass wand? Too much to bite off right now, she leapt into the sky from the back deck.

Antonia embraced the air; she could have flown there with her eyes closed. But that glowing broken wand, those silly pieces of wood had accomplished their goal: they seared wonder and worry (probably more worry) into her tired brain. She opened the door to the bar and saw Ezra sitting in "their booth," her eyes pinched closed, hands flat on the booth's table, *Fucking great—she's either in the middle of a migraine or a seance.* Antonia did her *moment meditation,* calming her everything as she approached the booth and their "happy" hour.

Stupid Party Tricks

✤

The end of something is always the beginning of something else... Tip looked back, continued jotting in her *Omnipresent Organic Journal.* She was keenly aware of how clunky her label for it was, but it summed up her "process" exactly: her ideas could happen anywhere and at any time and in any form—tangible, intangible, and otherwise. Much like one talking to oneself (which Tip did vociferously, happily, sometimes incessantly, and hopefully not too loudly). She *"streamed" her "consciousness"* onto the page:

It's Saturday again. Let's start something.

What do you mean 'something'?

*Let's do something, make something of all of this, everything we did and experienced—**are** doing, and experiencing...*

There's nothing really that new to say about it. Though; it's not like the rest of the world has never heard of Gandalf or Lena Duchannes.

And they and we just might be all the better if we never heard from either him or her or anyone making this stuff up ever again. It's not like they ever really lived it—not like we do. Or did. Or will...

Then, fortunately, breakfast interrupted.

The pancakes were already in the air, like Ed Sullivan plates spinning on sticks, but Antonia (once again) conveniently "forgot" the sticks. *Tom won't mind, he'll be too hung over to notice, and it's an old trick at this point. Helpful in its way, very nonthreatening.* (Antonia grinned at her magical *morning stretch*.)

She sat back and closed one and three-quarters of her eyes—which daughter would look first? Play with the spell first? *That might be hoping for too much. They're hungry, and my pancakes always overpromise—but they do look good.* Even at one hundred twenty-something years old, Antonia was an aesthete before she was anything else, with mother and then finally overwitch filling in any gaps when and where they might occur.

(Saturday mornings—typically more hung over than not—could provide a plethora of opportunity for all concerned.)

———— ⟨⟨⟨ ⟩⟩⟩ ————

WITH OUR MUDDLE of crafty teens and their organically, exponentially expanding wants and needs, hexes and anti-hexes, tweets that friend and unfriend, relationships of every sort tugging and taunting, it was no small miracle that crafting wasn't everyone's first line of defense (or offense). What's cool rules when all is said and done, and no one wanted to be the wannabe witch with the wrong wand stuck in the wrong—dare we say—hole.

Tom Boy had kinda-sacked Sasha and was semi-bewitched by Tip, Greg was troubled by Julie who, of course, couldn't get enough of (mostly just looking at) Tom Boy, and lastly there's Bitts who, ominously, had the most surprising and least natural (in a digital way of thinking) attraction for the Wicked (Under)Witch of Frenchtown High, Sasha. (That might lead one to assume that Tip would offer up the Glinda-goodness side of the equation—and there would be some truth in that—but hardly enough to manage the glare of Sasha's self-serving witchery.)

. . .

OCTOBER'S HUNTER'S moon seemed a shade minute or three early... *Pilar waves the notion away as silly, which in fact it was (Time does as Time is). She moves her text closer, into the glow, so she can see more clearly:* Here's a nice one, and it fits (mostly)—just change the boys to girls (as if it matters...)

> *The season, the signs,*
> *Are soon to describe,*
> *What's been twisted and turned,*
> *And who's fit to be tied.*
> *The knots, wrapped thrice,*
> *Leaves girls to delight,*
> *Which planets and dreams,*
> *Should be theirs to hold tight.*

An exaggerated fake yawn is Constance's considered response.

Pilar ignores the slight, then cautiously asks: We're here on this particular reality plane until we're told otherwise, right?

Constance: Yes. Correct.

Pilar: And our charge is simply make the *dots*—such as they are —stay connected as best as they can.

Constance: Yes, I suppose so.

Pilar: No, no 'suppose,' isn't that basically what's right there in stone in front of us all the time? We don't go rearranging anyone's dots just because we have a whim one way or another.

Constance didn't respond specifically; Pilar took that as a "yes."

She'd bring it up later when Abyssinia was back. She was always more effective with these kinds of discussions. (Constance respected Abyssinia... Pilar? Not so much.)

———————

ANTONIA'S ARMS fell with brush still intact. She glowered at her canvas and the angry reds and blue scowled back... *This music sucks.* Antonia pecked at the buttons, her preset stations seemed temperamental today, *There's something, finally—some rhythm.* Then this seemingly random song and moment took possession...

Antonia felt woozy, confused, but happy. What was so familiar? It was better-than-half, but a not-quite-full *deja vu* instant; then the colors—*oh, the colors!*—and then feelings—the emotions she was recalling...

A plump and mostly pregnant Antonia was semi-shocked, "Music?!" She peered at the email invite again, not quite believing, reconfirming what she'd read. "I didn't think The Coven even knew what music was. Must have been that new recovering Wiccan addict's suggestion." She smirked and sighed.

"They're three sisters from Cuba, and boy, can they sing! '*Like magic!*'" teased Marta. "And I'm not trying to suggest that one— their sorcery, their voices, and Cuba—has anything necessarily to do with the other... But maybe, who the hell knows?!" Marta had insisted Antonia should be there, and that bringing three-year-olds was hardly a problem. She wasn't a very consistent friend, but she and Antonia shared a long, enchanted history—she not only knew what could please her more than most, Marta intuitively knew what would inspire Antonia's insanely talented witchery and creative spirit.

Since these musical witches (these young Cuban women) had been so alienated from the world for so long, they had acquired unique abilities well beyond their already exceptional spell-crafting skills. Their talents had been bouncing off one another and the worn concrete walls of their small world, *What did they do —how did they manage till now? The world can be so perfect sometimes, taking care of its own.*

Antonia looked up from the runes, "They're the real deal! And the only thing *you're* excited about is their singing?!"

Marta sighed, "It's been a while, but we know each other

better than that." She perched her hand on Antonia's knee, and in an exaggerated fashion, peered over and around several people to smile at Antonia's twin girls. (Marta had always seemed to have one foot in, one foot out of their conversations, so the typically perplexed Antonia played along.)

She clearly remembers looking over at her two girls following Marta's cue, and her glance got stuck. It couldn't help but wrap itself around the young sisters—women- and witches-to-be: phantasms of their future lives burst across the crowd, through the room, and Antonia reveled in the moment. She'd surprised herself; glimpses into the future happened so rarely, and not in that way, not so intimately. Antonia's surprise was redoubled since she didn't believe she was actually able to *feel* these visions, have these emotions for what they *needed* to be—and not what she might simply want them to be.

A new song jarred her reverie, and Antonia turned back to her canvas; Marta and their shared time was a treasured memory. They had become unusually close and in such a short time, and it was one of the only few true intimate, almost spiritual connections Antonia would have. But mostly it was that searing vision of what might be possible for her daughters that had overwhelmed in the best sense, *The gods—all kinds—can move in strange and wonderful ways.*

UGH. The school, mostly an old brick building, was really hot—strange for mid-October. And it smelled like someone spilled a bottle of disinfectant something-or-other over another something that had crawled into a corner and died three times. When Mr. Stephen Clarke called Ali to get a mop or something, she responded (with a marked frustration) that *you teachers should make up your minds who gets the mop or not*. To which Mr. Clarke responded, in his typical pointed-finger tone, that Mrs. A. (that was Ali) was in charge of the two mops and who might be mopping, which she quickly acknowledged. He stated his case: "So, if you agree to that fact, then what real difference would it make what one teacher needed mopped versus another? It's necessarily a first-come, first-served kind of thing, no? That is, unless, there's blood every which place, and it's preposterously horrifying and grody—then *that* teacher should get mopped and as soon as possible. Wouldn't you agree, Mrs. A.?"

There was frustrated silence for a moment or three, and some animated grumblings in some form of Spanish. "So where's the blood?" Mrs. A. sighed an exasperated sigh.

"There *is* no blood. It's fine if I'm next or fourth or whatever. It just really stinks—somewhere."

"Stinks *where*—Charlie needs to know where."

Mr. Clarke persisted, "I don't know exactly—*somewhere* close to here. My classroom." Things became muddled twice over and again, but Mr. Clarke was clearly determined to be mopped. It was a pretty typical Wednesday afternoon, apart from the weird heat, the weird stink, and the weird convo; all of this was tough, especially right after lunch period when everyone had their blood in their stomachs and visions of caffeine in their brains.

The class continued staring blankly at Mr. Clarke and his phone, so he thought a spontaneous bit of levity might help, "Mrs. A., explain it again, but this time *without* the accent." He snickered, glanced at class—no one else was laughing.

Someone muttered, "Not funny, Mr. Clarke."

No response from Mrs. Ali.

"Mrs. A.?"

"Science Jones has the mop." And she hung up.

Mr. Clarke scanned the class for potential texting violators to deflect from his very public slap-down; he identified at least six— Tall Chance was the first culprit. "Chance, go pick up the mop from the Science pod." (Big groan, one must assume, because Chance was a *big* boy.)

"Where?" said Chance, expressionless, testing Mr. Clarke.

"Stop it. You heard me. Go."

"But you don't even know what's smelling let alone *where* it's smelling..."

Mr. Clarke didn't look up from his desk, just pointed at the door—Chance left for the mop.

TALL CHANCE—QUITE literally—walked into a wall; Chance was very tall but he wasn't *that* ungainly, so how? The simple fact of his face buried in his phone screen complicated by the muddle-inducing stink was the most logical explanation, but to Chance's now slippery consciousness it was mostly the issue that there is a wall where there wasn't one before. And after thinking about it for probably much longer than was necessary, Chance next ascertained that the Science pod itself had been repositioned. Then, more specifically, *it was gone.* Chance woozily, finally reconciled that if something doesn't exist, *why am I trying to find it?* So, he stopped.

Suddenly Tall Chance felt strangely and abruptly and completely inebriated, and then just as suddenly deciphered aloud that since the Science pod and especially the mop don't exist, *I really don't have a very good reason to be just standing here.* So, he walked out the exit (with over half of the school day still to go) and wandered (and then wandered some more), finally wandering (literally and figuratively) home.

"YEAH, that's what it says on the syllabus."

"Must be that temp's thing, the one they're trying to trick into full time."

"Hope so—Mrs. Tuck is cool. Like her."

"You would."

"Dick. Head." Tom Boy winked.

"You wish," Sasha replied, with her requisite sass.

Tom Boy bit and instead swallowed his ready response—*Not nice*. It was one of his usual quips, and he wasn't sure why, but it wasn't funny, not this time. He knew too well about Sasha's Type A Last Word Syndrome (i.e., always having to have it) and had always found it roundly fun, challenging. But that feeling wasn't there this time. Not even a little bit. He took a hard left in their conversation, "Yeah, weird choice. The teacher, I mean."

Sasha didn't budge, "No, I know. But I still like her. A lot."

"Didn't say she's not likable, but just after two years of everyone being so scared of anything or anyone with the teeniest ability witchery-wise."

"Yeah, but I think that was mostly because of the uncool factor, no real fear factor."

"Maybe. Not."

"Both then."

Tom Boy nodded.

"That's why this course *is* cool. Or it should be."

No one was in the classroom yet; Tom Boy peered at the syllabus one more time. Sasha leaned against him, whispered in his ear, then she almost burst open with laughter—Tom Boy appeared more startled than anything else.

"I'm not getting the joke," Tom Boy said, expressionless. He was not amused, that was clear; it was more of an overall frustration, and mostly with Sasha. This thing she was doing lately, some pseudo-intellectual attempt at humor (and still teen humor, at best), made him nuts. She'd always been a little on the pretentious side but seemed to maintain a sense of irony about it. Not anymore.

Sasha pressed on, "'Human *Witch*-uality'..."

Tom didn't look up, "I heard you the first time."

"It's *funny*."

"If you say so."

"Why are you being such a dick?"

Tom Boy still didn't look up, "Okay, I will stop being 'such a

39

dick.'" He started texting, ignoring Sasha. Now she was starting to not like him again. It was strange, especially lately, how it would just "happen"—seemed to suddenly hop over her shoulder and onto her lap, right in front of her, where she couldn't ignore it.

Sasha did her best to redress, in spite of her frustration save as much face as she could, "I'm thinking it better be all about the witchy ping commingling with the mortal pong. Remember? We were talking, kind of arguing with Tuck about that." she smiled. "And then we said if it wasn't, we would *make* it that way—twist her figurative wand, as it were." Sasha wasn't happy with Tom Boy's non-reaction, "You liked it two days ago."

Tom Boy looked through her, now sounding frustrated, "More like two weeks. And it's still first a seminar on *human* sexuality."

"Come on, Tom. Lighten up."

Now Tom Boy looked frustrated, "Just because your Aunt Ezra has you all hyped up about your 'newfound' overwitch whatever, *heritage or potential,* suddenly you're 'all witch, all the time.'"

"Jesus, you have the same amount of witch genes in you."

"No, not really. You talked yourself into that one a long time ago."

Sasha teased, trying to break the spiral, "That's because you were—you *are*—so cute." Big Sasha toothy, well-meaning smile.

Okay, *So things have been weird, and are only getting more weird.* Sasha sighed.

She offered, "People, most people, tend to make things worse than they really are. Or need to be." She deliberated a couple of seconds, "And I tend to set my expectations pretty high, for myself especially." She grabbed his hand.

Tom Boy looked at the wall, "That sounds—all put together—like I'm the problem?"

"No one is the problem," she pulled her hand away. "If there *is* a problem, we're all part of it." She grinned, "That's a little witch-tuition for you. Actually, it's not that exclusively witchy."

Tom Boy didn't have anything to add; he sighed back into his phone.

Sasha could feel her skin continue to tighten from her neck down her arms. Ezra had talked about that symptom (and not with a particularly positive resolve).

Mrs. Tuck leaned out of the door, starting to close it—she had walked right by them unnoticed. She baited them, "Are you two still interested—or not so much?"

———————————

THE NEWS WAS as plain as day but only if you knew where to look for it, and relatively few would be looking at the township's local newspaper that materialized, hopefully, once a week (if they had enough stories and news and stopgap ads to make it worth the expense). Even then the news about the Cortez family matriarch, Marta, barely made it onto page three; she was missing again, but this particular incident did not hold the mystery or suspense of the first: everyone *knew* she was gone—there was no *if*. The new and now undisputed fact that all her nostalgic talismans and inherited fetishes of (tremendous) sentimental value were also missing made clear that this disappearance was at least partially intentional; the real mystery was *how* she went where she went— her car, her bike, and any other mode of bodily travel remained untouched. And the real burning question was of course—*why?*

And what was equally bizarre was her daughter Martika's reaction: she went to school just like it was a typical Wednesday morning. But she made her breakfast and apparently forgot to eat it; she put the cat food in its bowl but with the can still around it; her two besties walked her off of their bus and beelined her into the bathroom to help put her underwear on *correctly*—they were on, but over her pants and not under. The rest of her day apparently happened without further incident (or embarrassment).

Then, almost two days and two and a half periods of class

later, the usually savvy Martika (like Tall Chance before her) wandered aimlessly out of the school. She eventually found her way home, but not before trouncing through two neighbors' gardens and another's basement, then alighting on her back porch, finally curling into a ball under the picnic table. By that point, if and when she spoke, it was in some half-formed gibberish that definitely wasn't English, maybe perhaps some tired oldish Spanish dialect (but probably not). The nasty and frightening buzz was that yet another young witch had been "emptied.'" (Sums up the circumstances rather well—apparently a *Body Snatchers* kind of thing.) The only person Martika seemed to recognize (but only barely) was her aunt. So that's where they put her—and that's where she'll stay until the moment her mother, Marta, and her wayward Mexican charms and magic find their way home.

"SO THAT MAKES IT FOUR, no, five," Jane groaned, as she gave that last hangnail one more twist to no avail. Like the last two, it only made it "hang" more, and now that the skin was torn slightly and bleeding, it added a painful twinge helping to reinforce Jane's habitual anxiety.

"Are you still talking about what I think you're talking about?" Tip slowly looked up from her phone, getting more impatient than was typical with budsie Jane. Jane was the worrier in the group, and everyone had, for the most part, grown to love that part of Jane too. She tended to pick the right things to worry about; her spell-making skills, even at sixteen, left something to be desired, but it was clear from a ridiculously early age that she was able to read minds, project very persuasive thoughts, and all before she could even cast the words in a hex. Jane responded carefully, "Well, given that tone—which answer do you want to hear?"

"So—that's a *yes?*" Tip put her phone down. "How do you get to five?"

"Chase, Stephen, Julie, Mark, and as of probably more than a few days ago, Martika..."

"*Julie* Julie?! But I just saw her—"

Jane shook her finger at Tip, "No, no—Black Clever Julie, not White Smarmy-smart Julie."

"So now it's *five?* Are you sure? How do you know? Marty's kind of an airhead to begin with—and I say that with all due love and affection." Tip smiled, but this new information was making her anxious too. She folded her angst deep down and within, sometimes two times over, so to always have room for more. To be fair to Tip, she didn't seek out hardship—she couldn't forebear any manufactured self-pity or Weltschmerz—it was simply a matter of balance, of fairness: first to everyone and everything around her, and then she would know how to best solve her own emotional equation.

Jane thought about it a second, "Yeah, I know what you mean. But I guess it was the floating thing that gave it away."

"Floating 'thing'?"

"Yeah, with Stephen, his feet weren't moving half as fast as he was. He looked like a bad animation project." Jane's already-anxious look furrowed again, she muttered, "And then there's the *shriveling...*"

Tip shook her head, "Now you're making your own evil *Sabrina* moment—there wasn't any shriveling. No one shriveled."

Jane's eyes widened, "Uh-huh. Sure. Well, *now* there is. Look at the inside of Julie's arms. They look like an old-Eva-Ernst witch's nasty arms." She shoved her phone at Tip, as if it were contaminated.

Tip winced, "How did you manage to get all of this—I have to assume—firsthand information?"

"Like I usually do. I just went over there because I was worried about her." For as overanxious as Jane could make herself, she could be equally overaggressive in getting what she wanted—or thought she wanted, "She was curled up in a ball, floating in the one corner of the ceiling. She'd be babbling some sort of nonsense, arms flailing, and then all of a sudden not. Then she seemed, with an infant-absent smile, like she was back in the womb. Or *something* womb-ish."

Tip listened carefully to Julie's somewhat rambling explanation. She jotted notes in her *Organica* journal—writing it down on paper helped her believe it (whatever it was) was real.

————— ◆◆◆◆ ◆◆◆◆ —————

ANTONIA KNEW the brush she needed (her *painting* needed)—where was it? Her best first guess was that it would have to be at least close to her *Love Box,* where she preserved all things of metaphysical (and more) value. It was a compendium of emotional knicks and knacks and (literally and figuratively) touchstones from her long personal history. She could never find the treasure chest easily—whether it was the *Love Box*'s fault or Antonia's, it was impossible to know exactly.

The *Love Box* started its long life with that meager wand collection she'd kept in that silly velvet bag—practically an outgrowth of her hip (and more of an emotional safety net than anything of real magickal benefit). Wands had for years garnered such a wondrous and enchanted reputation (which they still desperately clung to), but the sad reality is something quite different: they're silly pieces of mostly wood that mirror their owner's unique magickal talents—that's their *only* enchanted pith. So, sum told, the more powerful the witch—the more powerful the wand.

But there's all kinds of caveats: that maxim's true for just a witch's birth wand, or baby wand (your choice, but Wicca preferences—especially on this side of the pond—seem to be for the latter... Ugh. Trite.). So in spite of yet another popular myth—"the more wands, the better"—it simply isn't the case. Even a W's birth wand might only be good for turning the lights off in the house, or opening a jar that's stuck, depending upon how much preternatural *oomph* existed—or exists—at the get-go. Oh, and most important, to borrow a very adaptable and still popular adage: use it or lose it. (Like most things in this universe, it's not —nor ever will be—the Energizer Bunny.)

(These days you'd believe a cell phone could accomplish what some wands might have a couple hundred years prior, given how they're a veritable appendage to everyone, even most W's. Especially those silly Wicca-types. I'm a smidge resentful, I suppose, of all of this "streamlining." As if a stick of wood—perhaps very powerful, exquisitely magical wood—is such hardship. But I suppose I'm not being as objective as they'd prefer—in fact I *know* I'm not.)

(And in spite of all my prattling about wands, it was actually the wondrous *mix* of runes and makeshift talismans that were so much more emotionally valuable to Antonia. Wands are as wands do, but the rich personal lore that had crafted her enchanted history—now that was perfect magick. Plain and simple.)

So, Antonia's *Love Box* consisted of abused semi-orphaned wands and other assorted nostalgia—fairly much *anything* could be eligible. (Antonia had wisely limited her sentiments to just the one box—if something new went in, then something old had to go—otherwise, it would be a hoarder's magickal hell!) A second or two after she'd started digging through her closet, she'd forgotten why she was futzing to begin with... *Ah, that was it—paintbrushes! That one burnished beauty...*

Thankfully, the box suddenly resurfaced—Antonia bumped into it, knocking it to the floor. She stooped to pick, scoop up the charms and fetishes splayed around her feet—some seized the chance to stretch a bone or feather or bead—when she glanced at, just over her shoulder, her weathered red wand (one of her favorites) was dancing on its end a few inches above the stew of magical sticks still on the floor. They were barely able to accomplish anything interesting anymore; perhaps you could push a flame or a flower (a real one!) out the end of some of them (except for the red one). It was raising its hand high—that's a surprising amount of energy, all told!—as if it had an urgent question.

It seemed to Antonia the wand was asking to pause and affectionately remember a day some seven-plus years ago.

Soba's afternoons were spent at home; her kindergarten was in the morning. Antonia had finally resigned herself to that simple fact, and she'd make the better of it by painting her way around and through it. Of course, she loved Soba (all her daughters!) passionately, but there were times she simply loved her painting more. But one day, not far into Soba's sixth year, Antonia scared herself: she abruptly realized she had completely forgotten about Soba being home, *Certainly not winning any Best Mom points today...* But *where was* Baby Girl? What had she gotten herself into now? She wasn't typically this quiet (let alone that respectful of her mother's creative "space").

She wasn't downstairs—she looked there first. Soba's usual "hangout" with Sput.

She wasn't in her bedroom.

But there she was in Antonia's bedroom, with her hands in her (of late) favorite "toy box": Antonia's wands and such things. (Still mostly wands at that point: a couple very magical, the rest, well, not so much that—pretty, though... Waiting to become something, someday.)

"Soba, what the hell, I've asked you to ask me before—"

She was distracted mid-thought: true to form, Soba had aligned her favorite wands and knacks, from most favorite to least so, on the floor in front of her. Then, hovering flirtatiously just beyond Soba, was her totem of favorite-faves, hanging end-to-end: four of the wands doing their wand-like happy dance for Soba and her overwitch mom.

This made Antonia so very happy, and also shamed her into

acknowledging that she perhaps shouldn't continually underestimate her occasionally belligerent, mostly precocious Soba.

Antonia sat down with Soba and told her more stories, about her personal mythology and her wand menagerie. That afternoon, for a relatively short period, Antonia forgot about her painting—and remembered her daughter.

TOM BOY COULD SMELL Greg's thoughts already, from over ten feet away. And then there he was, in perfect Greg form, ready to pounce no matter what the sex of the wary individual might be. (An unintended exaggeration here: Greg was traditionally a tit man and the bigger, the better.) Then his typical goofy grin covered his face, which confirmed there was going to be some sex-related comment forthwith, "That new girl is so fucking hot."

Tom Boy obliged, "You already told me that."

"No, that was the old new girl. I'm talking about the *new* new girl."

"Uh-huh. Great, glad she's hot."

"I never thought I was into Latin chicks, but it appears I am. Guess it's that ol' Black Magic, or maybe Brown Magic."

"You better watch it—I hear those Latina witches like to eat blond boys' balls for a snack—you know, extra protein." Tom Boy's zinger missed its mark. Greg didn't respond; he loved his witch-bro Tom but only ever listened to every third word he said (Tom Boy did like to explain himself and often). Greg twisted in half watching the "new new girl" walk down the hall, turn the corner. He waited for a second more just to be sure she wasn't coming back for some reason, and then finally completed his careful, studied observations. "Damn... Sorry, what did you say?"

He looked at Tom; Tom Boy was dismissive, "Nothing. Wasn't anything."

Greg was flustered by Tom Boy's apparent "attitude." "So, what? You stopped thinking about girls because you're in mourning or something? I didn't get that you were so deep in it about Sasha."

"I wasn't, and I haven't. I'm just not so worked up about it at 11:32 in the morning, between second and third period." Actually, Tom Boy hadn't been "all that worked up" about sex in quite a while. He was curious about that—and just curious, not terribly worried or wondering, *Maybe next week I'll worry about **that***. He was currently more struck by his *socio-magickal hierarchy* (his words) fascination—maybe "obsession" would be more apt? Where everyone "fits" metaphysically and why, *And why is it such a big deal in my brain, and why the hell now?* (And not just Wednesday between second and third periods but almost every day, and pretty much all of the time. *At least it feels that way*...)

Greg wasn't sure if Tom Boy was being sarcastic or serious. He gave himself some emotional wiggle room and defaulted to, "Always Mr. High-and-Mighty..."

Tom Boy deadpanned, "No, but the mighty part isn't too far off."

Greg didn't answer—*he* was twisted and distracted again, and now he wasn't sure if it was a good or bad kind of distracted. "Oh shit, there's my other girlfriend. I hear she has three nipples, which is fucking brilliant."

"Why is that fucking brilliant?"

"Because that means she must have three tits. And you *know* how I love my tits. On a *chick*, I mean."

"Yeah, I kind of figured that out—you don't have to qualify it every time. Have to believe our gay bros aren't holding their whatever just for you, dude." Tom Boy closed his locker door and ribbed Greg, "I mean, you're cute and all. Nice ass." Tom Boy winked, "So, if she actually had three tits, don't you think you'd notice or see them or *it*?"

He was moving a little too quickly for Greg at that moment, so Greg proceeded cautiously, "I don't know. She probably has to be really careful about who sees it, where she keeps it. People would think she's a freak."

"Dude, there's no such thing as a 'freak' anymore, we're all fucking freaks..."

"Uh-oh, here comes another Tom Boy speech-a-rama."

Tom sighed, started walking, "Forget it. So, what the hell do you mean 'where she keeps it'? It's not like she can move her tits around wherever she wants."

Greg trailed after, "I don't know anymore, Tom-a-rama. Anything's possible."

IT WAS SLIGHTLY after 2:00 a.m., and the key was attacking the front door lock like it had so many other frightening Fridays— Soba and Sasha flew to the head of the stairs. They startled each other; it's not a simple coincidence to "run into someone" when you're outside of your body in your chimera, or spirit-essence form, nervously hovering at the top of the stairs. Clearly, The Sisters' shared anxiety was finally becoming a shared reality.

They had long ago given up any real expectation of anything genuinely changing; both Antonia and Tom Dad had become too comfortable with the labels "functioning alcoholic" or "addict" (depending upon that evening's drug du jour—tequila or pot).

But now, suddenly there was Soba too, which really surprised —*happily* surprised—her always-doubting sister, "You're here *too?*"

Soba bristled, "Is there a reason I can't be?"

Sasha offered, "Shit, no, not at all. Wasn't saying that, just didn't think you were that bugged by—"

Tom Dad, still clawing the outside of the house, suddenly burst into a slurry of song (usually Bowie's "Heroes" and usually with the lyrics misplaced); Antonia did not join the chorus tonight. The girls moaned.

"This sucks. I hate it. They're dumb, so super dumb."

"That sums it up—exactly-precisely."

The attempts with getting in the front door had been momentarily preempted by various forms of humping *against* the front door. The girls sighed so heavily, helplessly that their physical bodies almost felt compelled to support their incorporeal selves fluttering, simmering at the top of the stairs. The key stabbed at the door desperately, then more slurred giggling, laughter. Then success—the door swung open with Antonia and Tom Dad on top of it.

Suddenly the girls felt another presence—it swung directly center between them, seemed to pause for breath and then was gone. What, or rather, *who* was it? Tip was the only other logical entity, but she would have definitely said *something* (especially Tip, and especially *now*). Then out of the blue came another strange feeling and thought: it was all okay; it was nothing to fuss about.

Sasha and Soba looked at each other, bewildered and now too, too tired; they silently acknowledged their chaperoning was becoming as silly as their parents continued grinding on the couch downstairs. They dissipated back to their bodies and beds.

Tom Dad and Antonia slithered their way upstairs to their bed and continued their drug-fueled communion. Antonia was strangely quiet for someone who was typically much more vocal (The Sisters only noticed because they hadn't been woken by the rote yet random orgasmic moan or yelp, for a change.) Tom Dad hadn't noticed and didn't really care: all his favorite "parts" were fully present and accounted for. After two, maybe three (arguably) successive orgasms, their almost weekly Friday bacchanal came to a (one would *have* to believe) successful close.

The Ground Below, the Sky Above

❧

Julie L. wrote her BFF#3 Sasha a text, almost cracking the glass in the process; she was especially frustrated with Sasha this morning. (This was not unique to Julie; Sasha had this effect on the majority of her BFFs; it was simply one of the rules of engagement.) Sasha had run up and down Julie's BFF thermometer more than a few times, but Julie could not see through to entirely disenfranchise the friendship—the perceived value alone could be worth unknowable quantities of "friends" and "likes." Sasha was a social commodity not to be screwed with; no matter what you thought of her personally, her beauty and innate witchy potential demanded attention, and Julie would happily provide it.

Sasha saw Julie's tweet and intentionally clicked around it.

Then she relented, Julie was imploring: *I need you to be more sensitive to Tom Boy's needs. I'm telling you this—first and foremost, of course—out of my love for you, dear Sash...* (then two fat-finger indecipherables, and finally) *Don't think, just do.* (Then way too many kissy-wink emojis.)

Sasha was gobsmacked; Julie had finally crossed the line. Sasha glared into her phone, causing Julie's to momentarily asphyxiate—it was the perfect, proverbial diss.

Distraught, Julie was pecking furiously at her screen which, to her great alarm, froze mid-peck. Julie knew all too well what was happening: this wasn't the first time she'd inadvertently (or not) put her wand—along with her phone—directly "in it." Julie's lips curled tight, *Sometimes I just want to take that witch's tits and—*

"Which witch? *Whose tits?*" Tip was suddenly standing nose-to-nose with Julie, grinning gleefully, peering down at her screen, pretending to read whatever, whoever. She knew that would freak out Julie's—um, well, *everything*. (Tip basically liked Julie and Julie didn't give a decent shit about Tip, but it was Julie's arch gullibility combined with Tip's inherent witchiness that made Julie such a delectable target. It could be delicious and immediate.)

Tip started, "So who gave *you* permission to play in the Tom Boy sandbox?"

Julie was speechless—and pissed, "How the fuck do you know that? Reading my goddam mind again, witch?"

Tip smiled, "No, *witch,* you tweeted everyone on your shit list, bimbo."

Now Julie was stupefied. She groaned, "Screw me..."

"Yeah, screw you, but you know it was a very upright tweet. I think most people would interpret that as something constructive, as opposed to, *not* that. *No one* would think *you* were putting your own interests in front of whoever's." Tip's snark arrived intact.

Julie looked carefully at Tip, "Well, I wasn't. Tom Boy deserves to be as happy as any other witch here and I—"

"Oh, that's so very sweet—don't be a dick."

Julie's expression assumed its more natural and aggressive state, "Oh, Tippy Tip, I'm not the dick here." She glanced back at her phone, all was back in working order, "I just don't know why we can't all get along."

"Didn't think that we weren't. It's just that you seem to think you can wave or put your wand wherever you please."

Julie smirked, "You mean up Tom Boy's butt? I hear he likes that."

Saved by the bell (sort of), Tip simply grinned and shrugged and started her way to Mrs. Martin's English class.

Sasha might continue to dominate any beauty contests, but Tip was the more socially savvy of the two precisely because she really didn't give a newt's turd. Not to suggest that Tip was a slouch—far from it—it was more the fact that her natural interests lie somewhere far from what any phone might attempt to tweet or burp at her.

———————————

SISTER HILDEGARD SAT STRAIGHT UP: *Technomysticism? That's* what they're calling it now? How quaint! And trite. Had to be a group—probably a very small group—of boys that breathed life into that limp wrist of a name, no, sorry, "*term.*"

I'm doing it again, aren't I? My equivocating "thing." They're all nodding their heads—all four of them, and a tad too enthusiastically; I promised I wasn't going to indulge my blathering *thing* this time—*oops!* (I still haven't learned in three hundred years how to not start the conversation in the middle of the conversation!)

It's just that those boys have me in such a tither, they're moving so quickly—and about everything! Maybe I or we think too much about (now they're all shaking their heads) everything, and having a little spontaneity might serve us better. (But a *little* of it, and spread thinly and only where it counts!)

And, *To Whom It May Concern:* where did Tom Boy get all that money for renting the mall's dead Radio Shack store-cum-"portal"? It's hardly functioning anymore (the portal, not the store), so there's magic involved *somehow* and from *somewhere?*

Hildegard continued with her good-natured prattling but

overall, the Amstel Coven clearly wasn't pleased, *It seems every time we remind ourselves to 'check in' there's just another thing to worry about.*

TIP FELT STUCK; she wasn't sure why she even brought it up, and with Tom Boy? (She was already painfully aware of the subliminal implications.)

"So they like sex, so what?" Tom Boy shrugged at her comment, took another gummy bear.

"But do your folks like it *that much?*"

"Define 'that much.'"

"I don't know." Tip sighed with an emphatic exclamation point, hoping some semblance of a real response would fall into place. It didn't (kind of), "Well, Sasha and I always say it sounds like the last twenty minutes of *Poltergeist 2,* but only lasts for ten."

"Ten what?"

"Minutes, numbnuts."

Now Tom Boy had to consider his answer.

"I'm not sure my parents even have sex, not like real sex. Mostly just witch sex these days, at least those were the books I saw by their bed."

"Which side of the bed?"

"Mom's."

"Figures. Us women, we have real stamina, when it matters."

Tom Boy didn't want to talk about his parents' orgasms—if they existed—any further, "So what book is Antonia into?"

"Nada. The bedroom is a craft-free zone."

"I thought your whole house was now like "zero tolerance," spell-making-wise."

"Not so much, Tom Dad likes to sound tough. No one really seems to think about that much, craft-wise anyway, but then shit happens. Dad gets pissed, shit happens again... Tom Dad gets over it."

"Your mom doesn't care?"

"She's too stoned, or drunk, or both."

"No, I knew *that*. I meant the magic."

"My theory is the pot is some kind of metaphysical anxiety therapy—actually, that's her theory. I decided about three years ago to just agree with it."

"You know, your folks aren't the only ones who like to get stoned."

"Oh, what, now you're on their side?"

"What sides?" Tom Boy threw an imaginary ball of something at her, "You're freaking tough, you "Sisters"—perfect and *beyond*. Just chill it every now and then. What do you think—how about every alternate Tuesday?" Tom Boy grinned his adorable grin.

Tip took the gum out her mouth, thoughtfully balanced and molded it between her thumb and finger—then shoved it onto Tom Boy's forehead, "Fuck you very much."

Tom Boy couldn't quite believe it, something was definitely shifting one way or another *again*; he couldn't keep up, with Tip, with Sasha, with almost *everyone* somedays (like today). And maybe he didn't want to. He peeled the gum from his face, and then pressed the gum hard, methodically, deep into the crevices, the wood of his chair, trying to bury it. (Trying to make his thoughts more convincing, or make them go away altogether.)

He sat up, "That was mature of you—*not*." Tom frowned again, quickly changed the subject and the moment, "So what about Tom Dad?"

"He's a stoner, ex-party boy... Way too human for my taste, and Sasha too—especially Sasha." Tip laughed, even seemed to giggle, *Is she flirting? Or attempting to? Weird.* The difficult reality was that Tip was flirting, and the fact that Tip wasn't a flirter by nature only made the circumstance that much more uncomfortable. Why was she flirting to begin with? Maybe she felt she had something to prove to herself, that she was sexual and attractive and *valuable*. Maybe she knew Tom Boy wouldn't object, nor would he overtly approve, he could simply be a neutral sexual Switzerland.

Tip feigned concern, "If he wasn't my father, well then, I *just don't know.*" She laughed, grabbed the bag of gummy whatevers, "Why the test? You know all this—you've known it for, like, forever."

Tom Boy stood up to go, "A fucking day and forever."

GREG CONTINUED TAUNTING TOM BOY, "Sasha's going to be pissed. Turn you into a toad or a dork. Oh shit, wait, you're already a dork, so I guess the toad, or a turd, yeah, she can turn you—"

Bitts abruptly stood up, sighing loudly, apparently impatient, "Well, that's all well and fine. I'm outta here unless you butts have something else that was such a freaking crisis you had to call an "emergency session." Where was Sasha anyway?"

Tom Boy was suddenly agitated, "I don't know. And why does everyone keep asking like I would know?"

Bitts got even more impatient, and stared blankly at Tom, "Easy, Magic Man, I only asked because she's still a member of this club, right?"

Tom Boy bucked up, swallowed a few of his words, "Yeah, she is. Of course she is."

"Well, she sure as shit is going to be surprised by your mall maybe-portal thing. And Missy Maleficence isn't going to like she had nothing to say about it, the ultra-control freak that she is."

Tom Boy waved the concern away, "She knew about it and said no—there's only a limited number of ways you can interpret 'emergency meeting.' So, tough batballs."

They shut down their computers and walked out to their cars. The school was surprisingly unusually empty for a Thursday late afternoon and the early evening air damp and unfriendly, strange for a bright fall day.

STEPHEN CLARKE WAS VERY proud of the fact that he'd only screwed up three times in his entire adult life (he chuckled at his joke). Unfortunately, it seemed now that it was four—no biggie, it entirely fit with the overall shitty day he was having.

Right at the top of the shit list was that email—the morning's first communique—from that typically nasty bitch-of-a-witch he'd never met.

His cell phone rang, *No number—has to be her. And just as I happen to see her response to my response, I'll tweak that description to 'incredibly impatient nasty bitch-of-a-witch.' She's probably hovering in one of my ceiling corners ready to—*

Stephen interrupted his own thought, "Hello?"

No response, just a strange clicking, then abruptly, gruffly, he found himself dead center of a *pre-heated* discussion. His email from this afternoon must have triggered it—this anonymous she-bitch was unhinged...

"So you did *what again?!*" her voice bellowed. Stephen grimaced; this—*all* of this—was really not going well (but that couldn't be any real surprise since his whole crafting transformation had been half-assed from the very first incantation).

Stephen remained steady, "I juiced everything. Just seemed simpler, more efficient. And, it may be just my humble opinion, but a lot more effective and powerful too. Just like wheat grass used to be way back when."

She was dumbfounded. "You wasted all that time, all our resources?"

"Wasted? I would hardly say that."

"It didn't fucking work, did it?!"

Stephen was flip, and kind of intentionally, "What? You were expecting me to actually *eat* those frog and lizard organs? And..." he had to swallow some air to keep some measure of control over his head *and* stomach, "...a human *toe?!* I mean, I think it was human, don't know what else it could've been."

"Yes, dickhead. All of it. That's what the spell and elixir called for—it was even translated into English, for the more plebeian Luddites like yourself."

Stephen wouldn't give up, "I looked at the whole thing euphemistically—half that stuff I would never *actually* do. It was too *literal,* too silly. And just dumb."

Her voice fell off, "They're not going to like this at all."

"Who's they?"

"It doesn't matter. Actually, it matters a whole fucking bunch, but you're just another dickhead white man like all the rest of them who couldn't give a shit about anything other than himself, so like I said, it just doesn't matter."

Stephen stood up, puffed chest, "What the hell is that supposed to mean? Weren't we talking about doing this for the "greater good" or along those lines? And you liked me *'for my mind'*—those were your words, verbatim."

"Greater good? World domination is more like it—but the Greater Northeast would have at least been a start." (She was joking—wasn't she?)

Stephen poked, "You're kind of nuts, *aren't you?"* *No response, shit.* "Listen, I was just in it to, well sure, become the total brainiac I always wanted to be, but it was to be that amazingly badass teacher I've always wanted to be too. That was *my* interpretation of 'greater good,' anyway."

Complete silence again, but for the louder, now angrier clicking—maybe it was clucking? (Was she now possessed by some kind of oversized demon chicken?)

She was re-reading his email, then she said disgustedly, "So—you can throw your farts?! Like a ventriloquist throws his voice? *That's* your new 'special power'?!"

"No, not just that—sounds ridiculous when you say it like that," Stephen sheepishly stared at his laptop. "But it is mostly about, well, that part, no, that general area of my body." He waved the comment away. "Was just trying to balance things out a little more. Mind, body, you know what I mean."

"Yep, I know *exactly*..." Then suddenly she was gone, done, in a poof, nothing but a busy signal from the other side of his phone. Stephen could have easily convinced himself that the whole last sixteen minutes had been the result of yet another bad egg sandwich from Roy's.

He grabbed another beer and clicked on a fave "The Office" episode—the one about some crazy, wayward unidentified witch who crashes her broom, dies, and everybody lives happily ever after.

HE WENT to the bathroom mirror—he was correct—he looked twice as shitty as he felt. *That's not right—usually I just feel like* **one** *piece of crap in the morning*. But now two? One sitting exactly, agonizingly, squarely on top of the other? But Outside Tom was finally catching up to Inside Tom; he couldn't remember the last time he could say he was fully awake, alert, fully conscious, *firing on all cylinders*, one hundred percent (or whatever like-minded words you'd care to apply).

Yes, he knew this singular moment was simply that, but lately, he'd found himself once again grappling with the realization there were substantially fewer good singular moments in relation to the not-so-good. He (Antonia too, no doubt) would need a distraction, so he dug up that self-divined potion recipe from his great-grandmother Matilda's personal athenaeum. Even though it was a Saturday, they actually weren't stoned; they still laughed their asses off—it had been his family's *'Fountain of Youth, Tetersberg-style.'*

Tom had told Antonia he remembered Matilda was a bit of a cut-up, but never to the point of being *entirely* silly. (You try living to one hundred sixty-three and see how silly, or not, you feel; her sister made it to 159 and they both swore by this stuff.) *Good genes, and a couple shots a day of whatever it was in that brown bottle!* Oh, so we don't confuse the conversation: those "good" witchy genes were temperamental things—just like Tom Dad's great-grand-mother—and liked to skip around generations. Unfortunately, they mostly missed the year Tom Dad came into being, and he got just the teeny-tiniest smidge of that supernatural DNA. He was eventually too bored with the whole magickal craziness to even fret a little bit about his "handicap" and only later on, when it might have made a difference with a girl he liked, he'd get defensive and feel *really* sorry for himself. (That particular trait he became very accomplished in affecting.)

Tom forced himself back in front of the computer. He needed to finish these last two pages or he might as well not even go into the office Monday. He thought about it a minute more, *Yeah, I'll just not go into the office Monday.*

Tom glanced again at the email from neighbor Peter Steed—even fun felt like work, anymore.

The married Steeds knew Tom Tetersberg long before Antonia did. They had been the Family Tetersberg's neighbors on either side of their house, respectively: Rita in the house on the left and Peter lived to Tom's right. They all grew up together, went to school together, got drunk and high together, and then Rita and Peter decided to live together. Not so long ago, much to Rita's dismay, Tom, in a fit of *cannabis hysterium* ascertained that his years of friendship and appreciation of Peter, and to a slightly lesser degree, Rita, had *nothing* to do with genuine affection and everything to do with the number of joints they'd smoked. Antonia didn't have an opinion one way or another, the Steeds were just a little *too human* for her taste, and occasionally supercilious because of it. (She still felt this even though the societal status scale had been tipping much more in their majority mortal favor the last ten years or so.)

Rita also found every aspect of her emotional and psycho-sexual life supremely fascinating and enlightened. (She had stopped participating in actual physical sex about three years prior: "...just too, I don't know, *raw*.") Rita assumed other women would naturally find it equally fascinating and liberating—especially those of "mixed blood." (That was Rita's polite term for Antonia's "people": "'*Witch*' just seems so, I don't know, *primitive*.")

The remaining mostly mortal denizens of Tom and Antonia's block and a half were just slightly different flavors of bland, at least compared to the pompous Steeds. There was, though, one house that played home to a hard-core, true-blooded, heavy-metal witch and warlock couple that wanted nothing to do with anyone at any time or anywhere. Tom was convinced they were the pinnacle of evil and would have their young twins' spleens with shish kabob if given the chance, so he steered clear. Antonia, on the other hand, was intrigued but was most times too buzzed to fuss or bother.

It was the last nail in the cross: Rita's running joke (she found it *really* funny—all-the-time funny—for some bizarre reason) about witches in internment camps ("...they'd never be able to actually *keep* them in one place, to begin with!" Subsequent giggling and hissing...) when the Tetersbergs mutually decided with barely a word to disown the Steeds. They would continue their biweekly Binge Friday druggie holidays but at undisclosed locations. Tom quickly deciphered, from one thing or another the Steeds had muttered, that the sentiment was a shared one.

"That ugly stupid house of theirs could suffer some kind of terrible natural disaster, you know..." Antonia was just thinking out loud, as the Steeds happened to drive past.

Tom didn't even look up from his computer.

———————

IT'S a peculiar and difficult tipping point when it appears no one's interested in anything about anyone else... In putting any real time and effort into creating something more, something beyond soothing their id for the next minutes until the next illogical craving occurs to them.

It's like a curse. A hex. (No, actually much more than that.)

It's unnatural and it's creative; it's pitting one collective set of emotions against the other. Making something or someone so distasteful and disruptive that you can't ignore it, and you absolutely must react.

You'll respond in hateful and hurtful ways you're not even aware of or attuned to—your yin puts its fist through your heart; your yang is disabled. The Dark Enchantment made sure of that—it's been working way ahead of plan.

But everything else—the basic day-to-day, hand-to-mouth—that will forbear. (And things will eventually change back to what's best—what's been quietly existing for millennia.)

But at this point in time there's been a pestilence cast across the Earth's plane, a ruse of hoodoo-ridden disgust, compelled by the Patriarchy and its stronghold of all things enchanted and preternatural. The malediction is a simple one—which is a key source of its strength: mortal women and female witches and W's will devolve into two categories of temperament, either fawning and submissive or harridan, artlessness. The former will naturally find a place and a purpose as they always have, but the latter will discover (and have begun to see) that what is problematic and contrary only will become more so, and they will eventually, inevitably determine that *they* are the problem—the proverbial *whining wheel*, the *nagging gash* and wound that simply won't heal. And then they'll simply, sadly fade away.

It's remarkably difficult to find oneself in the very center of a problem from another place and time, but we all will make the best of it, the best we can—or die attempting that life-affirming effort.

Further Bizarre Behavior

❧

The bus was (finally, happily) exactly on time. Tip felt terrific this morning; she'd slept like a lobotomized warlock after three out-of-body orgasms. (Not that she had experienced an out-of-body orgasm—she wasn't sure she'd experienced an *in-body* one—but she found the analogy entertaining.) She was being greatly entertained by a string of tweets she'd received, until her scroll ran head-first into...

Four pubes... One more than yesterday. Go, Tip!'

(Then emojis: clapping hands, once, twice, letter space—probably unintentional—then a third for, maybe, good luck?)

That's what the tweet said—complete bizarreness. Tip, in a knee-jerk motion, shook her phone as if that would fix whatever awful thing had happened. She was horrified, overwhelmed, completely incensed—*why would my own sister do something like this?!* Then she thought for a second more and realized she really didn't believe Sasha actually *would* do something like this. *But then why, how from her tag?!* It couldn't happen any other way.* She looked across the bus at her sister—Sasha was smiling at her screen, oblivious.

Tip couldn't be rational and pounced: "*What kind of word is that anyway?!*"

Sasha slowly looked up, "Huh?" Sasha obviously had no idea what the question was about, but she was used to this from Tip who had a proclivity for starting conversations with herself and then engaging you in the middle of it.

"What? What 'word'?" Sasha's frontline defense was always prepared, ready for anything or anyone.

"*Pubes.*"

"What do you mean 'what kind of word'? Not a real nice one."

"Exactly right. Not nice." Tip glared extra glare-y.

"I know that face. Whatever you're thinking, I didn't do it."

Tip got up and plopped almost on Sasha's lap. "*You* didn't send this tweet?" She held her phone under Sasha's nose.

"Didn't do it."

"It's from your phone!"

Tip and Sasha had their basic argument drill down: Sasha would remain blank-faced and calm (whether she was lying or not), and Tip would continue to hyperventilate.

"I didn't send it! I'll prove it." Sasha took the phone. Tapped once, slid once. "Look, my number's not in your Recents."

Tip slumped. Breathed in. They frowned their standard quizzical furrowed brow at one another.

"Then, what the fuck?"

"What the fuck is right, sistah." And Sasha went back to giggling at her YouTube something-or-other. Then Sasha muttered, her eyes still attached where they were, "It's not true anyway so why go crazy, right?"

Tip continued to stare out the window. Her physical body hadn't always been her best friend, deciding to go left when everyone else her age had already gone right (physiologically speaking). Random patches of hair that came and went, an ovary that liked to play hide-and-seek—she'd won that last round. (There'd been more discomfiting scenarios, but those two had consistently clawed their way to the front of her brain more than any other.)

"What? It *is true?*" Sasha the Maleficent was trying hard to stifle her now ongoing gurgling-giggling.

No response. Sasha, wisely, ended the convo and went back to her Stupid Pet Tricks.

Tip had abruptly shifted from fuming to sulking during the turn into the school driveway. She mumbled some variations on, "That's just *mean...*" Sasha, surprised, looked up, *She's still on that? What is going on with these mood swings this week?* Then reassessing, *Me too, actually...* She glanced quickly at the month—nope, they both had their periods (the first one) just over a week ago, plus or minus a day or whatever. It had been a small blessing given everything else they had—in true twin formation—going on at the same time. Their periods could be mind-bending, shape-shifting horrific or life-affirming events. That, unfortunately, was typically true of the second one (yes, living-in-general is a mite more complicated for witches of the female persuasion).

"So, then *who did it?*"

Sasha broke, almost yelled, "I told you, *I don't know.* You're the one with all the geeky boyfriends—let them figure it out." Sasha started getting her things together.

"You wouldn't be saying that if it was *your pubes* in these tweets."

Sasha shook her finger at Tip, "Nada. I could give barely two shits about what anyone thinks about my body, let alone my pubic hair. Have you looked under my arms lately?" Sasha chuckled at her joke; Tip couldn't come up with a smart-alecky response because, for the most part, it was true. (But it was also true that Sasha had been blessed by more than a few gods and in more than a few ways in the Looks category, so she hardly had to worry.)

It was a strange subject title choice (let alone the actual email):

AN EMAIL FROM PRINCIPAL CASEN: To Staff:

Starting today, any implication of potentially prejudicial or racist polemic needs to be forwarded immediately and directly to my office. I think it goes without saying that the sooner that information is communicated, the better for all concerned. Be it of either a more rudimentary "Earth-bound" nature or something more far-reaching (and I mean far out far-reaching, even demigods-level stuff—as impossible as that may seem to some of you), I want to know about it absolutely ASAP—like, *yesterday ASAP*.

That's all.

P(S)C.

Various iterations of the message were shared via one platform or another with the school as a whole. The overall response and reaction seemed to fall into one of two camps: one, feigned shock and dismay, or two, no reaction at all.

Tip messaged Sasha:

That's weird

What? The PSC's?

Yup...

Yup.

What happened?

The locker graffiti, doodah!

It could sometimes seem that major departments of Tip's brain would shut down mid-texting (probably some sort mental health survival instinct).

Oh. Right. Didn't think that was such a big deal, not a big 'racist' deal anyway.

Now Sasha's brain skipped a beat, *You don't feel freaked about*

bloody graffiti on our school locker. Whatever it said? 'Hi, Tip! Have a
happy day!' in pig blood wouldn't freak you out? What's wrong with you?
Is it your period?

The second one always does make me a little looney.

A little?!

I don't know if anything actually happened-happened—how would I
know?

You always seem to know everything...

Uh-huh, I think you're thinking of you! Tip was worn down (best
to toss this sucker all back into Sasha's vainglorious court).

Sasha didn't have an immediate response to that; Tip was
thinking by this point she should have, but then still more dead
Sasha space.

You there?

Yep.

What's wrong?

Just saw something. Might have some buzz, see you at A&T's...

Then she smirked, laughing at her next thought, *Maybe those*
teen terrorists ransacked my Twitter account, too... Somehow that oh-
so-painful tweet had become inconsequential too—maybe, hopefully her witch's curse, part deux was going to help instead of hurt
this time.

THE ANNOUNCEMENT with its subsequent admonition had
happened with marked efficiency—no moss grows under Principal
Sara Casen's feet (or wand and craft, for that matter). She'd traditionally believed and had no qualms about employing whatever
means proved necessary to meet her desired end.

The lengthy scrawl across the Science pods lockers wasn't
exactly obscene; it was in a dialect that most high schoolers
(whatever their paranormal genetic mix) simply wouldn't understand. But given the reaction of the few that did, it was perfectly
clear that pranking had nothing to do with it. They—whoever

they were—intended to hurt and to intimidate. (And somehow Sara Casen was keenly aware of this.)

A loose translation of the archaic English statement-cum-quotation follows below, but please bear in mind it had been broken in parts, and across several walls, and through three of the district's high schools. (The circumstances demanded a swift, organized, and egoless response from all three principals.) Here then is a mostly makeshift conversion sans several of the Anglo Saxon unpleasantries (that would barely make sense anyway):

> As Demeter roams, to face her fears,
> The hate she suffers, fills the tears,
> For the child she lost,
> To those too pure, and pale of heart,
> Too weak with greed, shit stymies their breath,
> And too strong, she wails, vowing sure death.
>
> His horned white skin scoffs, and won't demure,
> To others with tints sharp or bland,
> It stabs its cock thru walls of fur,
> Leaving nothing fertile, nothing chaste.
> Their baleful cries, they mount,
> Demeter seethes, and must continue her count.
>
> The blood she'll draw, to salve the pain,
> For thousands more, then thousands again,
> Their terror foretold,
> Eternal pain prescribed,
> Demeter finds peace, only when she's complied.

There had to be some loftier mechanism at work here; this wasn't some bored white male witch or mortal dude with an itchy wand or spray can... And then there's the (too easily dismissed) *Trinity Concordat:* those final points in the triangle where every intention must comfortably intersect. These W's or otherwise—whatever color they are—must be rather free-spirited and not the least bit fretful that their pagan flirtations could easily offend certain Powers That Be. (It might seem fun now, but when all this shit finds a big enough fan...)

JULIE STARED BLANKLY at the crimson scrawl, "So I'm totally *not* getting why all the fuss—and it seems there's going to be 'fuss.' Hate fuss, and hate those stupid-ass Casen whine-a-thons. Maybe it's a big deal because it's some kind of trinity religious thingy since the three schools were hit?" Sasha found herself once again dumbfounded by Julie's singular ignorance; she decided to quickly change the subject to something Julie could better fully appreciate: Julie.

Sasha quipped, "Shit. Your Snapchat dysmorphia is 'showing,' witch..."

"You bitch, I thought we agreed no craftwork that was *biased* and *hurtful*. That's *so IDEK*..." Julie caught a glimpse of the spell's result in her locker door mirror.

"How so?" Sasha mocked concern, "You *loved* your Snap makeover, there isn't anyone that doesn't know that... Sorry, with that look on your face I thought you were looking at the other schools' graffiti pics. So freaky."

"What? What about 'other schools'?" Julie was distracted leaning into the full mirror—she needed its honesty. She was giving her new *Snaplift*, courtesy of her brilliant friend Sasha, one last formal perusal.

Sasha pressed, "The crazy locker walls... It's all over Snapchat."

"Um, yeah?"

"It happened at three other schools too—it was the first three parts of some ancient curse or spell or whatever—I haven't looked it up yet. So nuts..." (Sasha was patiently stretching the convo waiting for Julie to fill in Julie's blanks.)

"Uh-huh. Wait. I already *know that*..." Julie was barely paying attention anyway, but now she'd discovered three stray hairs (*Three?!*) where there shouldn't be *any*.

She was flummoxed, "*But why is that?* And *why* are there *three* of them?!" Julie held the phone's Snap image up to mirror as she compared, contrasted, and compared again. "What the *fuck?* They're not on the pic!" She started to whimper, Sasha hated that; it was one (number three) of the four things that Sasha hated about Julie. (Even though Julie desperately believed she was still inching ever closer to that vaulted Sasha bestie moniker.)

Sasha muttered, "It happens—what can I say? I can cancel the spell if that will make you happy."

Julie was stuck—she loved being digitized! "No, wait, *I don't know*..." the whimpering started again, "I'm going to have a dyke beard in two weeks at this rate!"

Sasha had run out of words and most of her patience, "So do you want the face or not?"

Julie pouted, confronting the whole mirror: *What is this shit? Some kind of payback?! I nicely ask my almost-best friend a Snapchat favor and this is my punishment?! I bought her **two** thank you soft pretzels! She probably thinks I'm trying to get her fat.*

Sasha muttered, "Barely. There's a spell for that too, bitch. Or witch."

Now a tad calmer, Julie engaged her digital Dorian Gray for a few seconds more... *My lips are definitely plumper... Though it does look like my left eye is stray, but just a bit...* Julie decided it was something she could live with (besides, Sasha said she could always undo what she did with a snap or a flit or *whatever*).

"Sorry, I thought I was doing you a favor. Ran into all this crazy didgie morphing shit in my last club meeting, and I thought of *you* immediately." Sasha was being intentionally inscrutable; the demigods (*I have to believe they're watching*...) would no doubt love how Sasha was helping and hurting (albeit just psychologically) all at once. (Now that's a gift—and to be that self-aware at only sixteen?! Not to mention the confidence and female/witch empowerment levels—off the charts!)

Julie started getting her social bearings again, "You realize what a witch-bitch you're being this second, don't you?" She actually put her phone down and looked Sasha in the eyes, waiting for Sasha's answer.

Sasha didn't like the abrupt and surprising honesty, "I'm not sure about that—you get something, I get something—*two fucking pretzels,* but it's something." Sasha thought a moment more, and added as patronizingly as she could, "Actually, you let me stretch my spell-casting wings, which I don't get to do all that much anymore, so it's a win-win."

Julie folded her fat lips together and smiled, "That could make sense. But I get a sense you don't know—well, maybe a tad—just how self-serving *you* are."

Sasha was struck, "Maybe. But you got what *you* wanted too."

"Not really," Julie pressed her finger into Sasha's hand, "I got what *you* wanted me to want. Or have... Same difference, at this point."

Sasha was happily intrigued when she would find herself 'tricked' into something she didn't want to do. "I wouldn't argue that..."

"Good," Julie pulled her hand away from the mirror, "Let's tweak the spell to be done by Saturday. I'll let you know if I decide something differently."

Sasha shrugged. (She definitely *didn't like* being told what to do.)

Twenty feet apart Julie swung around—her Dr. Pepper finally taking effect—and commanded, "Hey, witch, let's go check out those *other* walls after school today—you want to? We could rule the board on Instagram!"

. . .

SOBA WATCHED the bus pull away; climbing into a long, yellow sardine can at the moment made her want to wretch. She had panicked and all-of-the-sudden—just too many freaking *people*. And all at once...

She knew the walk would help. A walk would be just the trick —in more ways than just this one. Tip turned in her seat and looked back to see what Soba decided her mode of transportation home should be (this was hardly the first time, but it wasn't a terribly regular thing either), *Yep, she's walking again.*

"Soba's walking home again," she said, leaning into Sasha.

"So, who cares? Let her walk home. Why do you have to report to me every little stupid thing that little stupid sister of ours does?"

"Because you *always* end up asking me, somehow or other, so I'm just being proactive."

Thinking or considering why other people do or think or craft the things that they do was completely foreign to Sasha's current view of the world. Waste of time, which she had already determined was something—regardless of your witching quotient—of terrific value, *Time stands still for no witch—or W, or man-witch, or halfling, or...* (For as almost-brilliant Sasha could be some moments, she could just as often be surprisingly ridiculous.)

Finally by herself, Soba could sense the bits and pieces of many conversations—verbalized or otherwise—as she watched the square butt of yellow metal bounce and swerve slowly out of her view.

She knew things would begin to happen soon, and she was warmed, delighted to see that already she wasn't alone. Hardly.

The menagerie winging or winding their way about her had carefully started to quiz her about her day, picking and pulling at comments or questions that they thought might have interest. It was a test, Soba thought—whether intentional or not—to see how valuable she could be to them. *It has to be a mutually beneficial circumstance* was a pseudo-mantra of sorts; since she was three, she could remember grappling with that, with everything and everyone. (Maybe not those words exactly, but the intention felt the same. Certain animals were easier to understand than others, and her first and fondest memories of conversations had little, or rather *very* little, to do with other W's or human beings.)

———————— ❦❦ ————————

STEPHEN CLARKE TOOK A VERY CALCULATED and efficient snort of the concoction; from what he was able to further suss out online, the more the "elixir" smelled like a halfling's unwashed thong that had been lost in her laundry basket for three months, the better. So, the lid had barely left the lip when he slapped it shut—his eyes were watering, it was that putrid. Apparent success. At least at this stage of the process.

Stephen was still hoping for a positive ("upbeat" was the word he used) outcome; he had completely acknowledged to the still-mysterious Ezra that his "freelancing" the potion's recipe was an almost fatal (for the potion) mistake. This time he had only graced the tip of his tongue with that one meaty, fatty scrap off the toe's tarsal bone and it seemed to electrify every nerve ending from the edge of his hair to his own right fourth toe (he believed, hoped it was a "righty," *more magical 'oomph'*—that was the rumor anyway).

Anyway, he added the toe wine to the waiting blend of six-toed extra-cold-blooded amphibian "elements" and other sordid ingredients; the recipe did read like something written in the seventeenth century (which it could have been). Later tonight he'd imbibe and patiently wait for the desired effects; anything would be an improvement upon the morbid flatulence and the floating objects silliness from his first attempt. (And now he knew that bitch-of-a-witch's name so that had to mean something, *But it's not like we're actually 'dating' or anything...* He found his joke very funny.)

Stephen Clarke's *Master of the (Frenchtown) Witching Universe* evil plan (well, not *that* evil, but there were a few *slaves* attached to his Master concept) was, once again, underway and undeterred. *Oh, and lest anyone's still assuming the worst, I really am doing this for my kids.* (Really *and* truly. They lived with their mother in the next state, but still.)

With Eyes (Very) Wide Open

❧❀❧

Abyssinia couldn't see Constance anywhere, so once again in spite of herself, she wondered, *If I did just this one teeny, tiny adjustment, it's not a 'change'—it's a 'sugges-tion'—it's not going to make anything happen that differently.*

And in her next breath, she realized that wasn't precisely true, as true as it needed to be. She was trying (again) to have it both ways, and that definitely (still) didn't seem right, *But there's got to be some benefit to sitting up here wherever I am translating everything like some glorified extraterrestrial stenographer.*

Constance suddenly materialized, almost pressing her finger into Absynnia's forehead: You're doing it again—stop futzing! You wouldn't be here orienting if you hadn't figured out some way that made sense to everything—and everyone—else.

Abyssinia: No, it's good. I'm good. I just need to, I dunno, just to—

Constance: Just to read what's in front of you—or it is *now...*

Constance pushes the parchment page two inches from her nose.

Abyssinia: Great. That's just great. Another Dibbyuk riddle or whatever-they're-trying-to-be.

Constance sits glaring at her. Abyssinia decided not to stress her point, and continues with the statement:

> *When their timing was measured, they broke it in two,*
> *When it was fixed, it took three to view,*
> *Their hands where they shouldn't be, and when turned*
>   *right they were where,*
> *Just four eyes'd confuse, but six could compare.*
> *Then why not eight, or ten, or more that times two?*
> *Because that's one eye too many,*
> *And the hands—they're too few.*

THE VERY SPECIFIC audience pushed themselves into the auditorium, *Why just ninth and tenth grade witchy-poo types and only of the female variety?* Tip stumbled, half-dazed, toward the back of the assembly room; Mara was flailing away at her, *Something's up—that wave is way more than just seat-saving.*

Tip hailed, "What the hey! What is going down?"

Mara shrugged, "Not nothing but still no clue. Sorry—hope we'll find out. Such false advertising all this buzzy-boo. And since it's just us girls I was getting nervous and didn't want to sit by myself." Cheesy grin, *Please forgive antsy me. Love, Mara.*

"Huh? What? Worry, why?" Tip slumped down, dropping bag, books wherever they fit. A nasty glare from the anonymous strange-grader next to her almost missed its mark. Tip winked an excuse me, *All of it—and everyone in 'it'—had to be okay or Tip couldn't be okay. Hear that?*

Mara had to make her opinion clear, "You can't make everyone like you. Or do what everyone wants you to do *for them.* We've discussed this before." She smiled, helping Tip get situated, comfortable.

"I know, I know. At least I don't let it upset me anymore—not *all the time anyway.*" Tip knew she cared too much, worried a lot, but she'd also realized she really *liked* that about herself; Mara patted her head affectionately, maternally, *And how the fuck does Mara always seem like she's got it all figured out. It's starting to piss me off.* (Not entirely-really.) The two besties knew each other upside down and sideways; being careful and considerate did not necessarily prescribe a pushover or weakness. And they were made of opinions, strong ones; Tip's resolve was only matched by her empathy. Antonia and Tom Dad worried about her more than her sisters: would her magic interfere with her feelings too much or frequently? She'd always been deemed (dismissed?) as "too sensitive" by Aunt Ezra (but given most everyone's assessment of Ezra, Antonia and Tom took that as a compliment).

"Since we're finally all here—could someone tell me **why** *we're all here?*" Tip poked aloud. "And why is it only girls from ninth and tenth grades?"

Mara teased, "We're having 'the talk' again with Mrs. Severs. Us witches, you know, *Aunt Flo and Cousin Red* are always a year or so behind schedule. Plus, quite a few of us have the double whammy, you know: 'twice-the-curse.'" She said it with such a straight face Tip almost believed Mara didn't know about Tip's double whamminess.

"That's so screwed up, and seriously? Isn't it a little 'late' to be still talking about this now? Some of us might already have little witchlets in the oven, in one form or another." (Pregnancy could be a very creative thing for some witches if they so desired.) The anonymous, ageless student two seats away moaned in response.

"I'm kidding, *I'm kidding*—relax!" Then Mara shrugged, "But I wouldn't entirely put it past Casen's bunch, that's for sure."

Principal Casen waved for the doors to be closed and sternly gestured for the chattering to stop.

"Okay, ladies. Ladies?!" The room shifted and settled. "I need you to turn off those phones of yours—and I mean *turn* them off. Now."

Mara whispered to Tip, "Where's this new Principal Bitch coming from? She's never done this before, always so 'like me, please like me.'" Tip shook her head. Principal Casen tapped her pen impatiently; teachers winnowed out those reluctant to detach and yanked their phones.

"Wow, this must be serious, they're doing cell amputations."

Tip mumbled, "No shit." The lights fell, the room almost black. A photo of a Latina woman abruptly took over the wall over Casen and cohorts. Mara nudged, "Don't you know that girl?"

Then Mara leaned into Tip, "No shit—*I* know her! Isn't that the chick that went missing or dematerialized somehow almost a year ago?!" She suddenly sat up very straight, "I can't believe she went dinging around with that same crew again! So stupid!"

Tip gave her good friend the chill out tap-and-squeeze, "Let's not rush to conclusions. You should put on your glasses—that's *almost* who you're talking about. But not exactly, I don't think."

Principal Casen opened her notes, "My young lady friends, I won't keep you long. Firstly, I know all of this—the above photo, I'm only talking to all of you ninth-, tenth-grade women, etc., etc. —it probably looks pretty scary. Well, don't be scared, there's nothing to be 'scared' of—but we do want you to be concerned. And aware. And maybe just a *little* afraid—the healthy kind of afraid—if you think that would help."

Tip sighed, "Once a stupid bitch, always a stupid bitch."

Mara nudged, "Stop. Who's judging now?"

Tip leaned forward, whispered too loudly, "Wait, I *do* recognize her"

That triggered Mara, "You're *right*. That's, that's—"

"It's what's-her-name's mom! Not what's-her-name!"

"Marta! Marta Cortez. *Martika's* mother," Mara declared. "Yeah, she was pretty out there. But cool, definitely cool. Her mother, I mean."

Tip nodded, agreeing. The next photo of the family confirmed the girls' explanation. It *was* Martika's mom, Marta; she'd been finally, officially identified as *MISSING* (not that this fact was so newsworthy, even a little bit). Everyone had been painfully aware of the circumstances (rumored and otherwise) for days now, and this audience was especially aware and anxious about their friend Martika, who ostensibly had been "emptied" and meandered her way to her current nonexistence existence.

"But she's okay, right?" Mara leaned into Tip's ear.

"Yeah, yeah, last I heard. Kind of, mostly: floating in a corner of her aunt's guest room, comes down just to pee, eat, crap some more."

But the gist of Principal Casen's communication wasn't about either woman, it was the fact that this was the fourth attack in the last year and a half. And the perpetrator was victimizing Latina women—more witch-leaning than not—and *only* Latina women.

Principal Casen was clear and forceful, "This is home-grown terrorism, my young ladies, and we're sharing this first with you because we think you can help."

Principal Casen and her companion teachers explained by just living their lives as socially networked, as craftily, as Snapchat-ily, as rumor-driven and as normally as they could, clues could surface, and these awful horrific offenders or offender could reveal themselves. She'd taunted all the young witches in the room to shine up their Nancy Drew caps and wands and then finally do nothing else except 'be aware'...

"Use that sixth sense of yours—those that have it anyway—but like you've never used it before." Tip glanced at Mara, *What da freakiness is that supposed to mean?*

And in the next moment, almost magically, the lights went up and the doors opened and that was the beginning of that. Mara looked at Tip, Tip sighed at Mara and off they went to their respective fourth-period classes.

Tip groaned, *Like I need one more shitty thing to worry about.*

. . .

THE AFTERNOON DEVELOPED like the action sequences in the middle of *The Matrix* but without the bullets and the cartwheel variations: it moved painfully slowly, enhanced by a feeling of dread. The girls post-assembly all appeared drained, but that was hardly the only reason the rest of the school was already buzzing with curiosity. Tip caught a glimpse of Sasha and lassoed her close.

"So why weren't you at that meeting today?"

"It was that lab makeup test. Mrs. Stackhouse said she could slip it in then, so we did."

"Interesting. I wonder if she knows more than she's letting on. Not that it seems there's anything to let on about—not yet anyway."

Sasha's eyes widened, "No shit, what are you saying?"

Tip smiled, tight-lipped; Sasha potato-pinched her hard, nails and all (Sasha did nothing halfway), "Tell me..."

Tip winced, pulled her arm away, "Screw you!" Titters, then kind-of giggles, they leaned closer, looking five not sixteen. "You remember how much we loved Martika's mom?"

Sasha squinted, struggling, "Martika... Martika..."

"Marty!"

"Oh shit! I love Marty! What am I saying?"

"Like, nothing, that's what you're saying."

"All right, bitch. So—what?"

"It's her cool Mom. Just gone—*for real* gone."

Their teasing faded, now worried looks.

"Just like that?! That was the reason for all this discussion? But she would *always* just 'disappear'—right? And Marty always mostly knew what she was up to. She said it was 'for her art'—I always thought it was weird but a cool-weird."

Tip affectionately contradicted, "You always find stuff that you don't really understand 'weird but cool.'"

"I do too understand it—what's not to understand? She's a painter, she needed to go find things to paint."

"Uh-huh, it's not quite like that, but that's okay" Tip waved her next poke away, "No, they waited this time—Marty waited to be sure. She's *majorly* gone now: certain amulets aren't where they should be, lesser trinket-y stuff just dumped."

"So why did they just talk to you, or us?"

"For the reasons we're saying. She was so cool, so many of Marty's friends—and as we know, Marty has a lot of friends—"

"Who doesn't love Marty? Everyone loves Marty!"

Tip sighed, "You couldn't remember her name a second ago."

"Screw you, I *love* Marty..."

"Whatever." Tip started walking again, "Anyway, it's not like it's some awful secret or anyone died or—"

"As far as anyone *knows* nobody's died."

"God, Sasha, you always have to..." She let it go, "Never mind. They just wanted to have a smaller conversation with us first to see if we knew anything. It's not like no one else can't know or anything like that."

"Well that's kind of boring."

Tip couldn't quite believe Sasha said what she'd said, but then she thought about it a second more, always trying to give her sister the benefit of the doubt, and then a second after that, as per usual, and then wondered why she even bothered. *I love her to death but sometimes I could just rip her a...*

Sasha squeezed Tip's hand, "Gotta go. See you at home."

What does she have going on today? Tip just assumed it had another something to do with Sasha's ongoing obsession with all things internet-related, web-connected, or otherwise digitized. This one had been hanging around much longer than any other of Sasha's fixations, so Tip presumed this craze really mattered. *Tonight it'll be just more of the same basic blathering but with technomysticism as the obsession du jour. Whatevers.* (Once again Tip's Earthy yin was flipping off Sasha's tech-heady yang.)

. . .

GREG AND TOM BOY grabbed Sasha's backpack strap and spilled-spun her around heading the opposite way—Greg could have easily been penalized for unintentional yanking.

"Stop it! Why the hell do you—"

"It's this way—Clarke's class. They moved it."

Sasha adjusted her everything, "Well, you could have just used words like most people."

Greg smirked, "I'm not like most people." (No one acknowledged him one way or the other.)

"This is the second time since last week. Is it the same—"

Tom Boy interjected, "It's worse. You didn't smell it coming from the English Pod?"

Sasha said, "Maybe. I almost couldn't smell anything after that poisonous soft pretzel I ate."

Tom Boy saw Luis and high-fived him back around in their direction—the smell was back.

Luis looked surprised, "Clarke is usually pretty good at cleaning up his messes."

Tom, Greg, and Sasha's eyes widened. Greg muttered, "What da freak?"

"Oh, don't get all worked up. Just another of his backdoor attempts to justify magic again for the larger good. 'Bringing history to life.' Even if it's been dead for over a thousand years, if you know what I mean."

Greg was splitting his skin, "Fucking zombies! Real fucking zombies! Fucking *finally*..."

Luis deadpanned, "No, dickhead. Not dead people, dead *trash*. And trash that, for whatever reason, won't go back to where it came from."

Tom Boy quipped, "Hmm, how does that sound familiar?"

Luis grabbed the back of Tom Boy's neck—sort of affectionately, sort of not, "Laugh now, white boy. We'll see who's picking up that trash one day soon," a semi-shocked Tom Boy twisted out of his grip, wide-eyed, entreating Sasha to help disarm any further confrontation.

But Sasha was distracted.

Tom Boy said, "What's wrong now?"

"Nada," Sasha muttered. "At least, well... No, forget it. Just another weird feeling. Could just be getting my period too. Again." She laughed, but she was half-serious.

Greg grunted, "Sash, it's been great having you in the B.W.B. club—knowing you better, and stuff—but your bodily functions aren't *that* interesting."

"Tom and Luis aren't freaking out."

"I'm not freaking out. You know, I don't go telling you how many times I jerked off this morning."

Luis said, "You are such a dick—that's hardly the same thing."

Greg pushed back, "It's *completely* the same thing."

Then Sasha settled it, "It's not the same. I got my period like a year after everyone else, so I'm fucking thrilled *every* time it happens. You've probably been wacking it since you were two—so it's *completely* not."

No one knew how to reply to that exactly, so once again Sasha slam-dunked any rebuke.

She was, however, still trying to wrap her thoughts around this interminable smell. *And what 'trash,' Luis, exactly?*

———————— ◀▒▒◐ ◐▒▒▶ ————————

"WHY AM I always the last one to know?" Tom Dad assumed his 'Mopey Face in Hands' position #3.

Anna wasn't interested in co-worker morale at that moment, "I dunno, Tom. Maybe because you're the oldest?" Ouch-y. Snark delivered with an extra dash of snit. She did, though, give him a pat on the back or two before she left the conference room, and that was (mostly) sincere.

Tom looked out the bank of windows he'd stared out probably too many times before. He could easily recall when those windows were born (about two weeks after his remodeled office was). *Maybe that was the clincher?* Tom shouldn't have asked for extra windows; with these hard and ostensibly moral times at hand, with self-restraint and modesty moving to the tippy-top of the social decorum "to do" list, extra *anything* was generally frowned upon. And that held true for all beings—wherever you landed on the hoodoo scale.

And it just didn't matter, excess of any variety was simply considered distasteful. *And the gods know that being considered distasteful, well, that would just send someone straight home from school, with a note from the principal.* Tom's chronic sarcasm probably didn't help his broader case either.

"You weren't the last to know, you always just like to think you were the last to know. I know, because I was standing right there when Alice told us the meeting was moved." Tom's long-tine design partner-who-was-recently-promoted-to-be-more-than-that, Phil Esposito, seemed to appear out of whatever thin air was left in the room. Phil wasn't anything if he wasn't efficient, and Tom had learned to hate that about Phil. Most everyone—no, actually, everyone, all of them—felt exactly the opposite. (Poor Tom, old Tom.)

"Oh shit, you're right again Mr. Esposito." Tom pressed his pencil into his pad.

"It's not a matter of being 'right'; it's a matter of what makes sense."

"Oh, and now I don't make sense, either?"

"That's not what I was saying, but since you brought it up..." Phil grinned, he was clearly attempting to be the good friend Tom knew him to be. So Tom smiled too, eventually.

"You always make sense, Tom. I know you at least that well." Phil opened his laptop, "It's just that, lately, if I may be brutally honest..."

"You can leave out the brutal part if you'd like."

"You're not making sense to the people you need to make sense to—our client, specifically."

Tom wasn't surprised to learn that; actually hearing the words stung, though. He nodded, pressing the pencil point deeper into the paper.

Tom muttered, "So what do we do about it?"

Phil smiled a different kind of smile this time, "Sorry, buddy, but don't believe this is a 'we' thing."

Tom found his way out of the windows again.

"It all adds up, Phil. I'm a big boy. Something will change, don't fret."

Phil nodded. "Let's go drink more coffee."

"Sure. More coffee always makes sense."

More of anything can always make sense, one way or another...

ANTONIA TAP-KNOCKED THE TABLE, "ANYONE HOME?" Ezra opened her eyes, smiled slowly. True to form, Ezra was placed and pressed and folded, arms across chest, *Already on the defensive, I knew it, and hand into hand.*

"How'd I guess it? At least you're late exactly the same amount of time you were the last two weeks. Uncanny. Why don't we just change the time to 5:39?" She smiled slightly—so maybe this week's conversation would be a little lighter, the lecture a little shorter.

Always best—especially lately—to first chop her down to size, just a little bit, "So who's here today? Bitch Ezra, Politico Ezra, Sentimental Ezra?" Ezra squeezed Antonia's wrist, her passively aggressive way of saying knock it the hell off.

Antonia was favoring Sentimental Ezra recently. She seemed to have more in common with Sentimental Ezra, which made sense since their *sentimentals* were the same—they'd been kindred souls for at least half of their conjuring lives.

"I don't know, Ant, right now I really don't know." That was weird. For Ezra. Ezra never did oblique or ambiguous—well, maybe a little bit of oblique if it helped her point. Antonia signaled the bartender for her usual, waiting for Ez to sharpen the edges of her comment but nothing happened except a couple more milquetoast grins. Ezra now appeared lost, hollow—something that had never happened in the almost one hundred years that they'd been *blood sisters*. (Witchery-wise, one could readily expect the "ritual" to be more extreme than it actually is: it only involves the tiniest bit of plasma, even less than the movies would have you think. But they do more of the *ritual* talking, praising, mutual soul-sucking—I'm joking about that last bit, kind of, sort of...)

Ezra was nothing if she wasn't consistent, lucid, and committed. (We should add *passionate* here too, for good measure.) She'd been and still was the perfect complement to Antonia's warm, enigmatic, perpetually indecisive Earth mother. She waited again for Ezra to fill in some of the conversational blanks floating right in front of them. But her drink came and little else—only more concern.

"What is it, Ez?"

"I told you. Dunno. There's a lot. But I'm having a hard time putting my finger on it. Except for, well..."

"Well, what?"

"Your part." The booth shook ever-so slightly (but by which witch?).

Antonia squinted, trying to see through to any words that might be attached to those metaphorical blanks. Again, no luck. *Just going to have go along for the ride. Glad I'm still a little bit stoned for this.*

Antonia pushed ahead, "My part in what exactly? You're being really vague, and you're *never* vague."

"Yeah, I know. But there's so much I still don't know, and probably so much I shouldn't tell you."

Antonia glanced down at Ezra's inadvertent levitating (it always seemed to calm her): the various glasses, napkins, pretzels, and nuts floating anxiously just above the table's crusty surface. (Should they scatter? Get out while the gettin's good? Which corner would be closest? No, they stayed put—played their part.)

Antonia leaned in, "Well, what the fuck does that mean? We tell each other everything. Always have." *Guess I'm not that mellowed out after all.*

Ezra breathed out, sat back deep into her chair, now face in hands, breathed in. She then abruptly transformed as she unfolded, flower-like, eyes shut but smiling large, emanating some great pleasure and peace that shifted the mood of their conversation entirely the other way. It was a Super Weird Ezra Moment #2 (that was counting from just last week)—*what is happening?* Antonia anxiously took a deep sip, *And where the hell did he hide the alcohol today?* Ezra slowly opened her eyes, her smile even larger, but she now appeared to be looking right through her dear, worried friend.

Antonia pressed, "How many have you had? When did you get here—*noon?*" This kind of dig would always irritate the always-in-control Ezra. (Not now, though.)

On the other hand, maybe I'm too buzzed—didn't think so. Hard to tell anymore. Like any bad high, let's just wait this out... Then more bizarreness: in the next moment, Obtuse Ezra returned from wherever, and Blissed-out Ezra had fizzled.

"Sorry, what were we saying?"

"*You* weren't saying anything, even though you were talking," Antonia knocked back the rest of her double, signaled for another round, "Are you okay? You never act like this, not in the almost hundred years I've known you."

Ezra frowned, just a bit. "Yes, it's different. Something's different."

Antonia let her drink hit the table, "Okay, explain. This is where we started five minutes ago."

"I'm sorry. I feel like, no, I *know* I'm taking advantage. Our Fridays are hallowed; they've been that for how many years?"

"Fourty-four."

"Wow, you *were* paying attention. You know I never quite 'got' the drug thing with you guys. But no judgments." Ezra could almost feel Ant's impatience. "Sorry for making this all about me."

Antonia demurred, "Ezra, it's *always* about you. At least sixty percent of it." She meant that constructively and affectionately, *You're my best friend, you always will be, it's all fine.*

A big, broad Ezra smile eked through, and this time she was looking directly at her friend.

But the smile faded again just as quickly. Ezra spoke slowly, "Ant, I'll say what I can. And by that I don't mean to suggest that I'm not telling you something or keeping something from you. I would never do that."

Antonia had reached her limit, "*What* is 'all that you can say'?! You've never held anything back from me."

"That's right, and that's what I'm trying to explain, or maybe half-explain, is a better way of saying it."

"Uh-huh... So explain."

Ezra folded her hands, finger over finger.

"The last two to three months I started having visions again."

"You always have had visions. They were like your period—when you *had* your period."

Ezra nodded enthusiastically, "Yeah, thank the gods that's over with. Anyway, no, most were like that, but these are different. They're like comparing Bambi to Godzilla. And because they can happen just like some puzzle—the middle before the end before the beginning—and it can feel like Godzilla is standing on top of you and has to stop and think in which direction Bambi just scampered off."

"So *that's* why you don't know what you're talking about?" Antonia clearly wasn't satisfied.

"Very funny."

Ezra's expression abruptly changed again.

"It's going to be the most difficult thing or challenge—whatever you want to say—that's ever happened to me," she finally took a breath, "...*and you.*" Antonia took in the words and half-thoughts Ezra had been fumbling through, and she realized that Ezra was being as straightforward as she could, and that there really *was* something to be very concerned about. (Maybe even a little—a lot?—afraid of too.)

Every hovering glass, nut, napkin, and drop of alcohol instantly collapsed back on to the table, sloshing and splash-spitting everywhere. It startled them both. (Ezra clearly had forgotten about her misplaced spell and aggression.)

Antonia was struggling with her own thoughts now, bumping into words and feelings. There were a quite a few situations, things she'd said, and so on that she will always wished had never happened, and her dearest friend stayed close and understanding, persisting through every one of them.

But the memory of the incident and time that Ezra obliquely mentioned (*Did she say actually that? She wouldn't toss that out like so many lost weekends, boy toys, whatever...*) came rushing to the fore—and it was as awful, even more agonizing in hindsight. *Boy, I did a really good job of burying those three weeks...* (That was a sentimental way of thinking about it. Truth be told, it was a drug-addled binge that for even a "well-seasoned" white overwitch was pushing the limits. But Antonia had her reasons, her rationale for her defense—and they were almost impossible to deny.)

Antonia became mired in the pain of—*what?* What was it again? She watched more of Ezra's muddled conversation; the specific words were already gone, it had become one long inebriated meditation. Antonia saw Ezra's hand squeeze hers—their signal, it was time to go.

Antonia stumbled out of their bar and fell into the house—that's how she seemed to remember it anyway. The whole driving home thing was missing, gone; she did remember thinking it might be safer to just fly home, but the last time she tried that at this blurry stage she ended up trying to crawl in some older couple's bedroom window several blocks from Locust Lane. (Believing it was her own, of course. At least she got the town right.)

Tom Dad smiled his woozy smile and gave her a big woozy hug. He had her beer-wine-whatever-the-fuck-it-was waiting and mostly cold. He lit the joint and looked carefully at what seemed like an extra head of hair on his wife—he was wrong, "You're a mess. What'd you do? Fly home?" (Apparently, she had.)

"You're a fine one to point fingers." She smiled wide at Tom Dad. "Where are the girls?"

"Where they usually are—upstairs."

He smiled back at her, "Happy Friday."

"Yep, you too..."

They left for The Last Call a half-hour later.

SASHA JUST SAW BLUE, a lot of different kinds of blue, but just blue. She'd have to ask Tip, she knew this shit like the back of her several things (not just her hand). She thought it might have something to do with some natural cycle, the moon, or the seasonal something or other.

It's a good thing I like blue because, well, that's a lot of freaking blue. Blue is good, I think—single colors are generally a good thing. It's when that rainbow shit happens that means you're in the crapper.

Blue, blue aisles of blue. Miles of aisles of blue. Just outside, Sasha couldn't remember seeing a blue tulip before but there it was, right in the ground, right in front her. Tip eventually resurfaced and they sat on the front deck next to each other, looking at nothing in particular. Tip sighed, took a long slow breath, reminded Sasha it was just her aura in some kind of emotional overdrive, trying to help or something.

Today had been tricky, a little tough to negotiate. Not entirely out of the normal run for a hungover Tetersberg Saturday, but this one had pushed more than a few too-familiar buttons—and broken a couple too.

SUNDAY AFTERNOON, the inclement emotional weather began to clear. Antonia's donned her first (probably second, though she'd never admit it to them) Anthropologie dress...

"With all your powers and intuition and years of fashion sense, how did you actually *pay* for a dress like that? Sorry, I misspoke, a *ripoff* like that?" Sasha was trying to be funny, but it fell short; Antonia always seemed to wake up in a good mood—on Sundays, at least—so she followed along.

"I needed to prove to myself I could do it," Antonia sighed, joked, through her broad intentionally grinny smile.

"Do what?" Soba didn't bother looking up. "Bring back macrame jumpers?"

Sasha yelped, "Soba, *natch!* Didn't know you had it in you! Pretty good for a—"

"I'm three years younger—*just* three..." she kept reading, or appeared to be.

Tom Dad wandered in with his coffee, "Yeah, and you should probably consider underwear if you're wearing a dress like that."

Sasha crowed, even Soba chuckled now. Antonia mouthed *Fuck you all, very much* and slumped in her chair. "Seriously, why don't you like it?"

Sasha offered, "I don't like anything from Anthro. You look like you're trying too hard, and it's not clear at *what*—and no matter what age you are." Pretty sophisticated summation from a non-creative, linear-thinking almost-seventeen-year-old.

Tom Dad looked at the girls, gauging their reactions one way or the other; he wasn't convinced they were sharing in the spirit of his verbal spitballs. He felt tentative about *everything* at that second, still Soba seemed to be enjoying the moment with her mom all urban hippie-d up. Not much to do to try and correct for that, not that he should—Tom Dad slumped back into the couch, *Why would I think that to start with?*

*My wife used to be fun. Now she just seems, I can't think of any other way to say it than, she's silly. Sometimes she's stupid **and** silly, but mostly just silly.* He thought as he looked around doing a few more seconds' worth of introspection with the people, the family sitting around him. He thought that there's nothing wrong, nothing necessarily bad, but there's displacement, there's aggravation, and no one's creative about anything anymore.

Tom naturally turned the lens on himself; he was always fair that way. *I've made peace with my apathy—I can actually say I've **embraced** it.*

THE BROKEN END of her first wand, chewed and worried like a six-year-old's once-yellow number two pencil, rolled to the side of box. The torn paper with red marker x's, its corners rounded, pretended to be something it wasn't—a piece of a very makeshift heart maybe? Some urgent gesture of affection—love *maybe?* Yet another persistent Antonian memory—one she always welcomed but also couldn't recall exactly how or why; just another happy symptom of her foraging for magick and love. (She'd believed there were infinite varieties of both since starting her collection as a precocious seven-year-old.)

Antonia perused her enchanted history, *How sweet I was! How could you not just fall in love with me!* Antonia laughed out loud, rattling the box's contents in enthusiastic agreement. It *was* funny how much she once trusted in what those sticks of wood could do —even their broken shards, ends, nubs were hallowed; she wished she could recall more precisely when she started to grapple with the realization that she was the source of all things magickal—the sum of *her* powers, of everything that was good *and* bad. (That was the hard truth for *all* witches, regardless of their respective strength and competency.)

She reached up for her *Love Box*, the one that had (as I've mentioned) achieved a singular, strangely beatified presence. (Or perhaps "aura" is the better word, *It depends on the day.*) You'll recall it contained only the most rarified and personally fabled runes— Antonia's enchanted creme de la creme. Its contents were tired and old, appropriately exhausted, and desperately needed to rest —to sleep like the dead; her rationale was that its mythic contents needed to be more-than-ready, facile, and beyond powerful for the next... Antonia always resisted completing that thought.

(But the next *what?* Why was that such a difficult thing to answer? Or was it more to-the-fact that she was pointing that particular wand, with its obtrusive question, at *herself?*)

You're Gross

✦❀✦

Why there'd be two *new* substitute drivers for Bubby Welters was anyone's guess, and why two were needed for one bus driver position struck several of the students slightly unusual. (Only slightly because most everyone was aware of Mr. Ziff's penchant to overplan, as well as overdress—especially on a district staff manager's salary.) But there were definitely two, and clearly related given their physical resemblance, and both equally mysterious regarding their gender. The particularly odd thing was they were more *feminine* for the drive to the school and somehow more masculine (or better said: *less* feminine) for the return trip. The Sisters paid particular attention, though their fellow riders didn't seem to care much beyond that initial tweet.

Tip was late to the bus that Tuesday so instead of the back (which she was convinced was safer), she reluctantly sat up front. The frontest front. Directly behind Sub Bus Two, who finally had a name: Judy (or Jude?). It was that day that she discovered something else about Judy-Jude (apart from a gummy bear thing), and it worried her.

94

"She leaned forward—her hair fell forward—and on her neck was..."

Sasha knew too well of Tip's semi-obsessive compulsive disorder-*cum*-"great attention to detail" ("It *all* matters! It's *all* one big puzzle!) but was not feeling generous this afternoon. Stephen, her latest pseudo-flirtation, had dissed her—probably not on purpose but that didn't matter. They were walking, a block from home, when Sasha finally relented.

"What happened now, Tip? Just *say it*—I'm not half as fascinated by the bigender semi-twin sibling bus drivers... Did she eat yet another gummy bear off the bus floor or something?

Tip felt equally frustrated with Sasha, but couldn't put her finger on why exactly—she was swiping like mad through the diary of evidence of one kind or another she'd been collecting, she muttered, "Shit, it was just here. She probably hexed the pic as I left the bus."

Sasha said, "A pic of Judy? Why the hell would you want a picture of her? For this conspiracy 'campaign' you're obsessing about?"

"You're just as obsessive about it as I am."

"Yeah, but I'm not as obsessive *and compulsive* as you are."

Tip leered, "Don't be such a dick. She had jewelry—on the *back of her neck!*"

"Crikey," Sasha sighed, starting to walk away from her. Tip grabbed her by the hood of her jacket.

"*Bone* jewelry."

"Oh, crikey twice!" Major eye roll from Sasha, "Let me go. I'm hungry."

Tip shoved her phone in Sasha's face—she'd found the pic, "*But it's her **own** bones!*"

Sasha took the phone. It was definitely weird. Definitely some kind of bone, but too pretty, too sculpted to be just bone. She shook no.

"Open the shot. Look at the other edge."

It didn't look real (whatever it was) and was particularly grody (whatever *it* was.) The bangle was small but was definitely hinged to a horn-like protrusion from Judy-Jude's third or fourth verte-brae. It was just a small horn, but in any case it was definitely and exactly that. The leathery crimped flesh anchoring the bone seemed equally out of place given Judy's pale, oddly translucent skin. This was definitely some kind of out-of-town, out-of-sorts weirdness, something bigger and badder than what any sixteen-year-old underwitch could sort through (especially one from the suburbs).

BITTS ANNOUNCED, "LEAVE THE LIGHTS OFF!"

Sasha frowned at Greg and Bitts, but mostly Bitts, "Why? What is it about you and dark rooms?"

Bitts moaned, "Don't start bitching out already. I just want to show you guys something, *okay?*"

"I'm not bitching out, you always think that I'm 'bitching out.' What's that supposed to mean, anyway?" Sasha dropped her books.

"Exactly what you think."

"Do I keep accusing you of *dicking out?*" Bitts looked up and said nothing, Sasha pressed, "Because I could, I *should*."

Bitts got up and turned on the light. "What's got your panties in a wad today?"

Sasha was always ready for an argument, but even she knew, given her current mental state, more damage than good would come from it. "Nothing. No one. Sorry..."

Tom Boy and Luis tripped into the room. *The Boyz That Byte: Digital Machinations Society* had been meaning to change its name for over three or four months now (a couple weeks after Sasha had joined and made it explicitly clear she wasn't going anywhere, *I found my home, homeys...*). Not that any of the boys cared one way or another but they *had* gotten used to things the way they were (like anyone might, regardless of whether you had a penis or not).

Sasha unpacked her desktop folder for the meeting; the agenda was light today, but that was intentional. Sasha had been— and continued to be—rather distracted by the dearth of information about Martika's mom (it fell too easily into one of her conspiracy theory buckets). So, the boys didn't know it yet, but they'd been recruited for their brainpower, web prowess, and more, as needed.

Then with bold strokes, Bitts flipped the lights off and his laptop around and said cheesing widely, "Go Big *and* go Dark..." (Dark Web, to be clear.) He flashed the landing page of a site that also exhibited some *toothiness* with their surname (though not of the digital variety). Sasha squinted, "Gross. *What is it?*"

Bitts grinned, "Human and animal body parts for sale... But this section," he clicked down, "offers 'magical enhancement.'"

Sasha was now defensive, *They're just trying to freak-gross me out.* Luis leaned in, blurted, "No shit—*Brujas 'Bites'? Seriously?* What da fuck?!"

Tom Boy was surprisingly cool, "How did you find *this* sucker? The Dark Web's a pretty fucking big place."

Bitts scribbled over the screen, "Hacked a couple sloppy email trails—so easy."

They all stared unbelievingly at the slapdash site with its morbid flashes of depraved desires or needs.

Bitts now looked sullen, "Yeah, it weirded me out. And especially—look *where*..."

They gasped together: the Black Market, or rather *Brown Market* drug and sales locus—or one of them, a big one—was pinned just five miles from where they were sitting, in Riverton, USA.

———— ‹‹‹‹‹‹ ››››››› ————

THE PEN HOVERED, stumbled over that last letter—Constance kept writing in hopes it just might trick the solution to the problem word and puzzle into appearing, but alas:

Idea A: with Frenchtown pinned on her map:

> *The place had its sounds, its time, and its wits,*
> *To which all had some sense, but only in bits...*

Constance scratched-stabbed at the phrase—she refuses to finish the sentence (too pandering!).

Idea B: the Tricentennial event is nigh, and all things supernatural are a-light:

> *Spell,*
> *Sting,*
> *Witches on the wing,*
> *Blood red sliver moon.*
> *The rest will cry,*
> *That Time doth lie,*
> *And cuts deep—sword to whole heart's wound...*

> *Hex,*
> *Earth,*
> *Clever sisters all,*
> *Yet souls do go astray.*
> *The ground will swell,*
> *Bent till living hell,*
> *And precious few will stay.*

Pilar shrugs: That's sweet and clever and all that—but I'm not getting even a little bit, well, I am *a little bit*—that all hell is about to explode. But it's too *old school,* this should totally be your Kendrick Lamar moment. *Pilar smirks.*

Constance: You don't know that—none of us does! The Earth's plane could explode into nothingness—though I sincerely doubt it—or it could just rain horrendously and there's a whole bunch of nasties running around attempting magically nasty things. It'll most probably be some version of the latter; too much fuss for some sort of faux Big Bang. And Lord knows the gods aren't "into" fuss—especially these times.

Constance tosses the calendar to the other side of the table: They love to bloody the calendar with their crap, this Tricentennial jury-rigged hysteria. It's a bore... And try finding one portal that actually stays open long enough for even *one* entity to pass through, it's—

Pilar resists: One is better than none... Sorry, I'm just not buying that you were wandering around taking notes three hundred years ago in preparation for this very moment. You love to talk a good game, Constance, but you can't even remember where you touched down for your *last gig.*

Constance: None of us can.

Pilar, smiling cautiously: That's what they *like* us to think... *Pilar's impishness suddenly goes dark, she was distracted by Sasha's visage:* Oh, shit! Twice in one week?! She's back at Ezra's!

Constance: Are you really surprised? Those kinds of pustules always blister before they burst.

TIP WAS BED-BOUNCING, "So get in here, bitch! Why so cagey?"

Sasha waved away the comment, "I'm not! Just getting a little para-net-neurotic lately. Didn't want to leave a mark anywhere."

"Why? Thought you said everyone was already buzzing about the 'toe jam' rumor-thing anyway?"

Sasha chafed, "I didn't. You didn't know—and still don't, *right?* Plus I wanted to check my 'source.'"

Tip stopped bouncing, "Ugh. *Ezra?* You just said you were at Claire's."

"I lied. I always lie... About Ezra anyway. It weirds Mom out."

"Can you blame her?"

"Kind of and then not, can never really decide... *Anyway*, don't you want to *know?*"

Then Tip was cagey; she was never one for gossip, or any kind of manufactured truth.

Sasha shook her head; she'd plucked at a few of Tip's thoughts, "No, I think this is pretty darn real. It's kind of cool."

"So?"

"*Martika's mom is back.* Or found, at least. She's in hospital."

"What happened? Is she all right?"

"Mostly, except for her brain and her right foot."

"So, *it is true?* What's so cool about that?"

"She has no memory of the last few days, and she has no toes on her right foot. Well, she *kind of* has no toes... But nobody actually made any *jam* from them, at least as far as I know." Sasha chuckled.

Tip grimaced, "That's scary and gross—you think *that's* cool? That's horrible."

"But there's an upside. Her mind is coming back, and so are her toes."

"How? I mean, especially, the toe part. And—*what da freak?* —why toes?!*"

Sasha winked, "Maybe some black magic, no, *brown* magic thing?" She shrugged, "That whole Rodriquez clan is—this is what Ezra just confirmed—descended from Maria Solina kindred from Galicia, and ancestrally they're big on regeneration. Must have snuck into the gene pool somehow, because it seems to be *autocratic*."

"Big word..."

"Not that big." They looked at one another thoughtfully.

Tip said, "I guess you're right: it's weird but it's good. Mostly weird." She thought a second more, "Actually, a little scary too."

Sasha shrugged, "I just think it's cool." Suddenly Sasha jumped, "Oh shit, how'd I forget—hot off the presses. Remember that crazy bus shit? Well, I mean the shit you *didn't remember* but I completely bizarrely did?" Tip barely nodded, her eyes widened, "Ezra thinks it *is* a portal. Or shit, she *knows* it's a portal—it was a hundred or so years ago—she thought it was an 'obsolete gateway.' Isn't that nuts?!"

Tip was a bit stunned, "Um, well, *duh*—love that word 'obsolete.'" (She still hadn't entirely accepted Sasha's story, as semi-hysterical and long-winded the bus story was and especially for Sasha's typically stunted imagination.)

Sasha scowled, "Dude, are you *getting it?*"

Tip pushed at her sister, "*Dude,* don't be a dude! Of course I am! That's nuts... *The shit is starting to go down.* Whatever this 'shit' is!" They laughed, rolled back onto Tip's bed, "And that's all, um, just too weird for—" Then suddenly Tip held up a finger, which given the position of her hand could have meant to be quiet *or* 'wait a second.' Actually both were correct as Tip oddly announced, "You know this new habit of yours is not attractive at all..."

Sasha frowned, "What'd I do?"

"Not you," Tip sighed, "Get your ass in here." Soba curled herself around the door jamb and into the room.

"What the hell are you *doing?*"

"Just being the annoying baby sister," Soba mumbled.

"Just being a pain in our asses is more like it," said Sasha. "Tip's right, where is this coming from?"

"You *never* tell me anything, so what else am I supposed to do?"

Sasha leaned closer to Soba, suddenly very irritated—a few books, knickknacks took to the air, and shook violently, emphasizing how irritated she was, "Well, maybe there are things *we don't want you to find out.* Maybe they're things you're just better off not knowing."

Tip said, "Stop, Sash, she's not done anything really wrong—just stupid-wrong."

Sasha kept digging, "Well, it's that and this new attitude too—you've picked that up from that Dustin friend of yours. I never liked him either."

"Sasha, lighten up. Go help find missing toes or something."

Sasha looked at them both expressionless and went to her room.

Soba started to sit down, "Sorry, didn't think—"

"Don't sit down. You didn't think is right." Soba looked truly hurt.

Tip, exasperated, said, "I'm sorry too but I don't feel like talking to you right now."

Soba now suddenly felt as young as she looked and wandered back to her room.

SOBA CLOSED HER DOOR, grabbed for her "secret box" (one of her stopgap security blankets) under her bed. The last time was different, but she felt just as crappy as she did right now, so maybe the Owls would appear, listen attentively to her worries (at least they *appeared* concerned). Or maybe not. (It was never a sure thing.)

She unlocked the box, dug through the various trinkets. A couple tried to crawl out as they usually did (thankfully they were too old to actually fly anymore), but Soba carefully, most affectionately tucked them back inside. She found the two dilapidated pieces of wand, one was from Aunt Teresa, whom she never actually met but always kept sending The Sisters all kinds of mostly (to be generous) crap, old spell-making odds and ends. The other she couldn't remember where she got it—had to be from her mother (who else?). She just liked the color, or rather, the fact that it would *change color*. It reminded Soba of how she felt most days (especially tonight, especially at the moment); Tom Dad had joked "it" had probably given birth to mood rings (whatever they were).

· · ·

THE SISTERS CAME ROLLING down the stairs, a little ahead of schedule, which was unusual.

And there was Antonia, with breakfast almost on the table. (Speaking about unusual occurrences—The Sisters appeared unmoved.)

Antonia said, "Aren't you impressed?" She was a little peeved. (Rightfully so. Maybe.)

Soba peered under the top pancake, "All handmade? Craft-free?"

Antonia nodded.

Tip said, "What's the occasion?"

"No occasion. Just felt like overcompensating this morning."

Sasha said, "Lemme guess, you've already boned a joint and have the munchies and are just trying to distract us from the truth even though we don't really give a crap already?" (She was actually half-serious.)

"Okay, enough. If you don't want it, don't eat it."

Sasha laughed, "See, I told you!" The girls laughed, started inhaling their favorite starch.

Antonia positioned herself behind her tea; The Sisters did sense something out of the ordinary with their mother, maybe her aura was under duress for some reason (or maybe Antonia was striving to engage in ways even Antonia wasn't fully aware of yet).

Then, completely randomly, Antonia asked the table, "Whatever happened to Martika?"

Tip frowned, "Nothing happened to Martika—oh, you mean her mom? She's okay now, seems fine. Guess her toes have grown back by this point." The Sisters chuckled.

Antonia was staggered, "She wasn't freaked about her mom?"

"Not after she came home. It was like no big deal."

"They can't find parts of her mom's body and it's not a big deal?!" Antonia looked genuinely shocked, then pained.

The girls were apathetic. Tip said, "Kind of, but not really. Martika wasn't freaked so no one else was. Guess they're kind of

used to it as much as you can get used to something like that...
And not *just* her mother—all of them."

"Them?"

"That Bruja crew—*Brujeria*—they're totally cool, totally
amazing history."

Soba nodded in agreement with Tip, Sasha seemed strangely
oblivious. For some reason, Antonia was clearly hoping for a
different result—her pained looked remained, turning her tea
sour.

The Sisters were gone in a second, like magic.

They were half a block to their stop, and Sasha pulled Tip
back, "Why did you tell her Marta's *back at home?*"

Tip sighed, "Didn't want to get into it with her, did you?"

"You mean after all that fuss to get you three together, she just
up and left?" Antonia crossed her brow, aiming at the twins. *They
didn't learn to be this catty from me, that's for sure—but then again...*
(Antonia dialed that Hartford [Witch] Evil Eye down a notch or
two.)

"*Really*, Mom? You're blaming *us*?" Sasha almost stood up, "We
still don't know what all she was droning on about. It maybe made
a *little* sense around every five minutes, and it was a fifteen-minute
convo, at best."

"Even though it felt ten times longer," moaned Tip.

"Well, I wasn't there so I can't really judge—she wanted to see
just you two for something or other. And lately when the two of
you get on a tear you can be—"

The twins grinned in their evil twins' grin way, they mock-
shocked, "What?! *What* can we be?!"

This is bizarre, Antonia sat back in her seat, peering at her
offspring, *This is what they're becoming—no, have become?* They were
taking far too much pleasure in Ezra's discomfort; but then again,
to be fair, Antonia knew well how daunting her sister-in-spirit's

oversized personality could be. The twins were now sophisticated enough to hold their own in repelling their Aunt Ezra's will, a supernatural force in its own right (or at least it was the last time Ezra had to seriously think about it).

Sasha had snatched up her mom's last snippets of thought. (She could get into her head and out again before Antonia could think the words "pothead" or "you little shit.") Sasha blurted, "No one was unnecessarily *mean,* not even a little bit." Tip nudged her, "Well, okay, we always are a little bit—that's what makes it fun— especially with her. Besides, she's a big witch—she can handle it."

Antonia suddenly jumped to the defense of her dearest Ez, "You don't know that—not one-hundred-percent-positively know that." Antonia, still the fastest thought nazi in the Frenchtown *coven* (if you could still use that word: it's now more of a grumpy Girl Scout Club with sticks-for-wands compared to what I've experienced albeit a *long* time ago—I'm sure Antonia's well aware...). She skewered the thought-probing that Sasha, and now Tip, was attempting, *Pay attention to what I'm saying, not what I'm thinking!*

Then (lest anyone forget who was running *this* magic show) she tweaked a few nerve endings between their eyes to reinforce her point. The girls stuttered and were a bit overcome; today's Antonia was shockingly much more agile, and they weren't really sure what to say or think next.

Antonia said, "One thing I'll share: you don't want to get on Ezra's bad side. She'll turn you into a ten-nippled she-bitch faster than you can say *Wicked Twitch of the West.*"

Sasha peered at her mother, not quite willing to absorb the conversation thus far, "Where did *you* pick up that line? It can only be Ezra." The girls snickered (albeit cautiously).

Tip concurred, "This is getting a little weird, Mom. If you were sixteen and your pretend aunt—one that we most days love and adore—was suddenly trying to give you advice on sex with wizards and warlocks twice your age, 'protected or otherwise...'—

her words, by the way—you might throw some nasty shade her way too. And besides, who calls them 'wizards and warlocks' anymore? Let alone wanting to date one." (More sniggering.)

The conversation was becoming stranger, more unbelievable by the syllable, but Antonia remained undaunted. She said emphatically, "None of this changes the fact that this woman has sacrificed, relinquished so much of her own existence to make sure that all of you, me, and anyone with a shared history, like we all have..." Antonia seemed shaken; she barely managed the words, "Well, that only good things come from that."

They'd never quite experienced their mother being this direct, this absolute in her thoughts and comments. Ever. So, something (and something not very good) was up. You could usually tell who she was blaming, or most angry at, by the amount of times she'd look you directly in the eyes (Tip was the current champ, though this was by Sasha and Soba's count, so a little biased). But, nope. Nothing. No eye contact with either of them.

Strange times indeed.

TOM BOY COULDN'T GET comfortable, but that was a relatively new thing. Greg had always sucked as a driver, but in the last year or so, with the surprise appearance of a new sound system, it had gotten progressively suckier. The louder the music, the worse was Greg's driving; Tom Boy would try to tweak the volume lower, but Greg had the distinct advantage of the steering wheel master control, which made *everything* dangerous.

"Dude, that was a *red* light..." Tom Boy lamented.

"It was *mostly* red—it still had a little yellow in it."

"Whatever."

The app that Bitts had penned was, in its beta form, more a distraction than anything else. He wanted their BWB club to road test it (Greg had taken his request maybe too literally) and its aggressive promise of *extrasensory thaumaturgic perception*. The first read and results were disappointing—it was like watching a slapdash remake of *Ghostbusters III* but by eleven-year-olds.

"Point it at the intersection. See if it does anything," said Greg.

"We tried that twenty minutes ago, when we were coming instead of going," sighed Tom.

"Just shut up and do it again. Maybe it's left-handed."

"The app? Maybe *you're* brain dead-ed."

Greg tried to grab the phone from Tom who smacked his hand back to the wheel, "Just drive, asshole. I'll do it." And still there was nothing (not that they knew exactly what *something* would look like).

"So, who was the last W or whatever to find it? Or at least see it?"

"See what?"

"The Portal Gate, asswipe! The 'intersection'! Crikey!"

Greg who was immune to bullying of any flavor answered, "The site said maybe five years ago. Emmet so-and-so, never came back, so they were trying to sell him like the "legendary Emmet"—*get your Emmet Demigod of the Universe tee shirt here!*—and that he *meant* to never come back. At eighteen and *legend has it* a pretty freaking powerful and frightening eighteen, you might want to get the fuck out of Frenchtown but not the universe, or anywhere there might not be pussy."

Tom Boy looked at Greg, *Is he serious?* "Are *you* serious?"

"Why? Wouldn't *you* be serious? If there was the slightest chance that you might end up somewhere that you'd never have sex ever again in your life—assuming you've had sex by now." Greg smirked, "I mean, if I never had even fucked a girl once—or even a little bit of once—then I would probably not consider it. No matter how great the opportunity is."

"Why? You don't think females in this out-of-this-world world have sex organs?"

"I think you can't even assume there *would* be females. Maybe they're all descended from some strange bastardized sea horse-type creature—and they don't have a sex *at all!*"

Greg roared. Tom Boy had to confess it was kind of funny, *He's an asshole, but ultimately a good-natured asshole.*

"And even if they had vaginas, how would you know where to find it? Now *that* would be fucking awkward, forget even worrying about fussing around with a rubber."

Tom finally gave in, "Okay, okay, funny man, no need to get all gross about it."

"Who's gross? If you couldn't find a girl's pussy, wouldn't you ask her where she put it? Or last saw it—*if* she saw it? Maybe she's intentionally *hiding* it from you."

They laughed out loud, then suddenly the app on Greg's phone burst to life. "What the fuck?!" Greg slammed down the break, the car skidded to a stop. They looked around, then looked back at the meter: it was a weak signal, but it was definitely some kind of signal. Tom Boy locked and registered the occurrence as Bitts had requested—it was a bit piecemeal, but no one had expected the thing to really work (not that they were sure that's what was happening).

Greg peered out the window, "There's nothing around here, just homes, half-baked *covens*, and other various dens of iniquity."

Tom Boy smiled, "You're on a roll tonight."

"The only place I know that's right by here is—"

Tom Boy interjected, mostly joking, "Yep, The Sisters—'The Tetersberg Three *Coven* of Frenchtown'!" Greg laughed out loud.

They chalked it up as another failed beta test and drove home.

She loved laying them out from end to end—*loved it*. The memory and unmitigated sentiment she'd assigned to each piece of her treasure was perfect, complete. Soba's young years belied her ability to dissect and apply the most appropriate myth or invocation. If the power still existed (even slightly) in the talis-man, she'd sense it and adapt its future—their future —accordingly.

It was the only time that Soba felt comfortable leaving her physical body behind; she let her arms fall loose from her body and sucked in and swallowed whole the ideas, remnants of spells, old and dirty hoodoo. Commingling with the feathers and bones and stones of yore, kissing each other ever so slightly, lying all together from old to new. (Or that's what Soba loved thinking...)

Whatever their future was supposed to become wasn't of any concern to Soba, it was only the present (and perfect) happiness that mattered now. Sometimes—most times—it was this smaller, intimate magical world within her larger, painfully real and func-tional world that gave her peace. And thinking into it she realized it was much more than that—there was hope.

———————————

"THIS LITTLE PIGGY went to market, and this little piggy—well, no one quite knows where this little piggy is going, but he certainly ain't staying home."

Their laughter shook the room; the brown dribble hanging in their shot glasses started to crust around the mouth. He splayed the dollars across the table, as if revealing a perfect winning hand.

"Never seen this kind of money, let alone *touched* it."

"Never. How did you know?"

"I didn't, not for certain. But it just made sense. This site is so fucked up—there's an 'audience' for this kind of thing."

The shorter of the two crumbled back into the couch, now mumbling, "I still don't like that you hurt her, that you took *some-thing* from her."

"Don't blame me, blame that witch! It was mostly her thing. She started it." He closed his eyes, now nervous and impatient; he knew painfully well that their unaffiliated, unearthly "guns for hire" moniker had a very limited and precarious duration. "Besides, I told you, it fixes itself—it's the nature of things, all things. And she's part of that lucky tribe—they're almost super-heroes, that bunch."

It had been days since the "incident," but this wasn't their first time brokering on the Dark Web—the longer they tarried they knew the more valuable their "treasure" became.

There were two toes, snail-like, left in the bottle. And well over a thousand emails wanting to know about them.

Why's It So Dark in Here?

No one had seen Constance in, well, it was hard to know exactly how long—it could have been two hours or two days. And things seemed extra wonky this last while, which strangely and uncomfortably coincided with that cute graphical cue—some sort of "peak" or "bump"—on the Powers That Be's astral almanac.

Pilar: So maybe they actually know *what* they're doing, in spite of how Miss Perfect Constance would like us to think?

R.D.G.: Why? Just because of this wacky weather? No dice.

Pilar: Don't be a putz! Because of their wacky *behavior...* The weather's in there too, though—a tiny bit.

R.D.G.: Agree. It could very well soon be an all-hands-on-deck situation, so where the hell is she? She knows this better than any of us, *experientially.*

Pilar: Exactly. And so she got the hell out of here.

R.D.G. suddenly sits up, then stands up. He's clearly frustrated.

R.D.G.: Listen Pilar, it's the worst-kept secret, your contempt for Constance. And she's not exactly shy about her disdain either. But beyond you two pain-in-the-wherevers, you haven't seen Abyssinia either, have you?

Pilar: Holy crap, what do we do about that? And you're the senior guy on that totem-pole-of-an-org chart, aren't you?

Pilar's snark was becoming more forthright.

(If this was yet another "test"—one could only assume—by the Powers That Be, the demis were having none of it.)

R.D.G.: I'm not going to even acknowledge that kind of comment or rudeness... *R.D.G. slapped some paper around,* Here's that bus ride we glossed over—it's done finally. Read that and be satisfied with yourselves, at least for a few minutes.

THE BUS WAS TAKING that same "detour" again—Judy-Jude's preferred route. Sasha slunk back in her seat and re-analyzed the back of the substitute driver's head and skin decorations. She had finally been convinced of the skull shapes Tip had initially argued for, but today she was at a complete loss as to what Judy-Jude's tattoo was now attempting to portray—beyond a sort-of-spidery thing at the living design's heart-center. Then out-of-the-blue Luis walked by—on their bus! Luis didn't take their bus, ever; as a fact, Luis never took a bus—he walked to school, *So what the freak is he doing on **our** bus?!* He walked right by her and didn't say a word, a smile hello, nothing, *nada.*

Sasha looked over and back at Tip, but she'd missed the whole thing, her face in her phone. Luis had sat in the back and was staring out the window. The air abruptly was different: thick, viscous; Sasha recalled having the same sensation the other afternoon, *But I didn't feel this heaviness... Flat, dull numb.*

She was struggling now to stay fully conscious and alert. She wasn't sleepy, but the syrupy air was cocooning her like a blanket, encouraging her to not actually sleep but relax and seep into its warm folds. Not conscious yet not unconscious, somehow Sasha knew what was expected of her, of everyone, and that this anonymous magic was to help, not hurt.

Tip was now transfixed like the rest of the bus; Sasha was

willing herself free and it seemed to be working. She felt aware though her body was still sluggish; she maintained a vacant, woozy stare so no one would (or *should*) notice any difference. Then more strangeness: she knew where the bus *physically* was but there were impossible gaps of time between one stop and the next so *something* was distorting the logic of their physical plane. Next she grasped they were somewhere else *entirely*—she recognized nothing: the strange ambiguous suburban street corner with signs that ticker-taped some bizarre street name too many letters long; brightly colored home facades that seemed one dimensional (maybe two, *at most*). Everyone on the bus appeared drugged and oblivious as Luis confidently stood up and slow-step-floated down the aisle.

The bus door opened, he glided down the steps and slipped into the ether (as if some invisible monster's tongue slurped him toe-to-head). Sasha worried the world surrounding the bus's yellow skin was not as harmless as it first seemed, but then Luis reappeared, seeming focused and comfortable—a young man with a purpose.

Next Sasha saw something that truly did frighten her: the bus driver's piercing stare in the rearview mirror, angry and threatening—she'd been unmasked. Her guise and spell were tossed aside with a flick of his hand; she couldn't move or fully breathe.

In her stupor, she grasped *her* stop was the *next stop;* she felt two steps ahead of her body as she and Tip ambled down the aisle —Judy-Jude muttered some harmless version of "See you tomorrow." Sasha caught up to her body, fell into it, and turned to speak to her sister, "Um—and like *major* um—*did you see what I saw?*"

Tip glanced at her sister, "Obviously not, given the way you're asking." Tip pointed at the nearby bench that had lately become their stopgap "secret" clubhouse. "Sit. Spill it."

Poor Sasha unraveled in front of her twin, so much unlike the typically cool and disinterested Sasha that Tip climbed on the bus with just a short while ago.

. . .

PILAR LOOKS AT R.D.G., she scowls, twists her mouth in thought: Well, that's a bunch of benign bullshit. What was so hard about that? I mean, it's almost a week 'late.'

R.D.G. patiently sighs: I don't deny that it reads like some silly after-school special off the telly, but I had to determine whether it should go in at all, when it will matter—or not-so-much.

Pilar's scowl remained, now looking equally confused: What are you suggesting? I thought everything gets thrown into the pot, regardless.

R.D.G.: Oh sure, into the proverbial 'pot,' if that's your metaphor of choice. *He sneers slightly, then shrugs,* But not into the story, the document, whatever it's trying to become.

Pilar seems saddened, frustrated: So all of that pontificating about accuracy and verbatim? Just bunch of bull?

R.D.G.: Not at all, it's too much to grapple with at first so we keep it simple until, well, *we can't.* The *intent* is always to be accurate and truthful, but in *action,* or execution, things necessarily change. With every pulse, with every word that's written, spoken. It's just like that clever girl explained—I forget which one: *Wobbly things facts are...*

Pilar smirks: So we do change things while we *don't* change things? We get to have it both ways. Seems pretty screwed up to me.

R.D.G.: It is—*and it isn't.*

TIP SAT BACK into the bench, not exactly knowing what to think (or even believe) of Sasha's rather elaborate and enthusiastic tale, *Everything about the last five minutes was so un-Sasha-like that that's the only reason to believe her.* (Sasha couldn't make this stuff up—not Miss Linear Everything Always Me First.)

Sasha ran out of words, took a slow breath; she looked suspiciously at Tip, "You don't believe me, do you?"

Tip waved her hand yes-and-no, "It was a little silly, and boring. Like that old Nickelodeon channel crap we used to watch." Tip sniggered, "Maybe you just ate another bad soft pretzel or something."

Sasha looked stung, "Wow, witch, don't hold back. Why don't you tell me what you *really think?*"

"I'm sorry, and you do seem pretty freaked out, but on the list of all the weird shit that's going down right now, that's somewhere toward the bottom. At least in my book."

Sasha stood up in a huff, "You think it's just a *coincidence* it happened right as we were getting close to that *Fourth Street Light Portal* or whatever they're calling it now?"

"I think it's a Sasha brain-coincidence, that's what I think it is. I'm hungry; let's go home. We can talk more about it later if you want."

"I can tell you right now that I won't 'want'!"

Tip shrugged and started walking home.

———————————

SEVENTH HEAVEN. Antonia first thought it was another Ezra club somewhere on the other side of town. She wasn't right but she wasn't entirely wrong given Ezra's pissy, heady pseudo-psycho-philosophical mindset of late; Ezra reluctantly hinted it was on the opposite side of Antonia's family's *'getting-out-of-bed, making-the-donuts everyday.'* Antonia ordered another shot—another episode of *Aunt Ezra's Twilight Zone* had just begun.

Clearly Ezra was a little put off, even pissed off, *Why or how could she forget something like that? Even a little bit. What kind of witch sister are you, bitch?* Antonia was now convinced Ezra had one foot on the Earth's Plane, and the other had completely overshot, missed the

Astral but maybe struck the Causal Plane. She snickered into her shot glass, *Okay, I'm overreacting a tad*. But then, maybe not... She was now sensing something very *Alice Through the Looking (Shot?) Glass* as she was becoming small enough to fall into it, *My hands are getting smaller in proportion to my mind—or at least that's how it feels*.

Ezra was still ranting (or channeling some entity from some other plane by this point): "Diana, Zeus, and All Those Before Them—you don't simply *'forget'* about *Seventh Heaven*, Antonia! Maybe its real name is a little trickier—*Caelum Deus?* Yes? No? Sorry, not really, not even going there. It's not part of the curriculum; it doesn't happen..." *What the fuck is she talking about?!* Then Antonia realized that she had become *excruciatingly* small and was peering up at Ezra through the glass's facets as Ezra started to sprout a second head, and then a third, maybe there was even a fourth.

It's hard to comprehend it when you're first told about it (if you're actually given that opportunity), or read a mention of it, or have a sister or brother whisper that magical breath in your ear. Ezra claimed it sounds just like any other fairy tale, but when some witch tweaks the levels of hell, or slathers their own interpretation over why the *esprit de fee* ends without really an ending, well, that certainly isn't Maleficent just talking smack. (No one ever riffed on *Red Riding Hood* that way! *And certainly not in **our** Book of Spells, sister...*)

(Myths, in spite of what you might think, are so much easier to manage than people. *Real* people and W's [and variations therein]—to be extra-super clear—can be a goddam pain in the ass.)

As Antonia teetered on the edge of her shot glass, her attention waning, Ezra finally stated the main message of the strange reverie: "The Sisters—your daughters—are vital *to **your** survival*... And *you are essential to **mine***."

And with that especially bizarre and erratic resolution, another Aunt Ezra "dreamscape" came to its close. Ezra was hardly oblivious to her "dreamscaping" (one of her most vital spells) and its consistently mixed results, *But it's the only way I can freely express myself...* (So claims Ezra—I, however, beg to differ.)

This was the enigma of Ezra Prentiss: her shared realities were simultaneously magnificent and horrifying to everyone else but her.

Antonia woozily recalled Ezra's dreamscapes admonition from a few days prior, that it or they *will be coming...* They used to be a fun thing—many years ago Antonia recollected actually looking forward to them. Now she simply felt threatened.

Then, as if part of some buzzy-muscle-memory thing, Antonia recalled Tip chastening her (but when, exactly?): "Mom, Ezra's on the phone, trying to find you! You weren't answering your cell—so answer it!" screamed Tip. And if she wasn't positive a couple minutes ago, she was perfectly aware now—she was very and extremely wide awake.

Ezra was nixing their happy booze-time today—some silly ongoing argument with Ezra's friend Anne that needed hand-holding. *Thank the gods for small things...*

———————— ⟨⟨⟨⟨ ⟩⟩⟩⟩ ————————

"So what's the plan?" Tom Boy had finally said something. (The Sisters were starting to wonder.)

Sasha was curt, "What? You guys are doing your own thing?"

"For a little bit. Like the last couple times. We'll see you at Saxby's."

Tip locked eyes with Sasha, *Ask them. I dare you.* Greg was a little too animated for just another Friday visit to the mall; Tom Boy and Bitts were too much the other way—quiet and distracted —as if they were on some kind of bodyguard drill or duty.

Sasha didn't hesitate, "Have another appointment with that ominous empty ex-Radio Shack window?" Tip stifled her laugh, pursed her lips; Soba was like an excited dog on a leash.

Greg's eyes widened, stopped dancing; Tom and Bitts shrugged. "Don't know. Haven't heard anything yet." Tom Boy didn't appear the least bit flustered, "Probably." He and Bitts had strangely inscrutable looks on their faces—*that* was new.

"So you're not *surprised* by my question?" Sasha teased, winked, trying to eek a little more info from one or the other. Bitts said calmly, "Nope. You couldn't have been more obvious last time spying on us—if you could even call it that." He smiled. They all looked at each other once more, seemingly just to be polite, and then the boys started to leave, "See you in an hour or so." They turned and were gone.

Soba said cautiously, "That was weird. I'd ask if it was something *I* said or did—but I didn't say or do anything."

Tip peered after them for a moment more, "Nope. That was all them."

Sasha muttered, "And whatever's going on must not be any big mystery for anyone—just us, I guess."

Tip frowned, "Bitts isn't like that. He'll fess up." She looked at her sisters, "Where to first?"

Sasha nonverbally indicated "the usual" and they began their drill—twenty minutes later everything seemed ostensibly fine.

The Sisters were too distracted sorting out what the boys' last conversations should mean or shouldn't to notice the two (we'll just call them "individuals" for the moment) following close behind them. There was no real sense of foreboding or actual danger per se, but this anonymous troll-like duo were *very* much interested in what the group, and especially The Sisters, might be up to.

*SHIT, I forgot to leave a note—again... They'll figure it out—my bike's gone... 'She was either out riding—or someone killed her, got rid of the body, and made their getaway on **her** bike.' Not especially realistic,* but funny to think about, in that weird, esoteric way Tip preferred in deciphering the world around her.

But you'd have to press Tip—be *super-clear*—about which world she's contemplating. Because when it comes to the tangible, natural world: the small bright lips of scent and color that break out of the Earth's soil every morn only to be potentially decapitated or crushed back into the ground by some random shoe or action, she would have a very staid response.

'Tip wrapped herself around its cellular wall, its tiny green body, the cusp of every root and used her each and every twinkling, breath, tear, and smile to strengthen and lift it.' If it was *this* world—her alternative existence, her *meditation*—you would get a very, *very* different answer. She would offer her observations straight up, fearlessly, no more or less worried about what other beings, kids, stripling, anyone would think or do with that information, *Careless, perfect happiness.*

Tip got off her bike; the "nest" she'd created last week had only increased in beauty—its leaves, blossoms and Earth entwined. She plunged head-first into the happy melange and didn't move for the next hour (give-or-take a persistent scratchy twig here and there).

Living on the Edge

Here's the latest and the greatest: Mr. Clarke continued pursuing his dubious efforts at self-promotion and metaphysical evolution (doubly dubious). There clearly was no tangible limit to the quantity of World History facts, tidbits, and sound bites that he could consume; his class continued to be plagued with (albeit remotely) mysterious, putrid odors but the incidents apparently occurred less frequently—or much more likely, everyone just got used to it (people—even W's —can get used to anything). His brain and ego continued to swell to an almost unmanageable girth, at least for a man who was still mostly mortal no matter what he wished to believe. (His physical body, however, was oddly having the opposite outcome.)

MRS. STACKHOUSE MAINTAINED her irrefutably high standing with practically all Frenchtown High students, especially those that were missing that last helping of a healthy ego. She continued to struggle with having to compromise her great passion and talent for teaching (and the occasional hoodoo hit) with the color of her skin and suddenly, strangely, her sex. Her omniscient and ambisexual approach to Biology created a fan base among Frenchtown High's intelligentsia, but fomented an equally weighted (mostly male, mostly post-wizard) antagonistic troupe named the Suckhouse Six that threw shade and any nasty bit of craft they could get their grubby little wand-like hands on to resist the broader Stackhouse Movement.

FINALLY, Principal Casen's accommodation of the wacky ups and downs of the various and now rampant magical stops and starts was the brunt of unhappy tweets and texts. She'd recently ascertained that she barely gave a shit-and-a-half regarding what anyone felt. She and her three other principal peeps in her district had conferred, bonded and made a pact that: "... the wicked weak shall suffer the right and powerful might till—" They still had to finish it; she wasn't exactly sure of Principal Golden's general message—he wasn't the most articulate person, but she felt she had the gist—the runic nutshell. And it was this nut-in-a-shell that was going to give her what she needed: a license to do what she was put on Earth to do. (We're assuming good things, primarily. But we'll see.)

———————— •ııı• •ıı• ————————

"YOU'RE at one of three places when you're not eating: in the woods, in your bed, and every odd-dated full moon—or so it seems—in here with my, *sorry*—*our* wands." Soba didn't even look over at Antonia; she seemed transfixed by the blue wand this time, slipping the now glowing stick back and forth between her fingers.

Antonia kept talking; her daughter was making her uncomfortable in weird ways, especially lately. Soba seemed to be very precise, almost too careful with her choice of words, the ideas she would share or express. Very different from her sisters, jabbering on (or so it seemed to Antonia); maybe they were sucking all of the intelligent air out of the room, maybe the house... *It's not like Tom or I are that goddam brilliant every time we open our mouths—am I picking on her again? I don't know.*

Tip appeared at the door, looking (surprisingly) chatty and, well, happy. She looked once at the unfocused Soba and then her frustrated mother, sighed, and continued walking.

"You can take that one, sweetie, you know that was *your* baby wand." The wand swelled with its blue light as if acknowledging and agreeing with Antonia.

Soba looked up, "I know." She thought about it again, "I just like the idea of keeping it here, with its other wand friends."

Antonia considered the comment and decided not to say what she was going to say—just too mean, *I keep thinking she's too smart for her own good, and then she says something like she's five all over again.* "Well, you could take your sisters' wands too, for that matter. I'm sure they could give a shit."

Tip shouted from her room across the hall, "Not my wand, you don't! It's *my* baby wand..."

Antonia's shoulders tightened, "Oh come on, let's not have this discussion again. If any of you gave two shits about it they—"

"They wouldn't even be able to *make* two shits, they're such crap. But I get it, it's not about a hoodoo power thing." Tip laughed, thinking she was being especially clever restating what had been said so many times before. "And I absolutely understand: *you only get out of it what you put into it,* so then *why bother?* A good spell or incantation works just as well, and quicker—for as much as we get to play with any hoodoo, at least."

Antonia shouted back, "Don't blame your father for everything. No one's into my or your Aunt Ezra's kind of witchery anymore to start with—just 'not cool' enough." Antonia tried to sound as blatantly sarcastic as she could.

Tip muttered, "Well, it ain't. But don't feel bad, no one really knows what's 'cool' about anything anymore anyway—all your old hoodoo stuff or not. Some of it's fun, though."

Soba suddenly sat up, looked squarely at her mother, "I just don't get why you keep that chopstick if it's not even going to do anything."

"Sob, I've told you—and I don't get why it bothers you so much. It has its own 'special' magic. Of a sentimental variety, something I'll call love."

"Whatever, Mom. But if it's no one's baby wand, then why?"

Soba rolled the black shiny fetish in her hand, toothy imprints clustered at its fat end. There was an imprinted sentiment in Chinese, but just barely—one half was almost understandable, the other gnawed to its wooden bone.

Antonia persisted, "Because let's just say, for this moment, it was *my* baby wand."

"But you have three right here."

"No, I mean the other way around—my baby *birthing* wand— helped me will you three into being—*physically* being, that is." Antonia smiled gently.

Soba frowned as she left the room, content with the wands still safe in their makeshift treasure chest, "Whatever, Mom."

SASHA HAD RESURFACED FINALLY, claiming her study "immersion session" at Claire's only modestly successful; she abruptly appeared at Antonia's studio door—scaring the shit out of her mother. She was very animated and chatty, which Antonia was typically very charmed by (the few and very random times it would occur) but not tonight and certainly not in the middle of a creative (mini-) epiphany! And tonight's expose was becoming more random and anxiety-laden than was typical, *Just keep painting and nodding—maybe she'll just go away.*

Antonia was mid-brush stroke when she *thought* she heard

Sasha use the word *Dad* and the word *penis* in the same sentence. She looked slowly at her daughter, "Sorry, missed that. What?"

"His penis. When you first looked at it, it freaked you out... Right?"

Antonia was almost speechless, but it had much less to do with her first impressions of her husband's penis than with her current impression of her daughter's sudden, bizarre (maybe?) questioning.

Why penises and why now? Does Claire have a penis?

"And why, pray tell, is this a concern of yours? Right now? On a Tuesday evening?" Antonia put down her brush and measured her response, "Well, it looked fairly much like all the other ones. I wouldn't go so far to suggest I was 'freaked out.'"

"Oh, so there were other ones?"

Antonia sighed, "Um, sure, not *a lot* of other ones. But yes..."

"And *none* of them freaked you out?" Sasha now had that maddening matter-of-fact look on her face, *Just the facts please, ma'am.*

"Sash, what the hell—what happened? Are you okay?"

"Yeah, why? Just wondered, we were talking about it today. Julie had a pic she said she liked *a lot*, and um, me—not so much."

"So why are all of you walking around comparing penises all of a sudden?!" Antonia recognized immediately what a stupid question that was to ask *any* sixteen-year-old, let alone her daughter; she groaned at how much of a mortal suburban mom stereotype she'd become.

"I'm not comparing anything. And it's not all of a sudden." Sasha seemed to be thinking, genuinely considering what she wanted to say next (for a change). "They've always freaked me out —just seemed especially scary these last two days. Maybe I'm just getting used to my fertility factor."

Antonia's eyes popped, "Your *what* now?"

"The amount of eggs I've got swimming around my system."

"Your eggs don't *swim*, though it wouldn't surprise me to find

MY WEIGHT IN WANDS

out that yours had somehow figured out how to." Antonia couldn't remember whether she was breathing in or out, "How is it you're so bright about some things and so dumb about others?" She cheesy-grinned to make the question seem nicer than it sounded; Sasha looked a little wounded (at the rare times that that happened, it could break her mother's heart in a, yes, heartbeat).

Sasha suddenly looked ten not sixteen, her lips dropped, "I thought you said I could ask you anything about any of this sexy stuff."

Antonia caught up with herself, "Of course, sweetheart, yes, sure. It's not that 'sexy' but yeah, definitely." Antonia started to put her arms around her daughter when she jumped and blurted, "Cool." And then disappeared out the door, whining for Tip.

She's always preferred her father's hugs to mine, that brilliant little twit.

MRS. STACKHOUSE SEEMED in an especially good mood for a Thursday (at least someone was happy at Frenchtown High School that afternoon).

Mara squinted at her teacher, "I'm not quite buying it. Nobody's ever nice to her."

Tip looked hard at Mara then Mrs. Stackhouse, "I don't think that's really true, but she does seem a little extra upbeat today."

"Oh yeah it's true. Way true."

Mrs. Stackhouse stood up, smiled broadly, "Happy Thursday, everyone." She sauntered to the center of the room. Various confused, bemused responses of the same or *What's so happy about it?* answered her.

"What's to be happy about? Really?" She leaned up and on to her toes, "You're all way too young to be so disinterested. There's far too many things, people, *anything* to be inspired by."

Ralph G. sighed a very exaggerated, sarcastic sigh, and got the attention and giggles he was seeking. "Mrs. S., give us a break. We're not ten, you know. If this is going to be some speech or inspirational *whatever*—that is just so, really *lame*."

Mrs. Stackhouse's smile didn't hesitate, as she walked closer to Ralph, the books and phone and his *whatever* started floating up off his desk (just barely an inch over anything *illegal*, magically speaking). Ralph considered everything and everyone a personal challenge. He glanced at the spell cast inches below his chin then back at his teacher, "You're way out of line here, Mrs. S. I could report you to the authorities." His cheesy grin got his desired tittering, but it stopped hastily and slightly nervously when Mrs. Stackhouse's now slightly maleficent smile did not.

Ralph—more cowardly than most of the girls he was trying to impress—started out of his chair. Mrs. Stackhouse waved, willed him to freeze in place; he was stuck, his eyes twitching, searching for some way out of this silly, embarrassing circumstance. His audience was as much laughing at him as they were anxiously laughing at the moment—they had *never* seen Mrs. Stackhouse (or any teacher) behave less than teacherly, let alone seasoning her lectures with craft or hoodoo (actually, she did toss in a smattering here and there, but only in the rare instances she felt she was losing her audience).

Tip was stupefied, "What is she doing?"

Mara was equally surprised but excited by it, "I don't know, but I love it."

"What's to love? She's going to get her ass fired."

Mara play-slapped Tip, "What's *not* to love? A Latina wonder-witch showing her shit off—you *gotta* love it. Plus, they'll never *fire* her, she's a great teacher and she's the only brown woman working here. And on top of all those lawsuits, you don't want the wrath of all those Latin gods and goddesses coming down on you. You think you know pain? You *don't* know pain; I can promise you that."

"How do you have an 'in' as to what Latin gods and goddesses are up to?" Tip asked sarcastically.

"We do. We always have. You white boney-ass witches used to have that, but you started acting and thinking and pretending you were better than that—*and dat was da end of dat.*"

"I really doubt it was that simple."

"Well where the fuck are they? Your 'superpowers'? Which have *so little* to do with—"

Suddenly their desks scratched, shrieked one way from the other—the girls almost fell out of their chairs, "Ladies, are you going to make me have to embarrass you any more than you already have yourselves?" Mrs. Stackhouse had decorated her admonition with the desk dance, "You seem to always have a lot to say—both of you... Care to share? Should today be the day?"

They looked at each other at exactly the same moment and in exactly the same way. And then Tip said, "You're acting really differently. It's kinda freaking us out. Not just kind of, actually, it's 'a lot' freaking us—or rather me—out." Tip glanced at the grinning Mara, "She thinks it's really cool. Me? Not sure I get it."

In spite of what one might expect, Tip's comment only seemed to put Mrs. Stackhouse in an even better mood. She clapped her hands, eyed the class, "How many of you *like* what this feels like, this moment? Float your pens in the air."

John W., who was a little too bright for his own good, rightfully asked, "And what if we can't?"

Mrs. Stackhouse spun around, genuinely concerned, "Can't what?"

"Float."

"Then simply raise your hand, John," she smiled at him.

Which is what John W. did with two other people, with the myriad color pens, zipping, spinning joyfully in the air.

Tip pressed, "No teacher's *ever* done this before."

Mrs. Stackhouse smiled, "That's what you need to think, and what they want you think. But, big surprise, it simply isn't true.

Maybe they didn't 'own it' like me, but then no teacher could." Some of kids laughed and clapped their excitement. "So, this is already too much about me and not the real reason why I'm doing this. Does anyone know or can guess what this is about?"

There was a long thoughtful silence, their brains whirring. In the space between two words, Mrs. Stackhouse had shifted the conversation back to the more pressing goal (for her, anyway) at that moment, "What happened this day? Actually almost at this *exact time?*"

She was too good of a teacher and they were too young of a class. She relented, "The Renaissance of Science and a little bit of Magic—the *Bliss in Believing*." At which point she thrust her hands into the air and the floor then walls then ceiling swirled with multitudinous color and images. Each student was also seeing something that only their young minds could, and each would interpret slightly differently from the other. Given the vibrant mix of color and texture and image, the room was a surprising commingling of calm and exhilaration. But young hungry magically inclined brains can withstand a lot, and digest even more than that: this date from long ago—the beginning of the Renaissance and its residual wonders—would always be known as the omnipotent blessing it should be. The box of wonders collapsed back into itself and whizz-whipped back out of the room the same way it came in.

Mark S. threw his hands up, started breathing again, "What the fuck was that? Sorry, I meant that as a really positive and constructive comment." He blushed.

"It was like watching *Mary Poppins* super-fast and backward!" Tania was already scribbling notes in her book so she wouldn't forget the perfect "wonderfulness" (her word, made up or not).

Tip was a little overwhelmed, "That was pretty fantastic." She and Mara fell against each other, "I don't think my brain could take a lecture like that every day though."

Mrs. Stackhouse held up her hand, "No worries! That's a once-a-month lollipop of lecture, and that's at best. You don't know how much that kind of spell-making can take out of you—I'm beat to shit—um, sorry... Strike that last comment." She laughed, a couple of the students too. Then two of the boys started a slow, earnest snapping of appreciation, which swelled to include the room.

It was two minutes till the bell, and everyone started to gather their books, bags. Mrs. Stackhouse held up her hands, "Hey, my friends, here's my parting thoughts: *what happens in Life Sciences stays in Life Sciences.*" Everyone laughed nervously not really knowing what to do with such a loaded statement. "No, I'm kidding, but I'm kind of not. I know what's considered 'acceptable,' either by the school and even by you, other teachers, the world outside of this school building. But sometimes you have the bend the rules, and in only the best way possible, to begin making a real difference."

Everyone measured her words, the bell rang, and the enlightened bunch floated (though not literally) to their next class.

———————————

"Just stream it."

"What?! Where?" Greg's brow crossed.

Tom Boy tossed out, "It's on YouTube." Greg's mouth fell open; Tom had YouTube-phobia the last time they'd even mentioned it. "So, what the hell? What happened? *You* put your shit all over YouTube?"

(The Dynamic Duo was having a Subway craving—simultaneously, no less—so they decided to surrender to it.)

"No, dickhead, not me, that series I can never remember the right name of—you were just saying you wanted to see it." Tom Boy stared hard at Greg, was he high? *No, he hates pot.* But he certainly seems like he's stoned. *Maybe it's another 'kind' of pot...* "What's wrong with you?"

"Nothing's 'wrong.' Why? Just because I'm not hanging on every little word you're saying, mumbling, whatever?"

Tom Boy wasn't buying it, "Are you stoned?"

Greg started laughing. He knew Tom Boy would go right there. "And what if I am? What if I *'doobied'*? What if I did, Mr. All High 'n' Mighty and Better Than the Rest of Us?"

Tom did a triple take this time at Greg, *If he is stoned, it must be on truth serum pot.* Tom wasn't entirely wrong; the times he and Greg were together there was really only one thing that outweighed any general concern or worry, and that was *Greg*—a true megalomaniac just about to take off his training wheels. (It was a small blessing that Greg simply didn't have the patience for magic, at least magic he'd be able to *easily* swing; he fell more to the mortal side of the scale.)

(But something or someone—Tom Boy?—is diverting our attention somewhere other than it should be—and that is: first, what Tom Boy believes, or *likes* to think, will make a cosmic *portal* become more *portal-ish* and then two, that plague of locusts [they were locusts, right? Or am I making another *too general* of an assumption] that appeared at the Starbucks, and then just as quickly disappeared, except the ones that died—I counted about twenty-five.)

Tom was still perplexed, but intrigued, "Why the personal attack, dear buddy o' mine?"

"Who's attacking who? You just accused me of being a drug addict."

Tom Boy strangely enjoyed (this *was new*) the confrontation, "Don't be a dick. You just hate talking about anything other than you or cars, so you were totally gonzo. I get it. That's cool."

The line at Subway was too long—must be something in the air, water, *whatevers*—they retreated back to the car.

"And you..." Greg knew what he wanted to say, but the best words weren't handy, "Just hate *talking—especially these days*. You

never used to be like that, were always almost *too nice* about shit."
Greg frowned, "But now? *Nada.* It doesn't make sense."

Tom Boy straightened, "Wow, dude. Where is this coming
from? And you're right—it doesn't make sense." Tom's expression
remained strict and aloof.

Greg straightened, "At least when I talk, I say what I mean."

Now Tom was pissed; he could be generous to a point (that
was another thing, no, another *rule,* when you were managing
Greg).

"Well then what the fuck are you droning on about, dude?"

Now Greg seemed dumbfounded. "You just don't get it, *dude,*
do you? Unless it's got Tommy Boy in the subject line, lately you
just aren't interested." Greg abruptly felt someone grab the back
of his neck and push his face into the glass of the passenger door
window. It couldn't be Tom—he was driving (and smiling)—*so
what? Oh I see, it is Tom!* So Tommy Boy has finally grown "a set"
(as his contemporaries like to say). And suddenly now he has a
tipping point where his exceptional (and typically polite) witchery
doesn't apply. (*Bravo,* T. Boy!)

Stunned, Greg carefully peeled his face from the glass, "That
hurt, motherfucker. *What da fuck?!*"

But when Greg turned to confront Tom, he encountered *yet
another version* of his friend—the "old Tom Boy," the one more
familiar, the Tom Boy Greg liked.

Tom straightened his gaze and frighteningly, calmly considered his still-anxious friend, "I'm still hungry—you?"

"AND ON TOP OF THAT, I think she's ugly as shit. I've always said
it—and she's even doggier as a blonde." Julie was being surprisingly heavy handed with her editorializing, especially for so early
in the week. She was probably one of the cattiest and most obsessive gossipmongers at the school, but she took pride and precise
care in exactly *how* she would trash anyone she genuinely cared

about. Martika clearly was not one of those people, or maybe there were other issues at play. (Who's kidding who—there are and were *always* other issues at play...)

"Okay, clearly I'm in Bitchface Julie mode, and I'm referring to Marty as her *person*—I'm not *that* superficial to be so super-focused on just her *hair.* Jesus, Sasha, you know me better than that."

"You just called her 'Marty'?" Sasha tripped over her ongoing confusion, *Have to at least act like nothing's different.*

Julie's brow furrowed, "Well, that's what you, everyone calls her—what's wrong with you this morning? Maybe I shouldn't tell you about the other *awful thing* they just found."

"Just say it. What?"

"Another wall, more graffiti. Actually, it's the *same wall,* but just as they got it all spic and span, there's new now. It's as if they were waiting in the wings or something."

"More antiquated Spanish or Latin or Anglo-whatever it was?" Sasha suddenly had that twisting, stabbing sensation again, that same fearful nervous something-or-other: the feeling that she was falling behind, missing information she would typically be way out in front of, *Stupid, self-absorbed me—but with* **what?**

"Not sure, but that's why I wanted to tell you first, besides my usual reason for wanting to tell you *everything first,* my BFF for *life!*"

This was once again way too early in the day for Julie, but it was way too, *too super* early for *Needy* Julie. (Actually, there wasn't any time that was a good time for Needy Julie.) Sasha forced a toothy smile, *This will be over in moments—forbear.* "Okay, I'll bite. I'm already here. You're dying to tell me so just get it over with."

"Remember that amazing paper you did on that one John Donne poem? It so totally rocked."

"Yeah, but what does that have to do with—*what's wrong with you?* Why would *you* remember *that?* You must want something that doesn't have anything to do with any of this, am I right?"

"*No*, bitch! Why dost thou always *assumest the worstest?*" Julie grinned large, as if that would somehow make everything at least seem fine, that there was nothing to fret (not now, not *ever!*). "Actually, there is this *one little thing...* But first, it was your Old English curse words cheat sheet."

"Did you miscount and take an extra *Ativan* or something this morning? Just get to your point, I got to go."

"That was it."

"What was? The cheat sheet?"

"Yeah, I have it right here." And she did; Sasha almost asked Julie directly if she was under the influence of something or someone's hex (not that she would necessarily know that, but the attempt at an answer would explain a lot). It wouldn't be the first time, Julie was such a target—and fortunately a socially retarded one. Sasha watched how fast her mouth was moving, *Things are not only getting stranger by the day; it's by the hour now.*

"So, what the fuck does it matter?" Sasha suddenly decided she was done with this morning edition of The Julie Show.

Julie flipped her palms up to make her point, "The graffiti. It's riddled with it."

"Anglo-Saxon profanities?"

"Yeah, and there's this nasty animated woodcut that looks like a vagina with teeth that runs all over the place." In that next second, Sasha abruptly, completely empathized with Julie's erratic Julie-ness—it sounded like some serious sorcery that was going down. Ezra would want to know about this, like, *super pronto.*

Julie had Sasha exactly where she wanted her, "So, let's go."

"Can't. I've Clarke's class."

"They moved it again. Couldn't you smell it?"

"Yeah, but I guess I didn't want to believe it. Meet you right after."

Julie frowned, "Don't piss me off like the last time."

Sasha was already walking away, "What last time?" She blurted, "Kidding, bitch!"

"Oh, one last thing..."

Sasha sighed and looked back at her wiggly friend, "What?"

"They think *you* did it. Wrote it. Probably."

Sasha was dumbstruck. *What the fuck?!* "What? What the hell do you mean?"

"Just what I said. I don't know who told who what or who saw who what but that's the buzzy-buzz, bitch." Julie bit her lip in thought, "Actually, I shouldn't say, *he'd have a fucking exorcism,* but like I really care."

Julie was distracted by Sasha's eyes—the color was drained from them; she suddenly seemed more zombie than witch. Julie instantly flashed on the last time she'd seen Sasha in this semi-hysterical state, and the social massacre that quickly ensued, *Oh, shit...*

"It was Steve. Steve P., Blond Steve P., not the black one." Julie abruptly unhinged herself from Sasha's peripheral everything and ran like a bat out of *heck.*

In the figurative and literal sense of the phrase, "all hell broke loose" was moments away from becoming much more the latter than the former."

THE COLOR HAD STARTED to come back in her eyes as did a slightly more civilized approach to the problem. (She quickly rationalized that this was hardly worth being expelled or even suspended, let alone some silly—or not so silly—legal repercussions.) Sasha flew around (was she flying? Probably at this point...) the corner only to find Mr. Clarke strategically positioned at his new (let's just call it "current") classroom's foyer, anticipating her approach from either the north *or* south. The slightly maniacal glint in his eye made Sasha wince, but she didn't let that distract her, not yet anyway.

Something flared and quivered from her pack—*she'd totally blanked*—she still had her *baby wand!* (She'd brought it in for some wacky yearbook thingy—today of all days!) Without any hesitation she flailed her secret weapon at Mr. Clarke and the wall behind him, "Your new classroom wall seems a little bland, Mr. Clarke. Maybe some voodoo with racist obscenities will help?"

Mr. Clarke said through his toothy, nervous grin, "Sasha, you know you shouldn't pay him any attention; you're giving him exactly what he wants. And I'd *much rather* discuss this with you after class, after we've all thought about what—"

"Oh, don't patronize me! I know you're dying for a show and this is exactly the moment..."

He leaned closer, muttering, she could barely understand him, "Oh no, I do, I *really do,* but this is not, well—you *know it's not the place.* And your skills would be wasted."

The class was chaotic with anxious excitement (more worried than not). Steve Perez's toady Jeff was fueling Steve's performance, "She's trying to get out of it, probably blame *you.* That's real brilliant—like you'd want to curse your own peeps."

Steve grandstanded (you could hear him in the next classroom), "I don't freaking care what she thinks; she deserves whatever she gets, that stupid white witch!"

Suddenly Sasha was bowled over by a barrage of racist thoughts swirling around her, at her. *I'm a pig-headed hateful fuck?!* She could sense that was Perez; she could even smell him. She burst into the classroom aiming her wand, now aflame in reds, white light. Mr. Clarke was reaching after her, everyone froze— Steve was following his voice, already halfway to standing on his chair.

"I'm a *what did you call me,* shithead?! *Don't make me stupid.*" She glared at Steve, poised herself for attack, then a breath later, strangely hesitated, suddenly dropped her wand to her side. (*She wasn't thinking, lost it for a moment—you never ever do that... I'm talking about disconnecting from your wand when it's live— never-ever!*) She was more measured but not any less angry, "Go ahead, say it aloud, start your hateful speech with it." They locked eyes defiantly, Steve started to speak then swallowed his words.

"You know it wasn't me; you have no idea who wrote that crap."

Steve interrupted, "We don't know if it wasn't you or was—but you're the only one who knows the Old English crap."

"I did one paper on it, you dick!"

Mr. Clarke interjected, "Language, lady and gentleman, language!" Movement slowly came back into the room, phones magically appeared (without a smidge of craft, mind you) and started grabbing, stealing as many pics as was humanly (and otherwise) possible. (This fodder was going to help make the lunch periods rather "high energy"—wink, wink—today!) The dynamic duo continued their bickering as Mr. Clarke took them both by their weaponized arms—Toady Jeff had moments ago handed Steve's phone back to him (the phone was still recording everything)—and led them toward the hall to help soften their blows as best as he could.

Sasha was listening to the men, and halfway thru the doorway when she pulled away and turned back to the class. She seemed completely in control and confident, and said, "We *all* have the power to stop this, whatever it is. Plain and simple."

Everyone abruptly stood, crouched, sat exactly still. There were exactly two thoughts flying around the room: one, *Huh?*, and two, *Who the fuck would admit that??!*

And who the fuck would believe that? Steve's expression was as dry as the thought *he* sent around the room. They went into the hall and Clarke started his requisite teacher's reprimand.

Tip was in mid-pop quiz mindset when her hand—right palm, to be exact—became unusually warm and *fizzy* (no other word to best describe it); her chest felt something too, no fizz but definitely warmth, and quickly it became almost uncomfortably hot, not really painful but... Then she remembered that one other time, it had to be at least five years ago, when Sasha threatened (playfully, kind of) Aunt Ezra with her baby wand. Weird. And it was gone almost seconds after she started to think about it.

Tip wondered if Sasha was okay, and then quickly resolved she was fine. She'd know if something was *really* wrong. (Sasha would never have waved her wand if there was.)

For as melodramatic as the morning's events were, all it took was a few clicks, taunts, and texts for everyone to get it out of their system. Apparently, Frenchtown High was too excited antic-ipating the next crisis to put much energy or effort into any existing struggle or wannabe catastrophe.

SASHA FINALLY SAT up in bed, flicked the light on, didn't let herself look at the clock. *There is no going back to sleep until she stops eating...* It was surreal; the crunching decibels—tonight for some reason—made it seem as if she had found Sput's spare bone bag suddenly appealing and was going to eat the five or so left just to be absolutely sure she liked them, or not.

Tip materialized next to Sasha's bed, didn't even pretend to knock, "I have to see what the hell she's eating!" Sasha laughed and jumped up and flew after Tip, almost bowling her over at the door.

Typically overtired, buzzy, and pretty-much-always-still-stoned at this hour of the morning after her Fried Friday evenings, this particular point-in-time was proving slightly different. Mother Antonia—at approximately 1:32 AM—had once again experienced a small (maybe not so small and not especially positive) epiphany: her powers **frighten** her... It'd become practically a ritual by this stage, though these personal revelations had more control over her than the other way around; the (selfish?) gist of it was: she drank and drugged to escape her "overwhelming" and debilitating magick—*her powers had proven to be too much for her...*

This wasn't revelatory or even terribly recent—they always

had been a problem in some form or manner, but in the last year she'd felt incapacitated more than she had at any period before—and that, she'd hypothesized, kept her wanting (most times craving) to get high and stay high.

Antonia woozily glanced up from the extra-crunchy pretzel carcasses (Sput's Milkbones were still untouched) strewn across the kitchen table. Two empty Coke bottles (Antonia would never ecologically touch an aluminum can—she never had) towered triumphantly over the emotional battlefield and its residue. She looked straight through her daughters and continued her now rote sermon, "The stronger I felt my powers were, the more intimidating they became, and then the higher I wanted to go—get away as fast as I could. Didn't get that till I saw what you did —or rather didn't do—with Tom Dad that moment, and that second shot—maybe it was the fourth one?—tonight. The more important realizations always seem to have a delayed response or reaction time... Like I have to *digest* them somehow or other." At that moment she seemed strangely lucid and sober as she surveyed the table and its abused contents.

The girls were completely bewildered, "Huh?! *What?* With Dad and, um, *who?* Which 'you'?" Antonia would previously rally through her buzz, falling into one of her too-revealing "chitty-chats," which could leave Sasha and Tip howling (in a good way). But now it was getting weird again (for the third time in as many months), their mother's possession was becoming too hard to manage; Antonia's angst was not handing over the microphone.

Sasha joked as Antonia droned on, "Morbid Antonia we want to speak to Fun Antonia; Fun Antonia come forth on three—one, two, *three*."

No change. Tip and Sasha peered at their mother, then at each other. It was too hard to find the humor or any affection in this self-serving rant tonight—hope was completely absent from the munchie buffet (someone had already eaten it all).

Their mother could ofttimes be very entertaining with her

pithy though inebriated free association, but it was never *guaranteed* fun (always some emotional risk attached), and it was clear—as Antonia was sniffing through the crumbs on the table—that the latter was what was appearing on tonight's late-late show.

Tip looked thoughtfully at her mother, "I thought I was into it but I guess not—not when she's like this." Antonia's possessed jabbering continued; Sasha was usually the first to abandon any self-pity party. But that wasn't the case tonight. It added yet another layer to the weirdness (Tip was usually the more charitable of the two).

Then abruptly the prattle ceased; it appeared Antonia had swallowed her last few words whole, the conversation sitting in her throat and chest with a half-chewed Fig Newton. The twins watched the manifest pain slide the rest of her neck like a python ingesting another oversized victim; Antonia remained fine, still bleary-eyed and oblivious.

Tip continued up the stairs, "I'm *so done*—I can't be this sad anymore." She turned to Sasha, "Don't bother yourself. You know she'll be fine, somehow or other."

Sasha would have usually thrown up her hands and followed Tip to bed, but not this particular moment. She felt compelled too, but her conflict wasn't distorted or painful, not like her now semi-conscious head-on-hands mother. She grabbed an extra dish towel from the drawer, doubled it into the one by the sink, and after sweeping the crumbs and wrappers from around Antonia, pillowed them underneath her arms and head.

Sasha floated upstairs to her room, believing what she wanted was still somewhere at the bottom of her bag, *Where else would it be?* She pulled the piece of wand out and back to life. It's hopeful glow held her hand as she went to her parents' bed—Tom Dad was happily oblivious—and placed the blue light under Antonia's pillow where she knew she wouldn't find it, and went to bed. The glow quickly, sadly faded back to its tired grey wood.

PART II

The Shit Spies the Fan

R appatsi swung high and low through and around the surrounding blocks, homes, yards, pools, larger picture windows, streets—blah, blah, okay, enough. You get the upshot: she's thorough; she knows what she needs to do. And she's the best at what she does which also, unfortunately, is her bane, her "curse."

It's a blessing how the universe takes care of *all of us:* she would have unraveled eons ago if it hadn't wiped Rappatsi's mind squeaky clean each time she was born into a new position. And her fabulously delicious visage was an added treat this project! (I mean, it's not as if she had three eyes last time, but this—*this is trading up big time!*) It will definitely be fun and it's definitely well-earned; she's obviously been making the right impression on the entities she needs to—it's clear *they* (there's that ambiguous "they" again!) want her to succeed. (There must be big things in the multi-reality pipeline planned for Rapp.)

Rappatsi liked the physical environment; she liked the school —everything seemed straightforward, workable. The Sisters would offer a bit of a challenge (she'd sensed that straight away) but nothing that felt unfamiliar or uncomfortable; the bonds will take a little extra time—they always do—but *yes,* all very manageable.

R*APPATSI*—IT *is* a strange name. She could be "Rapp" or "Patsi," or both...

Pilar: It's at least easier to remember than some of those others.

Ditan: I don't think I was around then.

Pilar: You probably wouldn't remember anyway, not much memory-wise makes it past the etheric plane and names are the first thing to go. Just too *organic* for it to stick around.

Abyssinia smirks: That's a diplomatic way to say it.

Pilar: Why? You like to think there's *other forces* involved somehow?

Abyssinia shrugs, smiles slightly, and continues her writing.

Ditan glances around, looks at the notes and books on the desk, swings the log and diary around and glimpses at them: So Rappatsi will be living in that same space? Isn't that a problem?

Pilar: I know, I thought so too, but guess not since they dematerialized it—the guts of it anyway. It's been since half the town even existed or was born so I'm thinking not so much to fuss.

Ditan didn't look up. Something was distracting him.

Pilar: Not impressed, huh? *Ditan still didn't respond.* Guess not...

GREG HAD to go the back way; they were taking wedding pictures once again by the Frenchtown monolith and granite memorial of ill repute. It would never be settled whether Samantha Sturridge truly deserved this level of renunciation; there were equally weighted camps for and opposed and this was consistent with every other piece of history that found its way through Frenchtown—well before anyone "French" decided to claim these four to five square miles as their categorical "town."

The granite was pleasing enough, as was the history (or it could be) but each and every wedding party notoriously found their way there because there wasn't much else that was even remotely as picturesque. (But of course that meant that everyone's wedding pictures necessarily had a cloying and depressing similarity.)

"The groom's cute." Sasha was gazing at the dark blue velvet six-foot-three stick.

"Um, too thin. But not a deal breaker." Tip leaned across her to look closer, "Grooms are always cute. It's a rule."

Greg was oblivious, still fussing over having to drive out of his way *for a fucking wedding,* but Tom Boy was suddenly engaged, "How so? You're confused, it's the bride that's always beautiful."

Tip shook her finger at him, "Nope, *that's* the myth. It's just telling women what people think they want to hear."

Sasha wasn't buying it, "You don't want to be told you're beautiful on your wedding day?"

"Not if I'm not beautiful—you can't be beautiful *every day.* Well, I guess some women can be but not many."

GREG TURNED UP THE RADIO; Tom Boy was persistent, "How are grooms *always cute* then, if that's your logic?"

"It's their inherent *groomness.* It's unique." Tip smiled at her own repartee, "It happens naturally, absolutely. No magic necessary."

Sasha said, "And just for the wedding day? And why just the boys again?"

Tip bristled, *Once again Miss Linear-thinking Sasha blows up my whole convo moment!* She decided just to ignore it, "Absolutely just for the day. Some cases slightly longer—how lucky for those brides-to-be. Though it shouldn't really matter to them once their married."

Greg muttered, "Why wouldn't it matter? It would matter to

me. That's fucked up."

Sasha frowned, "You've stopped making sense. You were being borderline witty, but now it's just dumb."

Tip was still smiling, she'd made an impression, for better or worse. They got to the mall—the boys went their way (again), and the twins went theirs.

"WHEN'S DAD supposed to be done?" Tip asked Sasha while flipping through her new messages. No answer. She looked up—no Sasha; she swung around and then back, caught the back of her jacket. Tip threw her thought just far enough she hoped, *What the hell are you doing?*

Their conversation merged, *I'll explain, just get your butt up here.*

Why don't you leave Greg alone? You're giving him far more credit that he deserves.

I'm not sure you're—or we're—right anymore.

Tip saddled alongside her twin, "Is he by himself? Why this sudden change of heart?"

"No, Tom Boy too." Sasha stopped dead, and faced Tip square, "They stopped—are they looking?"

"No, not even a tiny bit, they're staring into that empty Radio Shack wannabe portal *again*. And Greg seems to be the one doing all the talking, which is *perfect weirdness*."

Sasha slapped at her sister, "*See, told you!*"

Tip almost dropped her phone, "Don't be a dick!"

(A Martika text tweaked them both—*nothing to fuss...*)

Sasha turned and said, "You said the Radio Shack, right?"

Tip looked up, "Yessss... Then where the balls did they go?"

The girls carefully snaked their path closer to the defunct store. It was at the one end of the mall, a lot of stores were gone or changing, and barely anyone within spitting let alone shopping distance. The boys were nowhere to be seen. The girls watched their bewildered selves in the black glass-mirrored storefront; the bottom hook of the "k" of the Radio Shack logo winked and sputtered red light at whoever was looking, and then not.

Tip spoke first, "They must be in there; there's no other way they could be—"

"Gone?"

"Yeah."

Sasha frowned at herself in the glass, thinking out loud, "It was strange that they were in a rush. Kind of."

Tip offered, "Yep, because Greg is *never* in a rush."

"Maybe it *is* some kind of portal?" Sasha proposed. "Whatever 'portals' might do these days, not that I've a clue— sounded good though, didn't it?"

Tip smiled, "Boo boo yeah yeah."

They scowled at their reflection again, thinking about not knowing exactly what to think.

Sasha hesitated, "Do we go in?"

Tip, *This is soo like her,* sighed, "Um, not so much. Whatever they're up to, they're already up to it. It's not like we won't see them in, probably-maybe, less than twenty-four hours at least."

Sasha bit her lip, this was such a "Tip response"—the prototypical passive Tip response. She was measuring her answer when (fortunately) Tip's phone buzzed.

"It's Tom Dad. He's done early, wants to know if we want to go or hang with him here." They both sneered at that thought; Tom Dad became blissfully brain dead at malls—some sort of nostalgic hypnosis—but F-town Mall in particular could have, for some reason, devastating effects (Tom Dad's stupid-ass grin, etc.) that lasted for hours. Sasha said, "Just tell him meet us at the usual spot." They started walking with Sasha flipping her gaze back at the store seemingly expecting to find someone or something "caught in the act." Tip moaned, "Give it up. It's not that big of a deal."

"How do *you* know it's not that 'big of a deal'?"

"I just do."

———————— ꞯꞯꞯ ꞯꞯꞯ ————————

LUIS PRESSED HIS FINGER HARD, then harder still—not that it was actually possible to accomplish what he was attempting to do. What he was attempting (at least in his mind's eye) was to push so hard on Sonja's forehead (just above her eyes—right through the hopeful center of her Third Eye) that at least the skin would break. He knew the bone wouldn't (though that was his desired goal).

You'd have to ask the question what could possibly have made him this angry? Especially since he'd never met this woman—or even knew if her name was really *Sonja*... But that was how every email or message had been, and continued to be, signed. *And now she "prefers" to talk to another woman. A female woman.* (Luis' frustrated sarcasm dripped into the keyboard.)

"I don't have women—that would be age twenty-five and above—as friends, Sonja..." Luis had carefully explained in response to Sonja's curt request. Luis continued:

"That would be bizarre."

Then Sonja messaged back:

Women are bizarre after twenty-five? Weird thought.

"Yes, it's weird out of context. Which is what you just did— and you've been doing a lot of lately—taking things out of context."

Oh, so suddenly the high school junior has all the answers?

"That's not at all what I said."

We all know who your mom was, and most of us aren't really that impressed, just so you know.

And here it was again, Luis almost leapt out of his desk chair: "*Who the fuck is this 'we'?*" He said it aloud. (Who wouldn't have?)

Then there was *nada. Silencio.*

Luis continued punishing his keyboard, "Hey! Speak up or type harder!" He was trying to keep the conversation somewhat on the lighter side, as much as he could without emojis. He hated emojis; they all just seemed so fucking *white* (in spite of their yellow, brown, or purple, or whatever skins).

And he got *nada* again. Now it seemed as if he was being taunted, but by whom? (Or was it by *who?*)

"So, what, is there actually more than one Sonja there?"

If there had been any opportunity given to pause and think about the better answer, that was it. But the response came almost immediately.

Actually, yes.

Which *now* gave Luis pause. He had been mostly joking—and then a little bit pissed—but generally in good spirits. Now he was in confused and slightly worried spirits.

"I don't know what to say. Why is this coming up *now?*"

Because it's time. Not all of us agree, but even here, majority rules.

That was too perfect: the Million Questions door finally opened, so he walked right on through, "So where's here? Oh, and how many 'Sonjas' are there exactly?"

Seven currently. But most times eight or almost nine. And if I told you where we were I would, um, have to kill you. Not really 'dead-kill' you, just take a limb or an organ you're not especially fond of. Luis swore he heard cackling (yes, actual *cackling*) though very faint as if it was coming from the neighbor's yard two doors away.

Luis stared at the keyboard not knowing whether to take their words literally or... Then a slew of irregularly spaced pre-emoji winks followed. It wasn't funny but then it kind of was, because whoever these Sonjas were, at least *they* thought they were *really* funny.

"Okay, well I don't want to do that... Why *almost* nine?"

She can never seem to transmogrify everything, don't know why it's such a problem for her. All the rest of us get here just fine; I think she just doesn't want to be here. She's just not that into it, and it shows: sometimes half a leg, no arms. Breaks me the hell up... Get it? And another slew of laughing actual emojis filled the blank space after her comment.

Luis stared at the screen again. *This can't be the same witch, it can't. If it is, she is completely schizo.* Luis looked at the server address and wondered if he had to completely get out of there, completely erase himself, could he probably do it. (Yes, he could absolutely do it.)

"So, all this time I've been communicating with a group of women?"

Well, yeah. A very small group and spiritually very aligned so in effect you've been talking to one woman, but physically that's about right, there's always at least three of us here.

"And 'here' is? Oh, that's right, I can't ask that for fear of penalty of death—or at least no email for the week."

Again, silence. *It's a joke, ladies. Not ha-ha funny. but at least one ha funny.* Luis was thinking that Sonja #1 had something of a sense of humor and wasn't simply nutty. But who could actually know? This was all becoming a little overwhelming.

Can we get back to our request?

"Which was?"

For a woman or preferably a young woman. At least your age.

"And what's been wrong with the work I've been doing?"

Absolutely nothing. You've done a remarkable job given the circumstances.

Luis thought this now had to be Sonja #1 at the keyboard. (Assuming it was that, wherever and whatever these witches— probably overwitches—used to text. Which was relatively wacky to think of, just itself.)

"Then why do you need a woman?"

Because you're a man. Or almost a man. I think...

"Thanks. For that."

Don't take it personally.

Now Luis had finger freeze. He really didn't know what to say, or do; plus, *why all of a sudden was having a penis problem?*

"I don't know anyone. That we can trust, I mean."

We think you might.

There's that "we" again. Luis pecked a big red emoji question mark.

There's that family you like, The Sisters.

"I don't like or dislike them. Actually, that's not true—I like Tip."

Yes, that's her. Tip.

"How the hell do you know about Tip?"

It's too complicated to put in an email. But I will say at the same time that once we share why—and we will—it will seem ridiculously obvious... Necessary, really.

"I like Tip. But I don't really *know* Tip."

But you should. And you will.

"That's sounding awful pushy. Not like you."

The air—the space that Luis was sitting in—got really weird, and suddenly crazy, like, out of the blue. I can say these things because if anyone knows weird, *I know weird* (and you're just going to have to work with me here. I know I'm breaking the form and context rules, but there's some serious shit starting to go down. So, my dear humanoids, hang, please, until I have a little extra time to explain, *which I'm not sure that I will since they seem to be giving us less and less time as it is.*

———————— ◦◦◦◦ ◦◦◦◦ ————————

MR. CLARKE TRIED DESPERATELY to not look—or even glance—at the jar for now the fifth time in the last three hours. Was today the day? *I don't remember—what an ass. I'm Mr. Anal when it comes to exact histories and times, dates, seconds, second cousins, second helpings at state dinners and who ate fast, slow—fanatical...* He looked dismayed and he should have: he could manage that level of detail history-wise but couldn't remember if he ate breakfast or not? (I guess he could be somewhat comforted that it wasn't the other way around, especially with Principal Casen measuring his every little action. *Would she actually do that? How does she have the time to do that?* He'd been surprised at the conversation; she was notoriously tough but a good kind of tough. *She won't fire me; she hate-likes me too much. I know it. I sense it...*) He started to turn on the TV—*what the fuck was I doing?* The jar was still sitting exactly where he placed it moments ago.

Godammit... He wondered if he could dig that email out of his laptop's trash—the whole chain would probably come with it. He knew there was no "instruction for use" anywhere, but the incantation seemed to suggest some kind of expiration date. She'd been anonymous through the whole transaction; said she'd know or "sense" when the transformation was complete—*'...this thing is so much bigger than the two of us.'* But as vague as the communication had been, Stephen could confidently infer via that small but powerful preternatural part of him that this was the "real thing." And this anonymous "overwitch" had been equally forthcoming: his evolution would be another very important feather in her pointed black cap (if she had one—in his mind, the bitch *lived* in one). Her *campaign* was and continued to be all-consuming—whatever it was she was "campaigning" for. *Halflings, half-breeds can't run for Congress, can they? I should know that.*

The toe looked more like a chick pea at this stage (at least what was left of it—he'd been shaving off nibs and nabs [for better or worse] since he'd gotten it), and *this had to be the piggy that went to market, no?* (The fourth toe, if he had his *piggies* sorted correctly.) Stephen smiled at his last thought: *thank the gods I didn't get the **last** toe—must be as intimidating as a Sun-Maid raisin by now.*

The first couple toes went to Canada somewhere—some transgendered coven in Winnipeg needed some extra *oompa-loompa.* He was surprised that the strange little guy—*At least he sounded like a guy, couldn't tell by just looking*—was so forthcoming. Maybe all of this wasn't as big a deal as Anonymous Overwitch seemed to suggest? But email can be tricky that way in any case. (He'd misread or miscalculated the implied emotion far too many times. Principal Casen's was a prime example of that.)

He found the emails, and the information he thought he

remembered, and probably needed. No real "end date," but it wasn't clear, so he wasn't as wrong as he'd thought. Stephen would have to—*well, not 'have to' but it wouldn't hurt*—reach Ms. Mastermind. Hopefully she'll respond, and hopefully she won't be angry, or at least too pissed off (certainly don't need any more witches frustrated with him at this point.)

So, he was now talking to himself, *I wonder who went home with that last little piggy...*

RAPPATSI HAD A HIDDEN TALENT. (Truth be told, she has several —actually more than that!) Sasha had been impressed from their meta-, non-verbalized "hello": Rappatsi had—from what seemed to be seconds—already learned the layout of their high school's makeshift building and campus layout. She knew all the teachers (their names, anyway). Even Sasha (the Perfectionist) needed a couple laps (and a few months or so) around the halls and the class syllabus before she had the teachers' names and faces where they're supposed to be, *What did she do? Go home and study the school roster, page after page?* And this was coming from a teenage girl-witch that felt sarcasm was too much effort, a *waste* of time. (What teen girl or boy doesn't practically live on sarcasm?)

It was immediately clear to Sasha (all the The Sisters, actually) that there was much larger metaphysical forces at play, both magickal and more powerful than anything Earth-bound. (It was the start of something that thrilled Sasha to her witchy essence, though she couldn't begin to explain how.)

None of The Sisters were that terribly shocked that the whole of the school believed that Rappatsi had been part of their *every-thing* and for as long as *forever*. It was as if some magnificent spell (or curse?) blanketed the community and rooted the lovely personal history of this lovely talented witch in their conscious-ness. The burning question was: *why and how were The Sisters unaffected?* Why are they immune to this new stranger? The only barely logical theory, Sasha speculated, was that the future had a distinct purpose for them—part of a shared destiny. (Sasha groaned at the barrage of cliches, but hey, *'if the wand fits...'*)

But this only partially explained Sasha's fixation with Rappatsi. She'd already abandoned the girl crush option, *Been there. Done that. Was over it before I even realized I was over it. Penises continue to intrigue me...* She was teetering on the young under-witch's typically aggressive *Territorial Imperative*, but tossed that because, *Maybe it made sense two centuries ago when you'd fly for two hours before even bumping brooms with anyone—let alone any full-on spell-casting—but nowadays?*

Did Rappatsi eat lunch? Did she sleep eight hours (actually, most witches prefer a robust ten at least)? Did Rappatsi take a ripe shit in the morning? These were the hot 'n' heavy questions that pervaded Sasha's analytical obsessive-compulsive-sorceress-hormonally-charged brain—sadly to no avail. Life was simply, blatantly confusing most times and no amount of magic or smarts would matter—*it was what it was.*

THE (CALHOUN) STATUE IS BACKWARD; I'm sure of it. Ezra was talking to herself as per usual; it evidently was integral to her driving a car—actually, better said: *driving a car successfully.* And the square was strangely quiet for a gorgeous afternoon... *Yep, either I'm driving backward or somebody or something is trying to pull a fast one.* Actually, it really seemed to have nothing to do with pulling or being fast, because the statue was exactly where it had been for the last one hundred twenty years; the dates on the plaque are barely readable, and the description of how, where, why, and what the industrialist Calhoun did to deserve the permanent commendation had been weathered clean, neutering any identifying or creative details (assuming the weather really had anything to do with it!). Ezra breaked hard when she finally ascertained what was what: the overall statue was as it should be, *it was just his head* that was facing the opposite way. *Who was it that said Calhoun always had his head on backward?* Ezra laughed, shook her own head, she couldn't recall—even though she was living in Frenchtown then, she was just getting her bearings, and still was young, mostly attractive, and somewhat (no, *very*) impressionable.

But, to be clear, impressionable has nothing to do with being gullible. Or lacking self-awareness. Ezra Prentiss was presented to Frenchtown's young and growing community as a fully intact woman: completely secure in her strengths and weaknesses (the few that anyone could identify). It was what had provided the crux for the fast friendship between Ezra and Antonia: both were brilliant women and witches (and not always in that order) with Ezra as Antonia's yang to her yin. Not to make less of all the astral projection and lucid dreaming that clearly reinforced their bond, but first and foremost, they were—and always would be—the best of friends.

What is the deal with your goddam horn, asshole?! Maybe he'd prefer looking out the back of his car, like Mr. Calhoun? Now, now, one must use—especially now—appropriate magic *appropriately.* And to be fair, she was the one who had abruptly stopped in the middle of the street, so his mortal-macho-shit horn wasn't entirely unfounded. (Though that *Exorcist* spell was always a fun party trick and it didn't hurt at all [well, maybe a little bit], but it might be a little disconcerting if you were sitting alone in your car.)

It was in that next second as she was driving away that she saw the statue was back to as it should be, *What the hell? This clearly isn't playing by the rules.* Though Ezra, much more than most, was keenly aware that 'rules' had nothing to do with anything. (At least not now, not anymore.)

SUDDENLY, happily, serendipitously (not really, but it felt that way) it was Friday again and time for their meeting of the minds

(and sometimes hearts) at the *Witch's Tit in a Brass Cup Happy Hour.*
Ezra and Antonia occasionally christened the event as such in
reverence to their singular crush on mortal wizard-of-song Tom
Waits. Mr. Waits had no clue—but that was only because of
Antonia fortunately talking Ezra out of a potentially disastrous
spell-casting fifty-some years ago. Regardless of this shared
nostalgia, this week's session was not boding well.

"You'll kindly remember that they're not *your* daughters. You
seem to lose sight of that way too easily."

"You're way too loosey-goosey with them. Drives me nuts."

"Did you just *hear* what I said to you, bitch?" Antonia wiped
the sweat off of her glass, "And I am not. They got a mouthful and
a mindful just the other day."

Ezra muttered, "I hope so—I couldn't get a word in edge-wise."

Antonia was surprised, "That's weird. They told me it the
other way around," she shifted in her seat. "What was all the fuss
about to begin with?"

"Fuss?"

"Yeah, you made me nuts—'*When are they free? Just them... Needs
to be now, can't wait.*'"

"Oh, well, yeah maybe."

"Not maybe. You made me nuts. And not a good kind of nuts,
just to mention."

Ezra teased, "Oh, please. Like your day is *so* high stress—*shall I
stretch this canvas a little tighter than the last?!*"

"So, Witchy-poo, what is your deal?"

Whether Ezra was feeling the first effects of the tequila or
whether she suddenly didn't want to elaborate on what was
supposed to be what, she waved the frustration aside, "They
weren't into it. I could sense it wasn't the right time. Sorry you
had to fuss... Maybe next time when I—"

Antonia sliced the conversation in half with her hand to Ezra's
face, "I'm going to stop you right there—I'm taking this right to

the tippy-teats of our dried out witchy tits: *the answer is 'no'. No way...* Whatever it is you're trying to do, '*find the right words for...*'" Antonia's eyes flashed anew, "You've *never* been so reluctant to say what you want or need so how come now? Not going to wait to know what kind of batshit you've gotten yourself into—as a fact, *I'd rather not know at this point.* Any of it. It will spoil everything—I somehow already *know* that much."

For the very first time in their long lives and friendship, Antonia had said no, and continued to say no. Ezra was perfectly stupefied, flattened; their last conversation—they both had acknowledged in half-sentences, half-thoughts, a half-hearted touch or squeeze of the hand or shoulder—had been an irrational catastrophe.

But what was now consuming Antonia were the apparent assumptions—the self-absorbed, megalomaniacal conclusions—that her self-professed kindred soul had made. (It was a tragic mistake for them both.)

Antonia spied the half-finished drink almost next to Ezra. "Is that yours?" She picked up the glass, "A little late in the season for a G and T, no?"

"They're seasonless now. Like winter white." Ezra took the glass, "Got here a little early. Needed to decompress."

"Or maybe *recompress?* Just so we—*you*, to be precise—don't have a 'this time' like the 'last time.'"

Ezra sighed, sat back in the new, hard cushions, "Yeah, I guess that's true."

"You guess? You were just *weird* last time." Antonia was attempting to be as diplomatic as she could.

Ezra abruptly sat forward, assuming her last defensive position. "Well, you weren't exactly the picture of abiding friendship and love either."

Now Antonia's neck was arched, *It's happening again and way too quickly...* And they both realized it in that moment.

When did the gloves start to come off? Surprisingly, actually, about two months ago, *Maybe longer.*

"I can't describe the pain, it was too much, when I realized. No, when I was almost forced to realize..." Ezra was clearly lamenting, "So you need to put that in my column." She hesitated but strangely didn't seem terribly upset anymore, "Because I don't think, I just *can't see* how you're going to even be a little bit happy with the rest of what I have to say."

Antonia was dumbfounded, *Why is this happening again?* "Ez, what was in that drink?" She couldn't think of anything else to say.

"Just something I've been thinking about for quite a while now..." Ezra slurred, smiled—her quip deflated in front of them.

"Well, yes, you've made the laborious nature of your struggle very clear."

"And now that it's all said and done, well, not quite yet, at least the 'done' part—I was being a little self-serving."

"You?! You don't say..." Antonia, now quickly a bright red, gauging her response. "That bizarre 'dream' you've been so beholden to—who slapped that together for you? It had to be your Coven cronies—so fucking deluded," she couldn't help the sarcasm, "I mean, to be fair, the visuals and production values were great—out of the park! And I'm always a sucker for anything *Alice* and her rabbit hole psychedelics: Cheshire Cat spitting toes into my shot glass—nice kinky touch..."

Now Antonia fumed, "But all the vainglorious bullshit—was that you as *Nemesis?!* I know you've always wanted to become more—*but a god?!* I think you're overreaching a tad, bitch. And with all now—I'm supposing—said and done, I still have *no clue what* or *who wants what!* Just answer the fucking question: *What the hell is going on?*" Antonia chewed through her last words.

Ezra refused to be intimidated, closed her eyes and slowly opened them, "Ant, you're just taking up space anymore. And there isn't a lot of 'space'—not anymore anyway."

Antonia sat stunned, silent.

"It's ultimately more of a compliment, so don't look so upset." Ezra, now bizarrely acting as if she were talking about a new series on Netflix and not her best friend's possible future state of being. "You're one of the most powerful overwitches in these parts—The Coven has committed to that. Always has. Completely *pissed me off*..." Ezra laughed. *Unbelievable!* "Just kidding! Lighten up, Ant, now you're looking like someone just died."

"Someone may be about to." Antonia flushed red again. "So, you're actually talking to 'them' now?"

"I've always been in touch with 'them,'" Ezra remained oddly serene.

Antonia countered, "Not always."

Antonia stared at her drink. For the first time in God knows how long she didn't want one. At all.

Ezra calmly continued, "And you're really just not *that* into it. Actually, you could say you're not into 'it' *at all*. Darling, you should know by now you don't have to pretend anything with me."

Antonia was seething inside, *I just might actually have to burn her—where the fuck is this coming from?!*

"I'm catching all of that, you know, your silly musings. It's amazing to me, you used to be so careful about that. Now you just let anyone in—your world is an open book. Just another sign you don't really give a shit."

Antonia's perfect anger was filling her seat, the booth began to swell, "Pray, what exactly is it that 'I'm just not that into anymore'?"

Ezra didn't hesitate a breath, "What *you* are—**your essence.**" She pulled a flask from her purse and half-filled her empty glass with some clear liquid—it started to steam, "Maybe you're trying to drink or smoke it all away somehow." Ezra took another swig of her "steam" and muttered, "Simply delicious. Even if I say so myself."

Antonia glowered, "That's new for you—what is it? Something your Coven friends gave you?"

Ezra smiled, suddenly appearing even more—albeit happily—sedated, "No. All mine. Something new. Let's just call it a protein drink for witches—oops, correction, for *overwitches*."

An incensed Antonia mocked, "Correction, bitch, there is only one *true* overwitch currently working this floor."

With that, the gloves finally, fully came off, and the "wands" (whatever form they might take) came out. The booth itself sweated and swelled.

"You really are *something*," Antonia focused her flushed stare, her ears folded up and back like an angered cat's scruff. Ezra shook her head and, leaning back, woozily laughed to herself—she couldn't move, the booth had sculpted a cast, holding her hard and still from her neck to her knees, *Ah, now I see, and this is becoming sillier by the moment.*

Ezra was starting to slur again, "Stop it, Antonia. We don't want to start threatening each other. We've never done that—we owe each other at least that much."

The booth's wood was animated, bracing Ezra; Antonia seethed, "*Start* threatening? You've been pressing and pushing me for the last god-knows-how-long and *now* you want to talk? You're different now... You're frightening my family—and you're pissing me off. What's changed? *And why?*"

Ezra was cloistered tight, but her mood and stream of thought still maneuvered itself easily around and through Antonia's anger. "Change is—and was—always inevitable. It was our shared wants, and a few serendipitous moments—actually, way more than a few—that kept things constant. Then everything else that you love started to pluck away at our bond. It wasn't the same—I knew it couldn't stay the same—so I opened my mind to, let's call them *alternative relationships*..." Ezra frowned, "Wait, I've told you this.

Maybe I'm buzzed, but I know we discussed the new planes and spheres of reality I experienced—*weren't you even listening?*"

"I was listening, but only half-believing," Antonia smiled a very small smile, "which was half better than all those other times."

Ezra stuttered, "It's bigger. It makes me better—I want to be better. I *want more.*"

Antonia frowned, "What's 'bigger'?"

"The Bliss, *The Realm*. Call it whatever you're comfortable calling it. The planes are *real*—they're not silly myths. The more we are part of them, the more they are a part of us."

Antonia was becoming blurry (in spite of herself), "That's what you *like* to believe, Ez, but you're so committed to Terra Firma, you're almost ridiculous."

Antonia wasn't any less frustrated or angry, but something was helping to smooth the sharper edges of their conversation—a feeling that was neither good nor bad. Just "slower"—with her sensing more control of, well, *everything.*

Ezra continued with her initial question and answer, "Remember The Ratios? We loved what The Ratios did. The yin and yang of it..."

"Yes, loved The Ratios, always will—it's always about balance, whatever words you want to use." Antonia softened slightly as she reminisced, but then quickly recalled her ire, her back arched, "*And your crazy dream!* It was like some bad Hulu doc about Scientology or whatever weird cult of the moment! And who the fuck played the lead? Teri Hatcher in a blonde *afterlife?*" Antonia sighed, smoke unfurled from under the booth for added effect, "The way you've been preaching about it, I expected to be reborn. Instead it I wanted to—"

Now Ezra became angry, interrupting, "Well, bitch, I don't know who the hell Teri Hatcher is, but if she's got the same wand-up-her-ass attitude as you do, then that makes complete sense. You'll always be the same self-absorbed witch you've always been."

"*Self-absorbed?* That would be a polite term for what you did to Marta and the black-market bullshit you tried to pull off—for your own fucked up benefit."

Ezra's face collapsed against the back of the booth, "How do you know that?"

Antonia was bemused, "Really? You of all witches should know you can't trust any coven—especially their Cheshire Cat—to keep a secret. It was one of the maybe two things that made a little bit of sense in that mess of a nightmare."

Ezra was struck but hardly surprised The Coven was double-dealing for their own selfish gain; it was more the harsh realization she was not necessarily a part of that. Now she was angry, "*They have no illusions about their fucking toes,* or any other appendage for that matter. And it's hardly as if it hasn't happened before."

"But not by any *witch* I know—and not in the last gazillion years."

"That's such shit," Ezra suddenly appeared far more drunk than seconds ago. "Those brown witches *brag* about their blood—their *meat!*"

Antonia became incensed, "And that's why you—of all people—felt *entitled?*"

Ezra looked confused, whatever empowered her a few minutes ago was gone. She sipped her drink, equivocated, "The toes grow back; they always do. It's no big deal. Everyone knows that."

"No, they don't know that. What you did was *criminal*. I could push it up to—"

Ezra blurted, "Push it up to *who?!*" She started laughing uncontrollably. (This only made Antonia more incensed, more self-righteous.)

Antonia announced, "You fucked up, Ezra—this is so crazy-criminal. These moments keep happening where I'm *completely* mystified as to why we've been as close as we are."

"Well, at least you and Tom agree on one thing."

The two women glowered at each other; everything surrounding them, whether under Antonia's wiles or not, became thick and slow.

Ezra finally acknowledged this was their turning point, and it was best to speak frankly, "So then you understand, you can't create room where there isn't any more. The Ratios, all that good alchemy, is set."

"I don't think I understand anything. If you keep talking to me like I'm one of your toadies, I'm going to just keep on saying that: *I don't think I understand anything.*"

"There are limits to everything, Ant. *Everything.* The amount of magic any one plane of existence can hold, the amount of joints any one witch can smoke. *Or should smoke...*"

Ezra had finally found Antonia's "line" and unblinkingly walked right across it—Antonia flashed, "You goddam bitch. How dare *you* lecture *me,* of all the women we've known. Of all the years we've done this... *What do **you** want? This is all about you—I'm sure —as it always usually turns out to be.* What's your fucking point? Or whichever measly crony clan you're involved with this time!"

Ezra was now expressionless, her eyes flat, black, "I, we, need you to let go, Antonia. You're too strong and, well, as I started to say you're wasting energy, time—*everything.*"

Everything that had been in some degree of swirling, smoking, steaming, or whatever abruptly suspended its play; the booth lurched and collapsed back to the ground and into it, everything elemental had shifted too: the air, the light, there was nothing there, nothing left to feel. Antonia was on fire...

"So, what is it, I just chop off my whatever and hand it over to you and your coven bitches?"

"No, Ant. No." Ezra smiled slowly, "Always so charmingly medieval, aren't you?"

"I don't know anymore. You tell me."

Again, flat, black silence.

"It's very simple and straightforward, or so I've been told," said Ezra. "You simply take a potion, go to sleep, and—"

"More fucking sleeping and then you, what? Just never wake up? Or never wake up on Earth again—something along those lines?"

"No, Ant. This isn't funny, Ant."

It was surprising but Antonia started to chuckle softly. Something seemed to snap, and not necessarily in a bad way. She thought out loud, "It would be a relief in a way, wouldn't it? I mean being good at something, really good, even though you never really tried or cared all that much about it—it becomes this weird responsibility. And one I certainly never asked for."

Ezra added her twist to the conversation and dropped her head to the table. Her fingers spidered her face up to look wistfully at Antonia, "I can't take care of you anymore, sweetheart. One hundred and twenty-five years is a *long time,* no matter which way you're looking at it—witch, mortal, whatever."

Antonia was once again debilitated by her soul sister's words, *Wow, two total mind-fucks—in just thirty minutes. A record...* Or was it? That's the kind of superior and unconditional trust that love can create, and for hundreds of years. And the sharp words from before forced Antonia to reconcile the jagged and painful edges of her reality.

She swallowed the last of her drink, "And in spite of all this discussion and awfulness, this decision, just to be clear, belongs to me. It has absolutely *nothing* to do with you." She looked hard at her now nemesis, but moments before dear friend, sighed long and deep as the tears pooled. "Yes, yes, there have been many times you, we, supported each other—but that one time in particular—that I know I would've never, ever made it through without your help. Your, well, *love*..."

"I know, I know," said Ezra suddenly, oddly nervous and dismissive, "but let's not bring back—"

"Not bringing back anything, but God forbid, if you hadn't done what you did. And helping me to find those women. And then hardest of all—or maybe not 'of all'—but keeping it our secret and protecting Tom from it for, for... Well, twenty years is a long time. And certain things, especially a certain love and the overwhelming pain connected to it, will never fade... 'Never' becomes something manageable."

Now Ezra looked lost. Blank. She had never forgotten (or ever would forget) what had happened and what she'd done for her friend, and Antonia was more than right, the fear and frustration felt just as real at that moment as it had throughout those three awful days. (Maybe because it hadn't happened *to her*—just *with* her—she'd been able to compartmentalize it. Cordon it off, down and deep where it could only be found by pulling long and hard on the heartbreak.)

Antonia felt weak, defeated. She measured her words, "So, this isn't a *yes*, isn't a *no*—just what do I need to do?" The question startled Ezra completely, then she quickly thrust herself back to the present, to the crisis that (she liked to think) had been averted. (Though, truth be told, there was plenty more that could skew things the wrong way for Ezra.)

Ezra hesitated, "I'll need to double check. But I'll get everything ready and bring it over. You won't have to do a thing except go to sleep. And when you wake, your power—or most of it anyway—is transmuted. I think it really is that simple."

Antonia mused, "If only the good things were as easy to do as the bad, that would be something indeed." Then she quickly corrected herself, "Oh but not to say this is necessarily a bad thing —right, Ez?"

Ezra looked at Antonia quizzically, "I know how much you love your sleep, so how could it possibly be something bad?" The whole room seemed to exhale and readjust its *everything*; Ezra looked at Antonia, smiled wanly and stood up to go.

Antonia took her hand, "You're clear that we're not clear, right?" Ezra's smile stayed exactly as it was.

Antonia watched her leave, then sat back, closed her eyes and simply, slowly breathed.

———————— ⟪⟫ ⟪⟫ ————————

"Why are *you* so hyper-focused and hyper-private about cycles lately—even, like, which *kind* they are?" Sasha smirked, "What does that mean, anyway? Like flavors? Chocolate or vanilla?"

Tip knocked Sasha's hands off her shoulders, "And why do *you* have to be so *gross* about everything lately? *Flavors?*"

"It's not gross; it's just a joke."

"Yeah, a *gross* joke."

Sasha persisted, "Tsk, tsk—so *sensitive too*. Must be having your period."

Tip glared, "You're such a dick sometimes—like *nowtimes*. You know exactly what I meant about 'kind,' and I'm not hyper anything—just because I don't feel the need to broadcast it to the universe every single time my witchy blood bath begins."

Now Sasha became indignant, "I'm spearheading a campaign: no woman, mortal or witch, should ever feel ashamed or whatever in talking about her body and its natural and perfect inner workings. Actually you—Ms. Earth Mama Hippy Witchy-Poo—should be totally into this." Sasha sneered, "And I do not announce it every single time!"

Tip insisted, "That's such bullshit! Every two weeks from on top of the toilet in the bathroom, or a cafeteria bench, or that's how everyone thinks about it." Tip tried to force a smile but she was too vexed with Sasha this moment; it was exactly this superior-sounding, bitchy attitude that notoriously made Tip want to turn her sister into a used Maxipad.

Sasha was relentless, "At least I don't feel like I have to sneak around going to the gynecologist—it's a natural part of just *things,* you know. I'm sure you could figure out plenty of other things to be ashamed about—give yourself a break. Jeez." She grinned her cheesy-nasty (in a nice-mean way) grin.

Now Tip was dumbfounded. And formally pissed. "You slimy little witch, you! What business is it of yours what or how many times I've been to the doctor?"

Sasha was on a scary roll, "I'll bet you wanted to see how you could bump your cycle up to having *three installments* instead of two, just to be one better than me." She laughed but she mostly wasn't kidding (pathetic, I know).

Tip launched out of her chair and hovered, livid, over her twin, threatening to do some real damage, "You asshole! *Only **you*** would think that, you competitive *cunt,* you!"

Sasha was only slightly intimidated, "Wow, shit, it *definitely* must be your time of the month, probably *number two* by the look of things." Tip's whole room shook; half the furniture jumped into the air and landed with a decided thud. After a few intentional and very deep breaths, she slowly floated back down to her chair and carefully said, "I think it would be best if you go back to your room now."

And then Sasha (always slightly retarded on the emotional sensitivity scale) started to realize her many and various faux pas and skulked out of the room, not entirely with her broom between her legs, "Guess I'll just tell you about Stackhouse's class tomorrow."

TIP SOON BECAME immune to all distasteful commentary, whether it skewed more to the preternatural side or the mortal side—she needed to ascertain what was genuinely wrong with her: she was delivering copious and unnatural amounts of blood through both cycles. She felt basically okay otherwise, but still, something had to be wrong; her period lasted sometimes for more than a week with no noticeable shift in her, shall we describe it, productivity. Tip scarred her calendar one more time: *Mom has to help you, or if she can't—or won't—you know what to do.*

The Family Deflates

✿❦✿

Wednesdays continued to be tough; Tom Dad had always promised that the figurative glass would become half full (as opposed to half empty), but The Sisters continued to feel differently. They felt stuck—that they were still waiting—in the middle, somewhere. *How appropriate for a Wednesday regardless of the time of year*, though it did feel particularly grueling this week, waiting for some sliver, a kiss of real change to happen. (In earnest—like *seriously*...)

Soba was once again mysteriously sibling-phobic this week; Sasha wondered whether she really had said something to offend Baby Girl. Tip wasn't that worried, "How could you have? She hasn't actually said anything to us all week." It was odd too that Sasha would worry about anyone but herself, but Tip could only accommodate so much familial duress before she would be required to imbibe at least three episodes of Liza Koshy (peppered with a little Emma Chamberlain) if only to maintain *some* semblance of Self.

. . .

TIP WAS super-late and basically fell into Mr. Clarke's classroom; she clambered back to her desk. She started to sling her backpack into the usually empty seat next to her except now it wasn't empty—there was an exquisite blonde sylph perched there. It was the first time in days that Tip had found herself close enough to really look at the infamous Rappatsi—*introducing Miss Gorgeous Otherworldliness...*

Rappatsi wiggled two fingers and a smile hello at Tip. "I'm Tip," Tip smiled slowly, fumbling through the moment.

"I know," Rappatsi acknowledged quietly; Tip was surprised at her response, *How the freak would she already know?* Tip wondered too why she felt so flustered? It certainly wasn't the first time a new student suddenly materialized (through the door or via other means) in class, nor were her powers that initially overwhelming. (Tip's innate witchy ESP was sensing above-average potencies, but nothing that made her skin twitch.)

But no one else seemed to be aware or care a bat's ass; Mr. Clarke interrupted Tip's trance...

"Rappatsi, you had an interesting comment about the World War II poster the other day—why don't you share it with everyone?"

The other day?! I've been sitting right here every day for the last huge bunch of days! Did she move from another class?

"That was a pretty rad story about your grandfather—or who you *hope* is your grandfather. That would be so cool if that works out." Jack volunteered his comment completely unsolicited, but then everyone else was grinning, snapping like they knew exactly about the "rad" story.

Tip was stupendously gobsmacked. (And a little more smacked than gobbed.)

She attacked her phone, her thumbs and fingers running over each other. She knew Sasha wouldn't be far from any text message: *Okay, so this shit just got real...*

Tip had barely looked up, when Sasha answered: *Rappatsi, right?*

Duh!

*And where have **we** been?!*

Double duh... And what the hell kind of name is 'Rappatsi'?

(Sasha lamented,) *A beautiful blonde evil one... I dunno.*

T.G.I.F (THE REMIX): The Sisters (sans Soba) were more than ready—let the *Friday Night Rap* festivities commence.

"Play it. I dare you." John glanced at the cheesy Lionel Ritchie cover art—cheesy then and, sadly, not even classic cheesy now. "They'll throw something at me."

Tip groaned, "What are they going to throw? A napkin? There's nothing—our cheap-ass student council once again decided dances aren't cool. So, to make their point, they're going to starve us to death."

John was not really listening, checking his messages. He was bored with everything, but he knew where Tip was going with her point. *Really* boring. "More class struggle? Play on words intended." He looked her, "I don't know why you keep trying to stir some shit up that really isn't there. Not anymore it's not."

Tip flipped John her peace V sign (those first two nails chewed to the skin), extricating her opinion on the subject. John kept protesting, "Okay, right. It's just *my* problem. I'm the only one experiencing this, um, *pain.*" He rolled his eyes. Tip finally waved her hand, *He can be such a downer!* shooing away the convo, "Just play the song. *Pleeeze!*"

Sasha sliced Tip's John convo in two, demanding, "Have you seen her?"

Tip was well-versed in speaking *manic Sasha,* "Who? You mean Rapp?" (Groups of ten or more typically brought out the crazy in her sister.)

"Of *course* I mean Rapp," Sasha snapped, "And her name is Rappatsi."

"Why are you lecturing me? Everyone calls her Rapp."

"I know what *everyone does*. Rapp is, it's, um, a *boy's* name. So it's just *wrong*."

"I didn't even think it was a *name*," Tip deadpanned her response; she knew it wasn't the most constructive thing to say. Sasha clearly was borderline *something-or-other* at the moment, and it wouldn't take much to... (There were distinct instances that Tip just *had* to let her inner witch come out and play—*Sasha can handle it*.)

Sasha nodded with a scoff, she'd agree to anything that would help chop this supposedly *not new girl* (witch, *please*—can we call a spade a spade?) down to a manageable size, though she wasn't as sure now as to what that would be as she was a week ago. Sasha curled her lip and Tip, decidedly out of character (*Everyone else has been lately so why not me?*), tucked in with her temporary besties to watch the action.

Sasha cornered herself as per usual and was again glued to her screen, her figurative asocial walls slowly assuming their position. Tip thought to channel, *What the hell are you so into? And why aren't you telling me about it?*... but decided to avoid any more potential conflict. But Tom Boy and Bitts, sneaking up on Sasha, did not share that concern and snatched the phone from her hand. The surprise made her grip the phone tighter and the hard corner, angled just so, cut through the creases of two fingers—deep enough that the blood didn't hesitate. She swung around, completely flummoxed.

"What the *fuck*—?"

"What the hell could be *so frigging* interesting?" Greg snorted, dodged and darted Sasha's grasp and even tried to toss the phone to Tom Boy but saw the damage. Sasha, though, quickly recovered, smiling strangely at her wound—a crescent smile of blood across the two fingers. (Tom Boy, too, seemed bizarrely pleased.)

Sasha joked, "Hey, dickhead, if you were hoping for some kind of Franken-weiner Viagra, eating *my* toes or fingers won't cut it."

Tom Boy got there first, "You're being a little paranoid for a very white, very powerful underwitch—don't you think so, Sash?" He wiped the phone clean, "Such a myth, all of that toe-eating or toe-sucking or whatever it was."

"Wouldn't really know since *I* don't have to worry about my *lack of powers*." The two glared at each other.

Greg was broadsided; never had he seen or heard these two supposedly kindred souls speak to each other in this fashion. (I warned you all the hormones were out to play to tonight!) He quipped but cautiously, "She's a friend, Tom Boy. She comes in peace..."

Tom handed the phone back to Sasha; he noticed the cuts were almost healed, practically gone. "You're at a fucking dance: an activity that involves other people and it's *not* on your phone. You're supposed to have 'fun,'" Tom Boy said now with a sly, out-of-character smile.

Sasha yanked the phone close, "I *am* having fun." She opened the screen, *I better not have lost that link, or next Monday's club meeting is a goner.*

A curious Bitts peered over her shoulder; Sasha'd been searching "missing persons" or "missing dead people" and then *Rappatsi* something-or-other. She caught up to the conversation, curling her phone behind her, "You assholes—you could've broken it!"

"Not with that cement-clad, safe-like case you have on it," joked Bitts. (Sasha had a tendency to be a little overprotective of her assorted hardware.) The boys' botched hello joke was reason enough for them to get the hell out of her line of fire, but then some yelping and laughing from the other corner of the cafeteria distracted all of them... Sasha fell back into her phone, Bitts moved closer to Tom Boy, "It couldn't have gone that perfectly? Do you have the tissues? I feel like I'm in some stupid-ass movie."

Tom Boy stared straight ahead, expressionless, dodging the flailing arms and music, "What does your mom always say? *'Don't count those chickens...'*? Yep, I got blood, or *we* got blood." They melded quickly into the anticipation and crowd just behind them.

Tip had been casually observing, and finally invaded Sasha's corner, "What's going on? Who or what's got you so worked up?" Sasha seemed to have forgotten Tip was there, muttered, "Nothing. Why?"

"*Why?!* C'mon, you're usually not this much of a bitch."

"Oh, thanks..."

"*And* you're usually not *that committed* to your screen. Why are you freaking out? What did the boys do?"

"They didn't do anything. Kind of." She glanced at her fingers and there was barely a scar. "And I'm not freaking out. Jesus, shit..." Sasha hesitated; she was confused and frustrated, "Can't sort out why 'Rappatsi' and why all of a sudden *now?* Something is just not right about the whole thing." The music got a tad louder (or it seemed like it did). Tip countered, "Tell me something we don't know." Sasha suddenly nervously scanned the room, "And something, *right now*, right here, just doesn't *feel right*. Or good." She started anxiously swiping her phone.

Tip knew the *manic Sasha* "drill" too well, so she continued trying to steer the chat back to what was right in front of them, "Well, for what it's worth, 'things' feels pretty good to me." Tip started bopping to the music, waved a couple fingers at Julie and her troupe.

Sasha's eyes flashed, "You're too easy. Someone could turn your arm into an eggplant, and you'd make eggplant parmigiana for dinner."

Tip laughed, a tad nervously, still trying to fend off her sister's visible distress, "That's funny. You're probably not too far off." Tip started dancing, "Love this song..." Tip suddenly, fortunately saw an opportunity to distract Sasha from herself, "*You*, however, have such screwed up control issues that if you could cast one of your precious fashion spells to color-coordinate the whole class every morning, you would."

Sasha blinked, shrugged, "No frigging way—such a waste of power." Then after a moment, "But it *is* an interesting concept."

"See! I told you..." Tip smiled. Julie fluttered at Tip to join them.

Sasha started deflating, "You don't think it's weird this whole Rappatsi thing, and how long as it's been going on?! This so needs to be figured out! We could wake up tomorrow and all have eggplants for arms!"

Tip smiled carefully, "Yeah, but I don't know that it's any weirder than anything else that's going down—here or at home, or wherever. And it's got to sort *itself* through—whatever '*it*' is—because it always does. That's just how the universe works."

"But the real stuff, like *life,* isn't making any sense. And the magic stuff, when you see it—*if you see it*—just doesn't add up." Sasha put her fingers over her ears (she'd never suffered concerts or dances or anything really loud very well), "And you don't even know which spell or craft-making would help the life part—I can't even *guess at it* anymore."

Tip had almost stopped listening, *Best to let her unwind all on her own.* She turned her body away from Sasha to the music then back again. "Not sure I heard the whole thing, but regarding that last part—I'm totally with you! Now, I got to go dance!" Sasha shooed her away and dived back into her phone.

WITH THAT CRAZY-SILLY Tricentennial thing fast approaching, and yet another red-blood-wolf (or whatever it wants to be) moon in place *and* a few X, Y, *and* Z hormones tucked under their capes —a cross-astral Eugenic Convergence was inevitable. (The Powers That Be had found yet another hole that needed to be filled.) Magic or spell-crafting hadn't been specifically prohibited at the dance (probably because no one thought about it, one way or another).

It was always the same old voodoo hoo-ha anyway, same old (and not so old) W's: the same witches, wannabe-Wiccans, etc.—whoever had the power to make the *fun* more "funner"—but were never inspired to stretch beyond their three or four token spells that got the laughs and the rote crowd response. (It even could get you the occasional hand job or even a little bit more and tonight seemed pretty flush.) But generally, the apathy was too pervasive—that extra "fifth spell" was simply too much trouble for a whole lot of not much.

(Even some of the new shit like that "Trans for a Day" spell was interesting, but for only a New York-second, like the new Apple phone.)

Yet even with the chronic boredom, there was still a tacit understanding that this wasn't the time (or place) for *fake* fun: love potions, breast enhancing (even of the non-magic variety), crotch-stuffing, transmogrification, and similar stunts. Depending upon which part of the country you found yourself, social decorum still frowned upon flagrant wand-waving (again, not that anyone even *thought* that much about *wands* to start with) in public spaces. If it was for a good cause —multiplying loaves of bread for a homeless person who had no to very few preternatural abilities (or their powers had dwindled to a crumb)—then that was fine. (Filling a classroom with bottles of White Claw to impress a *whomever* was not.)

But hold on, skip just one beat: why should a school dance be spared any of the hoodoo that had afflicted The Sisters' lives of late? Serendipitously, tonight *something* was converging with *something else, somehow* (sorry, that's the best information we have at this reading)—all the calendars stated as much and were at least consistent with their obfuscating.

(But for me and my demigod cohorts, this is just a way to help jumpstart and frame our conversations, where we might need to dedicate a little extra attention, or love... Even uptight Constance is starting to draw outside the lines a little bit!)

The cafeteria was now full and the energy high. Tip had lost sight of Sasha and was absolutely fine with that; the energy in the room felt—double meaning intentional and without a drip of irony—*magical*.

The weight of the crowd seemed to drift and ripple over to that one same corner again, but this time there were even more hoots, zips, "yeah mans," and other assorted yaps of encouragement. Then suddenly, wildly, the pairs of people that created a belt across the belly of the crowd were thrusted into air with one following the next—it looked like "the (human) wave," but instead of just their arms, "waving" their entire bodies! As the wave made its way to the other side it would begin again at the head of the malformed yet well-intentioned line dance, and somehow it was all perfectly choreographed to the unadulterated joy in the air. A second later, it all clicked into place for Tip: this was an enchanted interpretation of the renowned *Soul Train* dance line—and as one couple hopped off the boogie wave, another jumped on. Tip was overwhelmed, *What in the hooey?*, and scanned the room for Casen or Clarke, *Did someone get a special spell-casting pass tonight?* They did it once last year but only after a lot of major fussing around, and it was on a First Friday, and there had to be an extra chaperone to make sure nothing (or rather *no one*) got out of hand, and... And... And, by the go, *Where the hell is Sasha?!*

Tip was halfway across the floor before she realized and started to make better sense of how the wave was, well, *waving*: a chimera of a disco dance floor was undulating, flashing colored lights and strobes somehow intact. Tip could tell immediately that the master—or rather mistress—of ceremonies was the tall girl in black. From behind, her body and her very fitted outfit seemed to belie her (she was majorly guessing) sixteen (*seventeen,* at most?) years, *Who the hell is that? I don't recognize her at all—a new teacher? Did Mr. Clarke bring one of his escort girlfriends?* (That was a running joke about Clarke—kind of...)

Then this black-clad sorceress, her arms undulating to keep the floor moving and her people happy and high, turned back to face the crowd of dancing fools. Tip's jaw dropped: it was—till this moment—the ambiguous though omnipresent *Rappatsi*, attending, no, *holding* court at her first Friday night dance.

Tip beamed at the sight, *It looks like magick just got cool again...*

RAPPATSI WAS STILL WOOZY from the last "communication from the Beyond." Maybe the larger idea is on target, but the "beyond" part, *what the be-Jesus is that?* **Where** *would that be to be even a little more precise: up, down, all around us?*

Soon the communication became something more specific— yet another question (or concern) to add to her growing list. It didn't surprise her that so much still stayed so grey, questions cluttering her air along with the impending answers she'd been deigned to find (and confirm with that great, ambiguous Beyond). She'd quickly ascertained that her role here was once again merely the vessel, *My other witch-y friends love that term; I hate it. Don't find it 'romantic' at all. But it's my current lot in life—I'm the cliche to everyone else's originality.* (Don't listen to her, in spite of what she likes to think sometimes she's a megaforce; she's not even aware half of the time, which makes her—and keeps her—feet on the ground. Even when she intentionally has them in the air.)

Rappatsi knew one thing right now, right off the bat: her role might be limited but it was an important and specific one: she would *only help*—this was to be primarily the family's journey, everyone would grow and gain, but this time needed to be their burden as much as their reward.

(But she'd have some fun this time too—that was unavoidable...)

———— ◆◆◆◆◆ ◆◆◆◆◆ ————

EZRA HAD to have another glass of wine. That would make it *three nights in a row* of indulging in some form of alcohol, and Ezra had always strongly condemned the behavior. (To be clear, it was the "in a row" part—*not* the indulging.)

Ezra was desperately trying to discern what The Coven knew and what they didn't; they were agonizingly controlling (but only when they felt like it). If Ezra wanted to achieve and evolve to the next level of her existence, then she'd have to play by their rules. But the unnerving thing, especially for an extroverted control freak like Ezra, was that the "rules" changed all the time. (At least it seemed that way to her... *Oh screw it, just finish the bottle.*)

The overwhelming conundrum was *why Marta L.?* Just because Antonia didn't apparently care for the sand in their beleaguered sandbox? How did that even begin to insert itself into The Coven's (probably pathetic) conversations? To be fair, it was Ezra that introduced Marta Cortez to the clan, albeit for only selfish reasons (*Talk about "shooting yourself in the foot"—or Marta's foot*), but Ezra had been clear that Marta was only the teensiest bit interested in her preternatural talents (as powerful as they were) and was far more passionate about her broad, very rich Central American-cum-(mostly non-magickal) Spanish heritage. What was so tantalizing about that, especially for an old gaggle of tired, painfully white witches? (*And who'd actually want an occasionally deformed, disinterested Latina bitch as their next Supreme Overwitch anyway?*)

But then again, the pedestrian-sounding "toe thing'" was one of those impossibly unique synergies between myth and more than one level of subtle reality. Certain lineages of Latina witches gestated enormous metaphysical power in parts of their mortal bodies; Marta Lorca's clan and elongated sisterhood infamously had found their respective gifts in their feet, and ridiculously concentrated in their "Five Little Piggies." Suffice it to say that once word got out (how many eons ago), *none* of those piggies ever made it to market... But they'd grow back almost as quickly as they'd disappear—much to their perennial dismay.

Ezra recalled reading, any *toe potion* could offer additional powers, but they were temporary and had only to do with Natura-related matters, much like most of traditional Brujeria sorcery... How the Earth shed its skin on a daily basis was of little concern to Ezra—she had much loftier goals in her sights.

Rappatsi Rules

❦

"Isn't your 'friend' up for a YouTube Music Award tomorrow?"

"Not my 'friend.'"

Sasha insisted, "Yes, he's *your friend*." Bitts stared carefully at Sasha, *Why would she even give two whiny shits?*

"Just Snapchat. Hardly 'friends.'" Bitts was becoming less and less interested in words, or to be clear, actually *saying words*.

Sasha's sixth sense was yammering like a Santerian banshee; Bitts had a secret and it was a whopper. "'Friends' enough. I know he got you into that deep website, the one we thought was 'dark' and I'm guessing actually is...?"

"How do you know he's a 'he'?"

"Don't be silly, Bitts. He did, and I know he did—my heroic app tracked you mother f-er's and I'm f'ing proud of it."

Suddenly Sasha caught sight of Rappatsi aiming her steely grin directly at them, and before Sasha could think *Shit, we're screwed,* Rappatsi had attached herself to their convo. Sasha hadn't seen any witch move *that* fast recently, but then again no one was as obnoxious and flagrant with their craft until just recently—like Rappatsi-recently.

Bitt's face lit up; Sasha was almost offended. He spoke to

Rappatsi actually using fully formed words and sentences for the first time in weeks (or at least it seemed that way to Sasha), "Yo, Beautiful Bitch-witch, that was some rave of a wave you crafted together at the dance. It totally rocked!"

Sasha remained nonplussed for two fat reasons: why and how she keeps forgetting she's supposed to be best friends with this nasty witch just like everyone else. She could forgive herself even a little bit if any of The Sisters could wrap their pretty heads around why the *freak* just the three of them were 'spared.' (Sasha was starting to believe it was best, if not just easier, to believe they were the crazy ones.) The second nutty thing was why was Bittsface—*especially* digitally neutered Bitts —so smitten? What the hell was happening—all of the boy-bitches in her life were shapeshifting in front of her very eyes! It seemed almost too spiteful (and equally unbelievable...) She blamed it indubitably on the Beautiful Bitch-witch, now just inches from her face, *I take it back. She's not as pretty as I thought she was.*

"Well, you're as pretty as I thought you were—maybe just having a good day, Sash?" Rappatsi winked, the surprising snark landed intact, and then it was back to Bitts, "So, just wanted to throw it out there, you didn't sound *that* into it, but if you are, I can get us into the YouTube Awards. Not majorly cool seats but still fun—know someone who knows someone, blah, blah. So, lemmeno later... Oh, shit—there's Mara—" Rappatsi started to run, but suddenly stopped, turned to Sasha, "Almost forgot: thanks for 'stacking' me." She kind of winked-smirked this time.

"Huh? 'Stacking you'?"

"Yeah, the jeans in the store," Rappatsi laughed, "It's nuts. You'd crack up if you saw some of the places I've ended up floating to, in, around, whatever..."

Sasha was indifferent, "Sure... But that was Tip's thing. I could've given two shits—or stacks." Rappatsi smiled, ignoring the dig.

Bitts, oblivious, interrupted, "But it's in L.A.—were you thinking we'd just—"

"Yeah, do a transference or something. I'd think of something... And don't freak; it's never as nuts as most witches like to say—they just don't know what the fuck they're doing."

Bitts still seemed unaffected, hard to know whether he was in or not so much, "I don't know, I've got basketball practice and I wanted to check out that new site you said—if you just want to hang and do that later."

Rappatsi shrugged, Mara was wiggling a finger at her, "Yeah, maybe. Snap me." Then, fully turning to Sasha, her whole demeanor seemed to shift and calmly encircle her. Rappatsi said slowly, "You and I—and maybe your sisters too—but definitely *you and I*, we need to *catch up*."

And then she finally dashed, ran off (but it quickly became more of run-kind-of-flying dashing off than the usual jog).

Sasha was a bit speechless again, but now a little bit happily hypnotized too (she just assumed), "Man, that witch-bitch doesn't give a shit what anyone thinks, does she? Even with her spell-crafting whiz stuff?"

Bitts shrugged, "What? That's news to you? Where *you been, witch?* I gotta fly too—want to see that Dark Web shit you dug up!"

Everyone left Sasha standing in her own stupor. This was the first time in a very long time that she had no clue what to think or say next.

Tom Boy turned on the lights, but the lights didn't listen. He flipped the switch up and down a couple times, wondering at each flip why people respond this way to situations like this—as though doing anything again five more times in rapid succession would miraculously fix whatever the problem was. All of this mulling reminded him that there was no such thing as truly "simple" magic, *Nothing will do what you want it to by simply wanting or willing it, whatever it might be*; that *was* something he learned finally after poking (it had to be about) seven times at that pain-in-the-ass overlay on that alchemist's website *that I'm sure **was** possesse*d. He laughed out loud and wasn't even exactly aware that he had when Bitts—walking in the room—asked, "What's so funny?"

"Me. I'm so funny."

Bitts dropped his books on a desk, "Don't be weird, dude." He looked around, "And why are you sitting in the dark? Should I light a couple candles so we can do a little conjuring? A seance? Or something lighter?" (Bitts wasn't the wittiest guy, but at least he put forth an effort.)

"Careful, dude, the Dark Web gods might already be listening." Tom flipped open his two laptops, "Let's not do anything more to piss them off. They already shut off the electricity." He looked up at the lights.

Bitts offered, "I don't think anyone but us gives a shit about our little Occult Tech Nerds club. I don't even think the school knows we exist—which could explain the whole lights thing." Tom smiled, nodded.

Greg wandered in, his face perfectly framed by the light from his phone.

"So, Sasha *will* be here... in, like, ten minutes." He rolled his eyes. "I thought once you broke up with her—that would be that. That's what I hoped, anyway."

Tom Boy laughed, "God, dude, are you kidding? That only upped the ante. Everything's a competition with that woman."

Bitts turned, "She's a woman?"

"As much as you're a man."

Bitts turned back to his computer, "Uh-huh. Well I don't want to be a man. Not yet, not right now anyway."

Greg jabbed, "Too late, dude. They already held you back a

year. And you've got hair where most of us are just starting to think about it." Nobody laughed at Greg's joke but Greg (again).

Suddenly the lights came on. Bitts glanced at Tom, shrugged, but Tom Boy wasn't as comfortable with the coincidence. "Dudes—quick—show me your screens!" Tom looked at all four corners of his two computers as Greg and Bitts maneuvered themselves. Bitts fretted, "What is it? What's wrong?"

"Nothing. Nothing that I know of at this second anyway."

Greg said, "Nice. Get him even *more* worked up—we won't get anything done." Tom Boy looked at their screens and didn't see any evidence of what he *thought* he saw from the other day, right after their meeting. And maybe he was a little too much on edge given, well, *everything...* "It's just with the lights. With all that Dark Web crap we've been fussing around with and we already *know* the technomancers are vampires when it comes to energy—I don't know, just forget it..."

Bitts asked, "What's that have to do with the friggin' screen corners?"

Tom tried to play dumb, "I didn't say that."

Greg jumped in, "Yeah, you did."

Bitts said, "Yep, you said something happened the other day."

"I didn't say that, I *started* to say that."

Sasha had walked in and dove into their convo, "No, but you said enough of it. I even know what you're talking about and I just walked in the door."

She stared at Tom, "So you believe in the Corners Theory, huh?"

"Is that what they call it?"

"Who's 'they'? That's what I'm calling it."

"Oh, okay. *Witchy Woman in Control,* everyone." Tom Boy tried to joke. "Yeah, whatever, dude," said Sasha. "So, like I was saying, where'd you hear about the four-corner alignment being a port for the Dark Web gods?" Sasha then snickered, "If you tell me yours, I'll tell you mine..." That got a couple laughs. Even from Greg.

Tom looked around the room again, now a nervous habit. (His next thought always would be, *And what is it I'm so afraid of?*) He started to answer the best way he could, "Well, from the Dark Web..."

Greg blurted, "Ha! I knew it! I knew you did it!"

Tom frowned, "Did what?"

"You went there. You found Tor."

"So what? It's not that hard."

"That's not the point—the *rumor* is the point."

Sasha threw a pen at Greg. Tom Boy argued, "You mean for us half-breeds? The *Curse*? That's such bull crap. You believe everything you hear, dude."

"Really? You two are the ones already talking Four Corners. And unless you got to a Red Room, what or how would you know what to actually talk about?"

Bitts thought to mellow the conversation; it was getting a little too aggressive for his liking. Trying to be helpful (and on some level comforting) he suggested, "Yeah, you guys with those extra magic genes are like magnets for that kind of shit." And when everyone swung around, looking slightly panicked or irritated, he retracted, "Well, not every time. Just *sometimes*. If at all, if it's true at all..." The light flickered again but stayed on. Tom laughed this time though he wasn't sure why.

Then abruptly, very seriously he said, "Yeah, I got in and got out. That Four Corners thing was the first thing I ran into, and it scared the crap out of me." Tom Boy glanced at his laptop screen again despite himself.

Sasha said quietly, "So you *did* find a Red Room—that's the only way you'd see that kind of information, true or not. How'd you find it?" Sasha's competitive streak flared its prickly mane, showing no shame.

Tom frowned, shrugged, "Just clicked into it. Once I was in, I was in."

"Bastard." She laughed, started up her computer. They all sat down, assumed their usual positions and attitudes. Greg, with his mischievous glint, started to speak, "So..."

Tom Boy shut his computer, "Don't even say it. Let alone think it."

"Why not?! Show us your link. Or at least give us the path!"

In that instant Tom's eyes, his expression revealed how frightened he was really was, then almost as quickly he regained his manufactured cool, his sharp edges. Sasha looked at him carefully, *What else? There was something more. Tom's no hero, but he's no wuss either.*

"I looked. It was already gone." Everyone didn't believe him, "Take a look for yourselves. Feel free." He looked at the clock, "But do it now. Gotta go in five minutes."

"Where do you got to be in five minutes that's so important?" Greg couldn't help himself. (He did have some natural talent for certain magic tricks, but he'd inherited a couple extra asshole genes too.)

———————

FRIDAY NIGHT BASKETBALL (how could anyone resist?) and not only was their basketball team hardly performing, but Soba couldn't help noticing how the scoreboard was frizzed out too. She hated anything that involved a ball and people running to or away from it—it boggled her mind. Her older sisters didn't seem to share this sentiment, though they were clearly frustrated (toward the boring side of frustrated) with the circumstances. The whole of the scoreboard caught her eye again—something was different—or it could simply be she somehow found little lights peeking on and off more compelling than skinny (mostly white) boys running around in shorts that were too big for them.

No, something *was* begging attention, albeit very, very discreetly: some kind of digital computer worm wiggled across any available electrical sign, billboard, scoreboard—anything that had a plug for a tail, and the bigger the plug the better. It happened so quickly that just the handful with their supernatural radar and antennae always at-the-ready saw it. (Better said: *sensed* it.)

Of course, that would necessarily include The Sisters and Rappatsi. (You can't be surprised that Rappatsi had already insinuated herself—as much as she could—with The Sisters. It was very necessary, and inevitable—still just one of many moving elements.)

"Some *thing*'s trying to play catch up, and it doesn't have a shit to do with basketball... *Where the freak is all this magic coming from?*" Rappatsi started to flush red again, though for some reason this time from top down as opposed to tits up.

Tip tried to ease tensions with a lame attempt at basketball humor: something about Tim D., swingman (minor Tip crush from six month ago), LeBron and not "'passing' her up"... They all barely reacted.

But then, they *all* noticed the names on the teams' marquee...

"Look," Tip murmured, nodded towards the scoreboard.

Rappatsi suddenly jumped—they'd never seen Rapp react that way to anything.

"The names... I'm almost sure—" And then Rapp did something else they'd never seen before: she appeared to deflate, collapsing into herself. Usually so assured and flawless, it was frightening to see her bent, distorted, like a quickly crumpled piece of paper. This ball of Rappatsi floated up, just over their heads, spun once, twice... Then, as if someone stomped down on a rubber pump, she burst up and out, inflating like a Macy's parade balloon. Now hovering, facing down at them, deep in a trance state, she was blank, blissed out. Tip poked up and into her stomach, and then twice—no reaction. The Sisters were stupefied.

"What's going on?" Tip murmured, a little afraid, a little more than surprised that (once again, stupefyingly) no one else in the gym seemed to be noticing.

Sasha stayed strangely, remarkably calm, "The trance shit I've, *we've,* seen before, this 'balloon' thing—that's new."

Then Todd yelled from a few rows away, "What's Rapp's gig?" Still, most everyone else was more interested in Rory's halftime DJing. "She needed a nap?" The usual lame Todd joke.

Sasha waved Todd off and as if on command, Rapp suddenly spoke (but barely), "Names... Count."

The girls looked at each other and mouthed the words again.

What names? Huh?

Then more humming from Rapp, "*Definitely* not the home team."

Then Soba directed her sisters' gaze to the players' marquee, where the bright white-bulbed letters were featuring *names of women*, and names that were too long and complicated and demanded scrolling further down to the segmented box just below. Eight names ticker-taped their way down and around the marquee and then were gone. The board was black for a moment, then was fine again with boys' names back where they should be.

The Sisters were so hypnotized by this unearthly message they hadn't noticed that Rappatsi had neatly, nicely recovered and was sitting back on the bench next to them, sucking down her soda, "That shit can take a lot out of a girl, I'll tell you." She elaborated a bit further but was chewing on her straw at the same time so it was hard to know what "shit" she was muttering.

"Rapp, you *seem* pretty okay—are you?" Tip worried.

"Oh what, me? Sure, that kind of crap isn't hard, just saps the energy right out of you. A couple more Cokes and I'll be fine."

Sasha didn't appear worried, couldn't wait, needed to know, "Rapp, anything to *worry* about?"

Rappatsi was already absorbed in the game, "What? Which? You mean the names?" She sucked on the bottom of the cup, "I'm not sure. Have to double-check something later."

. . .

THERE IS a Superior Coven (as they like to label themselves), and they are preparing a battle (of sorts), or to do battle (or whatever description or mix of words sounds and seems the most horrific and omnipotent). Their long and sometimes sordid history would prefer to have you dumbstruck, stymied with fear and apprehension—but peppered with a blessed mix of awe, fear (there's that word again), and deep-seated regard. (The Trumpian parallels were uncanny—or probably not so much...) However, just glancing to Wikipedia's next paragraph's pathetic explanations would dispel delusions of any kind (let alone grandeur).

But that did not prevent this current (and happily more local) iteration of The Coven from trying and from doing some very real and perverse damage (almost in spite of themselves).

Ditan abruptly stands up and thrusts his arm out, palm first. He thumps, You self-serving bitch! You're only dissing their exemplary reputation—if I do say so—to shine your own! This behavior *must be reprimanded...*

Constance is unsympathetic. Really? Who's self-serving who here is the better question. Didn't you date one of those silly hags a couple centuries ago, D.? Not sure why this is even a conversation.

Ditan: You're older than the current lot put together—am I sensing some resentment, perhaps? Your days *were* the heydays— I'll give you that much. There must have been a really good reason you didn't subscribe or try to—or *maybe you did?* Rejection, *Ditan pauses for effect,* can be hellish—or was it that they never bothered to recognize you *either* way?

Ditan had been so quiet, so reserved, till five minutes ago—the group is dumbstruck. Constance likewise showed an aspect of herself that was almost equally surprising: cool, conniving, even self-righteous.

Constance: There will always be some of us that want things to stay exactly as they are—or maybe as they were—regardless of whichever reality plane you're subscribing to at that moment. How any thoughts, any prejudice, anything less than the truth is able to survive *at all* is mind-boggling—and to be fair, sometimes even humbling.

Pilar: The schools' graffiti terrorism was just dumb—another perfect example of the spineless shit they've attempted lately. It's only about finding the right eye-candy for this troupe of failed Morgan le Fays.

Ditan: How are you so sure it was them? It was more typical of the Brujeria's messy threats, and they're still *very* much around.

Pilar: Don't be such a dick—aren't you reading *your own notes?* The English text barely, clumsily translated?! They probably were also wearing blackface—no, *brownface makeup*—thinking they were fooling everyone into believing it was some Latino hoodoo hoods, violating all levels of borders and walls—geographical, cosmological, multidimensional, intestinal... *Pilar laughs loudly, punctuating her joke.*

Abyssinia stands up and holds out her hands, visually attempting to calm the conversation. The winds were shifting suddenly—somebody was getting a little too confident.

Abyssinia: Okay, let's all please chill. The facts are and always will be just as we see them, witness them, and—obviously—record them. We all know what can happen when we start to freely interpret or "spin" as they say, as we've all already probably done, at some point. Even despite ourselves.

Ditan looks dejected as usual, and Constance was barely present—a chimera of herself—with whatever else she was working on with her hands (also per usual) in too many "pots" or discussions. (Her extracurricular efforts weren't working to her advantage, by the way—can tell you that much.)

ANTONIA'S KNOCK was entirely original, it was the most unobtrusive and gentle interruption, one almost always became excited as opposed to irritated by it. She peered around Sasha's door, "You still up?"

(7:30 p.m. and Tom Dad was still M.I.A. Not terribly unusual but also not a common occurrence; it always surprised Antonia when she'd find herself wanting to talk to [perhaps actually *missing*] her husband, *The first available daughter will have to suffice.*)

"Yup." Sasha wasn't being successful with her search, so she was happy to have a reason to press pause.

Antonia had what appeared to be an old photo poised between her fingers. "I wanted you to see this."

It was exactly what Sasha thought it was, but *who* exactly was in the photo—apart from seeing it was an attractive woman playing with two, no, actually three, babies—was a mystery. Antonia continued, "I don't think you've ever seen this—actually, I *know* you haven't since I'm just happening upon it after who knows how long."

"Is this us? I mean Tip and I?"

"Wow, you *are* good, even I had to figure it out. Guess who the woman is..."

Sasha stared blankly at the smiling, dark-haired woman. She shrugged.

Antonia smiled, "Marta Cortez."

Sasha was stunned. "How did *you*—or we—know *her*? Or *them*?"

"That's why I was quizzing you the other time. I haven't seen Marta in eons—literally—but she and I were 'Krazy Coven' sisters, way, way back then. When Soba was already being the little witch-bitch she was destined to be, even curled in the comfort of my—at the time—*extremely* expanded and 'enriched' tummy environment."

"I've seen other pics, Mom—you were fat."

"That's so generous of you, Sasha. Thank you for that." She snapped the picture back out of her hands.

"Well, you were."

"Yes, and that time was really *hard*. That's why wonderful Marta took care of you more than just a few afternoons—when I just couldn't deal."

"So you were BFFs with Martika's mom? That's *weird*."

"Why's that weird? And no, hardly BFFs, and we didn't know each other that well, but we definitely liked each other. She was very nice to me, and I was very nice to her—when it wasn't exactly the cool thing to do, in either case."

"Hiring a Latina woman to babysit your kids isn't all that enlightened, Mom—hate to tell you."

Antonia love-smacked her daughter, slightly harder to help her point, "You little bitch, I come in here to share a special part of *your* history, and you can't even be pleasant about that."

Sasha, surprised and hurt, looked at her arm, "You left a mark!"

"Good. Hope so."

Sasha sighed, slumped back in her chair, "Sorry. Didn't mean to be mean. But I don't always get why people get so nostalgic—I don't remember any of that."

"You remember everything else—or you almost do—from when you were, like, *three!* It's always kind of amazed me—so why not four?"

"I do. I have. But just not that. Have no memory..." Sasha was thoughtful, "So we spent a lot of time?"

"Yeah, she was an angel. She took you both for a week, two or three times. Tom Dad was traveling for work, and I was so sick with the Baby Girl. Couldn't deal. Marta was a godsend."

Antonia turned to leave, and Sasha suddenly asked, "What did you ever do for her?"

"It was more coven stuff. She couldn't get pregnant; they were trying and trying. So there were a couple divinations—I had the powers, no one else did. I made it happen. Sounds impressive but it wasn't that big a deal, not in the larger scheme of everything."

Sasha smiled, "That was nice."

Antonia yawned, "Yeah, it was." Quiet smile.

"But I had no idea you guys even knew one another."

"It was strange. That was more her; she really kept to herself, her family. The coven—and it barely functioned as one, that Krazy Coven—was it, really. Once I quit that, nada."

Bitts messaged Sasha. "Oh, shit. I forgot about Bitts."

Antonia kissed her forehead and started back to her studio.

Sasha, fingers lingering over her keyboard, deliberated until she heard her mother at her easel before finally deciding not to impart that Marta had "passed on," left the Earth's plane several days prior. Martika had been careful to describe it as a happy and conscious decision made by Marta alone and that it should be perceived only as a joyful, albeit bittersweet, occurrence. Sasha muttered to herself, *Then why am I so afraid to talk about it, or even think about it...* She almost forgot about Bitts again and assaulted the blank email page in front of her.

TOM DAD SNUCK into his house. It was traditionally about the fourth, maybe fifth creaky back stairs step (he had committed to memory the *non-creaky areas* as opposed to the *randomly creaky areas* on each step) that he'd *traditionally* beat himself up for being such a spineless whiny bitch. Who was really going to give a shit about his M.I.A.? No one. But *everyone* would make some sarcastic or snippy comment one way or another about it, and that's what always ultimately unnerved him. He decided tonight, coincidentally (probably because we're talking about how silly the bastard is), that all of that whimpering would cease—like magic—at that very moment. And so it was (and it did).

Tom Dad turned and decidedly, naturally tripped down the stairs to the kitchen. He whipped the fridge door open and nonverbally announced his intentions of *yet another* beer, *you crafty, witchy motherfuckers!* He took a long breath, *And on the seventh day, he rested…*

Tom Dad now felt very happy, at the same moment being painfully aware how tenuous the sensation was; he suddenly felt compelled to see his daughters while they slept—they necessarily appeared beyond perfect in that almost-perfect place; he would fall to his knees (or it seemed like he did) every time this precious sentiment possessed him.

This time, this visit—a particular memory followed him. It was two days after their eighth birthday, and the twins still weren't speaking to each other. Tom Dad's charmed puzzlement became parental worry; Antonia was more or less concerned but happy to have peace and quiet the girls' battle provided. The party had been a modest success: the clown face spell got "stuck" on Neighbor Zack—or was miscast, or whatever the guest witch had explained. Anyway, his nose turned back to its normal pinkish and (usually) somewhat bulbous shape after a week or so. (Tom Dad had dropped off a good-sport bottle of red and a few joints as a kind-of apology.)

"I'm really concerned." Tom Dad looked up at the ceiling (where the twins might or might not be), his brow twisted.

"I know. I can see that. Why?"

"They might hurt each other."

"How?" Antonia's face tightened, maybe with concern.

"Sasha could burn a hole right through Tip just like she did poor Sput—his tail will never be the same."

Antonia deadpanned, "It was too long anyway."

Tom Dad was still absorbed with his anxiety, "That's if she wanted to… And if she knew how to. She's certainly powerful enough—God knows she didn't get that from me."

Antonia said patiently, a tad ironically, "She's not going to *kill* her *sister*."

"I'm not saying that—but a hole through *any* part of her body would not be a good thing."

Antonia stared blankly at Tom.

"You need another puff and a shot."

"Really? Both? I'm *that* bad?"

"You're probably asking the wrong person."

Just several feet above their hapless conversation, the two girls sat in the dark. One had their mother's frayed wand from God knows when, and the other was winging it. Against their parents' wish (especially recently Tom Dad's) they conjured eight wisps of firelight and floated them through, around, and above themselves. There was magic everywhere—and seemingly nowhere—*all at once.* Just like it was supposed to be.

———————————

PILAR SMILED: I pushed the water closer to the remaining potion —sorry, potions. Marta is still manifesting; it is a slow process even here, so on Earth it could seem like months, even years depending upon their will. But that love, their love, is immutable —Martika knows it because she feels it. (And at this glorious stage of things, it has so little to do with how many toes or arms or whatever she has or not.)

That woman, that overwitch is something overwhelming and stupendous—all the demigods agree. How and where everything falls or sets into place could bode well for her here; she certainly has ingratiated herself with the Great Mother and her means. Marta wears each of the elements as jewelry, one on each finger. Even Akna seems impressed (but she tends to be generous that way).

Martika will finally have her dream; she deserves it at this point. (And it will make her happy.)

Luis has more to do. And Lila will make it better for him, not easy necessarily, but better. And the Brujeria? They're most times our metaphysical 'feet on the ground' (*when* they're behaving). Everyone has their work cut out for them. Shit, we all have our crosses to bear (religious pun intended).

And I'm finally sensing something beyond OPMs—Other People's Moments; there's suddenly a hint of how I 'fit'—how I matter. But just a sense... (Go figure.)

———————— ⟨⟨⟨⟨⟨ ⟩⟩⟩⟩⟩ ————————

Every one of Rappatsi's six senses was flailing—the first incident already (and in just over two weeks). She followed her nose quite literally; the smell wasn't repulsive as much as it was—shall we say, diplomatically—*distinct*. But it was undeniable that each of her other senses was doing its own *Lost in Space-'Danger, Will Robinson!'*-hysterical-robot thing that confirmed there could be real Trouble in River City. (Indulge me, please—just spent a whole weekend cable TV surfing.)

Rappatsi peered into the now dark classroom lab—the force of the impact, pummeling her waist and back, grasping at the back of her head...

She sprang-twisted into the air leaving this monstrous thing spinning and spitting in its own threats and bile. She could now see, floating above, piecing together the shards of light and shadow, it was a man or what appeared to be such; his features were too distorted, bizarre to be human, but his scent said otherwise. He lunged up, she attacked, he grabbed her arm and seemed to thrust his body away leaving himself vulnerable to, well, *anything*. Bizarre strategy. Rappatsi (who was more surprised than anything else) found her opponent's attempts to fend off even the most basic defensive sorcery ridiculous. As they touched the ground again, she felt a searing pain abruptly engulf her whole right hand, quickly swallowing the rest of her arm. This troll—this *fiend*—had made a snack of her fifth finger on said hand! Rappatsi exploded, and her opponent was slung headfirst into the wall, several desks and chairs following, breaking many of his bones in quick succession. He slumped to the floor, whimpering, grumbling—and surprisingly, strangely stayed put.

So, that was that? *Really?* After such dramatic and smelly foreplay? Rappatsi was now poised for a healthy rumble (she actually needed a good stretch)... *Yeah, this sucks...* she took a better look at the tear, stub of bone, *But it'll be doing what it's supposed to again by tomorrow, at least I think I remember it was about a day for fingers, at least most of it. It won't look pretty, but you can't have everything...*

(This Lab Rat had a pathetically grotesque resemblance to the Bus "Judy-Jude" Rat troll... Rappatsi can't be missing that awful and glaring fact!)

"You should ask before you bite, dickhead. That finger will give you a morbid case of the runs before it'll give you any powers —which it *won't,* by the way."

"But I saw the emails, it was *all over the web.* This month, the whole Centennial moon thing—it's prime time!"

"Well, yeah, but it's not like you just grab *any ol' witch* and chew." Rappatsi peered at him; she didn't appear terribly worked up anymore, almost oddly caring.

"Now that I'm getting a better look at you, a fuller sense of your being, what are you doing still fussing around the school? Yetsi hired you guys, tweaked you up, paid you in units of magical potency, right?" He nodded warily. "The bus gig with Yetsi was a one-and-done—we got what we needed—I'm fine, we got enough of the portal to work—I'm here now."

Rappatsi held up her hand, "But here's the rub: *you shouldn't be.* None of you four should be—they aren't still hanging around the Earth's plane, right?"

Lab Rat coughed, still catching his breath, still trying to catch up to Rappatsi. "How the fuck would I know? I didn't even know there were four of, shit, whatever the hell we're made of."

Rappatsi sharply reverted back to her perturbed self, "No

need for that tone, putzface. You'd know—you'd *feel* him, sense him. Kind of like a vampire thingy."

"I don't 'feel' no guys. So no, he isn't around here." He was gaining his bearings, appearing threatened. His eyes darted about, searching for a way out, or a weapon of something... Rappatsi watched him for a moment more, studying his thoughts.

Rappatsi leered, "Oh Rat, I think you must know by now that *bad things* happen to *bad people*. And why you keep putting your greedy self into these circumstances—or why anyone would *choose* to do that—I suppose I'll never understand."

Lab Rat could still sense the power that Yetsi had bequeathed him, as limited as it was. He knew he'd be no match for her, he just needed to get out of there. He gestured, slinging three desks and a chair directly at her—she sprung cat-like out of the way, and up on the wall. The weapon crashed into the wall, missing her entirely. Rat lunged for the door but with a nod Rappatsi froze him in mid-step. Her voice was more measured, "Well, it makes complete sense you did what you did, but still, why waste the power?" Rappatsi looked bemused, "We can't leave things just like *this*..." she glanced around the lab's space and shelves, "Oh, there, that's perfect. That's what we'll do."

One of the test tubes floated across the room, stopping and staring Rat directly in the face. Rappatsi smiled, and said, "Get in."

"Fuck you."

"Oh dear, Lab Rat, this attitude—you're not doing yourself any favors. But since I *am* the kind-hearted soul I'm purported to be, I'll let you do this yourself: *you're **getting in,** dickhead. And it'll be a whole lot less painful if you do it yourself.*" Rat started sputtering and spitting again, but he knew things were going to be just as Rappatsi wanted them to be. He started to think small—very small...

Rappatsi willed the classroom and lab back into its original slapdash state as she capped and sealed the test tube, Lab Rat wide-eyed and whimpering from his makeshift glass dungeon. She found a space in the back of the specimen rack, in the back of the specimen closet. *He'll be perfectly fine there until, well, he isn't.*

Outside Rappatsi took to the air, heading home, *This 'cleaning house' part of the job sucks anymore... And Yetsi—if you're listening—this isn't reflecting well on your **white-knuckled sisters** at all.*

MRS. STACKHOUSE GLANCED at the clock one last time pretending to no one but herself that it wasn't as late as it was; she did, however, reprimand herself in equal measure. (She had a lovely and patient young family awaiting dinner for her—and she did have *a few more minutes* before that went from being a slight predicament to a real problem.) She stood up, scanned her class-room to be triply-sure she hadn't left any student issues untied, unraveled, or half-baked when she heard a distinct crack of some-thing—thick glass?—in the lab.

Unlocking the shared research space, after the lights flickered on, she was stunned, and a bit horrified (she didn't scare easily), at what was in front of her. The three rows of test tubes her chemistry partner had left by the window to dry, all twenty-four of them, were now each stuffed with a bloodied chicken foot—some with the blood still pooling at the glass base. It was a grotesque bouquet of scales with buds of claws, and the gross reference and threat to her personal history (Latina, Bruja) was precisely clear.

She calmly went back to her desk to get her phone to take a pic, probably many pics. But when she came back into the lab a couple minutes later, the episode was gone. Poof. A magical spic and span. She rushed to the window, looking into the adjoining classroom and saw nothing, no one. She went back to the window and fortunately (though this would probably mean nothing to anyone but her) she found the smallest bud of blood on the glass. She took and saved the pic (more fodder for Casen's next terrorism touchbase), carefully and thoughtfully gathered her things, and headed home.

What Mrs. Stackhouse had not been privy to was the specific reason for the ironic but perverse display of poultry: a certain gaggle of white witches, regardless of Rat's self-serving assault, hadn't appreciated how one of their "tribe" (albeit a gig economy hire, no real magickal affiliation) had been 'tortured'—*There could be no other word for it*—and debased. So, prior to whisking him away, they left a calling card spell that they'd felt was more funny than frightening. (Not to suggest that the *frightening* element wasn't a little bit intentional too.)

Too bad it was wasted on Celia Stackhouse.

No Bones About It

T here was a collective shrug...

Ditan: Those tribes of wannabes, they're always pissed at somebody about something.

Pilar is getting agitated. Again.

Pilar: Well, the Earth is worth getting pissed about. I know *you* aren't so focused on that anymore, but some of us are.

Ditan: But scaring the crap out of people isn't going to help.

Pilar: I don't know if I agree—especially if it's a smart kind of scaring someone... Especially a group. Especially a "tribe" that's got their head up their collective asses whatever the color.

Ditan: You're sounding more like I used to sound every day.

Pilar glares at him. I meant it as a compliment.

Pilar: I know you did. That's the most offensive part.

Ditan had always desperately avoided conflict, regardless on which plane he'd find it; it had worked for and against him in equal shares and he knew it. Pilar found his waffling silly and many times maddening.

Ditan: Lab Rat screwed up. How could he even begin to think he'd overpower Rappatsi? He must have known there would be repercussions.

Pilar: Repercussions, maybe, but left to decompose in some test tube in the back of some closet?

Ditan: Oh, so now the The Coven is right and the Brujeria wrong?

Pilar: Kind of like that.

Ditan's tone became serious.

Ditan: You can't have an agenda—*any* agenda. They'll skewer you.

Pilar: It seems your "they" is quite different from my "they"— and it's hardly an agenda. It was wrong—*all of it.* The graffiti, the test tubes, *everything... Pilar looks at her books, her notes.* The bloody feet was entertaining for what it was, and they got their ya-ya's out so now we should all be back on track. At least that's what I'm hoping.

Ditan: And you think a random, individual fire-bomb approach is the way to go for this Almost-an-Apocalypse?

Pilar: As long as the individual and sometimes *individuals* play *or fight* fair.

They sit thoughtfully for a while. Pilar starts to chuckle—the unremitting irony was absurd. Still unsure, Ditan anxiously does too.

Rappatsi stared at herself in the bathroom mirror: So I slept hard (unusual, given the messiness of everything—so stressful), that is, once I finally got to sleep: there was a raspy, whispery chanting that was gnawing and pervasive—I'm ninety-nine dash nine percent sure I was hearing myth being made real. Disorienting and discomfiting, like so much else these days.

Maybe I'm just too Earth-bound (and probably always will be), but these fancy obscure texts could mean anything, or *everything*, or perhaps, *nothing.* (Well, there is that semi-convention, unspoken rule that it can't mean "nothing"—at this stage of being were expected to rise above such sophomoric behavior.)

Now, there was something I wanted to do... Oh, right!

Speaking of selfish behavior, the boys apparently need a little reminder of their "place" in the larger scheme of, well, *everything*. It shouldn't be surprising that it's primarily my responsibility to make sure all of our striving and searching young souls keep their feet on solid (and especially Earthen) ground—all of that's moving along swimmingly. At least that's the feedback—paranormal and otherwise—that I've been sensing.

(And, by the way-go, if I'm going to forbear a reputation [and I *will*] then I'm over the moon to have finally ascertained it must absolutely mirror the glorious Tlaltecuhtli! [We can lose the human sacrifice bits, though.] When I finally die and grow up, I want to be exactly like her—*both of her*—she *and* he! I know how selfish it sounds, but to be a god of the female persuasion until those opportune moments when *she* decides that a male perspective would be helpful and plugs in a figurative penis wherever and as necessary? How is that not impossibly perfect and awe-inspiring?)

I scrolled the prologue to the hex (in effect, mostly a warning) across the blackened glass; they can't avoid it, the torn creeping script will only add to their dread. They're too cocky (like that pun?). We need to cut them and their male-specific appendages down to a more appropriate size.

I can't attest to the mythic nature or authorship of this curse, but as a solid piece of hoodoo, you can't cast any better (it's topped every list for centuries, one adapts where and as is needed).

This gem always seemed to me to have the hand and wand prints of those wonderfully ironic, characteristically nasty (but a fun kind of nasty) and ancient *Bru* sisters—they've always had some kind of small genius when it comes to a creative hybrid that can laugh and eek out even the most seasoned wicked sisters. It's also a perfect example of revenge craft when revenge craft works the way *you* would expect it to work. (That is, of course, a completely subjective argument—it just depends on which side of the teeth you're on... You'll see what I mean in a moment.) So sorry, boys, just keep your dicks where they're supposed to be and *everyone* comes out on top. (Last pun, I promise.)

To be clear: only chicks can infect chicks. Not that any warlock or witch with a penis would wish this particular fate on any fellow compadre:

> A place that holds wealth,
> So close to the heart,
> Would often forget,
> The other important parts.
> But lest the King feel less,
> No one muttered a word,
> And so he pressed, and twisted the truth till it tore.

> "Just grab it," he said, "take it—it's yours."
> "Whenever you want, whatever the mood..."
> "Your sex is king, and any cock will do."
> The Rod Supreme wandered through the land,
> Grabbing pussy by the handful,
> Laying waste to all but his future wants 'n' plans.

> But then three weeks and a day, fortunately and
>   then soon not,
> The King grabbed June too gruffly,
> So the kitty bit back,
> He leapt back in horror, his hand almost a stub,
> Less kingly by three, with five fingers at two.

> So the woeful King, his favored hand now a paw,
> Could only cum half save of the pleasures he saw.
> His body revolted, backing up his glans to his
>   throat,
> He choked on his orgasm, dying painfully afloat.

So when you see June,
You'll know quickly it's her, apart from her magic,
Her necklace of tarsals, skinned-to-bone meta, and
    more.

(Maybe now we'll finally begin to grasp how savvy our current batch of potentates really are...)

THE POWER SURGE tweaked the lights on just the left side of the mall (if anyone noticed at all). The Boys were finally ensconced at their dark-glassed altar in that dead, generic black box (the defunct Radio Shack, sometimes portal). They read the text for a third time. Greg harrumphed a second time; Bitts and Tom Boy continued to offer no opinion; Tom Boy remained especially inscrutable.

Greg grumbled, "Really charming. I don't get it; I guess that's supposed to scare us?" Greg kept babbling, "Where can I meet a witch like that? At the Caldrons 'R' Us store down the mall?" Greg, already laughing at his joke per usual, was counting how long until the rest of his audience caught up.

"For a Greg joke, that was actually funny," Bitts acknowledged.

Greg nervously persisted, "This is supposed to freak me out, right? It doesn't rhyme—I don't really get it. That's always one of the criteria, right? And—the *real question*—why just fingers? Why didn't she—or *they?*—go for the gusto? Nuts and all?"

Tom Boy looked askance, "Who said they don't? You have to start somewhere."

The threesome digested the comment, given the current social and physiological climate, grasping that teeth could grow *anywhere* and for any reason—perhaps in a very sweet place they'd *least* expect it.

. . .

THE NEXT TIME they were all together, the BTB troubadours made good on their promise: they just as calmly and casually explained their larger purpose behind that ostensibly threatening sheath of black facade they disappeared behind, '*Nothing more than a club within a club...*'

"*Huh?*" burped Sasha, "What the fuck does that mean?" She slumped back into her chair.

Tom Boy frowned, sighed, "Sash, could you take it down a notch? We're explaining it—not that anyone would expect you to be still paying attention to any answer longer than three sentences." Tom Boy (usually the model of tolerance) was reaching yet another tipping point.

Sasha was now more hurt than frustrated; Tom Boy had never talked to her with this tone before. "I hardly think I'm stupid, if that's what—"

"No, Sasha, just impatient. Probably too smart, your brain wants to move too fast sometimes—actually, most of the time." Pugnacious Sasha—words or witchery always at-the-ready—tried to think *slowly* of an answer to prove Tom Boy wrong and herself right.

And as she opened her mouth, nothing came forth. Not that she had any specific sense of what words were missing, but clearly something was awry. *Someone's up to no good and when I find out who it is...*

Tom Boy plucked her thought from her brain before it was even a little bit dry, "You're not going to find out because it's not something *you* can find out. Don't freak. You'll be fine in a sec."

And she was, but she did freak, "*You just did some kind of thought control, didn't you, dickhead?!*"

Tom Boy was undaunted, "Nobody here did anything, Sasha."

"Nobody '*here*'? What does that mean?"

Bitts sat up, "You are kind of being a dickhead, dude. Just talk about the fucking space, please." Bitts slumped back into position. (Everyone shook it out.)

Tom Boy suddenly looked possessed, his face red and full, "So, *here's the shit:* we needed a 'neutral' space. Something so dense with signal and web and net—in the air and not—that it would, in effect, cancel itself out but still maintain the right domain environment—to get through."

Sasha seemed like she'd forgotten the conversation from a few minutes before, "To go where? What do you mean?"

Tom spoke slowly, Bitts mouthed the words with him, "*From Dark to Light.*"

Now she was just being impatient, "That sounds like you're ordering coffee or something." Greg blurted, laughed out, "*Right?*"

"Sasha, c'mon, you know about the Dark Web stuff. You even said you were going to fuss around with something or other." She held Tom Boy's frustrated stare, trying very hard not to give away that yes; she had *indeed* been "fussing" with the Dark Web and had no intention of telling anyone (especially these three bimbos) about it. Sasha confessed, "Oh sorry, I did. I get it... I guess I'm not as into it as I'd thought I'd be." She pulled her laptop closer to her, "But what's 'Light'? *The Light Web?*" She started to laugh but stopped when she quickly realized—given their reactions—she wasn't far from the mark.

"That's mostly right. But what *is* 'Light'?"

Sasha scowled, she hated being tested or taunted. "Filling that void, adding energy where there wasn't any, the opposite of evil. Having hope... Whatever the fuck you want it to be."

The guys glanced surreptitiously at each other, *Anyone want to take this one?* Nothing with Sasha was ever simple.

"Kind of. Not really," a calmer Tom Boy continued patiently, "imagine all that crazy Darkness but with what its *companion,* its *complement* would be. Not its opposite—its *ping* to Big D's *pong*... Anyway, we think we've come in touch with it."

Sasha's face relaxed; she was finally intrigued, actually thinking about Tom Boy's words, watching him from across the mall that other night. "So, why the mall? It's seems counterintuitive."

"Maybe, still don't know. There are a lot of reasons. But the biggest was of all the Dark portals close to here, this one spot was one of the strongest and, surprisingly, least secure." Bitts was barely paying attention at this stage of the explanation, no, correction (both buds are in—he's clearly not worried or interested on any real level). Sasha glimpsed at his screen—just more code shit, *Why's he into coding so much these days?*

Sasha pressed, "So why all the skulking around?"

Tom Boy looked surprised, "Who skulked?"

"You guys—those couple times."

"No such thing. If you want to see skulking, I can show you *skulking!*" Tom chuckled, then Bitts (but not at Tom's comment, some pop-up on his screen...).

"Then why *so freaking casual?* Aren't you afraid that, of—"

"Why not? There's nothing to hide or be afraid of."

Sasha fell silent, then defensive, "Always so goddam cool —*nothing* is ever worth worrying about."

Tom Boy sighed, "And *you* need *everything* to be a battle—*good* versus *bad*. You're afraid of everything, everyone's an enemy until they're not." He said it so matter-of-factly, as if she had just asked him about the weather. And any inklings Seventh Sense-wise were now zilch, at least in respect to her ranking or *Tom Boy cred*.

The words cut quickly, deeply; she watched them pick and tear, somehow helpless to prevent the pain, or problems. *This is how I always do this—this argument convo thing...* So why did it all of a sudden feel so wrong? And not just the words but her whole, um, *process?* (Now awful, weird, and disruptive.)

Sasha captured the moment again, regained her footing. In spite of how shaken she felt, her audience had already moved on to their respective "machinations" (or so they liked to believe).

Sasha opened her laptop and stared at the screen, pretending to be fussing on something. She desperately needed to think about things—she'd never felt this unsure of herself.

When the Going Gets Tough, the Tough Get More Tough

❧❀❧

S asha was impatient and getting pissy. She'd been standing there like a dunderhead for the last ten minutes because "the boys" had once again "forgotten" to give her their new entry code. She could have easily crafted her way through but decided it wasn't worth the whining. Tom Boy suddenly popped into place disconcerting Sasha, *Some more 'different' from him...* They entered the Black Box.

Tom Boy had almost a sentimental look on his face (also weird for him—especially lately). He was transfixed by the glass altar—their reflections were exact, mirror-like. Then, completely randomly, he asked her if she could remember that one conversation from maybe several months ago...

Sasha had been making her point about spell-crafting hiding in plain sight, "So here's one: the clicking the heels shit really does work."

"It *so does not.*"

"You're so sure..."

Tom Boy shook his head, "Well shit, that's all that movie bullshit. Especially in 1930-whatever."

"Actually that's why they had to rely on us. Well, *magic* at least."

Tom Boy took a second to break it down, *She's starting to make sense. A strange kind of sense, but still…*

Sasha wasn't sure what Tom would do with her main point; he was a little too sentimental. Especially for (even these days) a boy.

Sasha offered, "The heels and clicking and stuff, you know?"

"Yeah, I love that. I know I'm a little weird that way."

"Nah, I don't think it's weird. Just misguided."

Tom Boy looked at her, "Huh?"

"Well, the click doesn't always take you *home*…"

He frowned. "Well, where the hell else would it take you?"

Sash grinned. (She actually *preferred* this concept; more *inclusive*.)

She loved her notion, "Nope, it takes you where you're **supposed** to be… Which may or *may not be* home—or some iteration therein."

Tom's frown dug deeper into his brain. *Not liking this. Again. What is it with Sasha? Always so negative.*

"I'm not always negative. Not even a little bit. Just realistic."

"So what? It'll take me to India to feed the poor?"

"If that's what's going to make things better for you."

Their shiny eight-month-younger selves stopped talking to them. Tom Boy slowly turned away from the glass. "Have no idea where that convo came from, or why…" He put the HDMI cable up. Sasha poked, "You're such a liar. I don't remember it that way at all." She smiled and looked carefully at Tom Boy. (She was kidding, of course, *It was exactly as I remembered it…*)

Sasha looked at the cable as it grabbed as much information and energy as it could, "Why do you need that? *More hardware?*" She looked out the window, still not a blip of Greg anywhere, real or digitized. "Is that going to make the truth more real?"

Tom Boy slumped laughing in a chair, his whole demeanor

flip-flopping, "You're so fucking snarky, I guess you think that's funny—W's these days might respect or even *like* you for it."

"I could give a shit if anyone actually *likes* me."

Then Tom Boy suddenly looked hurt, defensive. "You know during that entire 'home' convo? I wanted you to like me *so badly.*" He stood up, "And I *so* didn't want to do it any other way than *au naturale*—no artificial ingredients. Nothing crafty."

Sasha was laughing, "That's so wacky—*me too!* Except..."

"What?"

"I did potion you up—just a little bit. Actually, I started and then made myself stop." (She didn't stop.)

They abruptly stopped talking, looked hard at each other.

Tom said, "And now—now I'm having a hard time trying to remember why I even started wanting you to like me."

"You fucker. You mean you *don't* like me?"

"Not all the time."

Sasha scowled and willed the shard of red wand that was on the table, spear-like, into the deteriorating (etched) chant on the glass. (It looked like a sci-fi PlayStation version of "The Sword in the Stone.") Tom Boy remained indifferent. She slowly exhaled, then muttered, "Yeah, sometimes I don't like me either."

Tom Boy looked up, "Well, that can suck. Know that one too."

Sasha stood up and looked at her reflection in the glass wall again; there was this strange blend of wistfulness and pride. Tom Boy considered this new Sasha "version 2.1": one that seemed older, a bit wiser, but somehow younger too—vital, all in-the-moment.

She winked, "Why would two gorgeous, innately talented, mostly brilliant, gifted witches give a hairy rat's butt about what *anyone* thinks? Validation can be a mother-f'er."

Tom winked back, "Maybe because they're overbearing buttheads that only think of themselves the other *half* of the time?"

"I've never seen you be any of those things—though lately..."

Tom Boy grinned with an edge, "That's because I *used* to care what people think."

Something sparked and raced up the inside of the glass—it avowed them both, their pasts and their present.

———————— •◦◦◦◦◦ ◦◦◦◦◦• ————————

"THEY CALLED ME 'BIG C,' and you'll never figure out why, so don't stress your pretty little brains even trying to." She didn't finish the explanation. Big C was strikingly small, diminutive, especially given the name—but more especially for a god.

Big C was animated and aggressive, hands on hips, stalked the walls and the courtyard as if she was considering buying the place, *In some regards, that's not too far from the truth*... Then she was eyeing the three doors to the cafeteria as if her final grand prize was hidden behind one of them. (Strange and somewhat disconcerting behavior for yet *another* new person that no one except The Sisters considered to be actually *new*.) They were keenly aware of some of the Tricentennial godlore and myths that blew wide open every manner of portal and with all kinds of crap—immigration was a mess, *anyone* could go *anywhere*. But still there was nothing godlike about Big C, not even demigodlike.

Tip was passing through the courtyard and could sense Sasha's anxiety (or probably frustration). She found Sasha, her brow crossed, biting her lip; this small square person was basically shouting at her sister.

Tip purposefully walked into them (hopefully diffusing whatever), "Hey, Sasha, saw you and wanted to ask you something. Hi, I'm—"

Big C nodded curtly, and kept talking, "And I'm not, for all intents and purposes. I've absolutely zero interest in any of that demigod crap. I mean if they like you, they like you. And if they don't—you're screwed. They warn you about wanting bigger things but that's never stopped..." Big C kept talking, kept scanning the cafeteria. She now seemed oblivious to both girls; ranting about her brief stint as a god, planning something or other, then onto what the etheric plane did or wouldn't do, etc., etc.

While Tip tried to direct the conversation (if you could call it that) her way, Sasha mentally ran some situational analytics: *firstly, got to tell Ezra about this. She mentioned this year—especially these couple months—could be cosmologically messy...*

Sasha continued to observe, take in as many specifics as she could. If Big C was all that she seemed to suggest, how would anyone ever deduce that you're chatting up some entity that's a god (or some archetypal myth) come to physical life, or just some slightly older chunkier (probably held back?) new chick at the school? Ezra had started to warn her about the pieces and parts of what might or might not be happening now, but she'd been intentionally vague too (Aunt Ezra always left herself a way out), *Just keep in mind there could be all kinds of cosmic juju trash raining from every which plane—some of it can even walk and talk.*

Sasha caught the end of Tip's excusing them as efficiently as she could, "Sorry, Big C... What's your next class?"

"Something or other. Nothing terribly compelling."

This is friggin' high school, dude, not some trade fair.

The twins nodded and turned to go back inside; Big C pecked at her phone, kept looking up and around as if one cloud versus the other would give her more bars.

Sasha leaned in, "Can you spare ten minutes of your lunch?"

Tip jogged ahead, "You read my mind..."

They fell into the library and attacked the school's National Archives subscription—the search finished way too quickly. Sasha said, "That's bizarre. Shouldn't be that easy—it's not like she's Jennifer Lopez or Kiernan Shipka."

Tip clicked open and unrolled the illustration. (She'd Wiki'd it after all.) "That's her! *That's Big C!*" The name *Constantina* and her vast personal history seemed barely connected, but still possible. It was the eyes, the nose...

Sasha slapped at the image, "No way! No possible way. She's too big for fucking Frenchtown!" She nodded, "But what the hell? I know I keep saying this—*why here?*"

Tip tipped her laptop closed, "Well, at this stage, why *not?*"

(It did seem that had to be one of the weakest but still one of the most logical rationales: *nobody's really looking so let's see what I can get away with...* As if.)

ANTONIA GRUNTED, "Oh, now she's 'Big C'—interesting... Fucking ambulance chaser." The irony was strange, especially from their mother, but they clearly got the point. Actually, the fact that Antonia was responding on any level was shocking both of them. It felt as if they'd been living with a changeling for these last years, and the real Antonia finally resurfaced from some nearby parallel reality, or shed her final skin (or was too hungover that she actually *forgot* to get buzzed and could actually think clearly on a Wednesday morning)—she looked at them thoughtfully, deliberately.

Sasha sighed, "You don't even know who we're talking about. Or want to know."

Antonia measured her answer, "No, *you* don't know who you're talking about."

Tip came to Sasha's defense, "She probably never really *existed* in this century, let alone in this part of the world."

"That's so not the point." Antonia now appeared irritated.

Huh?

"Then what is the point?" Both girls felt supremely confident they'd finally caught their mother in some manufactured or fried synapse falsehood; Antonia was smarter than most functioning addicts—she'd actually only argue when she knew she'd win.

"Big C, Constantina—whatever name she's preferring now— she's only in it for the game, and the humiliation, of everyone else. The power grab, the opportunities around here wouldn't interest her. Too much work, everything's too piecemeal."

"So what's any of that have to with chasing ambulances?"

"Nothing, sort of. I'm just saying wherever there's an illegitimate opportunity, she'd know about it... Even got to be an Ubermensch at one stage—I don't know who you have to fuck on Mt. Olympus to get that done, but she completely squandered it. I'll bet you she's already blown town." The twins knew this particular raspy tone and manner too well (it didn't please them); Antonia looked at the clock, she grinned, "God, that took a lot out of me."

They were well-trained and knew not to spend any real concern or effort fretting about yet another *hour of happy before the happy hour,* they were still struck by their mother's response—her very assured response—about Big C. (Apparently a blip, but a rather important blip.)

————————

SASHA FOUND Tip in her favorite chair out front, wrapped twice in as many sweaters. "I didn't bother checking—are they talking yet?"

"Dunno."

"Are they screwing yet?" Sasha half-joked.

"Of course."

They barely snickered at their recurring lame quip.

"Actually, they were talking—and even before screwing—believe it or not. They're getting better at this fighting and making up thing every time—or maybe we're just getting used to it?" Tip squeezed herself tighter; Sput responded in kind.

"That's my guess."

"Which?"

Sasha shrugged. "Does it really matter?"

Tip threw a bolt of something or other off the tip of her right hand, pistol-like, at the dead tendril of the almost-brown plant hanging across the porch. It landed with a surprising thud. They jumped, laughed.

"*That* was weird. Didn't look like it would be that heavy..."

Tip nodded, "Like so much of this crap."

Sasha sat up, "Oh shit, wanted to ask you, did you see Rapp's Coven text?"

"Yeah, about the names at the basketball game that night—half of them probably real, semi-ancient coven-y stuff. Half of them *whomevers*... She did confirm it was all Coven shit though, finally. Silly bitches. Like, what was that supposed to do? Scare away the visiting team?" Tip chuckled.

Sasha smiled, "Oh, didn't see that last part—it was *all* Coven? That's interesting."

"You really think so? Complete silliness in my book," Sasha sighed, slumped back into the lounge.

Tip muttered, "Yeah, sure took her time on that one."

Sasha shrugged, "Like everything, *everyone else* these days."

Tip leaned back, thoughtfully peered at Sasha's moon-tinged profile, "You know you're awfully pretty, Sister Sasha. Has anyone ever told you that?" She sneaked her toes and feet under Sasha's thigh to keep them warm.

Sasha smirked, "Why no—you're quite gorgeous yourself, just to mention it. In that Earthy, erudite, *Game of Thrones* kind of way."

Tip twinkled, grinned, "So since sex is one of our talking points tonight, I have an announcement."

"It is? And you do?"

"Yes, I'm *not* going to have it. And I'm *not going to have it* with Tom Boy."

Sasha sighed, "See, I always knew you were smarter than me. Or at least more intuitive."

Tip sat straight up, "I knew it! I knew you couldn't keep it from me *forever!*" Tip laughed. "Okay, *share*..."

Sasha pursed her lips, "Sorry, I should be more specific: it was a *form* of sex, probably not the type you're anticipating... It was more of a 'mind fuck' than anything else—and again, *not* the type you're probably thinking of."

Tip winced, "'Mind fuck' is usually not a good thing, witch."

Sasha hedged, "Yeah, *usually*."

Tip affectionately pushed her feet out under her sister, "Bitch! *Talk!*"

Sasha was surprisingly bashful, "Tom Boy was horny. I was horny. We were *all* horny that night in Frenchtown, three months ago, regardless of your magical persuasion or abilities. It was inescapable: that Circadian Fertility event made everyone nuts, whichever plane you happened to be on—astral, etheric, Homeric... That's a joke, by the way."

Tip interrupted, "I don't remember this at all—didn't make me nuts."

Sasha snickered, "You were probably doing one of your *moon walks* or something... It was an *either-or* cycle that weekend. You're always an 'or.'"

"Screw you."

"*Yeah, baby!*" Sasha faux-leered. (Another feeble attempt at humor.)

Tip was rapidly losing interest; she didn't need yet another roundabout admonition about how ineffective she could be with the (mostly) male of the species.

Then Sasha finally elaborated...

Tom Boy was trying—*really trying*... Why was this beginning to feel more like a casual favor for Sasha as opposed to their first sexual *liaison*? He pressed, "What? Why?"

Tommy, c'mon, you told me you liked 'talking'... But Tom was sure he heard whining... Yep, sure of it—*what the hell is she doing?*

"Yeah, when Scarlett Johansson is doing it. And in a *movie*..."

Putz. If you felt that way, then why didn't you say so to begin with?

"Because I don't want to have sex—or whatever it is we're doing—with Scarlett Johansson. I want to with you."

Well, that's a funny way of showing it.

Almost at a breaking point for Tom: "No, *this* is a *funny way of showing it...*"

No response.

Tom breathed out, "Tell me *again* why we're not even in the *same room* together—the same *house together?*"

Still nothing. "Hello?"

Suddenly, strangely (or perhaps not so much), Tom Boy could now *hear and **feel*** the emotion in Sasha's thoughts, *Because, well, it's —I told you—an experiment. This major spell I found. I was curious and, well, you're the only boy that would do this with me. Or that I would want to.*

"That's the main reason now? Just process of elimination? Except there wasn't anyone *else* to eliminate?"

Even her breathing was now clear in his mind, synching with his.

Tom, no, c'mon, maybe not the two things together, but we talked about it... I want to have sex with you. Any kind. All of it, the "big one," the "first one," whatever you want. But this is just one part.

"One part of what?" Tom waited, listened, suddenly the strangeness was becoming enticing. He could actually *feel* her presence; it seemed she was *everywhere*. She didn't say anything more.

Tom smiled. Sweet. *Sweet, smart witch...* "Okay, I'm in, I guess. We've gotten this far. Just do whatever it is you're trying to do."

You're killing me... Sasha's smile matched Tom's—he could *see* that now too.

Tom put his hand in the air, "Let's just slow down. And maybe, first, just be quiet... Together."

Sasha stopped talking, she was sitting there eyes closed, smiling, blissful...

TIP POKED and soured the moment, "So, that's it?"

Sasha bobbed her head *yes.*

"Um, you *know* that's not sex, right?" (Tip was slightly afraid of Sasha's answer; maybe she'd already evolved to some state-of-the-art witch that didn't need men for *anything,* practically *godlike!*)

"Don't be a dunderhead, it's so way better than any icky bodily thing: the perfect *Mind Fuck*, a veritable Tom Boy fender-bender, and three times over."

"I only counted two."

"Whatever." (Sasha had anticipated Tip's lack of enthusiasm.)

And yet, Sasha was mostly smiling, still clearly sated; Tip was considering the evidence but had already determined that in spite of Sasha's boasting (such as it was), they were still on fairly equal ground as far as their virginity—figuratively and literally—was concerned.

The door to their parents' bedroom door opened and slammed shut; they looked blankly at each other. Tip sighed, "Tom Dad's on a couch again—it's going to be another long night."

Sasha quipped, "For him, anyway."

THERE WAS a red envelope on Celia Stackhouse's desk when she arrived that morning, *How the hell—I always lock that door...* It was wet (which was weird), as if someone had just dipped it in red paint. (It was too red-red to be blood.)

She gingerly picked and pulled at it—but her fingers stayed clean, paint-less. A little damp, at most... Way odd. And then— even odder—her finger slipped through it as if she was trying on a ring that was too large. In that next moment, she further discovered she wasn't truly *holding* the envelope—there was some invisible skin or "force field" that was containing it.

She impulsively tore at its lip, and it dissolved-spun into its hologram heart. Some text on translucent parchment with some visual, possibly video, floated eye-to-eye. Celia saw immediately, understood in that moment what this makeshift timeline and its content were proving forth: between the graffiti translations and the substitute bus drivers' possessed tattoos and zombie students to acid-laced water fountains (*How the shit did I miss that one?*)—she would have to really study it, but at first glimpse it seemed overwhelmingly (and bizarrely) comprehensive. *Could this be the handiwork of my partner in crime, Pearl Martins? How did she get this shit—maybe "crime" is more accurate than it should be?* Of course, Pearl had to have this same information; Celia would study it and *then* review with her at length. This was too good to be true. (And there wasn't a shred of hyperbole in her thought.)

Then she remembered Pearl's overexcited promise: she didn't have information, but she believed she knew someone that could get (or "dig up," as required) most of the (albeit broad stroke) particulars. The incredibly realistic projection—all ten pages—hovered patiently in front of her, and she almost swallowed the report's contents, its evidence, whole. It was almost as unbelievable as the first ten pages of the *National Enquirer* (but then again, she had always craved the *National Enquirer*).

So, now it was clear: two different networks (weird word, but it made sense here, with her mostly digital evidence and its two competing agendas). They had one common end goal, however: *to dominate the other. White magic* versus *brown magic...* But *which witch is which?*

(So, what else is new?)

She collapsed back in her chair; she had been basically feeling okay, managing to cope with yet another semi-hysterical verging on hyper-hysterical week, and now this bombshell—just enough to permanently exorcise any form of okay-ness. She wasn't categorically worried—she refused to be—she would figure things out as she always had.

———— 〰 〰 ————

THE SURREAL STATUS quo finally seemed to have gotten any last-thought bugaboos out of its system—things had been relatively staid for at least a week. People, halflings, and W's were still bouncing off the walls and each other. (Tell me something I *don't* know!)

There was one thing (though certainly not life-threatening), Rapp had been getting a little too full of herself (a case of *Earth People Are Easy* Syndrome or whatever you're comfortable calling it). It was Mara's last-moment decision to have a birthday something-or-other at Town Bowl; Tip graciously did all the inviting and social legwork, and Mara's aunt treated her to one of their party rooms in that nasty, kind of dank area downstairs. It wasn't concerning—there was food, Mara's various forms of besties, and everyone by this time was clearly in dire need of some unadulterated fun.

Rappatsi swaggered into the room and the conversation; forever-fickle Sasha resented this from the first moment for a couple reasons: a) this was not Rappatsi's convo to swagger into, and b) Rappatsi never swaggered—or (at least) she *shouldn't* swagger. (Not a good look; I don't care what Generation Alphabet you're leaning toward.) Rappatsi saw Sasha staring—correction —*glaring* at her, *What the Judas did she do to herself?* (Rapp never wore a stitch of makeup—she didn't really have to...) *It's like she's growing younger instead of older...* Sasha decided to ignore the whole situation, close her eyes, count to five, and maybe it would all go away.

But when she opened her eyes, Rappatsi was not only still there but bizarrely even younger looking, or more specifically she was (for lack of a better word) "moister." Now the room too suddenly felt very humid; Sasha glanced around and yup, the way everyone else was shifting and scratching, they were uncomfortable too (though probably not for the same reasons). A drop of water stung her forehead (surprise more than anything else).

Why is there water on the floor? Tip looked at Sasha who looked again at Tip. Too much happening all at once, but so what? Deal with it. Rapp seemed like she was stoned or something, *maybe too much "cold medicine" **again**? (I don't know how many times we're supposed to believe that.)* Tip looked up and around again—it was so damp everywhere... Rapp slid her way around Tip, almost running into her. Tip noticed the back of her neck; it was swollen and reddish, as if Rapp might be sick, the start of the flu. None of Mara's other friends appeared to mind Rapp's newfound brazenness; they actually were enjoying it. Sasha was following Tip's eyes and then gestured after she saw Tip's look of concern.

Tip said, "Rapp, you wanna sit down or something? You look woozy. Maybe some water?"

Glancing up then down, Rappatsi deadpanned, "You think I *need water?*" A strange giggle, a quick nervous look and glance around the room. Both Tip and Sasha could sense Rappatsi's uncharacteristic fear. *You felt it too, right Tip?* She nodded quickly, now nervous herself. *What was going on?* This was going to and supposed to be fun just a few seconds ago.

Tara, the friend of a friend of a friend, who had tweeted her way into this (at least in her mind) prestige gathering decided to make her presence felt, and elbowed—with a slow right and then quick left hook—her ego next to Rappatsi, who was getting exponentially loonier by the minute. "Why are you dissing my sister?" Sasha grabbed a hold of Rapp, who was tilting her way; water was puddling in random spots around the floor, where it was coming from wasn't clear.

Tip got right up in Tara's face and barked, "Dissing *your* '*sister*'?! Where are you talking?"

"Do you mean, '*What* am I saying?'" Tara flustered.

"Where are you coming from? You haven't said two words to Rapp. Like never, ever."

"I don't have to. Rapp knows where I'm coming from." Tara glanced at Rapp, whose eyes looked like the cherries or coins of a slot machine dial, trying to realign. Sasha was about to put her finger through Tara's claim when a big drop of water on her fore-head stopped the thought midstream. It drooled down around the corner of her eye. She looked up, Rapp looked at her, slurred, "Are you upset, honey?" She barely pushed the words passed her lips. Sasha heard her but not really—she was fixated on the ceiling, *You'd think this was a sauna, except there's no freaking heat...* Two more drops pelted the top of her head. Rappatsi stumbled backward still trying to stabilize her everything, her right foot splashing the now two inches of water across the ankles, some exposed some not, of her friends. Tara jumped on to her toes, shaking her ankle and the five bracelets around it, "Rapp, watch it! I just bought these."

Now Sasha peered at Rappatsi, "This is supposed to be a party —but *your party?*"

Rappatsi stumbled into conversation, "I feel fine," somehow managing to slur the word "fine." "Dunno why all of you are looking at me like that." Her heavy lids put the period on that sentence. Tip frowned, "Like what, Rapp?"

"Like your—" Rapp grimaced.

Tip scowled, "Like I'm *what?*"

Rapp struggled, she was resisting something, trying to stay focused. Her slap-happy grin was gone, "*Oshun...*"

Sasha flinched, she pressed Tip, "Is that what's making your Spidey senses antsy?"

"Probably-maybe. What's 'oh shoon'?"

A very anxious Sasha whispered, "Not what—*who...*"

The Sisters then frantically peered at the almost-three inches of water at their feet—Tip shot Sasha a mind bump, *Okay, extra-worried, maybe even scared now! You?* Sasha immediately nodded. They both stood up and back, started to let go of Rappatsi. In that second her eyes shut, her body elongated as if two cords, one at the crown of her head and the other at her heels, were yanked into some known position. She was pulled just above the water surface, that invisible cord forcing her in place.

Tip noticed first: the water no longer was water-like. Still clear and clean, but now the consistency of honey—smooth, careful, sensual. Sasha noticed everyone else: dazed like Rapp, blissfully confused. She'd been wanting to do it since Tara arrived, but now had a reason to and she smacked her upside her ear—no response, just a bigger grin. Apparently, Sasha and Tip were (once again) immune to whatever was going on; Sasha said frantically, "I think we've got to get out of here, Tip..."

A moment later the water-honey on the walls pushed out, bowled and squared in around the five young women encircling them from top, bottom, and every side. Sasha was already plowing through the almost knee-deep water and fell into the door, reaching the knob... She slid off it, losing her balance, tried again —she couldn't even grip it. *Shit*... This was a ton of crazy, clear, non-smelling most probably deadly *who-knows-and-who-the-fuck-cares!*

The Sisters' panic turned to horror when they saw that Rappatsi was quickly being subsumed by the water's surface—she appeared blissfully ignorant. "*Rapp!!*" Tip roared but to no effect; the viscous surface around them vibrated briefly then continued its hungry crawl. A gelatin headdress creeped down around Rappatsi's ears and eyes... *She'll drown, Tip! I know, Sasha—but what can we, anyone, do?*

The water box kissed the last spot of dry ceiling with the five girls suspended in their liquid death trap. Tip and Sasha were necessarily terrified; the other girls horrifically, blissfully oblivious to their fate. In that next pulse, Tip sensed Rappatsi, saw her twitch, her eyes now wide and lucid. She fixed on Rappatsi's face, waiting for the slightest shift or nod or *something* as to what to do next... Tip caught Sasha's eye, *Yes! I heard her too!*

There was nothing the tiniest bit nod-like about the sudden and violent spinning of not just Rappatsi's head but her entire body as it was—as if by the same invisible cord—being yanked down toward the floor. The event was overwhelming: this "cord" was somehow being pulled through an equally invisible hole in the floor where, when Rapp's pointed feet made contact, tore into the stone, drilling a hole black and wide. In the next moment, Rappatsi rocketed back up to the water's surface as the makeshift drain twisted the water away from the walls and ceiling; the more the water churned, the less viscous, and more water-like it became. The Sisters thrust their heads above the surface, gasping for air where they could; the other girls were startled awake, hungrily sucking at the oxygen. The floor's puncture collapsed out becoming larger, the spinning water rapidly becoming a whirlpool; the girls quickly realized they had to grab onto the nearest fixed object lest they get sucked into some aquatic netherworld. (This has been enough birthday party fun for one night, thanks anyway, *Oshun*-whoever-you-are...)

As their feet got close to the floor, the water seemed to recon- sider its violent intentions, acknowledging defeat as it emptied from the room. The last gurgle was best described as a loud burp; Rappatsi, wide-eyed and laughing, commented, "What a big baby! All bark, no bite." She glanced around the room that, surprisingly, didn't look a whole lot different than when the whole almost-cata- strophe began (apart from rather dramatic gash in floor). Rappatsi added, "Now *that's* a birthday celebration! Certainly makes you appreciate your next year of living, doesn't it?"

Sasha was mostly used to Rappatsi's sometimes strange and random comments, but couldn't let these pass, "Are you fucking nuts?! We almost died!"

"Uh-huh." Rappatsi was still flippant, "'Almost' being the oper- ative word."

Tip sank to the floor, "I don't believe you sometimes, Rapp. I really don't."

Tara was already blathering about how "fucking rad" the party was, and birthday girl Mara still had that pasted-on smile and was still bumping into things, but altogether seemed like she'd actually (the gods only know how) enjoyed herself. And in that next moment, Tara was yelling at her phone because it was too wet to text! (Life can *occasionally* be just one pain in the ass after another —don't you find?)

Rappatsi remained undaunted. "That's fine. You can thank Oshun the next time we happen to run into her." Rappatsi laughed out loud again, "Or—at the very least—buy Luis a coffee or a pretzel this week sometime..." What exactly Oshun or (perhaps slightly more rationally) even Luis had to do with wishing Mara another happy year remained yet another example of Rappatsi's obtuse commentary—the girls simply were thrilled to hear Lizzo playing upstairs and bolted hence. They bowled three mostly sloppy games, and all was once again right and upright (and mostly dry) in their worlds.

Tip sat next to her twin and tossed out the understatement of the year (if not the last few years), "Most friends don't have to save their friends' lives as some sort of test of their friendship, ya know."

Sasha scowled, her face twisting, "Is that comment pointed in *my direction,* for some reason?" She grabbed the Coke they were sharing from Tip's hand, "It's not like you've been Miss Rapp Cheerleader this last week or so either?"

"No shit, but come on, she's been a total arrogant pain for like the last week ever since that Big C ex-god-witch came and went, and, since we just had our lives flash before our eyes—I might as well just come out with it: you haven't been the poster child for underwitch decorum since, like, *forever...* Screaming from the desktops in Mr. Clarke's class from what I heard?"

Sasha was already too overwhelmed and mentally exhausted to express how angry she was—she was struggling, "Was 'decorum' a vocab word this week, bitch?"

Tip said coyly, "Maybe," then she shrugged, "but it works. And perfectly."

Then Tip became serious, "She knows we know about her... She also knows we don't know any more than we do—and that she's observing us as much as we are her." She finished the Coke, "So you're leading by example, Glinda, whether you—*or we*—like it or not."

Sasha felt bewildered, but at the same time knew her sister was right. "Well, what does she think we're 'leading'?"

Tip was finally irritated (she was a tad bit water-logged too, remember), "*How the fuck would I know?* You're the preternaturally gifted one; I'm just the hippy-dippy intuitive wanna-be witch."

Sasha slowly regained composure, her breath, her everything —that was her first experience that had coerced (permitted? allowed?) her outside of her very ingrained ego, precocious spell-crafting, chronic megalomania, etc. (insert appropriate obsessive-compulsive, over-bright underwitch adjective here).

Sasha looked up and around and then, lastly, maybe because she couldn't find some discreet way of letting go, a way "out," an edge to tug or tear at, she dematerialized and plopped herself upstairs away from everyone, hovering above the overlit laneways that appeared and sounded punishing. She was keenly aware there was suddenly no more grey, nothing that gave her an *angle*, a way to argue or bewitch her way out of this dilemma. (She was usually excellent at convincing or talking herself into *anything*.)

Rappatsi had saved her life, and the others' lives as a matter of course—would she have done (or even be able to do) the same? Just as selflessly? Just as *Well that was a trip—when's cake?*-casually? She didn't have a clue, but her best guess was if she did, she wouldn't have floated there, terrified, waiting for Rapp to do what *'Rapp always does...'* (Maybe Rappatsi did deserve a couple snaps after all.) Sasha hated feeling sorry for herself more than anything —*Screw you, you silly witch...* She resurfaced downstairs between Rappatsi and Tip.

Tip whispered at Sasha, "So who the freak is Oshun anyway?"

Sasha muttered, "Oh, only one of the southern hemisphere's major gods who manages many of the Earth's natural elements in her free time—you know, after she drops off her hundred-plus demigods at daycare... It's just a twenty-minute drive to the Orifice." (Sasha's "abrasive" humor had clearly survived unscathed.)

CONSTANCE SLAPS the desk in front of her—she couldn't choose the words to even start the argument.

Constance glares at Pilar: Why did you let her get away with that?

Pilar: Get away with what?! And "I" had just as much to do *with it or not* as you did, you white ancient bitch-of-a-witch or whatever you're trying to become.

Constance demands: Did you drop another of your "hints" to Oshun?!

Pilar puffs out her chest: And what if I did? More info is always better than less. And just because you're jealous of Rappatsi's success.

Constance explodes: You godless cunt! How dare you accuse me of—

Pilar doesn't flinch: What?! Trying to steal the life of another—

Abyssinia intercedes, flying directly between their venom: Girls, Women, Ancients, get a grip! *What* just happened?

Constance: Nothing that hasn't been happening for hundreds of years or eons probably!

Pilar: Oh, don't listen to it! I'm so tired of this self-serving, sniveling, too-white bag of boney shit. Nothing is ever right, and never will be ever again according to that witch.

The air had slowed, the light waned—Abyssinia knows this (whatever "this" is) isn't healthy or right.

Abyssinia: Stop it. They're not happy; we're supposed to be better than this. That's part of the reason we're here.

Pilar: I know that. But I can't ignore or pretend bad shit away, and I know that's part of the deal too.

They waited for Constance's answer, and when none came they turned to see just her chimera remaining (a placeholder of a sort); Constance had removed herself temporarily to what could best be described as "the quiet room."

Abyssinia: What happened? This is new. At least to me.

Pilar didn't express emotion either way: She's gone to one of a couple places—she did the right thing. It's a big deal; I only remember it happening here once before.

Abyssinia: Will she be back?

Pilar: As I understand it, there's no way of knowing. Even she doesn't really *know* her fate. *Then Pilar smiles wanly,* But she did the smarter thing by making that hard first decision herself.

CONSTANCE FOUND the same corner that she'd discovered when she'd "escaped" before—she'd fortunately been a bit more discreet about her intentions that last time. She was painfully aware of how *she appeared* to the others and—it was inescapable—the Powers That Be. And the difficult truth was they weren't wrong, their resentment and frustration was completely warranted, *I'm ridiculous sometimes—many times!—and I just can't see through to prevent it. It feels like some kind of involuntary reflex that I've not even a shred of control, and in the next moment there's all of these agonizing thoughts and words splayed all over the table, or the room, hanging anxiously from some other demigod's surprise or indignation.*

But the one thing, the one fairly recent constant, that unnerved Constance for better *and* worse was a *memory*—a memory where there *wasn't supposed to be any* (as you're probably very aware at this stage...). It was persistent and unchanging, so Constance had to believe—in spite of what appearance memories can assume if they seem to happen—that it was, or had been, *very real.* The most consistently frustrating aspect was the players were also persistent—*persistently anonymous.* Their role or function, however, was not: the *conduit* is to "sense" and to ensure that all the parts, pieces, and players are in their exact place and function so "things" go forward efficiently, smoothly, and primarily "as intended." (It's a big deal. And a big job.)

Constance had recently come to believe that Rappatsi had inherited this fairly coveted role but was, in Constance's not-especially-humble opinion, *"really screwing, no, fucking it up..."* But therein was her conundrum: how could she comment on an experience that shouldn't exist? Had she worn the *conduit* cape at one point? And how could she defend her position with something that was categorically illegal (her *memory*, I mean...). Poor Constance, old Constance.

Maybe the gods allowed her this insight to *promote her?* (Let's see how she'll rise to the occasion—she's always been a *diamond in the rough.*) Or was it precisely the opposite: to catch her "in the act," she could self-convict (so much easier; she could be disintegrated in a flash—*painless!*). But the foremost concern, at this moment, was there was no way to absolutely *confirm* Rappatsi was performing as poorly as Constance believed she was! It was a true enigma (and perfectly suited to someone with Constance's completely self-possessed disposition).

She decided to have another cigarette and think about it further after that, *Life—whatever plane you're on—is just one goddam test after another.*

ABYSSINIA PERUSED the space and the demigods in it; everyone was there except Constance (obviously): This is surreal, I haven't experienced anything like this before now—so somber, a purgatory *within* a purgatory... And I'm getting some sense of—what's the adage? *—the calm before the storm?* The disjointedness seems pervasive (up, down, everywhere) and so does the paranoia. (I'm picking on demigods and W's alike.) Completely undiscriminating... It seems equally surreal that as much as I seem to understand the problems, I don't know what to do about them. Not at all.

It has to be hard trying to put all your metaphysical ducks in a row to begin with but almost impossible if you don't have your feet on the ground (no word- or metaphor-play intended!). Rappatsi's "status report" was categorically late, but it wasn't as if anybody on a higher plane had given her a specific time—that would be impractical, to say the least.

Rappatsi, after all, is the *go-between*, that do-or-die role of *mystical conduit.* She's the channel that ensures all the parts are where they need to be before the next cataclysmic shift. I've learned it's typically when some being or entity is transitioning from something to something else, or someplace to someplace else, or it could be some cosmic calendar hoo-ha (but it would have to be some major hoo-ha if there's a "Rappatsi" involved). And as to who or where or what, that's the fodder of entities far more significant and influential than any of us.

AN HOUR or maybe a day later, the emptiness becomes almost too painful... Constance laments: I'm underused and overpaid (that's a joke, for your information), and I'm being moved to yet another "project"—don't ask, I can just tell... An enterprise in the making, I'm sure of it. (Yes, that was another anemic stab at humor.) And why yet another set of seemingly unnecessary quotes around another maybe irrelevant word? Because there is no specific notice or conversation—no truly fair way of discovering how ineffective you were, just a very hard-to-ignore "gut feeling." It appears nobody has or wants to put the energy into conversation anymore—apparently the way of the future.

(So I never breathed a word, not a dab of "expressed concern" about Rappatsi—I swallowed the *memory* whole... Was it the right thing to do? Did I live through a cycle as a conduit long ago? Is that why I had—*am having*—such a visceral reaction? *Maybe I actually was "promoted" at some point, only to be demoted just as quickly...?*)

Or maybe it's time for yet another "lateral promotion" (as we used to call it when you've failed without apparently failing). I'll walk through one of these doors and only know it's all changed and *completely new again* suddenly, and that's just fine because it's how it's always been. I don't believe I'll ever have any contact with any of you again, not because I wouldn't want that, but if I ever actually do find myself brushing cotton sand from my feet, breathing gardenia air, you'll be—all of *this* will be—the very last thing I'll want to think about.

So, um, shit, I digress. And it was a really elaborate and unhinged digression... And sorry for any inconvenience (but it's not as if Rapp is waiting on *me* for anything).

Hindsight Is Always Twenty-Something-or-Other

T om Boy froze—that next moment after flipping Sasha off (quite literally). He wondered what the hooey was happening: he absolutely knew what he was saying and doing—there wasn't the teeniest doubt that what came out of his mouth and mind was exactly as intended. But then, in that next millisecond, there came an intense desire to suck it all back through some red-striped mental straw to the back of his brain. Then that awful angst-y rush of guilt...

And then: *nothing*. Nothing but Tom Boy Robot Shell. It was hardly a new experience by now, but it was worrying that he had an acute memory of each conversation-cum-conflict.

*Maybe this is how a boy's brain becomes a man's? The softness becomes less soft, the mushiness just fades away? But why is it so clear, so precise? It's almost surgical how my yang is extricating my yin. (And I **like** my yin, don't want to lose it... Maybe I can keep it aside in a jar or something —like that grapefruit-size brain tumor I saw on YouTube.)*

*And there was Sasha all defensive and aggressive—nothing terribly new there—but the intensity **is** new. New and bizarre... And then those memory gaps, it almost seems as if she's yanking your—*

It was just after 2:00 a.m., and his phone tweaked. *What da fuck?* (As Sasha would say...) *Maybe it's that worm moon on top of the equinox on top that almost-Tricentennial thing causing all this?* Too much energy everywhere (with another possible hormonal overload menacing over and above any astronomical dysfunction).

It was Mike, and Mike never messaged him but now, bizarrely, Mike wanted to talk... About Tom Boy's "sudden, vital attraction" to Mike's bestie, Rachel.

Now? At three fucking o'clock?!

"'*Oh, Rachel said nada.*' She thinks you're cute and all but too crafty for her blood." (Yeah, he should talk...)

Mike was blathering away; Tom Boy was starting have another version of another out-of-body-but-still-in-his-body experience. He heard Mike ask why he was just staring at the screen—could he be *that upset?* He wondered why was he so distraught? This wasn't the first time he was dissed by a girl, or by anybody, for that matter. Why did this time matter?

"Hey, zombie face, what is it?" Mike peered at what seemed to be Tom's forehead. "Say something."

"No. Dunno..."

"Dunno what?"

Tom shot back, "I said I don't know—*didn't I just* say I don't know?"

Mike was still status-quo stoned, "Yep, you did, but you usually *always* know, so I thought it was weird."

Tom Boy always did seem to have an answer; it didn't really matter to Tom how accurate the answer was as long as he got there first.

Then, like just several minutes ago, the other Tom Boy—Evil Tom Boy—wanted to bite Mike's face off... And that was tame in comparison to what he wanted to do to that ungrateful bitch Rachel.

.   .   .

SASHA DIDN'T SEEM EVEN a little bit worried, "Doesn't seem strange to me, most other people are boring buttheads. Even those with the slightest magickal advantage don't know what to do with themselves, as if giving a cow a fifth leg was some genius stroke—a stupid stroke would be more like it. It's not any wonder to me you're losing interest... We'll be out of here—college or whatever—will happen soon enough."

"Yikes. Didn't know you had that so figured out."

"I didn't either, and I really don't. Sounds pretty smart to me too, though." Sasha smiled, but she was only half-joking.

"And you always seem to know what you want, what to do..."

Sasha sighed, sunk back into the two pillows that bloated and hugged themselves into the spot Sasha favored, and thought (for once) before actually answering, "I know I can tell you anything, so I'll tell you: I know it looks that way most of the time, but I somehow gained the skill of talking or answering before anyone else, so it appears like I know—and I *don't*. Not *every* time." She glanced at Tip, "And regarding *wanting something?* There's *never* been the 'perfect thing'—exactly the right book, or dress, or ice cream—I've *never* been satisfied. So, I grab for the closest thing or word, and just live with that... I feel pretty much like you but for the opposite: everything is looking at or waiting *for me,* and I haven't a clue—" Sasha fell silent.

Tip sat down again; they let all the ideas, thoughts settle carefully around them.

Tip said slowly, "Wow, who knew a couple random dreams about demon troll school bus drivers and brown overwitches would trigger all of this?" They laughed.

Sasha sat up, yawned, "That's true. But it's new and not new all at once, don't you think? It's every day, every moment—when you actually think about it."

Tip started to her bedroom, waving her finger goodnight, and whispered sweetly, "Sash, sometimes you *are* as smart as you look."

EzRA's WHINE had seemingly become permanent, "So she just came out and said it, like she was talking about the weather tomorrow." Her dreamscaping "nightmare" felt increasingly relentless and unforgiving.

"Why would you expect anything different. They're demi-g's, after all..." Book Store Anne was on her computer with her other hand, half-listening. She stayed a fair-weather acquaintance at best, in spite of their long history.

It had been three days since that demigod had tossed out that comment-cum-question about "How the hell is it a given that Ezra should be *'our* Ezra'? This is the first I'm even *hearing* about her..." blah, blah, bleh. And yet, what Ezra had tossed aside as easily as that goddess bitch had tossed out to no one in particular —she was *still* puzzling over what her answer should be. (Moreover, what the *desired* answer should be.) She found herself staring into her cup of tea... Everything, till a couple weeks ago, had seemed so clear and straightforward, *And how did Ezra the Good become this arbiter of what's fair and right? Going tits-to-tits with Ezra the Not-So-Good? Did Antonia put her too-talented girls up to this? On purpose?* (I'll remind you this is Ezra's *scarily* biased perspective.)

Ezra's problems were particularly difficult, mostly because—it could be argued—that a few weren't her problems at all: *they were the "other" Ezra's.* Seem confusing? It was and is, especially for Ezra.

Some told her it was a form of schizophrenia. If that were truly the case, then how could she be so clear, see each persona so discretely. So, if one was "good" and the other "bad," then why would—one could purport—the bad have any sway at all? And therein could that be the reason for her own omniscience. She'd known forever (at least she'd felt it forever) that sometimes a little bad would make the good so much better. And sometimes a little bad was good just as is.

The Phoenix Stones helped; their powers moved parts of

thoughts into a clearer whole. Ezra would arrange the stones until the colors stopped blending—the colors she saw just behind the lids of her eyes. It's when she opened her eyes, and the colors remained—that was the time to worry... Particularly if the color increased when and if someone was in her line of sight.

That last week Tip had turned a bright purple.

"Tip, what are you doing?"

Tip was just standing there. She looked left and right—and then again—exaggerating the motion, expressing her irritation. (Ezra could be annoying sometimes—sometimes *a lot* of the time.) Tip couldn't resist: "I'm standing here."

But that wasn't Ezra's real question, and Ezra was stuck. She knew what she saw and something *big* was about to happen to Tip, but how to ask without asking? (And even knowing that, how permanent can good or evil be? *And what dictates how "good" should be? And what determines how "evil" can evolve? Because like everything, it does and it must.*)

Ezra's sage sister Anne looked up finally, "Is that it?" Ezra nodded. Anne shrugged at the thought and questions, leaving any real answers carefully tucked away.

TIP LOOKED at her Sasha stuff after dinner. All of it. She needed some encouragement; she knew her heart was in the right place, but she had to figure out the best way to get her brain there too. She threw the myriad notes, trinkets, swatches of hair, shards of nail, a few worn threads of Sash's tee—her Sasha persona con grata grab bag—at her ceiling. She chanted the incantation right behind it, and it splayed out just as the recipe had predicted. So, for all her intents and purposes, she had the right amount—the necessary amount—of information. This was a crazy-good terrific result, but like that afternoon, it was equally angst-ridden. (And especially factoring in her *own* problems...)

. . .

It was a bunch of hours later (too late for Tip), and she was about to shut down but restarted instead; if she didn't change that old thought to a new thought, and do it now, she'd never get to sleep. (I know, I know, but a little OCD can be a good thing.)

Tip deliberated, negotiated with herself: yeah, a *little* OCD can be cool but not like this... *Am I really attempting to argue (with myself) about this again? The "how much is **too** much OCD" argument?!* Such a sad, pathetic puppy lately and then suddenly not at all... Those dreams of grandeur—*what else could you label them?* Who is that glorious woman that keeps showing up in one form or another? (In the dreams, to be clear.) *I keep hoping Mom will flit in and wave her dreamscaping wand, but no.* Maybe she's losing power? Or maybe she's just losing interest?

And while I'm milking this anxiety for all it's worth: *what's Sasha's deal?*

I had unshakable confidence in practically everything Sasha might think, do, say, dream, craft, on and on. *Until now—and despite my ceiling's happy communique.* There are two bugaboos that are threatening to do more damage than they should: one: *why the hell did it take Sasha so long to "confess" to me about her Ezra powwows?* My guesstimation is it had to be almost two years— that's some shit, sister... And two: *she hasn't breathed a word about that Digital Machoshit Club...* So, all of it is just weirdness—*major* weirdness.

You naturally think about these things—kinda-semi-major life moments like that; granted, it's not Earth's plane-shattering shit like when several Oshun brain children reincarnated *all at once* outside of the AMC theater (I'm exaggerating a smidge to make my point)—but then again, it's not *nothing* either.

But maybe it's my own bullshit sitting right on top of her bull-shit? *And she has every right to not tell me anything; she should tell me whenever she wants...* What da freak? I'm starting to fuck my own self up again... *Just not very good at this vindictive witchcrap*—the gods know I try. Not crafted or wired like all the other bitch-witches in my life. Especially Sasha... *Sasha Fierce sums her up pretty perfectly.*

A baby epiphany happening here (*you're my witness!*): I've always hated the fact that my kind of *hurt* has only ever *helped,* my inflicted *pain* makes *pleasure* (eventually at some point)—I've notoriously *killed* with *kindness!* Here's the epiphany part: I've always hated that wimpy witch, and now—miracle of miracles—*I don't.* Out of the blue, I think she's pretty fabulous and smart.

(I lost the "signal," *sorry dudes!* And it was just starting to *get good...* But there will *always* be limits and a respect of one's limits no matter how much synchronicity exists between your realities. Have no fear, dear Tip *au naturel* will be back shortly, I'm sure...)

Part of Tip's allure and intelligence was her obsessive self-awareness—it worked for and against her in equal measure. As the laptop screen refilled all the windows from minutes ago, she scanned it for those *exact* two sentences. Of all the myriad ifs, ands, and buts, it was odd that the stupid zombie bus ride was what persisted, kept chewing around her brain's edges. It was alarming and discouraging in pissy, frustrating turns that Sasha saw those bastards (or was it just one?) and *she didn't.* That was seventy percent of the conundrum, and then the other thirty: *Why the freak didn't Sasha do something?!*

(But what realistically would she have done? It's not as if waving a wand or crafting a spell on the spot would have done a morsel of anything—*that's* a fantasy... [You have to be an integral part of things—you can never truly just "wing it."] And certainly not during something like that crazy bus-to-portal-to-whichever plane of existence and then right smack back to the corner of Fifth and Main. *Give those ruby heels a freaking click, witchy-poo!*)

Wait, there, that's it... the page materialized. Tip was discouraged —her tired brain remembered it differently—it was just some silly blog. Someone's strangely anonymous, genderless blog *"from the black."* Tip now assumed it was something Dark Web-based, necessarily dangerous and unhealthy. But what she thought she remembered and liked—and suddenly, here it was again, in black and a slightly lighter black (*just call it freaking grey, Tip!*)—was this person's account of personal "responsibility and sacrifice." (Two of Tip's favorite words.)

Their stories were eerily the same: a *twin* (therefore, one "power source"), a reluctant witch (well, she/he was already an underwitch, so a little more proactive about their whole craft and spell-making heritage than Tip). He or she rambled on about an otherworldly experience of some kind or other; either this person was too upset to think clearly or was just a bad writer, regardless the gist was clear: Tip and their experiences were *frighteningly* similar and the necessary connection back to The Ratios (the hierarchy and balance of magickal powers, especially within families and doubly-especially between twins) was—surprisingly, given the free-styling penmanship—unambiguous and exact.

So, all told, the blog was a mishmash; some hit-or-miss digital voodoo that desperately wanted to *help* and not hurt. It did have heart, that much was clear... A broad concept of synergy, of balance, and that "everyone can't get and *have everything*" (with links front and center to dispel any kind of doubt) dominated every page. She was too exhausted to continue reading but something felt reassuring even though there was far, far too much information to digest. She bookmarked the page and turned the machine off...

And despite my grousing, my ceiling mini-ceremony seemed to want me to consider Sash in a more favorable light. It augured something—or someone—more benevolent than not.

Tip was a devout believer in everything happening for a reason, and so, as she woozily mulled over all of the testimony, comments (her defenses exhausted), one thing became instantaneously, precisely, and painfully clear: *her larger purpose in this grand equation was to become something **less** so she could, ultimately, become something **more**...* Tip collapsed back into bed, attempting to put these new thoughts into some sort of bittersweet logic.

(Tip will have another dream tonight—something comforting and perfect. Her "godparents" are never disappointed by their brainchild, but tonight they're especially, very pleased.)

TIP STARTED "TIPPING" into her reverie: I love this idea of myself! My Earth-bound *ping* persona to Sasha's Astral-plane-and-more bound *pong*. I'm glimpsing at a brilliant universe that's dust-to-dust—and then more dust and up and around again. My bliss discovered in elements that are as necessary as they can be unforgiving...

Magick-making is a wonderful, perfect part of what we are, but it's clear now: for both of us to live well and wisely; both Sasha and I can't be powerful. Not in the **same** *way. Sasha clearly has more power; she's always been stronger—especially magick that can matter every day, with everyone. So, it makes perfect sense she should benefit in the way we two never could—I will give what's mine to Sasha; I need and want to do this for her.*

So, Tip initiated her self-defined "self-propelled evolution" right then and there, believing that for every something that was lost an equal something would be gained. She was resolute even knowing she couldn't be sure what that "something" might be, or how this would help her too. She believed she had seen a couple clues mixed in with those sites—she'd review them again tomorrow... Or she could simply trust her own heart.

———————

DITAN GESTURED A FEW BRICKS, and then a few hundred more than that, to the broader side of the two walls that had been fighting each other for decades, at least... The demigods all looked at each other, really not knowing what to think and really, really not knowing what more to do— if anything. The school wasn't to be touched—nothing on the ground, ideally—but things kept progressing at an unprecedented pace. (It was the right decision albeit not the best decision.)

It was better already—you could see that. The air, the Earth, the things standing on or living off of the Earth were noticeably straighter, greener, fuller, happier. Pilar stood and hugged Ditan; Abyssinia wondered why such a simple benevolent gesture would feel so rich to her, as if there was more to it than simply helping something help itself. She walked out to the path; she needed some time alone to comprehend, fully digest this.

DITAN CONTEMPLATES: Note this first before you forget—Abyssinia's feeling it too, obviously. I can see her floating over yonder—something's amiss in Dreamland... Down below especially. It's like an Orgy of Randomness (my words), not sure how to even keep track, or even if I should try... Seriously, I know I need to "try"—I guess anything's better than nothing. Kind of has to be.

Could I build an argument, no, more of a rationale, around the Elements? No one would be *that* surprised, probably very few questions (some raised brows, but few real questions). I mean that whole fun, crazy water torture chamber thing, it was *so* Oshun and her kin's style—fun flavored with (almost) life-threatening elements—very cool, need to keep everyone on their toes or wand tips or whatever... But who would possibly be running interference in Dreamland? Who would be into that? Digging around everyone's subconscious—they have to be looking for something.

Not to worry, Tip's life will still be entirely magickal—her powers will still exist—just not *as powerful* or the same *kinds* of power. Sasha will become (as she was already beginning to sense) incrementally stronger. Tip will discover her new strength in exciting and different ways. (I'm sure *Gaia* will help unravel that for her.)

And someone *had* to get Rappatsi that deep "in it"—it wouldn't have occurred naturally. But who would pick that one conduit (out of, like, a *zillion*), and why? Besides, her methods may seem a bit random, but she's thorough as shit: the portals and their sense of place will be more than ready, *if* and *when* some entity passes through... *Who* am I referring to? Haven't a whit —*way above* my pay grade.

Or maybe it's just a tilling-the-soil thing? Getting ready for a Tricentennial "harvest" of some sort? Another "Spiritual SURVIVOR" reality show blitz, broadcast in parallel dimensions in 5DK?

(Need to tighten this up before I post it—still too loosey-goosey.)

———————— ⟨⟨⟨⟨ ⟩⟩⟩⟩ ————————

ANTONIA KNEW her girls were finally experiencing the Second Change (The True Flowering, as *her* mother had called it...). Their cycles—all three of them—magickal, fertility, metaspiritual—were now complete. Fully up and running, "hands-free"... Neither of them had uttered a thought or worry, but Antonia knew because of what Antonia suddenly couldn't do anymore: she was getting weaker—the natural ebb and flow of a witch's powers. (W's offspring preternaturally inherit more than eye or skin color, for your information.)

She knew that she was as similar to other witches as much as she was unique—her powers too had their limits and their strengths. She had always wondered whether longevity or even a teensy taste of eternity might be in her gods-given "witch kit." (She now was ninety-eight percent sure it was not, and that was bittersweet.)

Antonia further indulged her pensive reverie: she grabbed for her sappy *Love Box* (the second time in as many days).

Who really gives a shit anymore? Does "quaint" (the last *compliment* regarding her sentimental Love Box) *even register or mean anything at all?* Antonia would even admit, staring at the box, that it's a struggle for even her to really feel anything about them now, very different than just a year before when she'd clung (desperately) to the nostalgia, *Did they even do or make anything anymore? These batteries were for shit.* Antonia chuckled, threw the box onto her desk, *What's staring at this thing for one more goddam minute going to prove?*

The wands were her Trinity; it wasn't by design but by some cosmic serendipity that one perfectly complemented the other. (Of course it has *so much more* to do with the innate power of the sorceress. And Antonia had, well before the wands, proven her strength and wit.) So, enough with the eloquent arguments; things sucked right now. Antonia's life sucked especially and—worst of all—her family and her friends (mostly, *friend* sans plural) knew it.

Was Antonia giving the wands too much credit—or giving *herself* too much credit? Maybe, like so many other stories about witches, it was simply a sign, an *omen* (if that makes it more palatable). But each additional thing only added to the myriad excuses—her cloud only got cloudier. *And why?! I am a supremely talented witch—and not **my** words, by the way. The Dowagers ascribed that to me—each of them—and that had **never** happened before!* It had been the perfect compliment: as powerful as they were and as beholden as they were to their male counterparts, even one hundred-plus years ago they were able to recognize the consummate raw talent in Antonia. It was as much of a blessing as a burden for the young witch, who like too many others of her time, liked her other planes of reality—whether chemically induced or not—as much as the one she'd been born into.

"So is it that you think elevating your mind in as many ways as possible and as much at one time as possible is somehow a beneficial thing, Miss Stankberg?" Antonia's alchemy professor had been one of the few that had been able to detect the eccentric genius witch from the buzzed, inebriated eccentric genius witch. This was one hundred-plus years ago, and she couldn't afford to be high *all* the time. Even the best magic would only produce mediocre drugs—you always needed *quality* ingredients, and that cost money! Antonia was perfectly lucid when she pressed, "Elevating one's mind is a very subjective thing, Professor, wouldn't you agree?"

"Yes, I don't think anyone would argue that point, Miss Stankberg."

"And specifically the *precept* of elevating. Some individuals are perfectly content on the mezzanine, while others demand the penthouse. I, however, am very accommodating and to date, am generally happy with whatever floor I happen to land on."

"Well, that's very generous of you, Antonia."

"Thank *you,* Professor. I must say—" Antonia turned from today's reverie to face Sasha, examining her from her studio doorway, eyes tightened.

"You're talking to yourself again."

Antonia waved it away, "I always talk to myself."

"Maybe. But you don't usually answer yourself." Sasha maintained her very concerned expression as she continued to her bedroom. Antonia looked at herself, her reflection seemed to shift and morph even between thoughts. She took one more glance at her fave-rave of a rune—her debilitated, masticated wonder (still stubbornly unmagickal)—the Omnipotent Chopstick (her birthing and divining "wand"). The inscription remained inscrutable. (She had tried to trick the memory back into place many times, to no avail.) The first two words were ever-faithful: "Open" and "Your"... It was that last magical word that remained elusive. A perfect secret.

———————

"MRS. MARTINS, Happy Monday or whatever day it is." Celia Stackhouse had managed to sneak up behind Pearl Martins (she had been remarkably deft at avoiding her attempts to "chat").

"Mrs. Stackhouse, there you are. I keep missing you evidently."

Celia said in her most exaggerated, sarcastic tone, "I know! I keep watching *you* missing *me*."

Pearl's artificial grin faded, "Figured as much." She looked blankly at Celia, "What's the issue, Stackhouse?"

"Oh, so we're now on a *last* name basis? I get it."

"Good. So, what's wrong? You got the same info we all have, now go do your thing—whatever your thing is." (There was a very stinging, sardonic tinge to her comment.)

Celia Stackhouse took Pearl Martins' arms and sat them down at the cafeteria table. "The information seems fine. And nothing seems necessarily "wrong," except perhaps *where you're getting the information from?*"

Pearl peered at Celia, *Only this holier-than-thou witch would worry about shit like that...* She continued, "There's nothing 'wrong' about it—at least no one's getting hurt or losing a toe, if you receive my meaning."

Celia knew from her *toes*—and obviously (unbeknownst to Celia) Pearl did too. Pearl finished her critique, "You're just all wadded up because I got it, all of it, in front of Casen before anyone else did."

"But you did it anonymously?"

"Just for the moment—it was the more gracious, polite thing to do. No?"

Celia leered at Pearl, she took a couple very purposeful breaths before she said anything she'd regret (it wouldn't be the first time with this conniving witch).

Pearl couldn't resist—they'd been enjoying their "game" (for better or worse) for the last few months, "Now, now, Ms. Super-witch Superteacher-Everything—someone else can win every now and again, if you'd please." Pearl offered a toothy grin.

"Listen, *Mrs. Martins,* just share you source or sources so we *all* can leverage them and get this nastiness settled and as efficiently as possible, *wouldn't you agree?*"

Pearl started leave, "Not going to happen. They don't want to be known. Actually, even I'm not *entirely* sure who's driving that broom, well, that's not exactly true but just some days..." Pearl snickered. Then as she turned to go, she tossed out, "I just call 'em as I see 'em."

"What the hell is that supposed to mean? Is your info *real* or not?"

"As real as it needs to be, bitch—I mean, *witch.*"

LUIS DROVE a beeline to the mall, and yes—very-much-so yes—he knew he'd told Lila one thing and now, moments later, he was intentionally doing the opposite, *A guy has to do what a guy has to do...*

Luis felt empowered because if he pulled this sucker off, he'd be a hero on so many levels; no one could even begin to doubt, question, or turn his intention sideways like those Brujas— whether intentionally or otherwise—always managed to do. The upshot was this: between what Bitts Darkly (Luis's new pet name for Bitts and his Dark Web do-gooding) and Lila half-accidentally bumped into on that blog she loved (Luis hated), Luis had connected a few cosmic dots that revealed yet another Coven escapade: that silly ragged Covey was at it again, doing their chicken feet terrorism trick, only this time bigger, badder, and bloodier. Four district science department heads and their cohorts (that's where Stackhouse fits in) were having a day-long confab at a mall meeting facility. They were going to webcast their findings and concerns with several other counties up and down the coast; Luis had kept following the links, and was blown away by how bizarrely massive and somehow still strung together (but barely) the makeshift *"white-crafted but made to look brown"* terror was. (Not everyone was sold on the gross scaly feet angle, so they figured out their own "trick" that wasn't as messy but just as [hopefully] threatening.)

Luis landed; the "business wing" of the mall was small, and the parking lot almost silly. The marked cars were a cinch to find. He tricked-tripped the locks and plucked the feet from their various orifices. Luis used good ol' Fantastik and elbow grease to get the (mostly) fake blood with their fake terror off of the windshields.

Another job well done...

Luis walked into Mrs. Martins' class two minutes late. He was expecting the usual public lambasting, but none happened, just a nasty glare or two. Luis wondered what else he could've possibly done to piss off Mrs. Martins. (Whatever it was, he hoped it was extra-thwarting and frustrating.) He'd aced the test she just returned—but it couldn't have been just that, not really...

TOM BOY HAD GOTTEN the text in the middle of the night again, and for the third time. He was starting to find it irritating, a little childish too; one of the "group" (if in fact they were a group—he had no idea—which was the whole point) directives was anonymity, which made perfect sense, *But we don't have to skulk about in the middle of the night, do we? Maybe **I'm** doing something wrong?* He sneered at the thought.

Running over to the Altar (Tom Boy had adopted it as such— just him, though) at lunch was cleverer than he'd anticipated: not only was it a more convenient time, but there were fewer people —people that might know or would *know him* anyway—and it was less busy, blah, blah. The doors slid open without any complaining, *Someone—one of "us"—obviously has a very practical side to him, oiling the door this time, fixing that hinge last time...* Unless mall maintenance was just that thorough and that gullible.

Bitts and the other BWBDMSers were barely aware of Tom Boy's recent subterfuges with his anonymous cohorts. Tom wasn't sure how long it should stay that way, or if it should change at all;

the directives and the occasional initiative trickled down onto one platform or another, all originating from the some dark net somewhere, somehow. Tom Boy's conjoining with this ambiguous source (master?) was something inexplicable but very raw and real in his mind. His thirst was novel, undeniable, and relentless; something in him insisted he pursue this—whatever it was going to become—with every cell or ounce of his craft and (what was the word they'd suggested? Oh yes...) *consciousness*.

Tom Boy found the talisman his ally had left for him—he would add his portion of the spell later tonight.

He noticed the blood was entirely desiccated, the Altar (something in his gut told him) would need a "refresher"; it had lasted a surprisingly long time. (Maybe because things were still at the beginning stages then?) Tom Boy certainly couldn't just *ask* Sasha for *more blood;* she still wasn't aware she had "contributed" her life force that fateful (not *that* fateful, Tom and Greg had plotted the whole thing to the last detail) rather crazy Friday night. Tom Boy also intuited it wasn't necessarily an urgent thing, but it would be at some point soon... Maybe he'd finish everything tonight, get the token back there to be picked up for its last cycle, *Yeah, that would impress someone, somewhere... But by bit, it's the little things that'll matter*.

He sealed the door, was wiping the black glass clean, when just over his shoulder he heard, "Hey, Stud, what's up? You doing some part-time work during your lunch period?" Julie laughed, more to make her point than anything funny.

Tom Boy took a long, slow breath, *I knew this would happen at some point—but why did it have to be Julie?* Fuck.

"Yep, every cent matters." He looked at her, "Not really. Just checking something out. And you? What are you selling over here?"

Julie caught the slight, "Just the usual." Then she suddenly, even a bit scarily, became more pointed, "Had a doc appointment but extra-sensed something going on. It's that strong, you *know* that, *right?* Probably not—you're a boy." She seemed like she was joking, but then not maybe not so much.

Tom Boy knew loosely about that: W's had certain sensitivities respective to sex. But they weren't ever anything to worry about, but perhaps that's changed now too? Or maybe it's just another *"very individual"* quirk—with the boy or girl thing (with sprinkles and a cherry on top?).

"I don't think you're joking, are you?"

Julie shrugged, "I'll never tell... *No.*" She sniggered. "Yeah, and how opportune that my fave stud pup has his panties all caught up in..."

Tom Boy frowned, "Caught up in *what?*"

"That's what I'm asking you, silly boy."

Tom felt that same generalized frustration, irritation, whatever-ation, *Why do I have to deal with this kind of crap?*

Julie shook her head, catching the end of his thought, "I somehow don't think it's 'crap..'" She walked over to the shiny black wall—distressingly anonymous. "It's overwhelming and important—I can feel it... But it's hungry; I can feel that too."

Tom Boy said slowly, mostly truthfully, "I don't know... I mean, I obviously *know what's here,* but I don't know what it means —yet."

Julie's eyes flashed, "Okay. Well, if you show me yours, *I'll show you mine.*"

He sighed, "Dude, I've told you a zillion times, the sex thing is not where I'm at."

"Dude, it was more like a hundred, *okay?* And I'm not that much of a witchy bitch-asshole. I don't mean sex—at least not between you and me."

Tom Boy peered at Julie, "Why you crafty little something-or-other, what are you up to? Do you have your own shiny black wall somewhere too?"

Julie smiled slightly through her pursed lips. Now Tom Boy's eyes lit up, "I need to think more about this. I'll be in touch—one way or another."

They each offered the other a smarmy, fang-y grin, and walked out to their cars.

IT WAS A QUESTION—MORE a moral gauge—that gave Tip that extra filter she needed every now and again (and this was definitely one of those "agains"). Habakkuk, a seventh-century prophet (semi-self-proclaimed; one had to take charge of those things oneself then, the gods certainly weren't going to) gave Tip just enough of an ethical reference, a religious text she could pluck an idea or two from, just when things were getting a little (a lot?) wonky. Habakkuk and his oracles were obscure enough that even if someone actually recognized the concepts, it was a rare, rare thing that they could argue Tip's position one way or the other. (Tip would occasionally tag a query onto the epilogue of one of her lucid dreams; they were pretty rare too, and strangely had titles, sometimes prologues, *always* epilogues—it was a necessary thing, so you could be sure what you *think* you saw was exactly *what* you saw.)

So, would you answer the goddam question, please?

Tip didn't know what she thought or felt; the only thing she knew for sure was that she'd never felt like *this,* so void, a perfect blank—she was a figurative "shell." Tip had finally heard back from her OB-GYN who finally heard back from her doctor: in spite of how "rich" things seemed, twice or sometimes three times a month, she was—to use the doctor's "technical" term—"barren." Her doctor, however, did emphasize the more commonly heard phrase *extreme infertility*; some form of endometriosis had sneaked its way into her tubes *at this time or that*, had started its evil, dark-minded endeavors *at this time or that...* And that's when Tip just stopped listening. The deep, sad emptiness she'd been flirting with now subsumed her. Tip couldn't feel angry, sad, pity, or anything—she was full of nothing.

So, did Sasha get all the fucking eggs too?

The doctor said it didn't work that way, not for the "more human stuff." She was trying to be supportive when she offered that Tip's mortal body was fortunately—and unfortunately—hers alone. (Dr. Sandi's bedside manner had always lacked a certain tact.)

Antonia fell completely silent; her typical effusive heart-on-*both*-sleeves response to these kinds of difficult moments and circumstances was nonexistent. Antonia remained expressionless; she took hold of her daughter's hand and wouldn't let go, even during the drive home. Tip's situation was unique and terrible, and she didn't want it to feel any worse than it did, but her mother's bizarre behavior was having exactly that effect. Antonia gave Tip's hand a final squeeze and slowly walked upstairs to her room and shut the door.

Tip stood there for a moment staring at the stairs and then followed her mother's "advice," as indirect as it was... When she got to her room Sput was already in place on her bed; she crumbled next to him, took his paws, and pulled them close.

"So who's idea was this?" Mr. Clarke smirked.

"They've done this before. What are you saying?" Jones-y looked askew at him; Stephen Clarke had this remarkable (sometimes remarkable, sometimes annoying) knack for conversation and sentences that had at least one double meaning. (Jones-y assumed it was intentional.)

Stephen smiled, smirked again, "No, I know. At least it's not that babay ganoose crap."

"If you're going to criticize something, you should at least pronounce it correctly."

Stephen wheezed, "What? 'Crap'?"

"Oh, you *so* funny... Baba ghanoush."

They started into the queue, the variety and opportunities for filling the pastry blanket were overwhelming, especially for a cafeteria on a specific schedule and for students and teachers with much more on their minds than the kind of onion they'd prefer in their Mexican football. Then some commotion in the main room distracted everyone from building their lunch: Burritos Deflate Gate. The two quickly regrouped, refocused, and then doing their job looked in at the main auditorium space.

Stephen walked up and sighed at Mrs. Stanson, "Shit. I totally forgot about Casen's email, that she wanted to do this now." Stephen looked even more exhausted suddenly; he'd been hoping-assuming everyone had just taken a chill pill and moved on, but then the next thing or conversation would happen. He still couldn't intellectually digest why a little graffiti and a few zombie students (floating or otherwise)—*How are they that different than the usual? I mean, seriously?*—could incite such a fiasco. (Something else must have happened—maybe he'd missed that email too? *Again?*)

The situation reminded one teacher of an air raid as opposed to a spontaneous school assembly, even though that was exactly what was attempting to happen. "This is fairly scary shit," Mrs. Stanson declared.

"You're not even sure what it's about, so why stir the pot?" Stephen had to make comment.

"I'm the pot stirrer—it's what I do." (Mrs. Stan didn't bother acknowledging Stephen with her reflexive wink—something was *definitely* a little wackier than their normal.)

The auditorium's construction was still only half completed so the cafeteria would be obligated to serve lunch *and* the unexpected presentation. It quickly became a situation that had no room for interpretation; students perched two to a stool at least, certain boy- or girlfriends' laps were deployed, at a minimum, as a makeshift chair. Even though it was "uncool" (though far preferred by those that could conjure it), the random wand or incantation provided a temporary salvo—the invisible pillow chair. Principal Sara Casen decided to get in front of the (potential) problem, and in her most unforgiving and foreboding tone, declared, "Use your wands if you must. But only if you must. Remember, we always want to celebrate our differences but never in spite of each another." A big toothy smile helped reinforce her between-the-lines message. Sara was all about the declarative statement: *Just get the fucker done* was her mantra of choice.

It was the last period of three for lunch, so the cafeteria was a myriad of foodstuffs at various stages of transition to either something substantial or simply shit. (There wasn't an inch of table surface visible between half-eaten sandwich pockets, actual sandwiches, pizza, and many, many other forms of carbohydrates flavored with starch.) Tom Boy had been putting the exclamation point on his half-baked statements with a conductor's panache—a half-eaten soft pretzel subbing for a wand. The two hundred-year-old school's walls were finally beginning to show strain from the wild mix of realities they'd been recently required to contain; it had really progressed in the last five years, with much of the visible duress in just the last bunch of months. (Okay, the school was slightly older than I am, or I think I am, but I feel I'm fairly attuned to any symptoms of runic wear and tear.)

Sara held up her hand, the happily obedient room fell quiet. "I've one word," Sara began.

Tip leaned in, "And that's never a good thing..." Tom Boy nodded with exclamation points.

"Brujeria."

The entire room's faces twisted, "Bro *Areas?*" "Bra-*jeering?*" Other phonetic interpretations were offered, but another way to say "*A Place to Put the Bros*" was the most common translation. This silliness would usually have placed a big smile on Sara's face, and the kids knew that, but not now. There was abruptly an undercurrent of something very real and very wrong.

Sara answered plainly (and not especially patiently), "No, you heard me. At least I know some of you did, and definitely the few that decided to push the *Brujeria* envelope a little further than you should have. I know you know who you are." She looked up, her eyes flinting yellow, first left then right, *This is so snappably solvable, but we'll do this according the rules...* She placed her hands firmly on the notecards in front of her (so retro, *but it works for me*), framing the main thoughts she needed to impart. (As focused as she was, she'd always sucked at speechifying...)

"Those random 'few' need to rethink and reconsider their actions. This time, this period of our shared history, the history that we're making—together..." It was happening already, she was not only off-track but dangerously veering into gooey brain territory. She measured her words, *Bust it open, now. Take the fear out of the moment. You're the one in charge here.* (Uh-huh, sure...) "So, these tricks, these spells, I learned this a long time ago, they should stay where they work. Can't do any harm." (Still not exactly clear, but at least somewhat back on track. She started to see the reaction in students she'd been hoping to see.)

Julio decided to jump the shark (as much as he could see of it) and proudly stated, shouted, "*I'm* a Brujo... Or at least I am most weekends." The cafeteria—or most of the students—enjoyed the slight dig, laughed accordingly. Then suddenly he became rather serious, "Nothing's happened recently. Nothing dangerous, anyway."

"That's a lie, Julio." Sara Casen was abruptly scary, imperious.

Julio and the room were dumbstruck. Not only was it out of character for Sara, but *her words, her accusation* was the *only* acknowledgment of any (or even the *suggestion* of) Latin-flavored spells having been summoned—on any level, anywhere. And then why to decide that today, the cafeteria's Burrito Day, was the ideal day to "discuss" the matter? What was the new urgency? Especially given how random and desperate the whole situation had been—the figurative shit had been a little bit on and off the fan for the last few weeks (as much as the school had been aware of). It was funny how (more ironic than ha-ha) the scene became incrementally darker and more surreal in proportion to every incoming burrito and its hungry student. Still, people were quickly losing their appetites. (Thank God there were chips.)

Julio said plainly, "No it wasn't, Mrs. Casen."

She straightened, "You should already be very aware that any spells of any origin outside of well, um, *here,* are verboten."

"'Here'? You mean *here* as in *this country—'here'?*" The figurative student body sucked in almost all the air and held it, waiting for her answer, not quite believing what they *thought* they were starting to hear. She stood back from the podium and grappled for any remaining oxygen, "*Yes.* That's what I meant... Or I should be exactly clear: what I'm being told I'm supposed to be saying. Meaning. Whatever." (Her babbling now only made matters worse.)

It became imminently clear that Frenchtown High School was a hotbed of alleged cosmological immigration violations: magic in any other language than English was suddenly and sensationally illegal, at least that was Principal Sara Casen's assertion. And given students' general reaction, there was a remarkable amount of fucked up-ness in what the now very nervous principal was attempting to explain.

RAPPATSI LEAPT TO HER FEET—SEVERAL other student comrades followed her lead. To make her protest (and soon to be the students' point) even more pointed, she started chanting a fitting dissent in Spanish with the students gradually joining the swell. The room was now more than a tad uptight; the concrete walls now took the appearance of school paste. The angry Spanish declaration was lucid, glorious, and flowing; the various Latin American dialects were like powdered sugar mellifluously trying to sweeten something dark and hurtful; Sasha and Tip clambered through the unruly crowd.

Sasha nicked Tip's knee with hers; Tip read it as a cue that it was the right moment to join the chorus, even though she'd accumulated one year's worth of Spanish at best (and as far as dialects, well, don't be silly).

Tip thought wrong: Sash grabbed her bra strap and pulled her back into her seat. And now Sasha was, for some strange reason, apparently *very* pissed off. *Inelegant, T...* (Even if it was, it was a strange comment given the circumstances.)

An angry core was beginning to solidify, Sasha groaned, "What the hell is going on?"

Tip scowled at her sister; anything political always seemed like pap to Sasha, somehow beneath her. Tip reacted, "Shut up, it's fine. It's a good thing. You wouldn't understand anyway—not *really* understand."

"Try me."

Plain angry and more-than-ready to spite her sister, Tip stood up and started with her own version of the chant. She had played with some makeshift translation spell for about four months when she thought Juan was cute. (Then she'd decided he wasn't.) But fragments of the spell remained and were beginning to work. (What follows is the English translation, albeit with a spell that was created in perhaps 1959, so forgive any futzy, musty words or phrasing—like the word *futzy,* para example):

> Here 'tis again, the mountain on the wall,
> A sign, a word, just a thought that takes its toll,
> The people and minds, the soul that scorns this
>   hell,
> Finds love on the backs of brothers, from hand to
>   heart, we tell: (their stories...)

It even stayed mostly comprehensible between snarfs of

burrito! Finally and powerfully, the majority of students resorted to the singular statement (again, loosely translated):

Magic's for all or magic's for none.

WHILE TIP WAS TRIPPING over her Spanish, Sasha stood up, shouting at her sister, "This isn't going anywhere! Look at Casen, she's ready to burst—I've never seen her turn *this* shade of red before." Tip didn't even look at her sister; the dialect had clicked into place so she was shouting even louder.

Tip randomly, surprisingly flared at Sasha, "*Why are you such a bitch sometimes?*" She knew that would shut Sasha up for at least a few seconds. Sasha glowered her response; the din was becoming too loud, too political. Sasha was caught entirely off guard—why would this moment hurt more than Tip's usual jabs?

The cafeteria had become a cage, one that barely contained the banshee of emotions that was brewing. General discontent had been the flint and prejudice had been the spark, and the overcome Sara was realizing any responsible options were now gone. She carefully placed her hand on her wand, at same time accepting the terrible fact that there was no guarantee—not that there ever is—that her magic would make things better.

Sara bit her lip, winced, and thrust her wand at the students. They bit their lips as well, though not of their own doing. The pandemonium's only weapon—its voice (or the swell of teens' shouts and chatter)—was finally, albeit temporarily, disabled. An old principal's hoodoo from years on, it was a harmless ancient spell that turned vocal cords backward for just a few minutes, and that's all Sara needed. Of course, that did nothing to help the emotional temperature of the room, and all that tepid school wall paste turned to sour, dirty wax.

*We all want different things, but the only thing we seem willing to fully
share is our selfishness. And I say the time has come to embrace it—not to
nurture it, but to destroy it. Evil only thrives on evil, terrorism only
frightens those that have a reason to be...*

To be what? Casen's forcibly rapt audience were—evident even
through their semi-paralyzed faces and vocal cords—still shocked.
She was always a strong and proud woman and witch, but when
did social tyranny become one of her management styles or
specialty tricks?

(If she would have only answered her own fucking question:
Terrorism frightens because...?)

The ongoing mishmash being uttered by Sara Casen showed
no immediate sign of slowing—it was sounding more and more
like some perverted New Life Church text in spite of what was
actually happening. The rage in the room began to ribbon its way
in and around these, dare we say, surrogate disciples; the spell was
just starting to lessen its grip, but everyone's anger and frustration
was just at its frantic first stages.

Sara desperately, methodically folded her notecards in half and
confronted the throng, "So, to finish, *racism is terrorism.* Whether
it's one thousand years old—like the horrific spell text on the
walls recently—to the disappearing chicken feet trick or the
white-faced text messages Elisa got just two hours ago. It's wrong
and it ends now... So it may seem counterintuitive, but we're going
on a metaphysical lockdown for the next week: it's segregation
and limited personal freedoms but for all the right reasons."

Last Nerve Tito, true to form, was happily feeding on the bad
energy in the space, grand-standed, "Hey, Princess, where were
you the *rest* of last week? The 'Ricans' chicken feet was just the
appetizer!" Tito was used to the requisite sneers and scoffs, but
now no one even *blinked*; Sara held her focus, except for one mini-
moment when she had delectably visualized smashing a burrito in
Tito's face. The students' betwitched trance was now at its low

ebb, and they were expecting an answer—and one that they could believe, just a little bit. The air was almost gone, so whatever she needed to say or do next, needed to happen now—unfortunately (or fortunately), Principal Casen didn't have to make that decision —The Attack of the Burritos made it for her.

FOUR OF THE doughy missiles suddenly floated up and over the students' heads... The curious trick diffused the current roil, as silence rippled across the room. The starchy blimps did a brief pas de quatre, ending their dance above the heads of four students who dodged the dripping, dancing pillows. But to no avail, the burritos pursued their prey. The crowd, who a moment ago was transfixed, now burst back into noisy confusion—an equal mix of laughing and jeers.

While the burritos were hovering, making up their minds, another handful of students spied what was crawling up the wall and curtain behind Sara Casen: it looked like a second-grade student project that reinterpreted the Star Wars' ground battalion for three dollars or less: crab-like aggregates of pointed, hinged angular chips anchored by leathery avocado shells were quickly getting their footing. The ones in front were well on their way, their spidery grasp and grace improving by each nip and step. Sara spun around, *What in sacerdotal's name?!* The burritos seemed to take note of the encroaching front line of very aggressive corn-meal and gathered left to right to reassess. The students, teachers, humans part-witch, witches more so human were all gobsmacked: someone or *something* had to clearly be responsible for this *somehow*.

Sara started to lose her very tenuous grip, "Everyone—what is happening?! *And right after what we just talked about?!!*"

Tito was in his element, "*You* were the only one talking, Mrs. C.!"

Sara, in spite of herself, started screeching, "Whoever's

responsible for this fiasco, it is far and away breaking every law or rule there is!" She paused for effect, waving and threatening her wand, scanning the melee for any teensy bit of "normal" Then the principal finally imploded (totally abandoning any likability feedback), "Yo, assholes! *Knock it the fuck off!*"

Those must have been the magic words: every remaining burrito in the room, including the half-eaten one in Jimmy Parsons' hands, flew into the air and fell into formation. This burrito squadron would clearly have every advantage over the chip battalion. (But why would they be in any contest to begin with? More than that, whose fingers were on the control stick?) There was just as much attention on the pending Cal Mex civil war as there were eyes desperately surveying other sets of eyes as to who or whom was the instigator (or instigators?). Or did they even know, one instigator to the other, who was doing what food and why? (I mean the answer could be just as silly and obvious as the food!) Maybe it all shared some crazy, common end game? (I'm probably way over-complicating this... Or *am I?*)

Then, speaking of Baba (We were? How did I miss that?), Sara was once again first to notice: what she thought was a bit of burrito shadow play, turned out to be the pseudopods of the Blob from Baba Ghanoush. Tentacles of the eggplant miasma wrangled around, through, and under various feet, table legs, backpacks, and whatever else it could entrap. Then presto-change-o, to everyone's food-based horror, the Middle Eastern Blob took no prisoners from below as the Bluff from South of the Border played out above their frantic arms and yells. The food armies showed no bias; they attacked and slathered indiscriminately: human or witch, it didn't matter. The kids, and their present guardians, were flailing like flies—slip-sliding onto the floor, one another, under chairs, under each other. (The baba had too much oil—or just enough—depending upon your desired result; I'm probably going to get a bit of a talking-to—look at what bland hell Constance complained herself into just five cycles ago! But she was whining like an old tired hag from—well, I'll stop...)

Sensing some pending new insanity, Tip made a last ditch grasp toward Rappatsi thinking she would know what to do (since she probably *had something to do with this whole mess* to start with). But Rapp was lunging, slipping uncontrollably in the opposite direction and did not look happy doing it... *And you're wrong, Tip, I don't have a clue!*

(*But she was thinking as much when this whole thing was kicking into motion—so who's shitting who?*)

A minute later, when the adults thought they sensed the start of some semblance of order, a tray of food was catapulted (*slung,* would be more apt) from one side of the cafeteria to the other and splashed across the wall in grand fashion. The place *erupted*—decorum be damned! Four trays on complementary arcs, two heading one way and two the other, were suspended midair—Sara had jumped into the fray. But with the students now even more agitated, the ass't principal saddled up to Sara's side and advised, "Just let them finish it..." With *those* magic words, all kinds of therapeutic, good hell broke loose.

The next fifteen minutes were a conflagration of rice and bean shit bombs, slings of corn chip arrowheads, oil slicks of tahini, not to mention whatever else reanimated from any opened lunch bags. The cafeteria became one big salad bowl of a battlefield, tossed to and fro by some very vengeful entities, none of whom spoke a word of English or if they could, didn't want to. Yips, cries, tears of laughter, and otherwise were everywhere as students and teachers desperately, comically slushed or oozed their way to an exit. Sara had picked herself up off the floor and scuttled over to the closet to hopefully find a microphone that wasn't covered in oil or salsa. The always ingenious head cook Fred had started to scatter flour and cornmeal across the floor—people began to be able to put one foot in front of the other...

And then, just as unexpectedly, it was over. Apart from the

melee of myriad food groups, grains, and saturated oils, and some exorbitant dry-cleaning bills, the mood in the room was somehow lighter. Was this some sort of end game (or more likely, just the beginning of one or *several* someones flexing their magickal intuition)? Sasha, somehow relatively unscathed, wandered up to her sister, who was a mess. (She slightly qualified her thought: *more a mess than usual.*)

The students' communal daze shifted shape and tone again, becoming more confused, emotionally exhausted, and finally a little sad.

Tip declared, "Well, shit, an actual freakin' racist food fight—and with the food fighting back! And I do mean *freaking!* Apart from breaking every fucking rule of social decency there is, it was, um, *kind of a blast...* Sorry, Ms. C.!" Tip faux pouted, glancing over to Principal Casen's Last Stand.

Rappatsi sighed, "Yeah, it was cool, but the metaphors were so *obvious.* So heavy-handed." Unavoidable eye roll. "It had to be the work of one of those *Brujas...* Had to be."

"That's rather unnecessary," Sasha muttered, walking up to them after hearing Rapp's assessment.

"What is?" countered Rapp.

"Your opinion, I guess."

Big pregnant pause. Then Sasha continued (Tip winced), "That's just what they, whoever 'they' are, want out of us. No matter your color, your accent, your witching tendencies—good or not so much—it's a sock in the gut on every level. Physical, metaphysical, emotional, psychometaemotional."

Tip crossed, "Psychometa *what?*"

"I'm kidding. But kinda not really."

Tip was flabbergasted, "It took a fucking ethnic food fight for you to give a shit? You should be the new the poster witch for Unicef."

Sasha looked stung, sad; it could have been the fact of having missed lunch (who'd want to eat anything now?), but probably not. Tip was regretting her flip comments—her flip *everything* lately regarding Sasha. But why was she resenting her and especially *now?* No one twisted her broom in glorious sacrifice, coerced her into being an overzealous version of Tip the Martyr she'd too often fantasize about; she could have much more easily kept her gods-given powers right where they were.

More kids were starting to move in a more organized, dare we say, purposeful manner. The general feeling and conversation threading its way through the air or app or otherwise was good in the sense (as Sasha and Rappatsi said, albeit in two very different ways) that everyone in the school was bound together by this bizarre yet *shared* experience. What was problematic is what might transpire in the next hour or so, when the shared moments could become something potentially very different. Very specific. And maybe rather dangerous.

And Yet More Weirdness

※❖※

The idea that things might be turning the corner, one way or the other, was floated by Luis—and everyone in the room looked at him incredulously. "What planet have you been on the last twelve hours?" asked Sasha. She was joshing around (mostly), but Luis wasn't exactly sure; he looked around the room to gauge reactions before saying anything further. He, then and there, decided he didn't have to give a shit anymore—women, witches, and white people be damned, "I've been right here. Seeing the same miraculous—both good and bad—things you've seen. But I've seen them through this brown cloud, that I want everyone to know, doesn't seem so much like a cloud anymore." Everyone sat there with the same overwhelmed look on their faces. (Too much information for one—maybe two—miracles perhaps?)

"You were always such a dickhead about these kinds of things," burped Sasha.

"*And what the fuck is that supposed to mean?* When have we ever had something like 'these kinds of things'? And I didn't even fucking know you—I mean really *know* you—until about a month ago... *So what the hell?*"

Tip threw a chip at Sasha, and it hit her squarely on the forehead. (Maybe there was a little—tiny, little bit—of magic in making her point? I say that only because her aim usually sucked.)

Greg finally said, "Well, that was really compelling and all YouTube-like, but I'm really not sure what you're trying to get at."

Luis sat forward, now very agitated, "'Get at'?! It's the truth, dickhead. *Your* truth, for that matter... Who the hell got you out of your frigging burrito bomb mess?"

"I'm not sure. *What does it matter?*"

"You're such a white male post-warlock, barely-a-witch shithead. And I mean that in really uncomplimentary way, in case that wasn't clear enough already." Greg shot his stare past them and through the worn lead pane glass squares of the classroom. The glass stretched and whined in response; this was just the bazillionth time some W tried to throw their anger out the window—it certainly never got any easier for the windows (good thing they still made them like they used to).

Luis was full-throated, "I know your color-blind thing is actually a good thing, dudes. I know that you don't *believe* in prejudice, at least any prejudice that I give a shit about. But just because *you* don't, doesn't mean that maybe the person right next to you doesn't want to take one of those monster burritos and suffocate my Spic ass with it—it's every day and *all* the time... And, that wasn't just a turn-of-phrase; they actually *were* sitting within feet of us."

So it wasn't an abstract superpower, or gods' (demigods'?) wrath kind-of-thing?! It was some witch or W—or W's—in the room! Would have to be at least an overwitch! (Or an underwitch with some great connections.) And how did Luis sort all of this out, have these insights before anyone else had even fully digested their scary half-eaten burrito?

Now everyone was on the edge of their seats... Some had even started to float in anticipation of Greg's nervous answer. He mumbled, "Yeah, okay, well who was it?"

Luis, very flustered as the moment caught up with him, struggled, "Well, it was two of them. At least... But they were girls, I mean, *women*."

"Well, dude, I *knew* that. So, what's you point?"

"Appreciate it, dude! *That's my point!*"

It took a moment but the room caught up to Greg's too-casual remark—*what da freak?!* Greg knew *too?!* Everyone just glared at Greg. Poor Greg. (Or not so poor Greg...)

Greg suddenly rallied, "And I remember a blonde woman first, she was the first who spoke to me in my dream last night. And I do remember some weird convo about food, maybe she was just trying to warn me—*and **not** screw me?*" Greg sniggered at the limp joke and the strange story, but regardless, he wasn't making it up (not this time, anyway).

And as Greg and everyone continued their attempts to twist more truth from the motley mix of facts and maybe-fictions from sources conscious and not so much, what was clear was that the lines of battle had been drawn. (So much for any last-minute attempts at being politically correct or even a *little* bit color-blind.)

PART III

We'll Always Have Paris

S ee-thru Sasha floated into Tip's room unannounced (which typically meant something out of the ordinary or perhaps even a slightly *sensational* something had occurred).

"You know your *Almost Sex Theory* thing?"

Tip looked deadpan, "It's not a theory nor is it a 'thing'—it's what it is." She smiled through it, "But yeah, duh... By the way—" she surveyed all of Sasha's translucency hovering just a foot or two above, "your out-of-body schtick is looking pretty slick lately, if I do say so." Tip silently, appropriately gave *herself* a couple snaps, *Generous of you. Nicely done.*

"Well, why *wouldn't* you say it's a 'thing'?"

Labored eye roll from Tip, *Now that's the Sasha we all know and want to slap around every now and again,* "We won't go there. Just tell me about what you wanted to tell me about."

"Well, I did my own interpretation of it—like Martha Graham's free-styling..." Sasha had been recently wowed by Martha Graham's *'Oklahoma!'* genius even though she'd seen the film twice already (why the third viewing was suddenly so inspiring was a small mystery). She sniggered, "*And* I even flavored it with a little bit of the potion-spell-cum-voodoo love recipe you'd shared."

"That doesn't sound like *almost* anything, that sound like *way complicated everything*."

Sasha looked hurt, for someone so rationally bright and inspired on so many levels, she was many times (especially of late) strangely emotionally incompetent. "Well, I had fun. And it was just a blowjob."

"What? How did you 'not really' give someone a BJ? And who did you blow, you haven't said a word about—"

"Greg."

"Eew. Why? Oh, wait—you told me before—for most things he's like a living blow up doll that you can do anything to, and he doesn't give a shit."

"Yep."

"So, spill—I mean, in so many words..."

So, Sasha did. And shared how the spell allowed the specific parts or pieces—Sasha's mouth and Greg's penis—to be temporarily transmogrified so everyone got what they wanted out of it sensation-wise (mostly, kind of) but without any real physical contact, at least not in the strictly mortal sense.

Tip wasn't convinced, "So you actually liked it? Wasn't it like having a big invisible banana stuck in your mouth?"

"Well, it wasn't *that* big..." Sasha had to say it; they chuckled then Sasha shared, "It was actually fun. It was more a visual thing since he was sitting across the room, kind of like a weird VR moment. Actually, like most magic or crafty stuff these days, not that it comes up that often."

"You keep saying that, but you seem to be contributing your fair share."

"I do not." Sasha looked offended, "But anyway, it was fun. Had to give you snaps."

"For what?"

"Just the whole 'almost' concept."

"Well, that was the best *Almost Sex* story I've ever heard. Of course, I've only heard two other ones." Tip's voice trailed off, something was suddenly (or maybe not terribly suddenly) distracting her; a rose-like bittersweet scent edged the room. Their happy closeness hadn't soured but it had shifted somehow —Sasha could sense that Tip wanted her there even though something had forced its way in front of them, demanding both their attention, but Sasha was at a complete loss, *Did Tip just leave her body? Why now...?* Sasha then sensed her sister was *mostly* still intact, but not quite all... She slowly, carefully spirited herself closer, aligning with Tip, "I know you're still here—*what just happened?* Do you want me to leave or—"

"No, no... Wanted to share something, for a while I've been..." Tip's voice slowed again. "I just kept thinking it wasn't the right time but now I know it was that I couldn't believe it, or accept it —the last few weeks or however long."

Sasha warmed the space between them.

"So all our weird convos about our periods? Well, I found out —for *real*, from Dr. Senitz..."

"Yeah, all those appointments. And how heavy—so much blood. Scary. Like the Fertility Goddess what's-her-name..."

"Yeah, if only." Tip sighed, "That's weird you said that because that's what we found."

"What? You're a fertility goddess? You're pregnant—immaculate pre-conception?"

"Don't be a dick. Nope. That I *can't*. There's no there *there*— *no real eggs*. Actually, there's eggs, but they're malformed. Don't work. I think—it's just my theory, not hers—that all that blood was willed into being—it still is—by my eggs, my *'cursed'* zygotes trying to fix something with magic that simply can't be fixed."

Sasha was abruptly quiet, cooler. They floated there, their essences more unhinged.

Sasha muttered, "Sorry, I guess."

"You *guess*?"

"Well, why didn't you tell me sooner? What if I need to know something more? That something's wrong with me too?"

Tip seemed to smile sadly, "How the hell did I know you'd make this about you? Somehow you'd find a way."

Sasha was struck, mostly because she knew Tip was right. She wanted the security of her body again; she started to shift her presence back as she spoke, "I'm sorry. I'm sorry that's how things are. Still would have liked to have known—"

"Well, now you do." Tip was quiet a moment more, "There's nothing wrong with you. This has nothing to do with biology and genes and everything to do with metaphysics and the preternatural or rather, *unnatural* balance of things."

"Well, what the hell is that supposed to mean? The only meta I care about is metadata... That was an attempt at a joke, in case you missed it." Sasha immediately regretted the clumsy words.

Tip sighed, "I'm tired, and besides, you get you don't have to worry about it, right?"

Sasha said nothing.

The corner of the room lightened and then darkened again as the two sisters assumed their physical bodies, stretched to fill them, and slept as best they could.

THE TETERSBERGS CONTINUED to bump into and frustrate each other through the rest of the week; the emotionally disheveled school shifted uncomfortably in its hardening shell, and the pieces and shards from myriad W's, mortals, and inbetweenums that chipped up and fell away were large and painful. I had to look away (and I've no memory of feeling that way ever before).

Rappatsi had practically tripped over Big C making her way down her building's roof, almost through her wall—how did Big C get that close without any inkling, any jingle from the Powers That Be? The air and Earth around Rappatsi was clearly bloated and tired; she would have to be especially careful: any spells, aspirations, even the most elaborate, covert sorcery could become susceptible.

Big C interrupted Rappatsi with the palm of her hand, "This isn't *'that'*—what you're thinking..."

"Your social grace and charm is still unshakable, C," Rappatsi scoffed. "*So what am I thinking?*"

"That I'm here for the usual thing, my 'standard request..'"

"Well, *aren't you?*"

Big C protested, "Yes *and no.* Take a look at this..." Rappatsi sneered at the twig-like wand Big C just presented her.

"Well, that is just, um, *silly.*"

Big C persisted, "You're letting looks get in your way—I know you're smarter than that. Go ahead, give'r a whirl..."

She tossed the wand back, deciding it wouldn't be worth the effort to even try. Rappatsi had given up trying to keep up; every time a new project took her to what had been suggested as a "shared reality"—it wasn't. The last three triages were more different than similar. So it didn't surprise her that this old broad Big C would think a wand would offer some sway over Rappatsi's thinking—only the gods would know what reality plane Big C just fell out of! On top of that, she could tell Big C had no memory of the last time they'd bumped wands *and* heads a couple hundred years ago. (It was an anomaly, but then again, so was Rapp.) *We'll just say it wasn't one of our better moments and leave it at that.*

Big C still wasn't deterred, "Rapp, don't worry, I've changed— I've *upgraded.* I won't be in your way at all, it'll happen so quickly no one will even know *what happened.*"

"C, you so know that's not true, not even a teensy bit. Especially now..."

After her remarkable crash-and-burn in Seventh Heaven, Big C scratched her way back, becoming possibly the best *Repo Man*-witch of her time. Defunct wizards, warlocks, and witches actually welcomed her visage: it was finally their "time," and she'd made their recall and transition relatively painless. Then she got sloppy *and* greedy (again). And now, she was scrapping around edges of I-don't-know-how-many reality planes... Anyway, it wouldn't necessarily hurt anything to throw her a bone or two, but it definitely wouldn't help. And Rappatsi couldn't afford to have even the slightest spell go awry; like she mentioned, they were watching her and extremely carefully—she was so close to finally, actually expanding up and out. Her success was mandatory.

"So, what are you getting at?" Big C stared hard at Rappatsi.

Rappatsi frowned, "What don't you understand? Not here. *Not now.*"

"I don't think you're *really hearing* me, I'm—"

"C, don't make us do something we'll both regret. You know it'll hurt you more than it'll hurt me."

"But you're the *good witch*—the Glinda in this bit."

"That's where you're twice wrong and again, yes, I'm supposed to help the good parts more than the bad parts, but that doesn't mean you don't do some bad *to get* to the good."

Rappatsi started to bristle and flush, her hair flaring like she was part of some high school electricity experiment. Big C looked at her watch: not only was the time wrong but the year was off *again*—she was a mess, and painfully, sadly aware of it.

Then in some pathetic and desperate attempt to turn the circumstances to her favor, she violently turned and torpedoed her first wand plus two others (Big C always had *something* up her sleeve), smaller but newer, probably more powerful. If she could strike and impale Rappatsi with all three wands at once (and that was a ridiculously huge "if"), she could coerce Rappatsi to do her bidding, but only for ten minutes at most (much less if the intended was rather powerful, and Rappatsi was certainly that). It was an oldie but goodie—but the quality of the wands had a lot to do with it, too.

Anyway—hardly a surprise—she missed, and Rappatsi twisted and reversed the spell: the wands flung back, attacking their owner. They pierced both of Big C's open palms, and she crumpled into herself; she was gone with a whimper and would float in the ether until she happened upon another crack in someone's reality plane or another fissure in some burnt-out overwitch's reality.

━━━━━━━━ ◊◊◊ ◊◊◊ ━━━━━━━━

STEPHEN CLARKE STARED UNBELIEVINGLY, affectionately at the bones in his wrist, and then traced the crooked edges of the marvelous skeletal structure comprising his right forearm with his finger—it had served him so very, very well all forty-seven of his years on Earth.

He was delirious, *I guess it's "the third time's a charm." I can have that effect on witches... Plus if she was still so disgusted, why waste the drugs?*

He thought back to that "fateful day"—both he and Ezra had finally met and claimed it as such (stating it so just within moments of each other)—which made the whole day and conversation seem more auspicious. Even later, during the first "seduction" (as Ezra had labeled it), *There wasn't even an inkling of sexiness in any of this,* thought Stephen as Ezra continued shoving powder and then the *potion* in the appropriate orifices. This was their third "party," and to his mostly obliterated yet blissed out mind, *it just seems like just good—really good—old-fashioned buzzed-out drugs to my mostly mortal brain.*

I have to believe this is all part of the process, the transition. If I'm supposed to "revel"—that was the word Ezra used—in this next stage of my existence, it makes complete sense that I won't need bones, or organs, or blood to do it.

In Stephen's drug-fueled meditation, he laughed at the bizarre and yet beautiful coincidence of it all. Yes, he would have much preferred to stay on Earth and physically experience all of his newfound, newly born magical strength, but there was clearly some larger plan (Ezra had suggested as much) in which he was the mainstay; he would necessarily provide the immutable basis for its... He had to stop—he was overcome with the perfect beauty of it all. He suddenly felt himself propelled up and out though he had no clear sense of where he was going, what might logically happen next. He heard a strange muffled clunking as his bones collapsed and crumbled, and his skin dissipated.

Mr. Stephen Clarke had finally died—in body, mind, and sadly in spirit. And in spite of how much he had believed in himself, there was nothing left for him to offer this world, or any other.

Ezra heard the crackle of the hair and swaths of skin as they combusted—the hex was successful, the spell complete, *What a waste...* She sighed. She didn't care for him one way or the other personally, but if it had been successful, and if Stephen Clarke had transformed himself into his self-described, self-promoted "Mr. Magic," that would have been a bright, bold feather to stick in any cap she'd prefer—in any *overwitch's* cap, to be more correct (and maybe a shade grandiose). But not to worry—she had decided—there was absolutely nothing to worry about ever again —Antonia will experience The Ultimate Dream (The Coven's "conversion therapy"—they wouldn't, couldn't surrender to Antonia's disinterest that easily), and Ezra knew within a relatively short time, all would be right and correct with the world—especially *her* world.

THE TRADITIONAL PRE-HOLIDAY MONOPOLY ROUNDELAY! This random piece of cardboard and its makeshift oversized charm bracelet had inadvertently become a touchstone for the Tom Tetersberg clan's holiday traditions. The usual struggles and burning questions abounded: would Ezra be denied a turn at the board *again* this year? (*If everything continued to be a joke to her, that would be a resounding "yes."*) Would Antonia once again dominate the game, donning her fourth title in as many years? Would she once again try and psych out her opponents (for gods' sake, these still are her children...) by playing the last half of the game *out of body? (It could be slightly unnerving if your opponent appeared to be sleeping through a game you were losing...)*

But this year was especially unique: this Tricentennial celebration was occurring within seventy-two hours of the Thanksgiving moon, and barely twenty-four hours after certain planes of existence and planets aligning—something was destined to affect *something* or *someone*, some *way* or another.

A pounding, shattering thud from above shook them from their Monopoly game deliberations. It was Tom Dad again, he must have stomped his foot on the stairs or a couple *somethings*, and was moaning loudly and angrily. The Sisters immediately trooped upstairs to discover their next circle of family hell: Tom Dad's groaning was becoming more of a rant as he glared at the paintings hung in the stairs' hall. (Even his own simple pleasures —like his home's decor and design—apparently wasn't off limits.)

"Your mother did this, I'm sure of it..."

Sasha looked and saw nothing different, "Did what? The paintings?"

"Exactly, it's the paintings. Are you looking *at the paintings?*"

Then they saw the next episode exactly: the paintings had moved and had been arranged by color, mostly blue with mostly blues, red with reds. Tom Dad always struggled in placing each new painting (the wall being its own composition), so the girls completely understood this particular harangue.

Sasha kept thinking out loud, "But Dad, why Mom? You're blaming her for everything lately..." and after another thought added, "And granted, a lot of stuff has been *her fault* but not intentionally. Or consciously, anyway... And think about it: she's been buzzed most of the morning on the couch probably doing her Joni Mitchell Realignment bullshit, so when, exactly could she have done it—*all* of it? Did she *fly* up here while we weren't looking?"

Tom, indignant, said, "She could have."

"She could have maybe thirty years ago; she sucks at levitating now. Plus, we did establish certain *rules* in this house, didn't we, Dad?"

Tip mumbled, "They did. *We* didn't."

Sasha frowned, tried to nudge her and missed. She countered Tip, "Well, yeah, but that's *not* the point..."

Tom Dad snapped, "Yes, that *is the point!* Or certainly a big part of it."

A nervous moment later, Antonia suddenly resurfaced—but from her bedroom, not the couch. (Soba sighed, *Maybe my mother really* **is** *possessed.*)

"Everyone, I need you to see this." Antonia uneasily beckoned them in.

Her tone scared them; they rushed to Tom and Antonia's bedroom. They found her, looking stunned, and seemingly, strangely entirely sober, standing in the middle of the room as if afraid to move. She turned to face them slowly, now appearing more confused than scared, "So, you don't find this bizarre?"

"Find what bizarre, Mom?"

"They're right there. I'm waiting for *your* reaction... I mean, *why now?*"

Tom, strangely much calmer, asked again, "*What* is, Ant? You keep pointing—at nothing." She swung around, then swung around again. Antonia swore, "*Where did they go?*" Soba scanned the floor where Antonia had been flailing. "What are your wands doing on the floor, Mom?"

"That's the whole thing! They *weren't* on the floor! Just twenty seconds ago they weren't—they were floating *right here* in front of me, taunting me... At least that's what it felt like."

The four stood there for a few moments, not really sure what to do next. Was Mom being her usual weird and wacky self? The only catch was that as off kilter as Antonia's humor might be sometimes, you would always know the punchline way before she finished it (her half-baked attempts were part of her charm). But it was clear there was no "punchline"—so what was this? Just another freakish moment in what was already an especially memorable—*and not in necessarily a good way*—start to the holiday? Soba looked more closely at the accused rogue wands—something wasn't right about that either.

Soba had a theory, "Your main guy. The big one—it was your first wand, right?"

Antonia frowned, *Now what's she up to?* "Yes...?"

"It wasn't blue; it was red... Right?"

"Well, right. But they can change color, with age mostly."

Soba, the future litigator, knew then she struck a vein, "Just answer the question: it was *never* blue. Right?"

"Yes, right."

"And certainly never this intense or bright—whatever the color, right?'

"Oh yeah, that's *definitely* true."

Soba sat down, now very pleased with herself, "Well, that's the answer. There's the culprit."

Everyone looked at each other, not at all sure what was happening. Tom put his hand on his daughter's head, "What, exactly, are you suggesting, Baby Girl?"

"I'm not *suggesting* anything. The wand did it. All of it. The game, the paintings, freaking Mom out..."

"I wasn't *freaked out!*" Antonia waved the notion away, then not, "Well, maybe a little *freaked* out."

Sasha and Tip were conferring, "That could be it—but probably only half of it, if that."

Soba countered, "And *why?*" She never liked her sisters intentionally interfering (at least that's what it seemed like they were doing).

"Because wands don't have minds of their own... Not arranging paintings by their palette, anyway."

Antonia confirmed, "That's right. She's right. Someone or

something needs to be guiding it. Delivering either the spell or summons."

They all sat down, contemplating the possessed pick-up sticks. Antonia looked down at Red—her pet name for the alleged guilty wand—and said, "We were so close once, and now look what you've become." No one could tell whether she was trying to be funny or not.

ON SUNDAY EVENINGS, when empty, the school had an almost institutional appearance to it. The worn grey brick could inspire or deflate given one's respective emotional state—there was no in-the-middle sense about it. It was good *or* it was bad. To maintain whatever amount of positive attitude she had remaining, Principal Casen didn't let herself look up at the facade until she was either almost fully inside or if leaving, with her key in her car's ignition, *One day this too will change, somehow, some way...*

The stone structure, even though it was just tipping into two hundred years old, had this crazy aura of permanence: as if nothing could hurt or help it until it decided it was ready, when it finally decided to sit up and pay attention. Or maybe it was just waiting its turn; it perhaps knew something far richer, far more expansive than any human, witch, or otherwise's brain could comprehend. Maybe that's how the universe helped keep every little, bitty thing in check, by giving certain building and monuments their own special sanctity: a unique place and purpose, contributing to an overall scheme of all things. Once again, that could be a happy thought or not, depending upon one's current frame of thinking.

A Sunday late afternoon and pre-Monday morning pre-prep visit wasn't that unusual, but not only was her laptop on, her very old Wiccan calendar app was already open and chewing its way around most of her desktop. It was a calendar alert that wanted attention right now: the Tricentennial "madness" phase, period, celebration (in some circles, *the nuttier ones...*) was starting in a little over a week; she never had paid that much attention to the Centennial mythology, but a couple of her *Wiccanette* buddies had, *Strange that it's so close to the harvest moon and Thanksgiving, etc., etc. this time.* Could that be why? *No, too goddam easy.* Besides, it wasn't a specific "thing" that had been developed or caused or generated by anything nefariously evil or spectacularly wonderful (that might give it a little *oomph),* it simply was some (somewhat silly) alignment of planets and runic planes and *whatnots.* (It always felt like the Emmys to her: it seemed like they just presented them a couple months ago when all of a sudden it had been—it *had* to have been—a year.) She clicked the alert away and sighed.

Now what about that pain-in-my-ass Clarke butthead? She hadn't heard any grumbling in a few days, and that couldn't be right. And she overheard something about Stackhouse's class though nothing bad, but maybe too good to be true. And then there's the new English teacher whose name she could never remember

Then suddenly, as if prompted, an email that seemed possessed—she'd been blind-copied on it. Sara wasn't surprised by anything anymore: *'more zombie students,'* only this time they live underwater and are apparently very peaceful and happy...

Fuck me, *Happy Monday, Mrs. Casen.*

———— ✦ ✦ ————

JULIE PINCHED GREG. He didn't react; not that she was neces-sarily seeking a reaction but realized mid-pinch that might be a nice thing.

The was some more-truth-than-not rumor running around the halls that morning about the apparently indestructible graffiti hoodoo (yes, it can have Druid roots and still be called hoodoo—you don't even have to have a Southern and then a Louisianan accent for it to work!) and its surprising connection—or perhaps better said, just to be safe, *connections.*

The wall colors across all the different subject pods appeared especially bright, as if someone or some gnome or some spell had painted them just last night. But the irony of the colors, whether they were actually the way they appeared or just in how everyone had been hexed to see them, was perfectly clear given the cafeteria's bacchanal from just over a week ago. (It was especially to Principal Casen and her cronies—what was left of them.)

"Didn't you feel that?" Julie had her pincher fingers poised in case the answer was no.

Greg still didn't comprehend how most girls seemed to *consistently* choose the most-weird or plain-wrong moments to flirt (*Why the fuck else would she do that?*), "Well, maybe, not really, dumbass... What were you expecting to happen?" It was between periods, and he was looking for Tom Boy because, well, just because. And then Julie—*weird fucking Julie*—decided he needed to be pinched. Or whatever. He didn't even seem to feel the charm she'd wrapped around his exceptionally large balls (which, and she didn't understand it quite yet, she'd found erotically challenging, and in a good way)—so she just assumed, like the pinch, he didn't feel it. (But he had.)

Julie tried to keep the conversation going, "So you heard the buzz, right?"

Greg scanned the hall again for Tom Boy, "Who hasn't? Gross."

"Why is a dead teacher gross?"

Greg was forced back into the conversation, "I'm talking about the food rumor; what are you talking about?"

"Clarke's bones."

"Mr. Clarke?"

"Yep. A little teepee of white man bones, or that's how it was whispered to me. Actually, thinking about it further, no 'man,' probably just 'white bones.'"

Greg frowned, this was just the third time he was possibly, actually interested in something Julie had to say. He stalled,

"Everyone's bones are white, stupid ass." Julie just smiled quietly, her fingers still ready to attack. (Julie and Greg had a very healthy love-hate relationship—more so for Julie than Greg.)

Julie finally collapsed, sighed, Greg wasn't biting (or pinching back). Of course, it was the middle of the morning and on a Tuesday, but one never knows for sure when the best time for... "So, maybe the school walls are so bright and wet because they're in mourning."

Greg's brow furrowed ever further (though he did stop looking for Tom Boy), "Just because they found his bones doesn't mean he's actually dead."

Now Julie frowned, "Well, um, I think there probably is a *really good chance* that's the case." She thought another few seconds more, and smiled that smile again, recognizing the Gregism, "But you're thinking about those *Different Kinds of Death* theories you didgie guys dwell on, right?"

Greg started pulling on backpack, he kind of shrugged "yeah."

Julie smiled broadly, "I thought Bitts was the morose one."

"He is. I just think it's cool."

Julie kept talking to the back of Greg's head, "So who's teaching Clarke's class?"

He shouted back over his shoulder, "You're the one with all the secrets—and answers. You tell me."

Lunch stayed exactly as lunch should be that very slow and careful day; no one knew exactly how to talk about the events of the week before last, and only snippets appeared on the school's portal which—whether it was intentional or not—tended to belittle another potentially looming catastrophe by picking at all the messy recent *parts* as opposed to the whole. The school was ripe with misgiving and a good dose of dread; Princess Casen had seized the moment and blew it, though it was mostly clear the witching cards had been stacked against her and to some other witch's (or group of witches) benefit—but who?

. . .

TOM BOY STOOD there waiting till Greg had driven out of the mall parking lot; a somewhat confused Bitts stood there watching an impatient Tom Boy watch Greg leave. Tom Boy couldn't listen to Greg vex yet one more moment about the silly balls-in-your-throat spell. And then about the burrito that *clearly had a personal vendetta...*

Bitts commented, "He still talks about it like a recurring nightmare—it didn't even happen to him. I mean, I can't know for sure regarding the kamikaze burrito, but the balls thing."

Tom Boy glared at back of Greg's car, "Once a putz, always a putz."

"I guess it wouldn't ultimately matter where your balls were, assuming they could still do everything they were supposed to."

Tom Boy furrowed his brow, he seemed to be taking this conversation very seriously (or he was already anticipating the next one). He knew Bitts well enough that he would actually entertain the notion of testicular mobility, it could quickly become a dark, twisty rabbit hole of Bitts-isms. He wasn't in the mood; Greg had unwittingly tested Tom Boy's limits (that was lately happening more often than not). Tom had wanted to get to the mall, appease the Dark Web gods, then drive his white, boney-but-still-cute butt home.

Bitts, never to be outdone, leapt ahead to the *next* convo, "So, why are we here *now?* You still haven't really explained anything—not that you could have with whiny Greg going off."

Tom Boy looked disconcerted again, as if it was obvious (or if it wasn't, it should be), "Fresh *blooood...*" He drooled his o's, attempting a not very successful Bela Lugosi imitation. Tom Boy thought it was mildly funny, at least worth a chuckle. Bitts just frowned at him—they were on two very different wavelengths suddenly (that was the ill-famed Bitts Downside: abruptly leaving the moment and convo for other parts—and consciousnesses—unknown).

Tom Boy now sounded more like regular Tom Boy, "No, seriously folks, the sooner we get her blood on the glass, the better. Sorry, my bad: get her *ninety-nine point nine percent pure witch blood* on the glass... I need to show due respect to the source."

Bewildered, Bitts was still digesting the first half of Tom's statement, "Did it really say that? Gross."

"Not in so many words, but I think it makes sense. Don't you? Makes more sense than trying to wipe some kind of dried scabby thing into a piece of glass."

Bitts didn't have an opinion one way or the other, "So, whose blood is it this time?"

Tom Boy said plainly, "Fortunately Sasha's. Got her menstrual blood too—thanks to Julie."

Bitts grimaced, "How'd that happen?"

Tom Boy was now strange and flip, "Don't know. Don't care. They seem to be fine. Now I owe Julie one."

"What's that?"

Tom Boy deadpanned, "Rub one off and baggy it. She's got her evil magic going down—just kidding, don't really know if it's evil or not so much. Don't know, don't care."

Bitts took the information as Bitts typically would and shrugged—Bitts was the most linear and literal thinker of the group. (Mostly brilliant, but most times *too* literal.)

Bitts suggested, "So Sasha's kind of our sacrificial virgin once removed, and she has no idea, right?"

"That's making this whole thing sound so primitive and feral. And it's *so not* wanting to be that. Besides, I don't know how much virgin is still there or not..."

Now Bitts furrowed his brow, "Well, you of all people would know, no?"

Tom Boy stared blankly at the red light, "Well, yes and no."

"Thought you said you loved sex with Sasha?"

"I did? I wouldn't go that far."

Bitts went from being furrowed to being mildly annoyed to a

little more than that, "Well, dude, why *wouldn't* you say that? Are you saying you never screwed her?"

"Yes, and no. And *screw* is a very subjective word."

Bitts blurted, "No, it's not. What the fuck are you talking about?"

Tom Boy looked blank, shaking his head, as they walked up to the door. "It's too complicated and I'm too tired. Let's feed these monsters and get the hell home."

"Um, okay." Bitts suddenly had a too-smart-for-his-own-good realization, "But wait: how are we getting in there?" It was almost ten, and the mall was a darkened, boxy monolith... A boxy *impenetrable* monolith.

Tom Boy shook two keys and a glow-in-the-dark thumb drive in Bitts' face, "Stole key impressions and scooped the security code from one of your Dark Web sources."

"Shit. Who?"

"If I tell you, I'll have to kill you." Tom Boy didn't even pretend to smile after that usually semi-funny response. Bitts once again had his sense of being two steps behind the conversation (maybe three?).

Entry happened remarkably smoothly; it was clear this wasn't Tom Boy's *first time at the* —whatever it is—*opera?* Bitts' most times kind, generally brilliant, but mostly asocial personality fit well with Tom Boy's apparently newfound megalomania (though he was still, at this point, a *considerate* megalomaniac), but now Bitts was starting to worry. Without a word, Tom Boy swiped the bloody cloth across the window's etched yet fading inscription, whispering, almost mumbling the incantation at the same time. Bitts stared, *What da freak? Why am I even here?* The sudden heat from the altar glass almost overwhelmed them, and then a brilliant flash of black light—it was done (whatever "it" was...).

Tom Boy had caught Bitts' thought, "You're here because I want you here. But *mostly* you're here—well, you'll see the very next time you get your paws on your digital whatever." Tom Boy squeezed the back of Bitts' neck, "You're 'in,' dude. We both are. Probably should've asked you first, but what the fuck..." Tom Boy laughed and popped the door open with a snap, Bitts followed him out.

Tom Boy turned away from Bitts, reached into his backpack. He tore a couple small layers—barely a morsel—off of the "drug's" rough edge, evening it out. He noticed a sweetness this time as it (mostly) dissolved down his throat.

Tom Boy pulled up at Bitts' dark house. "God, dude, not even a single nervous light on... Your parents are so cool."

"Yeah, *when* they're cool, they're cool."

"So, dude, before you disappear, I've got a favor. More of a question. And it's completely cool if you don't—"

"Sure. What?"

"Want to make out?"

Bitts frowned again, he paused wanting to be sure there wasn't more to the question. He looked over at Tom Boy, "You mean kiss?"

"Yeah, I'd like to try kissing you. Greg was okay, but just not that into it."

Bitts thought a moment more, *Is he putting me on?* It didn't appear that way at all. Bitts slowly answered, "Yeah, well, thanks but I'm not into it *at all*..." then he joked, "I mean, I'll suck your dick, but I won't kiss." Bitts laughed out loud; Tom Boy looked like he was seriously deliberating the offer.

"Dude, I'm kidding! Aren't *you?*" Bitts still wasn't sure.

"No, I wanted to kiss you. But that's cool, if you don't want to kiss me." Tom Boy shrugged bizarrely matter-of-fact, and put the car into drive, "So, check out your new shit powers. And let's connect tomorrow, whenever."

Bitts started to close the door, trying to think of what the right thing (the nice thing?) to say might be, "Yeah, um, sure... So, sorry I didn't want to kiss you."

"Don't be nuts, dude, *everybody* doesn't automatically want to make out with *everybody*."

"Yeah. Okay. I get it." He shut the door, and Tom Boy drove off.

He shrugged and headed inside, *Haven't been hit on in a long time —it's kinda nice.*

———————

EZRA JUST DIDN'T GET it. She was never like this, not for as long as this—two days, *two whole fucking days! These stupid conversations with Ant didn't mess me up that much—or did they?* "Cutting yourself a break" was purely an ironic statement in Ez's waking world. There was never enough time for anything let alone "breaking" or cutting or *stopping doing whatever.* So maybe this mental fog was a way her body was revolting? Multiple espressos chased by that silly *Wizards' Wide Awake* juice had produced zilch. *And even spending this amount of time worrying about it is making me a little (a lot?) nuts...* She opted per usual to her default (typically comforting) activity: information gathering. Ezra's mental operating system functioned these days on one directive: *Information Is Power.*

So she'd finally heard from Antonia about her (and to a larger degree The Coven's) dreamscaping efforts, to be more specific and correct, her *failed* dreamscaping effort: Antonia remained resolute and disinterested. (There were multiple other excoriations and incriminations, but I'll save the paper and the time.)

So what the fuck happened? Maybe because it's about her? But that was never a problem before! Oh wait, *wait one moment!* There was just that one time, that one strange instance, when they'd just touched thirty (which in witch years is, well—just say it's nothing to worry about).

Ezra stopped herself then and there, she made herself—like she did that moment at thirty—quit thinking, quit rationalizing, stop denying. She made herself acknowledge the pain, an almost unbearable pain when one can't prevent, through magic or any preternatural power, the *truth*. And the truth can be a perfect and pure (omnipotent, some would say) force. *The idea that telling the truth is liberating is puffery at its puffiest...* Ezra chuckled but not in a happy way; she had denied this one lie, for so long and its ugly head and addled claw had finally found a way out, to be seen if not completely heard.

There seemed like there was every kind of reason to not tell Antonia and Tom at the time, *I didn't think he mattered... And the other sad truth is that I still feel that way.* The metaphor of peeling an onion wherein each layer revealed another reason for Ezra's sad logic; but those flimsy, translucent stratum finally presented her with just a putrid, black pit. She spun around, the walls, her apartment, everything was too close, had witnessed too much. She ran from her house.

The air helped; it always had. There was only one place she could and would want to go—*to see Anne.* Anne had the bookstore on Twelfth Street, the titular Twelfth Street Book Haven. It was an institution, much like Anne herself was—at least in Ezra's mind. Anne was also the oldest, truest, undiluted (commingling was prohibited in that distant generation—besides there simply weren't enough witches, let alone warlocks) bitch-of-a-witch sorceress of her eon. (Her peers were few and far away, if there were any left at all.)

Anne maintained a very low profile and struggled to keep it that way; Ezra was the spotlight-mongering opposite. How did they become such good friends? The answer was, and still is, *that they weren't*—they didn't really like each other much at all. But there was a deep-seated and mutual respect, and a shared devotion to their higher calling. Ezra was at the shop within moments; she saw her hand materialize just as she reached to knock, *I transported myself here and wasn't even aware of it? Things are worse than I thought...* It was late, the store closed, but Anne lived upstairs and had always gladly been available for personal catastrophes like these, *Though there's never been a 'like these'—this is weird, this is pissing me off...*

Anne opened the door, Ez's clenched hand poised to knock; she pulled Ezra inside. "I sensed you maybe a mile away. What the hell is wrong?"

"I wish I knew. I don't know that I can explain it in a way you'd understand."

Anne smiled, which is something Anne rarely did. Ezra felt slightly relieved, *Anne always has a way...*

"First, you need to get out of your own way. This isn't about you, this is so, so much bigger." Anne shook her head slightly, "I know you won't do it; you can't help yourself, but you needed to hear it."

So much for the slight relief Ezra clutched seconds ago.

Ezra cried, "I've *never felt* this confused. I always know what to say. And I've never hesitated to say anything to Ant. Anything."

Anne frowned and shrugged, she didn't care about that. "Are you listening to me? This is *way, way bigger* than you, either of you. Get out of your way, get out of Antonia's way. You pre-baby boomer witches got to get over yourselves. You *need to do this!*"

This wasn't what Ezra needed. And it wasn't what she had hoped this conversation would be about (though she wasn't really sure what she wanted. But knowing Anne as she did, this wasn't a complete surprise).

But then Anne did something entirely out of character: she reached and gently grabbed Ezra's hand. "All of this is going to be hard. It's always been hard." She reached across the table for a folder that felt as if it had been waiting for this conversation to happen. "Remember last time? When you wouldn't take my word as gospel? Play on words intended..." Anne smiled at yet another unfunny Anne joke. *Don't forget to laugh...* Ezra quickly corrected her wavering attitude; in spite of the enthusiastic welcome, Ezra wasn't feeling a whole bunch better, or even different. "Yes, I remember. But the pictures you had really didn't tell me or convince me of anything—since we're being honest." Anne didn't respond. She simply turned the folder to face Ezra and opened it.

The black and white prints immediately answered any and all questions, quelled any doubts: there was their infamous "sister" overwitch Martina, directly behind Gloria Steinem—it couldn't have been anyone else, especially with that hair. As if reading Ezra's mind, Anne turned to the next print: a blowup of the tattoo. The White Witch's mark, as black and sharp as cut coal, sat where it never could today (not without inciting some unwelcome comment from some coven group or another), across Martina's neck and down her shoulder. The size of the brand was a bold move even then.

Ezra breathed a long deep breath, in then out, *So it's all true— all of it.* She then did something she would never have done before: she took Anne's coarse hand, and when Anne didn't pull away, squeezed it very hard. Anne smiled and said, "So now you see. All your efforts haven't been for naught. The Sisterhoods' blood magic, and especially the White Witches sect, *your* sisters and all their attendant glory and powers. The wands, the alchemy, our community, on and on..." She turned to the last photo. It was another blowup from the same Womyn's March, though this time it was of Ezra and Antonia. Shouting at the wall of people, Ezra to one side and Antonia the other—it was their clenched right and left hands that had kept them so very, very close.

———————

TOM BOY UNRAVELED the ugly ball of crinkled plastic and desiccated flesh. It barely smelled anymore, or maybe it did (that would make more sense) and he had become immune. Once again it seemed as if he was sitting across the desk, or bed, or whatever from himself, confronting and wondering and concerned, *How the fuck did I get **here**?* He'd asked himself that simple question a gazillion times in the last bunch of weeks and the answer seemed within reach and impossible to say all at once. (It was a conundrum—*a true puzzle of the Tom Boy Mind*...)

And where that was once a challenge Tom Boy craved, now, in the next moment, he had no patience or interest in it. (Maybe he'd simply grown out of such simplistic pursuits.)

He took the last cusp of dried toe bone and flesh and swallowed it whole (the notorious last little piggy of the five). (I think Stephen Clarke had the piggy that went to market, but don't hold me to that...) Earth mother and overwitch Marta could now once again be *and feel* completely balanced with finally having (give her a couple days for everything to grow back where it belongs) ten toes on both feet instead of just nine.

Down to the Bone

✾✾✾

The *Grand and Extra-Deliberately Different Day of Thanks* was an event and "holiday" that was exceedingly joyous and cozily familiar all at once. It was impossible to find a W that didn't look forward to the biannual celebration with the utmost anticipation, glee, and any other fitting description you'd care to attach. The convenient timing (every other year) encouraged the lauded celebration to be big enough or small enough, grand yet intimate respective to one's wishes—it was a bauble of metaphysical bliss.

Every magickal being contributed in their own perfect way—a true communion of spirit, flesh, and dreams. Past celebrations varied greatly: fanciful buildings might be constructed, musical performances created, painting and sculptures expressed, but all would be embraced by gilt-edged feasts of food and every form of drink. These special days and feasts made the more familiar and purely mortal Thanksgiving celebration look like a bad lunch day in the school cafeteria.

The Sisters overthrew and fumbled the end of the Monopoly game (a record eighteen hours sum told, not including the one-to-two daylong breaks in play) with Antonia—even under wand duress—natching her fifth sequential title. Once the "lost" thimble game piece was finally located (dubiously under Tom Dad's seat cushion) and the box put away, formal preparations for the Tetersberg celebration slowly began.

———————

EZRA HAD to walk outside to her deck. She needed to breathe in a different room, a different place. Air that would help, and not hurt. Everything in her direct line of sight began to shrink, and then she realized it was in her and not what was outside of her; she was falling back and away and deep into a tight, darkening orifice. Her eyes cinched together, that miserable feeling of the front and back becoming one ocular bulb of painful messiness. She'd reached-clambered outside the screen door, the trees just next to the stairs, but to no real change... *What the goddam is going on here? Was the tea bad? Did that bastard bartender spit in my martini last night?* No, tea doesn't spoil (not without a lot of effort), and that barstool gin Ezra preferred would kill anything except Ezra. She saw Felix glimpse at her—and run-bolt in the exact opposite line from where she stood... *Fuck you too, cat... This has to be a migraine left over from that woeful weekend thirty-two years ago.* She started to feel a tad better; she was seeing just two of Felix as opposed to three... *Such an evil thing, but still love him madly.*

Next, she sensed something—*maybe several somethings*—strange and small trying to speak to her. She managed to maneuver, float, eek her position higher—her breath was getting shorter, *You're showing weakness!,* or was it actually a lack of oxygen? She slip-slided to the black edge of the circle and managed a slightly better view. More air, too! She suddenly saw what had to be the source of all that gibberish: it was her right hand and forearm, and perfectly positioned across her wrist were eight small human-ish heads, replete with eyes and mouths, some hair, ears were a bit randomly placed. The heads' necks were attached parasitically, rooted into her skin. (One would be forgiven for thinking it was just a bizarre piece of jewelry, a bangle created in really awful taste.)

Then the bracelet spoke, or the one side of it did, "So, if you're freaked out enough, we can stop this now. Unless you're into pain and dark tight spaces..."

Ezra still wasn't sure what the hell was happening—but she *was* rather intimidated (though would never actually admit that). She wobbled—the tunnel got tighter—she barely got her words out, "I'm not familiar with what being 'freaked out' feels like, so no, I suppose not." That was a lie, of course; Ezra, under duress, could be defiant and irrational as the next whiny W.

The heads sighed. They all spoke in fits and starts, finishing one another's thoughts as best they could. (And rather than attempt to parse *all* their random Ezra commentary, here was the general gist:)

(Heads #1 and #4, banter, to and fro:) "Ezra, dear, the time— your time—has come. If you haven't put two and two together quite yet, we'll just tell you: it's us. The Coven. Or rather one of the many iterations of our coven. Kind of fun, right? But kind freaky too—*a scary kind of freaky,* right?"

A strange cackling (sounding more like constipated bats than a gathering supernatural supposedly all-powerful W entities) ensued; Ezra didn't respond.

(Heads #1 and #4, #6 now, and in unison, mostly:) "So, here's what we need you to understand: don't get a *head* of yourself."

Now they all were hawing, snickering. It was kind of funny— the heavy-handed pun—though Ezra could be forgiven for not thinking so. She was simultaneously overwhelmed and under-impressed by this—her first real formal encounter with the region's legendary, hallowed *The Coven* sect. Ezra could now confidently (and sadly) confirm that their broken reputation was an accurate one.

(Then they all contributed,) "Our partnership is working well;

your contributions have been remarkably astute and valuable...
Well, at least until several months ago... But let's not make more
of this than what it's always exactly been: you're the *intermediary*
—*nothing more*." Then, as if rehearsed, all the heads stopped
babbling except Head #1, "There simply isn't enough *room* for
anything or anyone more. Oh, sorry about the hypothetical 'job
offer'—never *really* existed—but we trust you knew that on some
level."

The blackness started to loosen around her eyes and mind, the
circle softer, wider. Ezra felt emboldened; yes, she never really
fully trusted the notion of real *employment,* but something much
more—*bigger, badder!* (Maybe she was "winning"? *But winning what
exactly?* This was a test, *it absolutely had to be... Just another small
hurdle.*)

The head on the other side had been relatively quiet till now,
"Listen, bitch, it's not a matter of *winning.* It's not a matter of
someone having more, being better than any other. That's your
problem Ezra, and why you'll always be what you are, stay *as you
are,* until something shifts—and shifts *dramatically.*"

Ezra couldn't see which head started talking next, a tad defen-
sively, "Yeah, maybe there's an opening in that wacky Wiccan sect
—you speak that Anglican dialect don't you? They just got
elevated to the Etheric plane, though only the gods know how
that happened." More cackling again, "So, yeah, could be a "done
deal"; it would get a little lonely, though. And cold. And several
other shitty things that we won't go into right now." (Head #5
found that hysterical.)

Then #6 offered, "That's rather pointed, and not in a fair
way, no?"

"She's had over a hundred and fifty years—you're older than
that, Ezra, right?—she should be better than *this*." She looked at
the others who seemed to agree, "So all of that excruciating *Alice
in Wonderland* rabbit-black hole stuff at the start of our convo was

just a teensy taste of what could be if you don't, well, *play by the rules."*

Ezra muttered, "You mean *your* rules?"

The heads were surprised, "Well, yeah... That's what you signed up for, in one way or another."

And they weren't wrong, that was generally how these pacts worked, regardless of sect or history or any blind reputation: once you put your blood on the line, you had to follow the process and track until you couldn't—or didn't have to. And that would suggest you'd failed miserably or succeeded remarkably. (The only slightly bittersweet aspect to winning your new role is you generally don't remember—as we've suggested—what you were doing before... That's not *every* promotion, but generally thinking, the bigger the supranatural or cosmic responsibilities, the cleaner the slate.)

Ezra pressed, "And that last Clarke offering—the sacrifice and potion, the *'bone snow'*... That was a big nothing to all of you?"

"Not to all of us—but most of us... Actually, to be completely forthcoming, it was your means to an end—specifically the *end you wanted.*" There was some murmuring, discussion, then nothing—for an overlong minute or three, *Did they all go to the bathroom or something?*

Ezra surprised herself with her suddenly flippant attitude. *As they say, 'if you can't laugh at yourself'...* In many ways that adage holds true, but this really wasn't one of them. She glanced again at the grotesque bangle on her wrist to see what was going on when it shook back to life, the two on the end that had been doing most of the talking announced: "We *all* ultimately wanted that wunderkind Antonia... You were just the messenger, to be brutally honest."

Ezra became livid, "She hasn't finalized *anything!"*

There was a slow measured response, "Oh, Ezra. *Yes, she has*—it's not happening. She'll talk to you later today."

Ezra glowered at her wrist: she wanted to pluck each of the

morbid little outgrowths from her wrist and crush them one by one. Scream by scream...

But what would that accomplish exactly, except just more of her own spectacular, personal hell? Everything started to return to how it was supposed to be: the circle faded, the sky lightened, Felix resurfaced—Ezra's forearm became entirely her own once again.

———————⟨⟨⟨⟨● ●⟩⟩⟩⟩———————

ABYSSINIA WAS THINKING ALOUD: Constance had lamented—before she was gone—that anymore it was hard for her to follow who was who, what, where, or why. And that was part of *her problem*—not suggesting something necessarily bad—and she'll eventually end up at the place she's best suited...

We all think we want to be gods, and we all *like to think* we want that level of authority and responsibility, but that isn't how things happen... I can't exactly prove my simplistic theory, but it just makes sense.

We all *like* to think we *want* an omnipresent level of control and influence, don't we? (I'm asking ironically...)

But we all—Pilar, Ditan (wherever he went to), and I—*are* wondering *why us* and why this particular task and with this particular cast of characters? We'll never fully understand exactly how it all interconnects—that's an edict—but this, my here and now, *is unusual*. It's *unusual* to be so completely entwined with one school and this *one* family... One has to wonder: *why them?*

So, what I absolutely understand is that all of this will continue until a certain spacey, empyrean balance is found. Frenchtown is not unique: at this moment there's many other places in the universe experiencing dynamic shifts—stretching, condensing, twisting to fit—in their planes of truths and brass tacks. And Frenchtown was long overdue, just a symptom of a larger problem as the world struggles to discover the right proportion of yin for its yang.

For now, The Sisters will find solace in the hullabaloo: the mish and mash of their "newfound" or better, "refurbished" witchery versus the emotional tug and push of their family, their friends.

"I SMELL A PET RAT HERE," Bitts gibed.

Tom Boy waved the door closed behind them; he was either forgetting himself or very intentionally using his craft more and frequently. That was unusual in itself (Bitts made another mental note) but Tom Boy's blithe attitude—*that's* what was especially noteworthy. It wasn't as if Tom Boy had ever expressed any distaste or aversion to spell-making, it just never was part of his Tom Boy-ness. So, suffice to say, it was weird—ratty or smelly and mostly strange.

And *what da fuck?*: why this "emergency meeting" on a Tuesday night?!

Tom Boy miffed, "There's no other way I get you assholes out here on a Tuesday, right?"

That would be true—but also bizarre. (And not the "fun" kind of bizarre Bitts and Greg were used to.)

The door rattled in its jamb—maybe Tom Boy wasn't as Harry P.-smooth as he believed. Then it shook again, and abruptly flung-slammed open, the glass shuttered. Greg was standing there in its place, his arms still smoking. Greg (exactly the *opposite* of the Tom Boy finesse) whacked his way through his magic—it was almost comical—leaving a track of burnt troll dust and discarded runes in his wake. The boys stood there trying to decide whether the standard Greg reprimand ("*You putzface! I hope you're going to replace and/or apologize [respective to situation] for that fucking [place appropriate noun or name]...*") would be appropriate or a whole new iteration would make better sense.

But Greg wildly smiled and seethed—ne'er a word or threat was uttered. The door slowly slid closed behind him, a tad shaken but still functioning.

Tom Boy said, "*That's our Greg*—go big, or go home…"

"Screw *you*," Greg suddenly whimpered, rubbing his elbow, "That hurt. Why didn't you tell me that door was metal?"

"Um, because what the hell else would it be? You can't tell just be looking at it?"

"Yeah, well, screw you anyway."

Bitts was (also true-to-form) getting impatient, "Let's stop with the pleasantries, shall we? Why the hell are we here? And where's Sash?"

Tom Boy muttered, "Sasha's not coming."

Bitts and Greg were visibly surprised.

"I uninvited her—kind of. I told her we weren't meeting."

Greg continued whining, "And you think *that's* going to keep her from knowing what we're—"

"She couldn't get close enough to begin with—the door and entrance would reject her. *Naturally.*" Tom Boy was attaching another hard drive—the modem's several LED panels suddenly looked like a Times Square facade.

Tom Boy's detachment and curt reaction surprised his friends, *Yet another 'new side' in a series of new sides…*

All of which is fine and hopefully good unless your friend's new mindset seems more maleficent evil assassin than happily aggressive entrepreneur.

Greg assessed, "But it's her blood on the glass, no?"

Tom Boy got louder, "Not anymore it's not. That perfect bitch Julie helped us out, whether she knows it or—no, *she's no clue.*"

"So, you did like an autoimmune spell on the whole shit? Even Sasha? That is so *completely Gucci.*"

Tom Boy frowned at Greg, "I knew it would happen eventually—now you're even *talking* like Julie."

Greg looked struck, Bitts too. Neither of them could think of anything appropriate (or inappropriate) to say.

Tom Boy sighed, "Sorry, distracted. Didn't really mean it... And no—I don't 'do' spells—but the blood worked exactly as it was supposed to. Almost exactly. Julie's pool doesn't have the same spunk of Sasha's—but desperate times equals desperate measures, no?"

Bitts swiveled to the glass, the black-red crusted blood had buried itself deep and hard into the etched incantation they'd discovered (or that *Bitts* discovered; Tom Boy had seemed indifferent) that Friday night (when he also wouldn't make out with Tom Boy, just to remind... *I mean—what the hell*... And, like, whatever Tom Boy's into Tom Boy can be into; no one's saying that can't be down...). Bitts had to ask, "So, then, what was all that running around for? *Just to get me alone with you?*" Bitts gimped at his joke, Greg raised an eyebrow, and Tom Boy pretended not to notice either way.

Tom Boy said, "Just to let them know we were serious."

Now what?! *Who?* The boys stared hard at Tom Boy. Greg said, "And who is this 'they'?"

"The Dark Knights, the Deep Web Dudes—or, I don't know, they might not even have a sex. But they seem like dudes... But they *only* want to deal with dudes."

Greg wondered, "So, there was *no* craft or hoodoo going down?"

"Nope. Just looked that way... I'm such a clever boy."

Greg and Bitts got mentally stuck, stammered; *He just went ahead and did that—just decided 'whatever the hell'? What did this guy do with the other, better, kinder Tom Boy?*

Bitts joked again (cautiously), "Is *that* why you wanted to make out that night? Some hazing thing?"

"Uh-huh, right..." muttered Tom Boy, placing two thumb drives in the stopgap main frame. "You've been in touch with a couple of them already, Bitts."

"I have? Who? Baba Yaga and her sidekick, Ivan the Terrible?"

"Don't be a dick. You know you have." Tom Boy now seemed to be coding the equipment from his phone, *What the hell is he doing now?!*

Bitts scowled. "Didn't know that I had."

Greg leaned in, "Listen, dickhead, before you get too intimate with your hardware there—you want to tell us *what the hell is happening?*"

Tom Boy shrugged; now he was getting as impatient as Bitts.

"Just plug in tonight—just sent you both the code—and you'll get the picture—the *story*." Then Tom Boy hesitated, his face softened, "Listen, I'm not *not* trying to include you guys, but everything started to happen and happen so quickly the other night, so I just went for it. It's what we've been talking about, like, *forever* so I thought you'd be cool. It was a now or never thing—or a *then or never* thing, I guess."

Tom Boy suddenly collapsed and sat down right where he was standing, his breath was rapid, anxious. Greg and Bitts were simply trying to follow along at this stage when in the next moment Tom Boy stiffened, his eyes sharpened again—he was staring at something on the floor. "Pick that up," he directed Greg.

Greg glared but did as Tom Boy commanded; he picked up what was at first glance a stretch of blue tattered wood, a sad twig-like toy. Then they realized it was wand "remains"—just the grip and the top, most of it was missing.

"Who has blue power that we know?" Tom Boy pressed, waspish.

Bitts rolled his eyes, "Dude, here you are preaching all futuristic and now you're asking about something as common as fucking wallpaper?"

"Uh-huh. And who has wallpaper in their house anymore?"

"Huh?"

Greg jumped, "Sasha's a *blue*. *Okay?* I'm somehow shocked you didn't know that. But I *wouldn't* be shocked to learn that was a baby wand remnant—though left over from what I would fucking love to know." Greg snickered uneasily trying to dampen the tension.

Tom Boy chewed his words, "So—she was here?"

The boys shrugged at each other, "Well, who else would it be? You told them about this. All of this. Made it a 'thing.'"

They watched Tom Boy shift, change. He was more intense, severe. He spitted, "Yeah. I did."

LUIS GLANCED AT HIS PHONE; Lila was rambling on about something or other. She just needed to get things off of her chest (or very substantial tits, as it were), *Celia's fat-ass tits can hold an awful lot of problems*... Then Luis wondered aloud how it was extra-weird that his mother had never, ever asked him who the female voice was she had to be hearing most nights, from who or where the hell it was coming from. (Either she was too drunk or too tired, probably. Or she was just happy to know her plump, occasionally good-looking son was getting laid somehow or other. *If only*...)

In any case, Lila would be spending the night but happily ensconced in her "Jeannie" bottle in a snap, crackle, and/or pop moment, so he had to forbear yet another spontaneous counseling session just a little while longer. (Luis and Co. had crafted a way to make their resident *sprite* Lila's *Dreams of Jeannie* come true.)

Luis clicked on the text, another message from Martika: right now everything seemed okay, but he shouldn't turn his phone off *just yet*. And she promised she wouldn't reach him unless it was an "emergency"... *So what's a fucking emergency? Under her bed she finds another wannabe El Cucuy next to her old* Us *magazines...?*

All this attention from all of these W's—it had to mean *something*. (Luis always mentally kept that glass at least half full...)

Or should he now put a little more love in Bitts' direction? It was pretty Dark and intense what the boys were doing, but at least they were *doing it,* and not *just talking* (or texting) about it.

ABYSSINIA: Here 'tis. A few more enchanted words to help things along—I hope... Not terribly tricky, pretty straightforward. Guess we're getting close—or closer?:

> *The time is near, the space is nigh,*
> *To push the Earth, pull the sky, to make the*
> *Will of things subside and listen, watch, shift to*
> *Fill the gaps that widen, the space between the love*
> *And fear. Make room, find heart, patience from the start,*
> *When all things end and...*

It's changing, fading already—I can't make the rest of it out. It's almost done anyway—the incantation that is, not this crazy-randomness... I'll just keep lining up those cosmological ducks as best I can.

ALMOST ELEVEN—SO he really had been staring at the same sentence for the better part of a half hour, since he fell into the office. His phone twitched—Antonia, *Can't think about her right now.*

There'd been a Facebook post that was strangely familiar and unfamiliar at the same time; he absolutely recognized the face in the post but absolutely couldn't begin to mentally put him anywhere. He was starting to toss the thought aside as yet another symptom of brain farting or Mary Jane Madness (one key symptom: *everyone* looks familiar on *some* level...) when another message bumped the first one up and out of the frame:

Tom, it was the wrong day, never the wrong drink or girl. (Wink. Wink. Chortle.)

Tom stared at the scroll. Adele, his new semi-boss, walked by his office for a second time, *What **is** her problem?*

He clicked through to the file... *Shit, how could he possibly forget Teddy Z.!* His "co-conspirator" from his community college days and beyond. Pre-Antonia (kind of). As to what exactly they had conspired for or against, that was definitely now a mystery (probably at least three mysteries, if not more). All very Earth-bound though since Ted was as mortal and red-blooded as they come... Ted blurbed something about moving or meeting—then Adele leaned into their office.

"The client's here. I'm assuming you want to be a part of this...?" *Fuck.*

Tom jumped, "Oh shit, yep, *yes!*" He grabbed at the stack of papers, the pad across his desk. He slapped the laptop shut, ran out of the office as Adele sighed after him.

Tom was keenly aware of how things were shifting and evolving around him at work. He was also aware that he remained separate and apart from what was developing, and strangely, sadly, he didn't seem to give a shit. Even a tiny shit. He was more anxious about *his* lack of interest in *general* as opposed to the office's lack of interest in *him*. He had gotten glowing notices from Drs. Zane and Tartan, the therapists that Adele had "recommended" he see, but the sticky status quo persisted. The net effect (in Tom Dad's getting-smaller-by-the-second brain) was that it had been at least a week since he "knew" he was going to be fired in any case, and it struck him as more of a quirk than an anomaly: *nothing seemed to really worry him or thrill him one way or another anymore.* He had achieved a whole new level of personal ennui—he simply wished he could be a little more excited about it.

The meeting was a bore. "His team" once again wrote, presented, and brainstormed well-worn circles around him while he drew circles on his notepad. He was once again deemed unnecessary; he'd make up some excuse and hope Sean was still boning that joint on their office roof deck.

———————— ♦♦♦♦ ♦♦♦♦ ————————

"WHAT GOOD IS BEING my mom's BFF if you don't really give a shit *what* she's thinking? No—*feeling!* What a fucked-up generation! Or actually a *few generations* if you think it through—maybe that's why you guys are so messed up..."

Sasha hadn't even been there ten minutes and she was ripping her Aunt Ezra a new one.

Ezra quickly decided she'd needed something stronger for this session with her Bunny, Dear—her term of affection (off and on—more off) for Sasha from over ten years ago. She had no idea why that had somehow abruptly resurfaced, fell out of her mouth—especially now. (Perhaps some desperate plea to Sasha's more developed sensibilities, which had sadly started to disown Ezra about three months ago.)

Ezra knocked back the Jack, "Bun, I'll just skip any pleasantries because I can see there's nothing pleasant about—"

Sasha proclaimed, "That's it! I'm *so done*. All of you grown-up witches—*under, over, supreme,* **whatever**—are *ridiculous!* There's *nothing* 'grown up' about any of it!"

"Any of what? And hold on, don't include me in their mess." Suddenly Ezra was feeling defensive—that had *never* happened with her Bunny before! She was at a loss as how to respond. She would typically shave off one side of her adversary's hair with a snappy flip of her hand—it was notoriously successful (at the very least) at changing the subject. But she couldn't even consider that with her Bunny, Dear... *Maybe just an eyebrow? Half an eyebrow?*

Sasha's aura started to flare—not a good sign (or look). She fumed, "*You* put yourself in the middle of it—I had nothing to do with it."

"*What* did I do?"

"I don't know. But it's something you said or did, and I don't know what that was, but it so obviously sucks because Antonia's on a rampage... All I can figure out is that it's about you *and me,* so she's tormenting me." Sasha's blue spectrum was glinting red —*really* not a good sign, "*Did you tell her about our thing, these convos?!* I hate her more than ever—she's *so* selfish!"

Ezra grappled for the bottle of Jack and saying the "right thing," whatever that might possibly be, "I'm almost sure I didn't mention you—" (Only her Bunny could push her to this diminished state.)

Sasha achieved lift-off, "*Almost?! Shit!* She's *so over you* anyway, I wish I knew what you—no, maybe I don't..."

Ezra blanched, "Over *me?* What? Why?"

"I don't know! That's what I'm saying—*are you even listening to me?!*"

Aunt Ezra was desperately reconsidering the head-shaving spell; she measured her words, "We didn't talk about anything that..."

Sasha, wild-eyed, interrupted, completely changing the topic, "And that other dickhead! Who's *out of a job* evidently! And also evidently decided to not tell anyone about it for a freaking week..."

Ezra stared, "Tom Dad? He quit?"

"*Fired.*"

Ezra drunkenly shrugged her non-surprise, and muttered, "Well, if he ever had the balls to..."

"You knew about that *too*?!" Sasha's glare unnerved Ezra.

Some tragic and precious invisible line had just been violated by both of them, and the distinct sense of having lost something very special, invaluable, hit them hard, cheating their breath. The air became too heavy and sad.

Ezra murmured, "No. I don't know, didn't know..." Ezra sensed tears, her eyes wrestled with the moment (she couldn't remember the last time she'd cried), "No, I can't tell you about any of this...

Can't help you with any of this." *Did she really expect me to know? Or to actually explain this to her?*

Sasha desperately looked around the room, as if someone had whispered that her next clue was under some book or behind some chair cushion. She looked terribly alone.

Sasha picked up her pack, "I think I just need to go home, Aunt Ezra."

And so she was gone, her bike left slumped by Ezra's back porch.

———————

THE RAPPATSI BIRTHDAY party that Julie *tried* to host was a bust (kinda, sorta mostly). That probably had to do with the fact that, like most Julie parties, it was ninety-seven percent about Julie and then the feeble other three percent would be the proposed person or theme. Sasha confused herself, *But I thought Rapp just had her birthday?* Maybe tonight was the Rappatsi Thanksgiving Thinga-majig? *What da fuck—same difference anymore...*

She was too frustrated to sleep (as if that was anything unusu-al), so she landed at her laptop. She knew it wouldn't help her feel better necessarily (probably have the opposite result), but she lit up nonetheless.

What da shit? An invite to Skype with Tom Boy Stud?! Sasha had—to use her parents' words—very much "moved on" but even hindsight had confirmed that there hadn't been a whole lot of *moving* to do in either direction. Her Skype invite dinged and pleaded with her for a third time to say hello; it seemed as if there was some urgency this time in its bleat—it was very distinct. Everything about Tom Boy had always been amiable and lightly humorous (i.e., mildly boring) but now, suddenly, was the mirror opposite. Even stranger was that Sasha now seemed to find him sexy *and* attractive, and not just around the edges, *So freaking bizarre—the W mind, especially mine...*

The screen on her laptop looked wobbly; she attributed it to her overtaxed and overtired state, the many unwelcome contact highs she'd had through the party, and then (this one part, she was sure of) second-hand pot smoke... But she looked closer—it was definitely *there,* definitely part of its plasma life force. She didn't think that Tom Boy's Skype was still active but she accepted anyway—*I'll talk to anyone at this point...*

The frame opened up, its wobble still wobbling.

"Well, you certainly took your time," she recognized Tom's voice, but his face looked strange—as if it was backward and its inverse, its negative.

"Why are you up? Since we're already complaining..."

No answer.

Tom Boy kept falling in and out of focus. "Yeah, I'm tired. Listen, I needed to ask: isn't this yours? Or from one of your brood?"

"Brood"?! What da freak?

Sasha peered at the barely recognizable image—which she had no problem recognizing (unfortunately), *So that's where that wand —or piece of wand—went.* But hold on—where did *he* find it? Major exasperated sigh from Sasha; gaps in memory are one (not great) thing, but leaving parts of it behind as evidence is another thing altogether.

"That would be a 'yes.' Part of my baby gift wand—or baby wand *gift,* whichever makes better sense to you."

"People still did that when you happened?"

"Evidently. All of us three. It is, or was, weird..." Sasha knew she had to talk about the strange coincidences—*some sort of preter-natural simpatico?*—except she had wanted to be in control of the conversation (like she always seemed to be) and not the other way around.

Tom Boy abruptly abandoned any niceties, "So what were *you* doing there?"

"Comparing this and that—'this' being the wand inscription

and 'that' being the new etched glass message—*'from beyond.'* It's changed again, *right?*" No answer. Sasha continued, "You didn't say anything otherwise, seemed to suggest the space was for the club. Am I wrong?" She leaned into the screen again, "And what the fuck is wrong with your face?"

"Nice. When did you become such a dick?"

"Probably right about the same time you did..."

Tom Boy smiled, "I mean, you've always kind of been *kind of a dick*—that was part of your 'charm'—but you haven't been such an *in-your-face dick,* almost more of a cunt, really."

What evil wizard invaded Tom Boy's body? And ate that sweet, adorable brain behind that sweet, adorable face?

"So, what *is* wrong with your face?"

"Nothing. Nothing unusual anyway. I mean when you're Skyping from your own brain, it can get a little dicey."

'Dicey'? What da— "You're Skyping from *your* head?! How is that even possible?"

A crazed, glazed Tom Boy visage zigged up, zagged left and somewhere off the screen, then back. "Sorry, what?"

"I said: *how the fuck are you doing that?*"

It was hard to say for sure, but Tom Boy seemed to be smiling, and with all the fizzing and static-y dust it started to have an almost Batman Joker-like perverse sneer to it. Tom Boy said smugly, "Um, *magic.*"

"But you always turned your nose up at magic. You never once let me even show you how well—"

"Oh, I already know how well you think you do *everything.* So no, I didn't need to see you turn poor Julie's tits into—"

"'Poor' Julie?! You were grossed out—still are grossed out—by Julie. And talk about stupid magic tricks, she's the one, boy, is she—"

Tom Boy disappeared from the screen again—*how could that happen if it's transmitting from his brain?* There was nothing but static filling the tired air. Sasha was starting to fade. "So, whose magic? Which craft?"

Tom Boy offered, "I mostly figured it out. But it started with a few tricks I took out of that dark net portal I found."

"Well, that's nuts."

"Not as nuts as—what were you trying to do?—use your baby wand to turn the glass obelisk into a friendly pet or bootlicker you could take home to your wacked family?"

Sasha didn't like that comment at all, "What did you say, dick-head? No, it was the new inscription, the similarities between them—and did you have anything to do with *that?*"

Tom Boy muttered, "This is boring me now. I'm done."

Now Sasha was angry, "*Who are you? What* are you? You were never such an ass before! No, *I'm* done before you're done!" And she scrambled with the keyboard to quit the app before he did—but alas...

"SOBA LEFT before breakfast *again* this morning. That makes it four days, almost in a row." Tom Dad was frowning out the window.

"Isn't she allowed to have her private time? I don't think it's worth worrying about." Antonia slapped the spoon on the counter next to the wrong tea bag that was now drooling across the worn wood. (She hated chamomile, *What are the odds that I would choose the wrong tea bag two days in a row?*)

"Oh, okay. So what might you consider worth worrying about? If she walked in with her tits on her back you'd probably say 'chill out—she was just tired of having her tits on the front of her body.'" This was now Tom's adopted tone for anything and every-thing he communicated to Antonia. (It was the first time in a long time he'd been consistent and consistently good at one thing.)

"That's bizarre."

"Yeah, right, it is a little bizarre, but I'm *a lot* bizarre so I guess it makes sense."

Antonia knew he was justified in feeling and behaving the way he was, and she knew—in spite of her real feelings—she had to allow it to happen. "No, it's bizarre because she already had her tits on her back. But just for about a day and a half. Someone was trying some potion, and she wanted to see what it felt like."

Now red-faced Tom abruptly picked up and put down his glass hard, the crack sounded as if the glass broke, but it hadn't. "That's fucking great, you're letting our daughters drink any old drug or potion '*just to see what it feels like.*'"

Antonia stared hard at Tom Dad—she could so easily and comfortably reenact that whole *Carrie* death scene with the kitchen utensils, right here, right now, with her husband as the evil mother turned sacrificial lamb. It would be so simple; it would feel so good, *We aren't called "witches" for nothing.* She even could do it with her eyes closed and her back to the target. She thought about it a moment more but then couldn't remember the antidote spell, at least not all of it, so she stopped wanting to put Tom Dad in some kind of awful and agonizing pain, *Ugly, bad Antonia.*

Antonia calmly sat down across from Tom, "No, I didn't 'let' them. No one asked me."

"Even better. The only one real responsibility you have and you continue to fuck it up in ways that consistently surprise me."

Antonia sighed deeply. She noticed her hands were fading, doing their translucency thing. She wasn't consciously trying to dematerialize, but she decided right then wasn't going to prevent it. It was bound to happen (for the third morning in a row), so sooner was just as well as later.

Tom Dad saw what was beginning to happen and seemed to simply shrug. "That's fine. Disappear... Wonder where you float off to, not that I really give a fuck." He poured the rest of his cereal into the sink, grabbed his keys, and was gone.

Antonia clearly had some more thinking to do: she became the size of a small insect then thought the better of it and embraced the small grey patch of mold in the far corner of the ceiling. No one would even think to look for her here. *Corners must be my thing these days—shouldn't surprise me...*

SOBA LOOKED UP, "So they were arguing *again?*"

White Owl said yes and did another circle over Soba.

She suddenly stopped walking and collapsed, legs crossed, on the grass next to the sidewalk. She counted her breaths—the counting *with* the deep breaths helped—as she stared at the tops of the trees of the woods close by. She'd been having this discussion with herself that she wouldn't *really* be running away since she'd be—relatively speaking—just several feet away from the house (actually, quite a few more than that). It would be true, however, that she wouldn't be *living* at the house anymore. She argued she'd outgrown the house, and especially the sad and annoying people in it—it was time for a change. White Owl sat next to her watching her think. (She didn't listen to Soba's thoughts this time; it would have been, given the circumstances, a very rude thing to do.)

Soba promised herself she'd make a decision by week's end. She stood up, took one last deep breath, and continued walking to school.

———————

SO THE FIRST day finally arrived. And not actually the day but the day before the day, which was generally accepted by all within or hovering around the Tetersberg clan to be just as important as Thanksgiving Day itself... It was the Eve of Thanks. (Tip had muttered the moniker one especially precocious year and the term stuck.)

And so it would be that this year's Eve of Thanks, with the twenty-some guests all with varying degrees of connection (by blood, by witchery, or some cosmic blend of the two) to Tom Dad and Family would become something infamous, for both wonderfully good and bad reasons (and nothing in between).

Tip herself had completed the soup; she felt a responsibility given how much she'd hyped up this mushroom soup recipe and how badly (between tequila shots) her mother had botched her first attempt with it earlier that afternoon.

"Soup's on!" Tip squeaked, *Why the hell am I so nervous about this?* She surveyed the table and its immediate vicinity; she was glad to see no Mom (even though Antonia was in no position to criticize, would do so anyway...) and thankfully no Aunt Ezra (whose tics and snorts condemning a meal—any one that wasn't prepared or influenced by her—made it unbearable, at least for Tip). But where the hell *was Antonia?* If she was missing at this first juncture in the evening it did not bode well for what was forthcoming, *Maybe that's why I'm freaking like this?*

The soup was a hit. A hard act to follow, and Tip wasn't really sure who was following; the dinner was up, down, and all around behaving happily, even joyously by some accounts, and still no sign of either elder stateswoman. Antonia's soup and place setting remained untouched, as if in a museum.

Then Sasha fell down. Sideways. And on top of Sput.

The room was suddenly confused and stuck; it appeared, out of the corner of one's eye, that she'd been shoved—it was that sudden. But who would have done something like that? And upon a closer anxious glance—as she was gathering herself, her wits, her ginger ale—it was clear that she'd fainted or something like that.

Ezra seemed to appear out of thin air. Embracing Sasha, she pulled her upright and into a nearby chair. Tom and Antonia slowly turned the corner from upstairs with Antonia, in spite of all her promises (mostly to herself), stoned and drunk again. (For that matter, so was Tom Dad.)

Aunt Jane was first to fully realize what had taken place; she reached for the scattered pieces of broken cup and plate, "Whoever's in the kitchen: emergency rags, paper towels, *whatever's* handy, please!" The socio-politics of magic-making, especially lately, was a scary thing; one treaded carefully in such mixed company—it would have been an easy Mary Poppins snap or a Samantha twitch for any one of them, but instead everything got stymied and stuck (and could quickly, unknowingly become more sticky). It was Aunt Jane's girlfriend who finally appeared with things that absorb; Sasha had almost immediately regained consciousness and appeared more embarrassed than anything else.

Ezra and Jane had already helped Sasha onto a chair by the time Antonia slow-motioned her way to her daughter's side. Sasha looked up at Antonia; she didn't say a word, but smiled slightly, touched Sasha's cheek, took her hand.

Ezra said, "Ant, unless you want to help, can you move one way or the other? You're really just in the—"

Antonia, in spite of her woozy appearance, responded clearly, firmly, "I *am* helping, Ez. Just because it's not something you'd do doesn't make it wrong."

The dining room fell silent. Everyone there, regardless of their personal connection with Antonia or Ezra, was keenly aware of the tensions between them.

"Well, she's not *my daughter,* Antonia."

Antonia smiled, and not in a friendly fashion, "That's right, Ez. She's not."

The two women looked carefully at each other. Everyone else in the room, in the house, stood very still.

Ezra spoke slowly, "What happened to the guilty mother from last Friday?"

Antonia shot back, "And where is that selfless, optimistic magical maven from a few days ago that I was about to melt, but she convinced me not to...?"

Jane's girlfriend quickly tried her best to diffuse the obvious

317

strain in the air (and in the punch). "Okay, girls, where's that holiday spirit? Or *spirits*?" Her smile was big and earnest.

Ezra continued, looking back to Antonia, "She's right here, where you left her." She smiled but barely, spoke slowly, "With everyone here, together, and especially tonight, it forces one to re-examine things."

"I thought that's what *we've **been** doing,* Ezra."

"That's very true. To a degree."

Antonia sighed, exhaling all levels of frustration. People sighed with her, began to mill, find polite ways of removing themselves from the room (picking up empty glasses, etc.) and the necessarily uncomfortable impending discussion. Antonia considered nipping any potential argument right then, while it was trying to gain its balance, but then thought no, *Let this go, let it finish. Let her have her last words. And then I'll be able to really make a change, make something right happen...* It was, after all, an unwritten but enthusiastic part of what made the Eve of Thanks as special as it was: the *truth-telling*, the honesty, the cleaning-the-slate aspect of it all. And desperate Aunt Ezra had seemingly come prepared to showcase the best of her waning abilities. While everyone finally, anxiously settled themselves, Ezra stole another swig of what was apparently her new potion-y signature "cocktail," steaming garnish intact. As Antonia scowled her disapproval, Ezra raised her glass and blew some steam in her direction. Antonia sucked in some more air while she could, rallied her matriarchal sensitivities, and announced (with as much snark as she could muster), "Okay, Ezra, since you're so shamelessly prepared, please proceed..." Ezra swung around from the couple friends she'd been (strangely) giggling with, she blurted "Why, yes! Certainly!" She spitefully toasted the room, blew more steam-smoke in their faces and spoke, "So, Ant, in front of this *Court of Everyone,* let it be known that I've checked all my various hoodoo, wands, incantations, and magickal predilections *at the door!*" There was a smattering of snickers; the room tilted anxiously in Antonia's frustrated direction.

Antonia jeered, "Well, that's so generous and trusting, Ez, I'll hope you didn't leave your brain and self-respect there too?"

The room suddenly burst into sundry hoots and catcalls, all good-natured, but all bizarrely (from Antonia's perspective, anyway) directed *at Antonia*. The general mood seemed abruptly upbeat and, dare I say, in the "holiday spirit"; Antonia was baffled, *I know I'm stoned but I'm not **that** stoned...* But then how did she get the emotional temperature of the room so wrong? The Sisters didn't seem persuaded either way, and Tom Dad's opinion didn't matter at this point, so then *how?* Antonia quickly determined another shot and a toke were mandatory before another thought or word was offered.

Aunt Ezra turned back to the room after another sip and more strange giggling (sounded more like *gurgling*, to be completely honest) with her toadies, she steadied herself and muttered, "Okay... [more laughing] *where was I?*"

Uncle Zack shouted, "You had me at 'hello'!" Everyone actually laughed at that—the-joke-that-wasn't-really-meant-to-be-funny joke... (Most everyone there knew that you could rely on Zack to put the *a-r-t* in party, somehow or other.)

Ezra kept it up, "*So here we all are* at the beginning of another year, another season. And let me be the first to tell you there's going to be some big changes around here..." Everyone laughed out loud at that comment; Zack took note but wasn't dissuaded. The infamous Aunt Ezra and Uncle Zack's year-end review or *schtick* was perforce a "spontaneous" event—either their crafty stars were aligned or they weren't. And they—somewhat surprisingly to the woozy and wounded Antonia—were clearly fully charged, loaded, and ready to roar.

Antonia sighed and quietly started to "disappear" herself, remembering there were a couple things upstairs that needed to be painted and smoked. She glanced over at Tom Dad who was blandly futzing at his phone, *Should I ask him to join?* Antonia sighed again, *Nah, screw him...*

ANTONIA HAD SEEMINGLY EVAPORATED; Ezra (now several toots and shots to the figurative wind) had *really* wanted Antonia's audience—this was going to be their "big moment" (for better or worse)—and her absence was glaring. She determined that she would *absolutely not* chase after her supposedly dearest friend until, moments later she decided, no, it *absolutely was the right thing* to do. (Even if she had absolutely, undeniably, in boldface hoodoo calligraphy, *fucked her over* by not (well, it was a teensy bit lopsided) doing and becoming the paranormal powerhouse that Ezra had demanded of her.

The house was at its peak: the pervasive merriment belied the calamity that was unfolding. The too-drunk Ezra was beginning to resent anyone and everyone that seemed to be in her path so she astutely determined it would be best to take a moment, take a breath, and pluck Antonia from the front of her brain until a more advantageous (for Ezra) moment. She sat and counted to ten a few different ways (only one of them correctly). Then she noticed Tom Dad walk (barely) in from the patio and blearily decided, for this particular truth-sharing, he would work just fine as an Antonia surrogate...

Dinner happened without Antonia, but it was a little always like that on the Eve (an Antonia tradition). The more potluck-than-not makeshift feast (any blood-letting aside) always had seemed to take on a life of its own respective to who was *crafting* that part of the celebration.

Antonia slowly began to emerge from the block of pot-addled smoke that was her "office." (She wasn't even sure Tom Dad knew about the closet off of her closet—she would describe it as her *office* or her *panic room* depending upon the conversation in front of her.) As buzzed as Antonia was, she was now again fuming about Ezra and her too recent and too presumptuous treatment of her girls—let alone their friendship, *But again I digress—this is a party and this is* **the** *Annual Thanksgiving-a-rama—show it the respect it's due, bitch!* She slapped her own wrists and floated back downstairs.

Everyone was still hovering around the dinner table, including Ezra (which Antonia had been hoping might not be the case).

Tom was seething, trembling in the threshold; his face burning, his eyes almost black. Antonia knew in a breath that something was terribly, awfully wrong, *I can't leave for five minutes (fifty minutes?) and this (whatever 'this' is) is what happens?*

Everyone was glowering at Ezra and wouldn't let go. Antonia, *What the fuck!,* tried to put any available, obvious pieces where they might make sense. Even as most people attempted to return to their chits and chats, they all had that clear guise of social desperation—any real conversation was dead in the air. Another quick glimpse of Ezra confirmed she'd accomplished whatever it was (emotional duress?) she had been hoping to accomplish.

Antonia knew it was best to avoid any interaction, but how could she? Everyone was clearly depending on her; she glanced again at Tom, his beet-red flush had graduated to a look of unmitigated rage. It seemed as if Ezra's next utterance might have the equivalent effect of a spark to a bloated hydrogen tank.

Antonia bit, "Okay, *so who died?*"

No one moved. Ezra shrugged ever so slightly, kind of smirked.

Tip said, completely without emotion (which was never a good thing in Tip's social vocabulary), "Um, I would say *Dad did.*" Ezra shifted in her chair, giving away the slightest bit of discomfort. Suddenly Antonia had a really, really good guess as to what or rather *who* just transpired.

"*Ezra*, what did you—"

She startled Ezra (she knew she'd have to defend her actions but so soon?) "Nothing. I didn't do anything."

Tip cut her off, "That's a matter of opinion." Tip was very angry, and apparently so were her sisters—varying degrees of very, *very* angry.

Then even Soba confirmed, "Yeah. Definitely a matter of opinion." Wobbly Ezra gave her a dismissive frown, *Twerp*...

"Well what the hell happened? I go and have a little dessert—"

"*A little?*" Aunt Jane couldn't help herself. Antonia ignored the dig. (Jane was always easy to ignore.)

Antonia was struggling to focus, "And I come back and every-one's ready to kill each other."

Sasha finally spoke up, "No, not each other, just a couple people."

The room kept looking at Antonia and then Tom and then back again—everyone but Jane, her twins, and their two friends who already were halfway out of the dining room by this point. Tom finally, slowly raised his head looking as if he was about to make some kind of pronouncement (which he was) when Soba blurted out, "So did you really *only* marry Dad because he sucked at hoodoo or magic *whatever?*"

Tom stayed silent, his expression assuming the enraged posi-tion it was in a few moments before. Antonia looked around the room—now all eyes were on *her*.

"No. Who told you that?" As if Antonia didn't know—she glared at Ezra. *"That's what your 'year's revelation' was about?!"*

Tom finally sat up and forward, and spoke, "No, not just that. Among a bunch of embarrassing moments for us that made them —mostly *her*—look great, some choice tidbits about your long-ago affair with Daniel and the 'vacation' that we took a bunch of years ago."

"*What the fuck?!*" Antonia was incredulous. Now Ezra sat up, placing her hands on the table, poised, lips pursed as if she was about to say grace before a meal. She had an innate talent for—when required—presenting a persona that was exactly the oppo-site of her intention. *Evil, selfish bitch*... Antonia glared at her, Ezra glanced up at her apparently indifferent. She'd caught the thought.

Ezra took a breath and simply, calmly said, "It was time. It *is* time."

Antonia was dumbfounded—and furious. "*Time for what* **exactly**?!" she demanded.

Everyone and everything froze; Tom Dad, Antonia, and Ezra's presence filled the space: marshaling the air, any available emotions, the past and present... The future was about to be discussed.

"What else—the truth." Ezra stared at the table. She said what she felt she needed to say and was prepared to accept the consequences. (Within reason, that is...)

Antonia fumed, "Whatever the facts might be—*do you really think this is* **your** *truth to share?!* Were you as forthcoming about Marta and her five little piggies that *you* decided to take to market?! Fortunately, she's more the forgiving type than I am."

Ezra's neck arched, she leered, "It wasn't really Marta's decision to make..."

Antonia was stunned, "That's preposterous! It was *exactly and only* her decision! You're perverted, Ezra—something's gone very wrong with you."

The air became very heavy, everyone around the table suddenly felt bloated, weighed down too, as if all the food they'd just eaten abruptly exponentially expanded. Ezra remained unmoved—as resolute as if she'd just requested the check in a restaurant. She said calmly, "The truth belongs to everyone, Antonia."

Antonia was suddenly airborne, arms, legs, any available appendage splayed, poised for attack—"shooting daggers" and "breathing fire" would be an understatement. People dived behind, ran from, grabbed onto or did whatever they could reasonably do to find shelter, safety. (Those lucky souls who were magically inclined just disembodied from the moment; they didn't care where they ended up, the roof, the middle of traffic—anything would be better than being there with these banshees.) In the next instant, the dining room became a vortex of wind, fear, fury, and surprisingly painful, slightly dangerous pieces of projectile stuffing cubes or whole cranberries...

Ezra—*never* one to be outdone—rose (in more ways than just a few) to the occasion: her whole body and chair, her various accoutrements arranged themselves around her in as threatening a position as possible. Her visage, ironically, was one of utter calm and control. The pressure in the room suddenly forced the French doors to the patio wide open and everything moving and whirling blew through them, out and everywhere. The women quickly repositioned themselves outside well above the patio, taking full strategic advantage of the air and space. Everyone but Tom Dad moved to their respective edge of the house to get the best vantage, play-by-play.

Ezra spoke first, "Very impressive, Antonia, I didn't think you still had it in you. Even stoned you put on a pretty good show—I would've imagined the opposite."

"Always so smug, so above it all. Isn't that the case, Ezra dear?"

"It depends, Antonia. Are we actually being honest with each other now?"

"It doesn't seem to matter *what I think,* Ezra. Does it? Everything is suddenly open for interpretation. How is it, after all this time, I never knew this *about you?*"

"That's because I didn't even know it myself, but now I do. Connect the dots from our earlier conversations, bitch!"

Antonia bristled at Ezra's patronizing tone; flames spewed, colors flared.

"Be careful, sister! This is *your* house, not mine..." She smiled but it was particularly telling and particularly evil; the twins and Soba witnessed it, and closed their eyes not wanting to believe it.

Antonia blared, "That's true... So where does this end?"

"This? This right here? I'd say we're just getting started, sister.

Antonia seethed, "That may be, but if there's one scratch on anything or especially *any one* of the Tetersbergs, there will be an unremitting hell to pay."

Ezra, apart from all her flailing, still seemed unmoved, "You're about as threatening as this cube of stuffing, Antonia. What are you going to do—fly over and blow my house down? You big, bad witch, you!"

The whorl of activity seemed to slow time, a discomfiting and surreal feeling overtook the next couple minutes.

Then bizarrely, perhaps all the activity dampened Antonia's high or her oxygen levels had fallen conspicuously, out of the blue she burst out laughing—*hysterically* laughing... "That has to *one of the stupidest things I've ever heard you say!*"

Everyone stared unbelievingly at Antonia, who was now laughing uncontrollably, her witchy bells and whistles starting to sap and fade. Then they all quickly shifted their attention to Ezra's next words, with which she was at a loss, hemming and hawing through the wind and the dust.

Ezra muttered, instantly embarrassed, "Well, what the fuck else *would* I say?"

They floated there, now with absent sheepish looks on their faces. The scene had gone from fiasco to farce in a not-so-enchanted second, *Maybe things spun out of control just a tad...* The twins slowly turned to each other having caught whomever's thought in the still-reeling air, and mentally agreed at almost the same moment, *What **dis** shit?*

Ezra cracked first, "We could blow something up—would that make you feel better?"

Antonia sighed, "Yeah, let's blow *you* up. That would *definitely* help my mood."

"That's a little harsh."

"*What?!* And talking about Daniel and me with everyone *else* in the room is just regular coffee conversation?"

Ezra pouted, "I didn't think you were taking me seriously the other day... And the day before that..."

Antonia's witchy appendages started to flare again, "All of *this* was about *that?!* This isn't the first time I've said no to you *or* the first time I haven't gone along with one of your grand plans. *But this?* What the fuck *was all of this?* Maybe you should start smoking pot again—something's definitely come undone in there."

Antonia maintained, "You're being a real bitch lately, Ezra. I don't mind telling you that, right here. *Now.*" Antonia alighted on the patio stone; squinting, frowning, laughing to herself, she was scrutinizing the damage done. Nothing particularly noticeable in respect to the house, but her reputation as mother, wife, and witch (and in that order) had taken a significant blow, *I can sense how desperately the girls—they're wanting me—but if I look at them now, even a glance, it'll be suicide.*

Everyone resumed their party-ness as if little, if anything, had happened—picking up wayward pillows and sideways chairs as if they were just clearing the dinner table. All three sisters found each other and huddled in the far corner of the hall. They looked at each other, overwhelmed and exasperated—no one had any words to offer. "To be continued..." muttered Sasha, "We'll talk about it before bed."

In that next moment Antonia sensed that Ezra was abruptly gone, seemingly disappeared. There was a smudge of something here and there and a few singed leaves and branches but otherwise you'd barely know anything had happened. Then Antonia sensed her again but in the kitchen, *This is a very misguided time to play coy...* She curled her head into the kitchen's bustle, "I was talking away and you doused your flames, up and left. A tad rude, no?"

Ezra was oddly flip, "What more was there to really talk about, at least right there with everybody watching... Besides I had to pee like a banshee."

"Why didn't you just let it fly like everything else?" sniped Antonia, but Ezra was already on to her next topic—talking to Jane, hands and eyes flailing. The last several minutes caught up to Antonia, she sighed, *So bizarre—everything...*

Even in her post-performance stupor, Ezra was able to sustain a guise of genuine interest. "Aunt" Jane (from Tom's "side of the family"), who was boring, narcissistic, and had no interest in anything sorcery-related (one of the "I couldn't be bothered" generation), was rambling on about her three orgasms with Friday night's fling while Ezra became keenly aware of an itching-cum-burning encircling her right hand and arm, *Strange place for an allergic reaction—Jane usually just makes me slightly nauseous.*

Ezra didn't like the thought that popped into her inebriated brain, *This is exactly where those Coven bitches found their nasty way through the other night...* She grabbed another shot of something and went back to Jane's orgasms.

The Sisters discreetly evaporated to the cold comfort of their bedrooms, deciding there was nothing (at that moment) to think, feel, or care seriously about. The adults continued their wallowing, dissolving into their respective puddles; eventually they meandered home or to bed. (Don't fret, there's plenty left to argue about tomorrow...)

———————

A MISCALCULATED DOC'S appointment for Soba happily coincided with Tom Dad's desperate need to escape the house that morning. The moment they left the doctor, Soba was chatting a hundred miles an hour—a completely rare and almost unnatural occurrence. Tom Dad was barely beginning to comprehend the happily convoluted brain dump as he decided a special Soba Delight was in order. He pulled into GreenStuff—their Chickpea Cheetah Chips were the Baby Girl's heaven-on-Earth since age whenever.

She bounced into the store; Tom Dad had more than earned

his points for the day. But then, something else as it winked around the corner of the chips and sticks: it could only be the Imp of Smiles. Imp's dimpled happiness was infectious. It was impossible to avoid, to steer clear of its powers simply because it had nothing to do with sorcery or spell-crafting—it simply was as *Imp was:* a perfect, pure, and powerful expression of happiness. Imp's very rare appearances were more fortuitous than not, but it certainly wasn't a guarantee of something great, good, or even a twinge of luckiness, but the odds were significantly tipped towards the positive. (And Tom Dad was going to take any and all the help he could find or if it found him.)

Soba looked surprised, "It's cute. And it's certainly happy," she searched about, its puckish twitters bouncing here, there. "Where did it go?" Tom pointed around the corner mouthing the word "maybe?" But the sing-song quickly faded and Imp was gone, or so it seemed.

Soba said, "I thought they were like Santa Claus. Real until they're not."

"Hmm, nope. But I've seen them only once, and a really long time ago."

Soba peered through the shelves.

"I don't see it. Or hear it now."

Tom Dad smiled wistfully, "Maybe that's it up there..."

Soba saw the whitest bird just outside the open sill.

"Imp's a shapeshifter too? Man, that *is* lucky."

Tom's smile widened, "That's what I heard at some point. And that could have been the Santa Claus part, but maybe not." Tom Dad wrapped his arm around his daughter, crowning her opinionated kinky hair with something more than just luck.

Tom Dad leaned into her, "I've a gut feeling that girl-boy-bird or no girl-boy-bird, there's enough goodness *and* luck for both of us, sweetness."

"And Sput. And maybe Tip."

"Why maybe?"

"I'm still deliberating..."

Tom Dad twisted his mouth and winked, "Where's that holiday spirit, Baby Girl?"

T-DAY: everyone arrived at once, for better and worse. Antonia was mostly, basically prepared; Thanksgiving and all its happy trappings, especially for W's of her generation was an *event*. (Especially when you factored in all the before and after witchy parts and parties.) As far as Tom Dad, his tradition was to duck and dodge; he had learned the hard way that he had very real limitations as far as Harvest Week was concerned. So, as you might expect, any hopes, highs (chemically induced or just the contact variety), and expectations were occurring in a heightened state.

(We thought it was worth revisiting the hopeful status quo since it was about to shift dramatically again in about *five, four, three, two*...)

Tom Dad had started early, having ascertained that tequila would be his only true friend today, and The Sisters found themselves all agreeing on *one something*—a single "strategy" for once: wayward wands or spells be damned, they would take care of *each other* first and foremost... But there was a shrewish elephant in the room exactly because she *wasn't* in the room—not yet, anyway. It was Aunt Ezra. Where the freak was she? (Or did she hopefully realize her bodily presence wasn't high on anyone's invite list today?)

Antonia was just about to close the door when an uncomfortable surprise slipped through, wrapping her arms around her before she could do or say anything (that probably was Ezra's intention). Antonia could smell something alcoholic in Ezra's trail, *Shit—I should've expected nothing less.*

"I feel like we haven't been here in weeks!" Ezra buzzed sarcastically, caressing the new painting in the Tetersberg entryway.

"The real you probably hasn't." A fang-y, agitated Antonia handed Ezra an already messy glass of white, "But who's counting?"

"Once a bitch, always a bitch."

"Takes a huge one to know one..." Antonia walked right through her back to the bar.

Ezra assumed the banter was simply that, but Antonia's state was painfully familiar—she was never one to easily forgive and forget. Ezra tried to pluck a few thoughts while Antonia wasn't on her particular wavelength and angrily realized she'd been "unfriended." She grabbed Antonia aside...

"What are you still steaming about? Just the *Daniel* thing? Can't be. You're not that petty."

Antonia almost couldn't believe it, *She's not even twenty feet inside the house and she's trying to fuck it up all over again.* "Daniel is a conversation waiting to happen—no, it's your *ongoing, undying bullshit.*"

Ezra swallowed the wine, dumped in more from an abandoned glass, "You said 'no,' I mean, you didn't actually *say* it to me—which would've been the polite and nice thing to do—but I got your point loud and clear: *Ezra, take your grand plan—your future—and fucking shove it.*"

Antonia measured her words, "I'm not so sure what you understood, Ez. There were two things—two really big and important things to me—and you seem to once again have turned them into what you needed them to be—what *you wanted.*"

"No, I didn't."

"Yes, you did."

"No, I—"

Antonia chewed her words, "Have you spent time with Sasha alone since we talked?"

Ezra gulped the glass of whatever she had, and then after a deep breath, answered, "Well, shit, of course, but not like we had before..."

Antonia swiveled desperately back to the bar; Ezra traipsed after her, still attempting to defend herself.

"I thought you were speaking *euphemistically*..." Ezra was stretching for anything to make sense.

Antonia's eyes clenched, she howled, "*I wanted you to stop!*"

The room and its inhabitants stood exactly still; there was a clear sense of preparedness, to be ready to "go" at any given moment...

Antonia measured her words, "*You don't belong—not anymore. Not here, not with us certainly...* I can't defend—" Antonia's broken voice spilled across the counter.

"Defend *what*, Ant?"

"*You.*"

Antonia grabbed her too-full drink and left the conversation. There had been battles through the years, but never had Antonia been so exacting and resolute. She quickly removed herself lest they risk losing part of the house again, until she regained some of her *thankful* spirit and outlook.

AUNT EZRA TOTTERED into the middle of everyone's everything, getting a decidedly mixed response. (The living room tried its best to afford Ezra her desired "platform" but the size triple XL elephant she'd brought with her this particular visit was too unwieldy.) Sasha was rapt, and not in a good way. She was nervous about two things: Ezra's right hand (which was shaking) and Ezra's ongoing quiver (from the top of her head to about her knees and back again); she knew Ezra did neither of these things together unless she was (very) nervous and drunk. Ezra's absent stare made everything seem potentially worse; people standing, sitting close started to do the pretending-to-clean-up thing again, to get the hell away from what had to be an inevitable disaster...

Aunt Ezra took a long, slow breath and wobbled her last wobble. She was slapping a small knife against a large glass in an attempt to help speak through her stupor. "First off, you all know what this come-to-Jesus part of the celebration's all about, and if you don't, you'll figure it out soon enough. It's kind of a really groovy, witchified New Year's resolutions, but without the smarmy New Year part—*right?!*" Ezra fell into the side of the couch as if it had attacked her first, *I shouldn't have taken two of those pills.*

"And here's something else: I'm not going to apologize or feel guilty about being as buzzy as I am right now," she squinted at Antonia and Tom, "especially given present company, as much as I love them—most of the time, anyway..." Tom barely smiled; Antonia was not as forgiving.

Ezra kept jabbering, "Sorry, I digress... Seems to be my 'thing' these days." She smiled, a big crunchy smile, "So, the big news—I promised big news, or *maybe I didn't?* Well, fuck it, the news is that *I won.*" The entire room froze still. *"Does anyone else here know* ***that I won?"***

Uncle Zack, too drunk and always too willing with Ezra, answered right on cue, "You won *what*, Ezra? *'A trip to the moon?*" He laughed feebly, a couple other people followed his lead.

"Oh, okay, so you don't know. *Why would you?*" She was now stumbling on her words and her ego. "And most of you don't even pay attention to your moons, your emotional physics, your spiritual health, yada, yada, yada..." *Is she trying to be funny again?* "I'll bet a good chunk of you don't even know how much witch or wizard you have in you." She started slurring, flailing her hands around dismissively, "I know, I know it's a non-issue, society doesn't even think about those race issues or prejudice, black or white, witch or mortal, anymore. Right? You don't, *right?*" She stopped to breathe, no one knew what to say, or think. She moaned on, "You know you *all* have a little bit of hoodoo in you, right? Just like we all have a little bit of African in us from how many millions of years ago." Ezra fell emphatically into the couch again as if she was trying to underscore her point.

Antonia remembered to breathe and said, "Ez, no more sermon. What did you fucking win?"

Ezra perked up, "*Win?* I didn't say that I—oh yeah, I did. It was just a turn of phrase, but they picked *me*—The *Coven* did, their *Panel*—over those other two bitches. I told you the other night..."

Sasha looked at Tip who looked back at Sasha, *Who the hell is The Coven's "Panel" and what did they do with our Aunt Ezra?* Sasha tried to finish the thought; she knew *very well* who The Coven was, or what they believed they were, but Tip had stopped listening.

(This was now feeling more like an ill-advised remake of *Invasion of the Body Snatchers* as opposed to a pathetic, tragic *Bewitched* update.)

Tom Dad, poison in his voice, finally spoke, "Ezra, make sense or die."

Antonia nudged Tom, "Ezra: what the hell did you win? *What did they give you?*"

Ezra blatantly lied, "Permission. And power."

"For what?"

"To 'Make America Magical Again.'"

The joke—was it a joke? *It had to be a joke!*—fell splat on the floor in front of Ezra; she focused hard on that spot as the thought fizzled. She appeared as if she was expecting it to jump up, hands extended and waving at the crowd, grinning obnoxiously.

Uncle Zack (who was still nursing his Ezra crush from probably decades ago) laughed and clapped and blurted, "Ezra for Overwitch Supreme! Supreme Overwitch! *Whomever Bitch!*" Zack feigned chagrin, "How you going to do it, *Aunt E.?*"

"Women, mostly. Us witches, mostly."

Some other voice tossed out, "But we're not mostly women." Heads pivoted, *Who would dare make such a proclamation? Especially here, and now?*

Ezra tut-tutted, "Oh, *now,*" she smiled broadly, "That's giving yourself away, you *have to be smarter than that.*"

Tom Dad moved to take Ezra's arm; she wobbled again trying to swat him back into place. "Ezra," Tom had a tired (very tired), patronizing tone, "you know better than this."

Ezra slurred, "And look who's talking. The model of father-dom. Forbids his daughters to be who they really are..."

Uh-oh, that crack in the floor that's a beeline to hell just opened up again... Sasha glanced at Tip then at Soba—The Sisters began measuring their collective breath.

Antonia slumped into the nearest chair, head in hand, *Where the fuck is this coming from?* It was more rhetorical—she had started grieving for her dear friend last night, but right now was some-thing very, very different: Ezra's transformations had never demanded this level of melodrama.

Tom Dad shot back, "I do no such thing and you know it. Just because you're holding onto your quaint notions of what your magick wants to be doesn't mean anyone else does, *or wants to.*"

Antonia reached out, "Tom, don't egg her on. Look at her, *she's a mess.*"

Ezra flushed red, "*I'm a mess, bitch?!* Is *this* where we are? You and that ridiculous excuse for a whatever he likes to say he is? Mortal, not-so-much, blah, blah..." her voice floundered.

"*May the gods **damn you, Ezra**!* You're acting like some pathetic twenty-something mortal now with—"

"Oh really, Antonia?! And what happened when **you** *were twenty-something, give or take a decade or two?!*"

Antonia was too tired, too everything to fight anymore, *Always fighting everyone lately for some strange, tragic reason...* She cupped her face with her hands, not wanting to have anyone see the start of her tears. She would be shattered if Ezra continued explaining as she was now praying she wouldn't, "If you're talking about what I think you are—I just don't know what to say... **Why are you doing this?**"

"If I've said it once before I've said it—" Ezra's eyes flared, "**it's *time*,** Antonia!" She was shouting, leering at Antonia. "It's all about time. And we can't afford to be anything less than *who we're supposed to be*. We just told each other that—*declared that*—at our last happy hour."

"'Happy' would be the last way I'd describe it."

There was a painful, terrible silence; Antonia started to really cry, she pleaded, "Stop, Ezra. If you need to talk about this, let's not do it now. Not in front of everyone that we love, respect..."

Ezra announced, "Respect is *exactly* why we need to do this now. And here."

Tom Dad looked more confused than pained now; he didn't know what he should do or say next. It was pitiful how these two *whatever they'd become* were so inconsolable, *It's the same strange shit over and over and over again...*

Ezra straightened herself, relinquishing the couch... Now bizarrely lucid, she began, "It was twenty years ago, two weeks after we baptized this day, this holiday, that Antonia and I first began to realize our potential: the possibilities that her newly established family and my soon-to-be marriage created, in partnership with this very powerful part of the world—and universe—where we lived—and still do—*right here.*"

The Sisters were thunderstruck; half the room felt the same, the other half were holding their breath, waiting for the next words Ezra would utter.

"Then Dennis, my fiancé, disappeared. Somewhat mysteriously, somewhat not. It, needless to say, devastated me. Then Antonia's *first girl* was born... And tragically—we had to believe—didn't survive..."

Sasha wide-eyed Tip, Tip blinked back, both were completely bewildered, *I'm standing right here—we're standing right here... She really has gone off the deep end.* Sasha looked at her mother who still had her face in her hands, her father was now facing the wall, as if he was being punished... Sasha then deduced that, given Ezra's calculations, this "first girl" was not only dead but would have been dead five years longer than she'd not been alive, *Such a Sasha factoid to think, helping to dull the awful reality in front of me...*

None of this—especially stressed-out Sasha's haphazard math—was making the least bit of sense... **Unless they had another sister.** Another older sister whose memory and meaning was intentionally lost and buried by their parents almost nineteen years ago.

A bleary Sasha pulled her mother's hands from her face. Antonia's swollen, streaked eyes peered at her daughter, she barely muttered, "We'll talk."

"But is it true?" Sasha sensed tears when she wasn't anticipating them at all.

Tom Dad held Antonia's shoulders tight, each person in their small way acknowledged it was. The Sisters almost collapsed, their one rare moment of communion had imploded, becoming something tragic and not the least bit joyous.

Aunt Ezra had, one would think, spoken her peace, but that was not the case. She puffed out her chest, "*Everyone listen*: here's what I need to finally say—to confess, really. What absolutely needs to be known..."

Now the whole family, the entire house, fell to its figurative knees.

"The blessed young thing—a girl—*didn't die,* the underwitch midwives took her... They took her from a family they did not think was deserving of a child they believed was so powerful. Or would soon become so." Ezra mustered enough wherewithal to focus her gaze on Antonia, who sagged into her chair.

Tom Dad was stunned, obliterated—*he had no idea.* Antonia could not take her eyes off of him. He looked down at her, "*You knew this?*"

She barely nodded.

"All these years—**you *knew* this**?!"

She couldn't respond; she couldn't form the words. Tom

turned away, he started to stagger, and it seemed as if he was going to fall into the wall—but recovered. He glanced over at his daughters, couldn't look them in the eyes, and suddenly, tragically ran from the room.

"Ezra, what the fuck is your end game here?" shouted Zack, springing from his seat, finally offended, mystified. A few other people echoed his frustration and anger. Ezra had no friends left in the room—this Tetersberg household—and if she did, they certainly weren't about to help or defend anything.

"This needed to be done, Zack, nothing could move forward if it hadn't—The Coven made that oh-so-clear to me. And I made it so to Antonia."

At that millisecond, it became hard to breathe wherever you were in the Tetersberg home. Another power—something very keen—was very invested and on its toes (whether Antonia wanted to acknowledge it or not).

She was barely able to form the words, "You've made none of this clear to *anyone*, Ezra. In spite of what I have believed for years, it seems now you—very suddenly—have a tragic and very sad understanding of what friendship can mean, what sisterhood should be..." Then the tears started again, uncontrolled, cathartic, "The many, many years we helped, we cared, we..." But somehow everyone knew it wasn't the broken friendship but the very maternal and unmentionable loss—until moments ago—that was overwhelming her.

"I'm sorry you feel the way you do, Ant," Ezra appeared immune, unmoved, "there was never any ill will in—"

"That's a fucking lie. Your Coven friends should deny you for that alone. It's just, it's just..." And with that she lost her words, became inconsolable. Everyone just sat there—no one had any idea of how to help, or what to say, not say.

"Antonia, this conversation needs to be complete or—"

Antonia shook her head violently, and with a mere flick of her hand she summoned her substantial talents and carefully, quietly,

337

simply faded from view. She dematerialized leaving Ezra in mid-sentence—standing there with empty glass in hand. Where she went was anybody's guess; The Sisters sat stone-faced, emotionless.

Ezra collapsed into the nearest chair and grabbed the closest glass of whatever she could find. Two women all aflutter descended upon her, adorning her with praise ("...so brave of you!"), questions ("...did Dennis ever find you again?"), and other assorted fawning behavior. Ezra was finally starting to relax into the conversation when Sasha appeared directly in front of her and coolly, firmly stated, "I'd like you to leave now."

And without another word—and very much in spite of herself—she did.

<hr/>

LASTLY AND, actually, least-ly, there was the Sad State of Affairs that was The Aunt Ezra. The Coven had started popping and cyst-ing around her wrist again even before she had the car door shut, and during the drive home they made their final reprimand and denunciation painfully, horribly clear. She fell out of her car and hysterically crawled up her steps and through her door. Felix sat there watching and wondering if she would melt, or combust, or if he'd see an entirely new unique way for a witch—and a fairly powerful one—to be, somewhat sadly, eliminated.

That physically didn't happen but *metaphysically* (mentally and emotionally speaking) it did: said simply, The Coven informed Ezra that she would not humiliate them or any of her ilk one millisecond more.

For once The Coven was focused and uniform in their decree—Ezra was to, in effect, *cease and desist.* They were tired and irrefutably disappointed and uninspired, as were a few other similar sabbaths that had *volunteered* their opinion.

Ezra was devastated. But from Ezra's shrinking perspective,

she would as she had many times before simply (or not so simply) discover *yet another door*—the next one, and the next after that if things went awry (again). Rebirth was something she'd come to rely upon, not terribly different from keeping an extra metaphorical meat pie in the freezer for when and if you just can't get it together to cook that night.

To be sure that Ezra fully grasped her circumstances, The Coven entwined their knobby protuberances and severed her hand and some wrist from the rest of her—"We trust we've made our point exactly clear? *'To the bone'?*" Some cackling again, then they were gone.

With a silent scream, Ezra picked up and placed the thrashing appendage against its matching component. She compelled it back into place; she wouldn't know till morning if the magic worked. And if it didn't, well that would be another story she could tell, if anyone was willing to listen.

In that next second Ezra decided it was time to not so much right the wrongs perpetrated against her, but to *wrong those wrongs, over and again,* until she got what she knew was right and good and deservedly hers.

———— ·|||)◊ ◊(|||· ————

R.D.G. SLOWLY CLOSED that section's parchment covers making it clear he'd come to the end (of that part of the story, anyway): So once again, to sum up (and I'll be sure Abyssinia gives you the next play-by-play —such as it is—so you're getting a *truly* balanced perspective), the Tetersberg emotional climate, in spite of the holiday forecast, is currently overcast with malaise with some dark and threatening behavior in the vicinity. Which direction will it decide to go? We'll know better in a few hours... (See, I at least make this shit interesting—if only certain someones would just try a little harder.)

· · ·

DITAN SNEAKS OVER TO PILAR: This is what I think I'm under-standing: their thoughts are a mess—the girls' father, who's self-ishly and defiantly mortal, becomes very sick. It perforce creates a tension, a tangible stress within the family and especially the girls. Each deals differently with the situation and him, as it should be, and each day raises the stakes, the emotional commitment, chal-lenges. So, regarding The Sisters, they should hew closely to these catchwords—keeping the emotional thread crystal-clear: Tip: sad, questioning; Sasha: detached, resentful; and Soba: confused, alienated.

Their words should be strong, clear, yet plaintive:

"Dad's sick."

The girls stared a hole into the floor, and then the ceiling too.

"I mean, he's sicker. No change. Actually that's wrong: there *is* a change, it's still not good, though..."

Ditan looked at the next page—it was still forming itself, the text staining and shaping the thoughts, motives.

Pilar: But that doesn't change *anything*—where's the "win"? *Ditan seems dismissive making Pilar anxious, oddly paranoid. He waves her fretting away, she presses,* Why? Have you heard something different? I've never changed or even tweaked the course of any subject's destiny path. It can't be done... *Or do you know something I don't?*

Ditan: It's a grey area—kind of while "nobody's looking," if you receive my meaning... You can nudge. As long as you're *helping* their situation, you can nudge. Make it a tiny bit better.

Pilar: So, because Tom Dad wants to kill himself, we can make that not so?

Ditan: No, that's hardly "nudging." And you—we—*have no idea* if he's going to actually do the deed.

Pilar: So, then what?

Ditan: Change the gaze. His perspective. But it will take all of us to do it, and if he doesn't like it or respond, it's a demerit on all of our logs—somehow or other. Everybody's is so different, thank the gods.

Pilar: So, if I really think my idea could work, I just need to convince everyone?

Ditan: Yep. All four, or better, the other two... Unless one of us is gone by then.

Pilar stares carefully at him.

Pilar: What are you saying? What *else* do you know that I don't?

Ditan shrugs coyly, looks at Pilar who is now playfully ignoring him.

Pilar: So how do you know all this, um, *criteria?* You seem to be just a little bit older than me.

Ditan: Probably. But let's just say I'm a whole bunch sneakier.

Two Steps Back

❧

Ezra still felt worried. (Turning the world upside down didn't seem to help at all.)

Everything happened as it was supposed to happen, *at least as far as she knew*. (But maybe she really *didn't know* everything there was to know. It wouldn't have been the first time...)

Things appeared correct—it certainly seemed that way to *her*. But to be fair, it can be worrisome when everything *looks* fine but doesn't *feel* anything close to resembling "fine." She was outside, watching the approaching maelstrom (no other way to describe it) when she thought it probably best to go inside... Unlike the storms from the other day during which she'd determined it to be part of her inherent supernatural responsibility to stand in the middle of to help guide its apex, to garner any new information and powers she'd been deigned to receive (all of this from the convenience and comfort of her back deck—*imagine it!* You're missing the very exaggerated rolling of my eyes), but the fat drops of liquid ripe with new knowledge seemed to intentionally avoid and dance, splay around and away from her. Ezra slouched her way back inside, her visage wind-torn and rearranged, trusting whatever new competencies she'd just absorbed needed time to come into force...

But they didn't because they hadn't, not even a smidge; the only tangible results from the Furies' mystical tumult were a few bugs between her teeth. It was a teaching moment, but Ezra, though dismayed, still staunchly believed her recognition was long, *long* overdue, *Simply put, it's inevitable...* ***I'm*** *inevitable...*

THE PATTERNS ARE TAKING SHAPE—THE *sky, the Earth's gaze— defining their precise position... It's a wonderful thing to see.* The singular messages, like possessed snowflakes, slip-slided down around and through her, everywhere. She knew they were experiencing this too, and there still wasn't a word from The Coven, not a whimper of an apology... At least her spell *mostly* worked: her hand was *mostly* where it was supposed to be, and she *mostly* had the use of two fingers and a thumb. (The opposable aspect of it was still a big question, however.) Speaking of forgiveness, Ezra was still ambiguous about the whole Marta Cortez brouhaha, but hindsight (and most everyone else) had not been as charitable—could she have gotten that one wrong too? Apparently so. (She wondered whether that was the wand that broke The Coven's back?)

She had always felt superior; she's always believed most beings —simple humans, pedigreed witches, maybe even wizards (when they existed, if they existed) and any iteration in between—thought the same. Ezra was a life force to be reckoned with; her idiosyncrasy was that she truly felt that she was absolutely the premier version of herself. On the other hand (when she had one), she'd been equally passionate in the belief that her being and life did not hold any more *value* than anyone else's. *No one's did.* Everyone ultimately was intended to be the best version of themselves whatever your chromosome map, however many cheeseburgers you ate or didn't, however many hits of acid you could do or couldn't, however many gods you worshiped or didn't... Ezra passionately believed that *every soul mattered* and had a place and a purpose; she also passionately asserted that respect did not always equal likability. (Of the thousands-plus people she'd encountered in her long life, there had been only a few that she'd genuinely liked. And as to how many genuinely reciprocated? She would never know.)

And of the thousands *upon thousands* of times she'd met, spent time with, talked with, argued with, loved with Antonia and Tom, she'd *always* liked—*sometimes even loved*—Antonia. She sadly never came upon a reason to actually like Tom Dad, but as suggested, she also never felt there was any wasted effort: there was something even more exceptional in spending time and a certain quality of conversation with someone you already knew *you didn't like*.

The next storms came and fell hard, the prognosticator's maps and schemes had cut their paths correctly and efficiently. Life and its residual magic had a big job to do...

———

SPUT WANDERED BACK DOWNSTAIRS—STILL nothing, no sound, not an inkling of feeling or life. The air was numb, unsustainable; Ezra's emotional genocide had been rampant and most thorough.

It was almost a full day and a half later that everything (and we do mean every *last, little thing*, regardless of its corporeal "quality") shifted mental states from manically depressed to manically surreal... There was suddenly a violent clinging-to-clanging mostly from the kitchen—The Sisters flew-floated downstairs immediately. Antonia was dead center kitchen table, flipping through the latest *Vanity Fair*, the tips of her (at the moment) very enchanted fingers guiding the erratic ballet of purging surrounding her. It was as if she'd flipped the "Self-Cleaning" switch on for the whole of the downstairs (a much more smarmier, aged-out hippy-er, drug-stained version of when the toys and etc. responded accordingly in *Mary Poppins*). As The Sisters dodged and ducked the various pans, brooms, and other cleaning accoutrements, what was most upsetting was their mother's blandness, her simple disinterest. Granted, it had been awhile, and this certainly wasn't the first time Antonia had given her wands and her house (and her family?) a good whack, but it was marked how sad and perfectly disaffected she appeared.

This could take a while—so The Sisters retreated back to their rooms anxiously anticipating the next mini-cataclysm.

PILAR DECIDED to stop pretending not to notice, she looked up at Abyssinia: Why the angsty look? Where's your holiday spirit? *Pilar sniggered,* I'm kidding, mostly... Seriously though, you've never looked *this* freaked out?

Abyssinia didn't look up, collapsed back into her chair: I think I screwed up—no, *I know I did.*

Pilar looked disbelievingly at her, but Abyssinia had become a little "rambunctious" of late (maybe just a Tetersberg party trick?)

Rappatsi will feel unsettled, anxious. Sleep won't be the simple and straightforward thing it typically is... She'll find the terrible words and images—remnants from the event hovering by her tea in the kitchen; she'll sense their awful sadness before she begins to understand...

Abyssinia mulled: What's that maxim we just learned—probably for the hundredth time—"Hindsight is forty-forty"?

Pilar joined her very real concern: What the fuck did you do?!

Abyssinia: I talked to her—well, *directly* communicated. "Left a message."

Pilar: Rapp?!

Abyssinia nodded.

Pilar: Why?!

Abyssinia: Because the hole in the family is real—I'm sure of it —and only getting bigger.

Pilar crumbled into her chair, then in the next breath, was suddenly (oddly) indifferent: Well, it is one of those perfect storms—you're getting screwed from both sides. Or ends. Or whatever you have there.

Abyssinia: I couldn't stop myself, they needed *help...*

They stood there looking at each other; the silence was agonizing. They were waiting for something dreadful to happen and had no idea what it could be.

Pilar relaxed, shook her head: So Rappatsi will try, and hopefully it'll all be okay. And if it's not...

Abyssinia paled, wide-eyed: What?

Pilar shrugged: You might find yourself somewhere else tomorrow or sometime soon—it won't be anything bad; you had only the best intentions. They should understand that...

LATER THAT SAME NIGHT, within minutes of one another, The Sisters and then Tom Dad woke up, sat up (in bed), and realized the same basic piece of information—a mental "text message." The gist: *Antonia would be "unavailable" for an indeterminate amount of time.*

No one was sure exactly what that phrase meant or was attempting to suggest, but they all knew their mother and wife, respectively, had, once again, wooed them during their most susceptible and willing states of mind—while they were sleeping. (Antonia's spell-making intuition was shrewd but cowardly, as per usual.)

Tom Dad turned and looked across the bed, still half-believing what he'd supposedly slept through, but it was true—she was gone.

There was also the notion of how she *Needed some time away*...
(Maybe that plea went just to Tom Dad?) And again, whatever
that was supposed to suggest or mean, was open—way, too open
—for interpretation and bitter, spiteful confusion and fear. (I have
to say, I don't blame them.)

*And **I'm** the passive/aggressive one in this so-called marriage?* Tom
Dad rolled over, clenched his eyes tight, and summoned all of his
very (*very*) limited witching ability to send a thought to all of his
daughters, who he could see, now, in his mind's eye, flailed, lying
in their beds, emotionally exhausted.

*New rules, kiddos: **have at it**—unleash those wands. Make your
magic until you can't make it anymore... But most important: only do unto
each other—and especially **other** others—as you would have them do
unto you.*

Tom Dad couldn't breathe let alone go back to sleep; he got
dressed and left the house.

IT WAS SUPREMELY IRONIC, and equally surreal, that for all the
horrific and agonizing pieces still lost in the air, The Sisters found
themselves in the same position—floating, free from their earthly
shells and skin, hovering above the hall in the foyer—at their
"spot," their makeshift 'safe-cum-panic room.'

Antonia's dream state musing and farewell—albeit temporary
—had left them too frantic to sleep again but too exhausted to be
fully conscious. Another odd realization: they agreed without
words they were worried and comforted in equal measure—very
worried about their parents yet very, *very* happy the both of them
were, well, *somewhere else.* (That's diplomatic of the girls, I should
add.)

"Where *is* Dad?"

"Walking, I think... I *hope.*"

"But it's 3:30, where would he walk for an hour? And around
here?"

As if on cue, the key in the door announced Tom Dad's return. The Sisters quietly observed their father, floating unseen just above his thoughtful, methodical steps up the stairs. Just as he started into the bedroom, he turned as if he'd forgotten or just remembered to do something...

And with that careful thought, he went into each of his daughter's bedrooms, gave them a kiss, rolled their blanket just so, turned back to gaze one more moment, feeling blessed and awestruck by their—*there are no other words for it: their utterly perfect-perfection.*

Tom Dad collapsed into his empty bed, finally happy—he'd done all he could possibly do for the people he loved.

To Our Readers

The Sisters and I would love to know what you think about their story thus far.
Your thoughtful input can help guide their ideas to the page as I finalize the notes for *My Weight in Wands, Journal Two*.
Please share your comments on Facebook at My Weight in Wands@mixcobooks or at mixcobooks@gmail.com